REUNION

"Throw down the strongbox!" called a voice that seemed vaguely familiar.

I was sure glad the stage was carrying a strong-box, because I didn't figure the robbers would search the passengers, too. But I was wrong.

After the strongbox clunked to the ground, I heard the same voice say, "Everybody in the coach out." The door opened, and a man with a mask stood there pointing a gun at us.

I was the first one out, and I got close enough to the robber to get a whiff of his breath, even through the bandanna over his face. I swallowed hard. Only one man I'd ever encountered had breath that bad.

That man had pulled my wisdom tooth.

That man was Doc Holliday.

The Memoirs of H. H. Lomax:

THE DEMISE OF BILLY THE KID
THE REDEMPTION OF JESSE JAMES
MIX-UP AT THE O.K. CORRAL

Mix-Up
at the
O.K. Corral

Preston Lewis

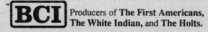

BCI Producers of **The First Americans,**
The White Indian, and **The Holts.**

Book Creations Inc., Canaan, NY • Lyle Kenyon Engel, Founder

BANTAM BOOKS
NEW YORK ʋ TORONTO ʋ LONDON ʋ SYDNEY ʋ AUCKLAND

MIX-UP AT THE O.K. CORRAL
A Bantam Book / published by arrangement with Book Creations Inc.
Bantam edition / April 1996

Produced by Book Creations Inc.
Lyle Kenyon Engel, Founder

ISBN 0-553-56543-5

Published simultaneously in the United States and Canada

Bantam Books are published by Bantam Books, a division of Bantam
Doubleday Dell Publishing Group, Inc. Its trademark, consisting of the
words "Bantam Books" and the portrayal of a rooster, is Registered in
U.S. Patent and Trademark Office and in other countries. Marca Reg-
istrada. Bantam Books, 1540 Broadway, New York, New York 10036.

PRINTED IN THE UNITED STATES OF AMERICA

RAD   10 9 8 7 6 5 4 3 2 1

Introduction

My original intention had been to hold off on publishing this volume of the MEMOIRS OF H. H. LOMAX, but my editors convinced me, rightly so, that interest in the so-called gunfight at O.K. Corral had soared as a result of recent Hollywood portrayals of the famous shoot-out. Though I had always had a passing interest in Wyatt Earp, his story, like George Armstrong Custer's, had been told so many times in print and on celluloid that another telling seemed superfluous.

As I began to read H. H. Lomax's account, however, I realized I was wrong. I had in my hands a fresh perspective on the events of 1881 and 1882 in Tombstone, Arizona Territory. Several things make this account interesting, not the least of which is Lomax's relationship with both sides in the dispute. While most accounts tend to favor either the Earps or the Clanton-McLaury-Behan faction, Lomax's perspective falls more in the middle, primarily because he seems to have been at odds with both sides. He evidently had a knack for making more enemies than friends, which may account for his peripatetic course across the Old West.

What makes his observations all the more startling is that they challenge the conventional wisdom on several events and several people who are central to the lore that has grown up around the gunfight. In most accounts, an unsuccessful robbery attempt on the Benson stagecoach seems pivotal in the events preceding the gunfight. By

Lomax's account, the robbery of a Bisbee stage almost six months later was the actual catalyst for the gunfight and the final breakdown of law and order in Cochise County. The Helen of Troy of Tombstone has long been identified as Josephine Marcus, who was first Sheriff Johnny Behan's lover and later Wyatt Earp's wife. Lomax, however, mentions Josephine but a handful of times. The woman more responsible for the events, as he tells it, was Hattie Ketcham, who is familiar to aficionados of Earp and Tombstone history but likely to few others. Finally, the Lomax memoirs provide new explanations of who fired the first shot at the so-called O.K. Corral gunfight and who killed Johnny Ringo.

While it seemed rather foolish of me to challenge the record as it has come down through the years, it was exciting, on the other hand, to read Lomax's entirely new perspective. The problem, though, lies in determining what is true and what is not. Narrowing in on the truth was intimidating for me because the truth has always seemed so murky, the waters often intentionally muddied by proponents of both the factions involved in the troubles in Cochise County.

For instance, in the hearing after the gunfight, nearly every witness with a vested interest in the outcome lied—and that included Wyatt and Virgil Earp. Doc Holliday and Morgan Earp were not called to testify, although impartial observers thought the two of them had actually fired the first shots. Under oath, Wyatt and Virgil took the blame, likely to protect Morgan and Doc.

Though the original transcripts of the hearing by Judge Wells Spicer into the gunfight have been lost, a typescript of the handwritten documents was produced by the Federal Writers' Project of the Works Progress Administration (WPA) during the Depression. Though far from complete, this typescript is the best record of the hearing. Lomax claims to have testified, but his testimony was not included in the typescript. It was that kind of distracting inconsistency that told my instincts to withhold publication of this volume until I could dig deeper into the background of the dispute.

However, the more I delved into the story of Tombstone, the more convinced I was that the facts had become so entangled in the legend that the unvarnished truth could never be extracted from the available evidence. Consequently, such popular recent movies as *Tombstone* often offer as good an interpretation of the events as some of the early accounts by Stuart Lake or Walter Noble Burns.

The most glaring of all falsehoods about the gunfight, of course, is its location. Legend places it at the O.K. Corral. History does not. Those who have studied the gunfight know that it actually occurred behind the corral on a vacant lot known on the plats of Tombstone as Lot 2, Block 17. Consequently, the title of this volume of Lomax's memoirs is *Mix-Up at the O.K. Corral*, which pays homage to that misconception about the battle's location and about the events that, according to Lomax, really started the dispute.

In my own evaluation of Lomax's memoirs, I came across several minor inconsistencies that I did not attempt to remedy as they did not seem as germane as the bigger issues. For instance, Cochise County was not separated from Pima County until 1881, though Lomax generally refers to the county as Cochise throughout. Also, Lomax often refers to Virgil or Wyatt as marshals, either city or federal. They were not marshals throughout their tenure in Tombstone, and since Lomax doesn't always supply specific time frames to place them in, it is difficult to know exactly what their official capacity, if any, might have been at any given point.

Beyond that, Lomax's account generally follows the documentable facts about Tombstone during that era, and the people he mentions generally show up in the records. For readers interested in comparing the Lomax narrative with a solid historical interpretation, I would recommend the work of Paula Mitchell Marks in *And Die in the West*. That account comes closest to unraveling the personal and political animosities that exacerbated the tensions in Cochise County.

Now, the question of whether Lomax's perspective is nearer to the truth than previous accounts by contemporaries I will leave to the reader. But whether or not his recollections are completely accurate, Lomax still makes entertaining reading.

Those unfamiliar with the first two volumes in the MEMOIRS OF H. H. LOMAX—*The Demise of Billy the Kid* and *The Redemption of Jesse James*—may be wondering who H. H. Lomax is and how I came across him. Born in Washington County, Arkansas, on January 9, 1850, Lomax left home after the Civil War and became a frontier vagabond. He tried his hand at just about everything, from cowpunching to bartending to bank robbing to mining. He was unsuccessful at practically everything he tried and went to live the later years of his life with his sister on an Oklahoma farm the family later lost to the Depression.

The final two years of his life he lived in Hodges, Texas, in the Camp family home just north of the gin. He died May 22, 1933, leaving behind little of material wealth except for two trunks of handwritten papers about his adventures in the West. Those papers, found by Hodges farmer John Bracken when he demolished the stone house in 1975, were given to the Southwest Collection at Texas Tech University. It was my great fortune to review and edit them for publication.

Though I was able to track down some of his relatives and find out a little about his later years, particularly in Oklahoma, I have been unable to ascertain why and how he came to live in Hodges the last two years of his life. Though I have talked to some old-timers around Hodges, I have yet to find anyone who remembers him. That should not be surprising, of course, since he had been dead some sixty years when I began that search, and at any rate folks could not be expected to recall a man who by most accounts was not the most congenial fellow ever to leave footprints across the Old West.

There remain, then, several mysteries about H. H. Lomax that may one day be resolved, but for the time being his words will have to stand on their own. He was a good storyteller. Whether or not he was telling stories is another matter, but who among the principals wasn't stretching the truth about the events around the gunfight at Lot 2, Block 17, Tombstone, Arizona Territory, October 26, 1881?

—PRESTON LEWIS
Lubbock, Texas
January 1996

Chapter One

Things might have turned out different in Tombstone if I hadn't had a toothache and Doc Holliday hadn't had bad breath. A lot of men died as a result, though not likely as many as needed killing. If it hadn't been my tooth, though, it'd probably have been something much less important that started all the trouble, because there were more mean folk in Arizona Territory at the time than you'd find anyplace else in the country short of a suffragists' convention.

The law was crooked in Tombstone, and it didn't matter what side of the law you were on. The politics were crooked in Tombstone, too, which made it no different from most every other place else in the country. You couldn't even buy a town lot without some greasy son of a bitch trying to claim it for himself. Nothing was straight, not even the liquor. I knew that for certain because I owned a saloon there, and I'd cut my whiskey with just about anything I could, even water—which was expensive at three cents a gallon—when nothing else was available.

Running a saloon is as respectable an occupation as, say, running for political office, and you get to meet a higher class of people. That's how I met Doc Holliday, who threatened to cut out my gizzard, and Johnny Ringo, who offered to blow a hole in me wide enough to drive an ore wagon through, and the Earp brothers, who were rightly named because I always felt like throwing up around them. They made me that nervous because I never knew what side of anything they were on, save their own.

Though the misunderstanding out back of O.K. Corral eventually cost dozens of lives by the time the killing was done, it saved my hide. Were it not for that shoot-out and some accidental gunplay of my own, I might have been buried in the rocky soil outside Tombstone.

It must've been late 1878 when I first arrived at Watervale, Arizona, a couple miles west of where Tombstone would be platted out the next spring. I'd tended bar for a spell in Beaver Smith's saloon back in Fort Sumner, New Mexico Territory, and might've stayed there had not the hot-tempered señorita I'd been courting decided she didn't want to get married after all. I was never certain I really wanted a wife, but I knew for sure I'd always wanted to get in ahead of the boom on a mining camp. I pretty much did that in Arizona, although I couldn't hang on to my cash, through no fault of my own. I'd been in mining camps before and always spent my money staking out a claim and hoping to open the door to the mother lode. About all I ever opened, though, were blisters from all the pick-and-shovel work that went with mining.

On the other hand, Old Beaver had given me quite an education at running a saloon. I learned that it was easier to empty a bottle of liquor than an ore cart and simpler to slip money out of a thirsty man's pocket than to pry ore from the ground. Another thing I learned was that saloon owners cut more than the cards. Fact was, Beaver taught me how to make a small fortune from a thimbleful of liquor. First you thinned it with a couple gallons of water, then added a cup of kerosene for body. Next you poured in a cuspidor of tobacco juice for color and flavor. Then, for a little bite, you added some hot pepper squeezings or, if you knew how to catch and milk a rattlesnake, a little of his poison. Now, don't get me wrong. I never served this concoction to my customers the first round or two. No, sir, I saved it for later rounds when their judgment and taste had been dulled. By then they seldom cared what they were drinking. And if they didn't care, why should I waste good liquor on them?

When I rode into Watervale on my mule, Flash, I had a hundred and seventy dollars on me and was due another ten or eleven from Beaver Smith for tending bar. I could tell Watervale was a prospering place even if it was little more than a jumble of tents and shacks thrown up between the rutted trails that passed for streets. I counted four saloons, all of them operating in tents, and decided I would open up a new one after I inspected the others. I knew sure as rain I could make my fortune once I was buying whiskey by the barrel and selling it by the jigger.

After riding around the camp, I took aim at a saloon with the name "Bloody Bucket" scrawled on the door flap. It was the dirtiest, greasiest tent in town. If business was as bad as the tent was filthy, I figured I just might get the owner to sell cheap, and I'd be in business. I jerked Flash's halter in the direction of the mangy tent, but the mule balked like I was on the road straight to hell. The harder I fought the halter, the stubborner Flash got. I would've taken to beating him, but a circle of men were pointing and laughing at me so I decided to beat up one of them instead. I picked out the puniest of the bunch, but the moment I loosened up on the reins, Flash bolted ahead, and we went lurching down the street. Flash saved that scrawny spectator a terrible whipping and found me a saloon in the process.

When the mule finally came to a halt, he was standing outside another tent where liquor was served. He tossed his head a time or two, a sure sign his stubborn had kicked in. I looked at the sign propped on the ground against the tent wall. A slash of green paint identified the place as "Saloon." I had to give the owner credit for deciding on such an original name, but the strain of coming up with it must've tired him so much he didn't have the strength to mount the sign at eye level. Maybe he was going for the rattlesnake and scorpion trade.

Deciding to find out for myself, I dismounted, tied Flash's reins around a hitching post, and stepped toward the tent flap, pausing to ponder the sign some more and wondering if the owner was going for the stumble drunks, too.

I ambled inside and laid eyes on Joe Campbell for the first time. He was standing behind the bar, a handsome fellow if you ignored his crooked nose, stained teeth, humped back, nubby ears, long arms, and unruly brown beard and hair. If he'd had horns and hadn't been wearing britches, shirt, and apron, I'd've sworn he was a buffalo standing on his hind legs. He was so ugly his momma must've taken him everywhere as a boy so she wouldn't have to kiss him good-bye. Even his half-dozen customers sat with their backs to him so they wouldn't have to look at him. I moseyed up to the plank bar.

"Afternoon, stranger. What can I get for you?" He adjusted the garters on his shirtsleeves as he eyed me.

"Whiskey," I answered.

He turned around, bent, and grabbed a bottle of whiskey from one of the wooden crates lined up against the back wall. He picked up a jigger glass and studied it against the yellowish light.

"Clean enough," he announced.

I shook my head. "You ever wash your glassware?"

With his brown eyes smoldering, he looked at me like I'd slapped his momma. "Damn straight I do. Once a week for certain."

After he filled the jigger, I reached for it, but his hand stopped mine.

"Two bits!" He didn't think I was good for the money.

As I pulled the wad of bills from my pocket, his jaw dropped. I peeled off a one. "Can you handle that?"

He nodded as he snatched the dollar bill from my fingers, shoved his hand in his britches pocket, and tossed the change at me.

I grabbed the drink and downed it in one gulp. It was good liquor, uncut, and a lot of it. This barkeep wasn't just born to be ugly—he was born to be broke, too, serving full jiggers of straight whiskey. The way he was eyeing my roll, I took it he had never seen so many greenbacks.

"You wouldn't be interested in playing a little poker,

would you?" he asked, staring at my money and licking his lips.

Looking about the tent, I didn't see a card table, much less a dealer. "I don't play with strangers," I declared.

"You're the stranger, mister, because I'm Joe Campbell." He offered me another drink.

Though I was tempted, I waved him away, figuring if we did get in a card game, I didn't want my head muddied with whiskey. "Who's your dealer?"

"Just me," he answered.

If he didn't deal cards any smarter than he poured drinks, I figured I could beat him like a rug. "You got any money?"

Campbell nodded.

That wasn't good enough for me. "Let's see."

He fished a handful of coins and my dollar bill from his pocket.

"That's it?"

He nodded.

I don't know what he'd spent his money on, but it hadn't been brains. "There's no more than a couple dollars there."

He shrugged. "That's more than some people got and less than others, and that's a fact unless less is more."

"Huh?" That was when I realized Campbell was a barroom philosopher. In some of my schooling, which I hadn't taken to very well, my momma had made me read some highfalutin words by one of them Greek philosophers. They made about as much sense to me as a hog bubbling in slop. That was the way with philosophy. None of it made sense. And if that was the case, Joe Campbell was as good a philosopher as ever lived anywhere. I waded into his philosophical discussion. "How can less be more?"

He got all excited, wiping his whiskered face with the back of his hand and grinning at me with those dirty teeth. "You ever cross an Arizona river?"

"I've crossed every river between here and New Mexico Territory, at least what there was of them. Back in

Arkansas, we'd've called them cricks at best or good leaks at worst."

"Well, sir, that's my point. When there's more river, there's less bank, and when there's more bank, there's less river. So more can be less, or less can be more. You see?"

Well, I didn't, but it didn't matter. I just hoped Campbell never turned to politics. The way he talked, he could wind up as governor or even something more important, like justice of the peace.

"You ever play with yourself?" Campbell asked.

"Say what?" I cocked my head and would've cocked my pistol at him if I hadn't run out of ammunition shooting rattlesnakes on the way into town.

"Do you ever play with yourself? Cards—you know, solitary?"

"Maybe. What's it matter?"

"You said you didn't play cards with strangers. If you don't play cards with yourself, you must be a stranger to yourself."

Campbell's philosophizing was getting to me. I was tempted to borrow a bullet and go outside and shoot Flash for ever stopping in front of this saloon. I thought about shooting Campbell, but evidently there were already enough holes in his head to air out his brain pretty well.

"Do you know your name?"

"Of course," I replied.

"Then what is it, and we can play cards."

"H. H. Lomax."

"What's the H. H. stand for?"

"Henry Harrison."

"Well, Henry Harrison Lomax, we ain't strangers anymore, so I reckon we can play cards." He reached out and grabbed my right hand and shook it to seal our long-standing friendship.

He'd made me so mad with all his gibberish that I decided I'd play him cards long enough to take his few coins or go broke trying. "You don't have enough money to make it worth my time."

"I got my saloon to bet."

I perked up. Maybe Flash did know something I didn't. I looked around, studying the place, figuring it wasn't worth my money roll, but it wasn't as greasy as the Bloody Bucket back down the street. "I've been in better outhouses."

"Less is more," Campbell repeated.

"More or less," I conceded. "Pick your table, Campbell."

He shook his head. "I got to wait bar."

I looked around at his customers, drowsy over their afternoon drinks. "What's wrong with a table?"

"I need to be here in case a customer comes in."

Not a man had entered since I came in, though I couldn't speak for whatever snakes, scorpions, and tarantulas the low sign might've attracted.

Campbell turned around and pulled out a dog-eared deck of cards from the bottom of one of the wooden crates. He scattered the cards on the plank and began to mix them. Some of the cards were torn, some missing corners, and others creased. They were so cut up I figured a den of bobcats had played with them last. I'd seen marked cards in my day, but none like these. A blind man could've read them.

"Don't you have a newer deck?"

He shook his head. "Can't afford a new deck."

"Looks like a marked deck to me."

Instantly Campbell lifted his hands from the plank. "Then you mix 'em and deal."

He must've thought I was ten kinds of fool. It didn't matter who mixed a marked deck if only one person knew the markings, but by then I was determined I was going to take the son of a bitch, marked cards or not. I mixed the cards. "Five-card draw?"

"Suits me."

I offered him the cards to cut the deck, but he left it pat. *The cocky son of a bitch,* I thought as I dealt out five cards to the both of us. He picked up his hand and fanned out his cards, grinning all the time.

Picking up my own cards, I discovered a pair of deuces and an ace of spades with the corner missing.

Campbell licked his lips. "We forgot to ante." He put two bits in the pot.

I matched his bet. "How many cards?"

"Three."

I dealt him three battered cards for the pair he held. "Dealer takes none," I said, watching him closely.

His eyes dimmed, and his face fell. He bit his lip, then tugged at his ear. Campbell didn't have a poker face, that was for sure. He pondered, then nodded without upping the ante. "I'm in."

I shrugged and revealed my hand, exposing my pair of deuces.

Laughing, Campbell threw down his cards. "Three aces!" Reaching for the pot, he explained, "Less is more here. My three cards've got less spots than your two deuces, but mine's the winner."

While he explained his philosophy to me, I retrieved his three aces and studied the markings on the back. The ace of clubs was creased in the middle, the ace of hearts had a bite out of the side of it, and the ace of diamonds had two bent corners. While he counted his money, I restacked the cards and palmed the ace of spades that had been the high card in my hand.

We played several more hands, me winning one by accident and Campbell taking the rest. As we played, I slipped the aces out and up my sleeve until I had all four, then started herding the kings in the deck. After all, I didn't want to give myself a fine hand without also giving Campbell one. My only fear was that he was smarter than he was letting on and was going to pull a surprise—or a gun—on me.

By the time I was ready to deal the rigged hand, I was running behind thirty dollars and Campbell was beginning to feel the snap in his sleeve garters.

"Let's up the ante to a couple dollars," he suggested.

"How about ten dollars?"

Campbell didn't hesitate. "Yes, sir, that's a fine idea."

We shoved our money to the middle of the plank. Then I started dealing, giving him a pair of kings and myself a pair of aces.

He examined his cards like a preacher studying the

Good Book. I grew worried that maybe I'd dealt him two pair or a full house, but he finally nodded and looked across the plank at me. "I'll up the pot fifteen dollars."

I looked at my cards, folded them like I was going to give up, then grimaced and nodded. "I'll see you and raise you another ten."

Campbell matched my raise. "Three cards."

As I dealt him two more kings and a throwaway, his eyes widened, and he licked his lips. "Dealer takes two," I announced, trying to make him think I had three of a kind. For show, I grimaced when I looked at my cards, then bit my lip, trying to get him to go for the idea that I hadn't gotten any help with the new cards. Four aces sure looked good staring back at me.

"I raise you," Campbell said, pushing the remainder of his money into the pot.

I hesitated, then pushed a wad of bills atop his wager, knowing he couldn't match it. "I see you and raise you."

"All I got's the saloon."

"You betting it or not?" I inquired.

He nodded like he had a sure hand. "Against the rest of your money, I am."

"Then show your cards."

He fanned out his pasteboards and laid them before me. "Four kings."

I shook my head and watched a smile crease his beard. "All I got is four spots. I believe they're called aces."

Campbell just stood there, staring at me with those muddy brown eyes. He looked sick as a dog passing peach pits. "I got beat, didn't I."

"Less is more," I reminded him. Campbell didn't have the common sense God gave a rock. I never knew a fellow who could get beat with his own marked cards.

He stared dumbly at his cards, then at mine. Finally he reached behind his back. I was sure he was going to come back with a fistful of knife or gun, but he merely untied his apron, slipped it off, and tossed it atop the pot. Then he slid his sleeve garters off and dropped them on the apron. He started toward the door, looking sad enough to bring a tear to a glass eye.

I feared he planned to shoot himself. "Where you going?"

"A man's gotta follow his piss," he mumbled.

"Huh?"

"To take a leak."

"Don't flood any of the rivers," I told him.

He stepped outside and shuffled away.

I turned around to greet my customers. "Gentlemen," I proclaimed, "my name's H. H. Lomax, and I'm the new owner of the saloon. Drinks are on the house." I gathered my apron and money from the plank bar, then poured liquor for my six customers, careful not to fill their jiggers as full as Joe Campbell had.

It was a proud moment, owning my own saloon, even if it was a tent. But I needed to come up with a new name for the place, something appropriate for the occasion, although I didn't figure the Crooked Hand or the Stacked Deck would draw many customers.

As one of the men stepped outside to call his friends over for free drinks, I glimpsed Flash, standing there proud as the new poppa he could never be. That was when I hit upon the name: Stubborn Mule Saloon.

When word got around I was offering free drinks, business at the Stubborn Mule picked up. By eight o'clock that night I'd made a friend of every man in town. By midnight, when I ran out of whiskey, I'd lost every one again.

Even with my liquor supply dry I still had a saloon, which I hadn't had when I rode into town, and I still had money in my pocket to buy more whiskey. Only problem was, I didn't know where to get it. I figured Tucson was the likeliest source, but I didn't know where to order it or the cost of freighting liquor in.

It was a problem I figured to tackle the next morning after a good night's sleep, but just as I was ready to crawl atop my plank bar and rest, Joe Campbell returned.

"You just now finished your leak?"

He shook his head. "I've been thinking."

That told me right then trouble was ahead.

"You might need a bartender."

"What I need is whiskey. I'm bone dry from giving it away. You know where to get more?"

He nodded. "Done it before. Can do it again, if you hire me."

Campbell was too ugly to tend bar for me. I wanted to run a fine establishment where customers didn't gag at the sight of my barkeep. "You look like you were born downwind from an outhouse."

"I can get you whiskey."

Crossing my arms, I pondered the problem. I doubted Joe could adapt to my being the boss. On the other hand, he probably wasn't smart enough to steal from me. Still, I didn't want him scaring away business. Finally I nodded reluctantly. "Get a shave and a haircut and bathe more often than you clean your glassware. Then you can stay on for fifty cents a day and any money you find on the floor."

"That's slim pay. Miners make four dollars a day."

"Just remember, less is more."

"Can I sleep here?"

"Once you get a shave and a bath."

"Okay," he said. "I'll do it."

Joe Campbell ambled off into the night, and I blew out the lamp. I decided to get a little sleep, rise before dawn, visit my two competitors, and maybe steal a few bottles of their liquor. Unfortunately, the sun beat me up.

It was well past dawn when I felt a hand on my shoulder. I awoke with a start. Standing over me was a man I'd never seen before, clean-shaven and smelling of tonic water. Then I realized it was Joe Campbell. He didn't look half bad for an ugly fellow.

"Less hair, more face," I said, wiping the sleep from my eyes.

"Do I get the job?"

I nodded. "What about more whiskey?"

Campbell tugged on his nubby ear, then grinned slyly. "The Bloody Bucket's got a freight wagon coming in today. I'll take a wagon out and talk the teamster out of a barrel or two, if you can spare thirty or so dollars to bribe him."

"Won't the Bloody Bucket be mad?"

"Nope. They'll get their whiskey. The freight company'll pay for replacements when the teamster tells them the barrels fell off the wagon and busted."

For a dumb man, Campbell was getting smarter by the minute. I just hoped he didn't play cards with the freighter. I fished money out of my pocket and counted out fifty dollars for him.

"I'll see you later," he said as he grabbed the money and left. "By the way, I stabled your mule."

When he returned that afternoon, he had two barrels of whiskey and fifteen dollars, which he returned to me.

Over the next few months I came to depend on Joe Campbell. No man in Arizona Territory was as honest or as dumb. Though he was a bit squeamish about cutting liquor and spreading rumors that our competitors were cutting theirs with horse piss, I finally convinced him of the wisdom of my way of operating a saloon. The Stubborn Mule did a good business for Watervale. I saved close to seven hundred dollars without Campbell realizing it, and I upped his wages to a dollar a day. He was happy as a boardinghouse pup.

After wintering in my tent saloon, I was thinking about building a fine wooden building come spring with all the money I'd made. The only thing that held me back was talk about moving the mining camp up to Goose Flats, a mesa that overlooked the Tough Nut claim. Though it was farther from water, it was a level site that had more room for growth than Watervale.

The land at Goose Flats was patented, surveyed, and staked out. A townsite company was formed, and one of the speculators, a redheaded fellow, took me for a tour.

Speculators were a lot like philosophers: They saw things no one else did. When we rode up to Goose Flats, the fellow pointed out lines of wooden stakes with bits of red cloth tacked to them. Where he could see Fremont Street, destined to be the town's main avenue, I saw only a line of stakes. Where he saw buildings and houses, I saw sagebrush and cactus.

"The future's here, not Watervale," he told me. "The town of Tombstone will be the mining center of the Southwest. Kings, governors, and princes will one day come to this site in awe of its wealth. King Solomon's mines themselves will bow before the mines of Tombstone. And *you've* got a chance to buy into the wealth now."

"Tombstone's not a promising name for a town. Sounds like it's already dead," I replied.

"Aha!" the speculator cried with a sweep of his arm. "But it's a name you won't forget, I daresay, and you have the chance—no, the golden opportunity!—to buy into Tombstone. I can give you a prime location on Fremont Street where you can make your fortune and move out of that tent back in Watervale."

When I looked around Goose Flats, all I saw was thorny plants and those wooden stakes. But I'd always wanted to get in early on a mining camp. This would be my chance.

"Fremont's eighty feet wide," the speculator continued, "five feet wider than any other street in town." He pointed to a corner stake and nudged his horse ahead. Flash followed.

"Here's Fifth Street, bound to be the center of town," he said, as excited as a horse on locoweed. "It's an excellent site for the Stubborn Mule. I can let you have the northeast corner of Fifth and Fremont for three hundred dollars."

"Three hundred dollars?" I spit. I looked around again and could still see nothing but stakes and brush.

"A bargain at that."

I didn't want to be the first to buy unless I was sure others were moving. I hesitated, reluctant to give up three of my seven hundred dollars.

All the way back to Watervale the speculator tried to sell me on Tombstone, but I held him off, saying I needed more time to think about it.

It wasn't a day later that I heard people were warming to the idea of moving to Goose Flats and scratching their names in Tombstone. When I was sure the interest was genuine, I returned to the speculator.

"You know that lot at Fifth and Fremont?" I began. He nodded.

"I'll take it."

He smiled. "It'll be five hundred dollars."

"I thought it was three hundred."

"The rush to Tombstone is on," he replied, "so the price has gone up."

I cursed him under my breath.

"I can let you have a lot for three hundred on Allen Street, a block south of Fremont."

Gritting my teeth, I shook my head. "I intend to be on the main street. I want Fifth and Fremont."

"Then it's a deal," he said. "You've just bought the best lot in Tombstone."

Chapter Two

Over the next year, Tombstone gradually grew from a camp to a town and was incorporated in late 1879. I never was certain what "incorporated" meant, other than it gave lawyers something to do and created a small kingdom for even smaller politicians to fight over, which was what started all the trouble rolling. Tombstone was not without its shootings, knifings, robberies, thefts, and other crimes, but looking back on things, it seems like all the real trouble started after the town became legal.

There were still Apache troubles in the territory that touched me periodically, but I managed to hang on to my scalp and fatten my wallet enough to build a fine false-fronted saloon with wood hauled from the Huachuca and Dragoon Mountains. The saloon had a large front room with a dozen tables for drinking and poker, plus a faro layout. I had three rooms in back, one an office and storage area and two with beds where the dance-hall girls could take their customers and where I could sleep until I got my house built.

When the building was finished, I purchased a fine mahogany bar and backbar in Tucson and had them freighted to Tombstone. Some saloon owners put up large mirrors on the backbar, but I decided against it. With Campbell so ugly, I didn't want customers getting more than one view of him at a time. Being one who believed a saloon should also offer cultural attractions, I bought paintings of plump maidens with less clothing and more flesh showing. Those paintings were better for business than the beer company posters of "Custer's Last Stand" that other saloons tacked to their walls because they got my customers pining for my girls, the prettiest of whom was Corina DeLure. Corina had hair the color of corn silk and a bosom that stood up well against the Huachucas and the Dragoons.

Tombstone kept growing, business kept getting better, and I'd've probably become a millionaire if "the best lot in Tombstone," as the land speculator had called it, had panned out. Problem was, there was nothing but stakes and a speculator's dreams marking the rest of Fremont Street. Tombstone sprouted up around Allen, a block south of Fremont, which became the main street in spite of the speculator's vision. Granted, Fremont was five feet wider than any other street in town, but it still ended up that I'd paid two hundred dollars more for five more feet of street and less business than if I'd bought on Allen. So, to keep business up, I had to spread rumors about how the other saloons cut their whiskey or cheated at cards.

"That don't seem right," Joe Campbell told me one day after I'd passed the word that an Allen Street saloon was carrying buckets of horse piss from the O.K. Corral to cut their beer.

I philosophized so Campbell could understand. "If less can be more, why can't wrong be right?"

Campbell shrugged his humped shoulders. "Huh?"

"The less business there is for them, the more there is for us."

"That's a nasty thing to say about another saloon," he countered.

"What saloon did I say that about, Joe? Name it." I had him, but it took a minute for him to figure it out.

"You didn't say a name, just a saloon on Allen Street."

"How's it wrong? You know how many saloons are on Allen?"

Campbell lifted his hand and started counting his

fingers. He hadn't reached his third finger before I started naming them.

"There's the Criterion, the Miner's Exchange, Mount Hood, Alhambra, Bank Exchange, Doling's, Park Brewery Depot, Green's Headquarters, the Diana, Cosmopolitan, Palace, Oriental, and McCann's. That's thirteen of them, all trying to get our business."

Campbell was still counting his fingers.

"How many are there on Fremont? The Stubborn Mule and Kelley's Wine House. Then there's Scully's on Fifth Street. That's it, Joe. We got to fight the Allen Street saloons if we want business."

Campbell just stood there scratching a head so thick I could've whacked him with the biggest mining timber in town and it would've been morning before he yelled.

In spite of Campbell's doubts, the rumors—plus a couple buckets of piss I left behind the Alhambra and the Cosmopolitan one night—helped business at the Stubborn Mule. I made enough money to erect a fine sign over the door with a likeness of Flash painted in black. Above the mule's profile in big letters were the words STUBBORN MULE SALOON, and beneath those, in smaller letters, was H. H. LOMAX, PROPRIETOR. Joe and I were so overworked that I hired a couple barkeeps—Ned Nichols and Til Walteree—to help out.

Ned Nichols, a mean-looking hombre with a handlebar mustache, thick black hair, and dark, brooding eyes, was as jumpy as any man I'd ever seen. He was as skittish as an old maid in a room full of mice. Til Walteree was a reed of a man with an easy gait and a fishhook nose. He came from Louisiana and talked like a drunk Frenchman.

When they took to bartending, I had more time to spend my money. For two hundred dollars I bought a lot from the townsite company on Safford between Third and Fourth Streets. I hired a couple drunks to build a house, the first I could truly call my own since I'd left my folks' place near Cane Hill, Arkansas, almost fifteen years earlier. It was a little clapboard house built on a stone foundation with a small parlor, kitchen, and bedroom. I even had an outhouse. So I was leaving my mark on Tombstone.

I also invested in mining properties, but I didn't spend *all* my money. I bought a tin lunch box like the miners carried and stored cash and stock certificates inside. Then I pried a floorboard loose under my bed and cached the box under the floor. I figured to become fat, rich, and respectable.

It was easier, though, to become rich and respectable in Tombstone than it was to become fat. The problem was rats and mice. They lived there by the millions, and you couldn't leave a scrap of food out without the little pests eating it and asking for seconds. I heard of one miner actually starving because rats sat by his plate and took food from his spoon before he could get it to his mouth. I don't know if that was true or not, but I do know those critters could make more noise at night than a convention of drunk Democrats. It was so bad a man couldn't sleep for the commotion. Goose Flats would've been better named Rodent Flats, Rat Hill, or Mouse Mesa, because I saw more rodents than I ever did geese or anything else save scorpions, tarantulas, flies, and centipedes.

Around the end of 1879 and the beginning of 1880, a couple things happened that pretty much ruined my chances for staying in Tombstone. First, it became general knowledge that the Tombstone Townsite Company had failed to get a clear patent on the land they'd laid out and sold. Their title—and those of everyone who had bought lots from them, myself included—was challenged by the Gilded Age Mining Company. Until the issue was settled, the town was held by the city commission. That made everyone who had bought property nervous, because our titles apparently weren't any better than the paper they were written on.

Second, and worst of all, Wyatt Earp and his brothers came to town.

I guess I'd heard of Wyatt Earp before, but I'd never paid much attention to the name. He was like a lot of men with reputations: You didn't think much about them until you ran into one, and then that was all you thought about. It was one thing to hear a coyote yelping and quite another for him to bite you on the butt. Earp'd apparently made a reputation for himself as a lawman in Dodge City, Kansas. He and his four brothers arrived in Tombstone within a few months of one another.

The three that were to play into all the trouble were Wyatt, Virgil, and Morgan. I came to believe there were several nooses hanging in their family tree. They were lean, lanky men with wide mustaches, grim eyes, and generally humorless dispositions, excepting Morgan, who had a knack for playing pranks and for getting to the bottom of things, like a mug of beer, a glass of wine, or a bottle of whiskey. Virgil was probably the most decent of the three, and he might've been outright respectable except for a temper that could burn hotter than three shades of hell.

Virgil's wife, Allie, was a looker whom I learned to like because she seemed to needle Wyatt like a seamstress. I never saw much of Wyatt's wife, Mattie; word was she took a little laudanum and drank whiskey now and then. If I'd been married to Wyatt Earp I'd've probably done the same thing. Morgan's wife, Lou, was a fine-looking woman as well. To help support their men, the women took in sewing and ironing.

The other two Earp brothers were James and Warren. James, the oldest, arrived about the same time as Wyatt and Virgil; Warren and Morgan joined them later. With a bad shoulder that still carried lead from a Confederate sharpshooter, James was the puniest of the Earps. He came to Tombstone with his wife, Nellie Bartlett Ketcham, and her daughter, Hattie. James tended bar and drove a hack but otherwise pretty much stayed to himself. Warren was the kid brother who always talked big but never seemed to be around when trouble happened.

It was a cold winter afternoon the first time I saw Wyatt Earp. He sauntered into the Stubborn Mule and stood at the door for a moment, letting the heat escape outside before shutting it. The way he studied the place with those narrow, squinting eyes, if the saloon had been a bank, I'd've figured he was planning to rob us. Under his long coat I could see the bulge of a pistol on his hip, and he looked like he didn't mind using it. He was as cocky as a rooster with a hard-on as he stepped up to the bar, glared at us, then looked around at the handful of customers.

"Never seen so many bartenders for so few customers," he drawled, as if we gave a damn.

"That a fact?" I answered, figuring to start him on the bad stuff without letting him have a couple jiggers of the good first.

He eyeballed me. "Are you the owner?"

"That's another fact. I'll be damned if you aren't the smartest customer we've had since Flash strayed inside."

"Who's Flash?"

"My mule."

He bristled. Campbell, Nichols, and Walteree eased away from me.

"You ain't so damn smart yourself," Earp informed me. "Only someone dumber than a barrelful of hair would open a saloon on Fremont when Allen is the main trail through town."

"Let me get you a jigger of our finest," I offered, reaching for a glass that hadn't been washed in a month and a bottle that had been cut with turpentine.

"I don't drink."

"Neither does Flash, but he came in for a reason. Did you?"

He looked from me to Campbell, Nichols, and Walteree. I could tell he didn't want our conversation to be overheard.

"I'll tend the bar if you boys want to leave us be."

Nichols was wringing his hands like he expected trouble. Walteree eyed Earp suspiciously.

Campbell nodded at me. "Less of us is more of you for him to shoot."

Earp squinted at Campbell. "Who said anything about shooting?"

"You said shouting, didn't you, Joe?" I asked.

Campbell shrugged. He probably couldn't remember. He backed to the end of the bar, trailing Walteree and Nichols. Then all three stared at me.

Earp leaned over the bar and spoke in a half-whisper. "I deal faro, and I deal square. Wonder if you might be needing a dealer?"

"Why'd you want to work for a place on Fremont when there's thirteen on Allen Street that're busier?"

"I figure you get a better class of customers, rather than just drunks stumbling from door to door. Anyway, I hear some of the saloons on Allen Street cut their drinks with horse drippings."

"So I've been told." I didn't like the looks of Wyatt, so I shook my head. "I don't think I need you."

"Do you know who I am?"

"You haven't introduced yourself."

"Wyatt Earp. You ever heard of me?"

I scratched my chin. "Can't say that I have."

"Lawman, Dodge City."

I turned to my bartenders at the opposite end of the bar. "Any of you fellows ever heard of Wyatt Puke?"

"Earp," Wyatt corrected.

"Vomit," Campbell said.

"Where?" asked Nichols, shifting nervously from foot to foot.

"The name's Wyatt Earp." He slammed his fist against the bar. "There ain't a brain among the four of you."

"You ain't met Flash," I countered.

Earp growled. "There are some men who'd threaten to kill you or burn your place down for insults like that."

"There'll be hell to pay if you try."

"To kill you?" He laughed.

"No, to burn my place down. Dry as Tombstone is, you'd burn the whole town down."

Earp cleared his throat and spit at a spittoon. By the *splat* rather than the *ping* I knew he'd hit the floor instead. "I bet you don't even know how to do long division."

"Why would I need to know that?"

"To take your cut from my faro table."

"Don't need to know it if you ain't working here, and you ain't."

Wyatt Earp shook his head. "Be a bad thing if rumors started floating around about the Stubborn Mule. It might hurt business."

I figured I could spread more lies about him than he could about me. After all, I was an upstanding Tombstone citizen, and he was an upstart who would soon develop a reputation for slugging people with his pistol.

"Adios, Mr. Earp or Puke or whatever it is."

He scowled, then spit again on the floor, not even aiming for the spittoon. He spun around on his heel and strode for the front door, jerking it open. The door banged into the wall, then bounced back as he marched outside.

After that confrontation, rumors began to circulate about town that I had stood Wyatt Earp down. The rumors didn't displease me because I started them. I had to watch out for my own business, and I figured Earp was just the type to tell bad stories about the Stubborn Mule.

He kept throwing his weight around, trying to intimidate some saloon owner into taking him on as a partner. He managed to get an appointment as a deputy sheriff, then resigned after Milt Joyce sold him a quarter interest in the gambling concession at the Oriental Saloon, where Wyatt started dealing faro. That suited me fine.

By the end of the year, I was doing good business. The mines around Tombstone were producing half a million dollars a month in silver bullion. But trouble was brewing. Probably the first sign of what was ahead was the shooting of town marshal Fred White by Curly Bill Brocius in late October. I didn't see the shooting and never saw Curly Bill until months later at a dance, but folks said he offered the marshal his gun, which went off and struck him in the chest. Some said it was an accident—even Fred White himself said so before he died—but others said Curly Bill had been put up to killing White because he sided with lot owners like me rather than the mining company that was trying to take our property.

After White's death, Virgil Earp was appointed acting town marshal, a position he held off and on until the big gunfight. As soon as he started wearing a badge, he and his brothers saw to it that ordinances were passed like the ones Wyatt had enforced as marshal in Dodge City, which kept a man from carrying a gun in town or riding his horse on the boardwalks, foolish things like that.

As 1881 began, though, I wasn't too worried about those ordinances—or anything else—because I'd managed to save better than a thousand dollars and to stay off liquor. Whiskey was an occasional problem of mine, but fact was, I didn't want to drink any of my own because I couldn't remember what I had cut it with.

Then I got a letter that weakened my resolve and got me to taking an occasional nip.

The letter was from the señorita I'd been courting a couple years earlier in Fort Sumner, New Mexico Territory. She wanted me to return, and I had trouble resisting her charms. Though Rosalita was a fiery sort, she'd offered me a warm place to stable my mule as often as I wanted, and that was a hard proposal to turn down. I gave it a lot of thought and downed considerable amounts of whiskey before I decided to give her another chance.

Business was slow the day I called Joe Campbell, Ned Nichols, and Til Walteree together to let them know I was returning to New Mexico to see Rosalita. I told them I trusted them to run the saloon honestly in my absence and that I was giving Campbell the chance to run things. He suggested I see a lawyer to draw up any papers I might need so there would be no question he could do what he had to in my absence. He even suggested one Henry Guinn as an attorney who could be trusted. I didn't know such an animal existed, but then I wasn't the philosopher that Campbell was.

Before I left, I visited the lawyer to make sure my saloon and lots would be protected from that damned Gilded Age Mining Company, which was still claiming much of Tombstone as its own. Guinn's office was in a front room off the parlor of his house on Allen Street.

His wife, Amelia, answered the door when I knocked. Her name should've been Ample because she was the most ample woman I had ever seen. She had ample hips, legs, and ankles, ample shoulders, stomach, and breasts. She had an ample neck and ample cheeks. She'd've made a half dozen of the nudes on the paintings back in the Stubborn Mule and still had enough left over for a tub of lard. She didn't look half bad, though, from the forehead up.

I introduced myself as owner of the Stubborn Mule Saloon and explained my need to see her husband on legal business.

"This ain't about any of your saloon girls, is it?"

I shook my head. "No, ma'am."

"It better not be. I don't want him dealing with any of them loose women. If I ever caught him with one of those dance-hall girls, I'd kill him with my bare hands."

I took off my hat and held it over my chest. "Mrs. Guinn, not a one of those soiled doves is half the woman you are."

"Them's mighty pretty words." She blushed and let me in to see her husband.

Henry Guinn was a frail, slender man with sloping shoulders, narrow waist, and almost no hips. His clothes hung loosely on his narrow frame, and I wondered if it was the rats or his wife that was stealing all his food. He wore thick spectacles and had a girlish grip when we shook hands. He didn't say a word until Amelia closed the door behind us.

"My wife didn't scare you, did she?"

"Nope," I lied.

"She's the jealous type, but I'm not the kind to run around on her. I took a vow to be true to her when we got married, and I intend to live by it. She provides a lot for me."

Like shade in summer and warmth in winter, I figured.

Guinn motioned me to a chair. "How can I assist you?"

I explained I had a lady friend in New Mexico I intended to take for my wife. "Joe Campbell suggested I make legal arrangements for my business and other affairs should the Gilded Age Mining Company try to take my saloon or my home."

"Joe Campbell's a wise man and a friend of mine," Guinn said, sitting down at his desk and picking up a pen. He dipped his pen in an inkwell and took a few notes as I talked. When I finished, he nodded. "Give me a couple days to draw up the papers, and then you can sign them. What I'll do is give Joe the power of attorney to make any decisions necessary in your absence."

Knowing that Joe wasn't smart enough to be an attorney, I didn't see any harm in that, so I agreed. I figured I'd found an honest lawyer, but what I didn't know at the time was that he was no better than the rest of his breed. In fact, he was worse off, having a wife as big and ugly as Amelia.

When I stepped out of his office, Amelia was standing by the door like she'd been listening in on our conversation. Again I admired the cut of her forehead and thought how I'd hate to be yoked to her for life—though I had to admit it might be safer to have her as a wife than as an enemy.

Amelia smiled. "You're welcome back anytime, as long as you don't bring one of them saloon girls with you."

"Yes, ma'am." I tugged my hat and left.

Two days later I returned to sign the legal papers. I read them, but they didn't make that much sense to me. Amelia Guinn was as ample as ever, and I expressed my regrets that I couldn't stay and slop her trough for her.

I took my copies of the documents home and hid them in the tin box under the floor. I had a growing stack of money as well as several stock certificates. In spite of the rodent noise, I slept soundly that night because I was certain I was going to be rich.

The next day, after giving Joe Campbell instructions on how to handle business in my absence, I mounted Flash and headed for New Mexico Territory and Rosalita. The nights were still cold, and the ground wasn't as comfortable as my feather mattress at home, but I slept undisturbed by rats and mice scampering about the floor.

After about two months in New Mexico, while Rosalita was trying to decide whether or not she wanted to marry me after all, I got anxious to check on my saloon and make sure Campbell, Walteree, and Nichols weren't robbing me blind. I started back for Tombstone to give Rosalita time to think about us getting hitched.

On the way back through Mesilla, I stopped for some lunch at an eatery and watched a cat lounging in the corner while I downed some tortillas and beans. He was an ugly cat with piss-yellow fur and mean eyes, but he was also either lazy or hungry because his ribs were poking through his homely fur. I thought about shooting him to put him out of his misery, but then it hit me that this tomcat could get the size of Amelia Guinn feasting on all the rodents in Tombstone.

Now, I tried to be a law-abiding citizen whenever I could, so I considered the law as I knew it. It was against the law to steal cattle, but this wasn't a cow. It was against the law to steal horses, but this wasn't a horse. It was against the law to steal chickens, but this wasn't a chicken. I had never heard of a law against stealing cats.

"Here, kitty, kitty," I whispered when the cook wasn't watching.

The cat just stared at me, finally lifting a forepaw and licking it. He must not've understood English, because he didn't move no matter how many times I called him. I finally dropped a piece of tortilla on the hard-packed dirt floor, and the cat rose lazily and ambled my way. He ate the food, then took another bite from my hand. I put a piece of bean-smeared tortilla on my leg, and he jumped up in my lap to eat it. I stroked his fur and got him to go to sleep. The woman cook seemed indifferent to my scheme, so I took a long time finishing my meal and my cup of coffee. I put a little extra money on the table to cover the cost of the cat. When she wasn't looking, I slipped the cat under my coat, rose, and started out the door.

Just as I reached Flash, the cat clawed me through my shirt. I about screamed like a crazy Apache before I managed to lift those claws from my flesh. I couldn't ride all the way to Tombstone with the cat clinging to my skin, so I walked over to the mercantile and talked the owner out of an empty gunnysack. When I got outside and was sure no one was looking, I dropped the cat in the bag, tied it to the back of the saddle, hopped on Flash, and headed toward Tombstone.

The cat was none too pleased with this riding arrangement. Once, when the sack slipped down beneath the saddle blanket, the cat took a swipe at Flash, digging those claws into his hide. Flash jumped and the cat screamed, almost scaring me out of the saddle. As soon as Flash calmed down, I secured the sack and made sure it wouldn't slip again. Once a day I opened it enough to drop a slice of jerky in. Whenever I came to a stream or a water hole, I would douse the sack to give the cat some water.

I had a lot of time to think on that trip. I thought about how good business was in Tombstone and how I might make even more money if I opened up a second saloon in another town. Benson came to mind because the railroad stopped there. By the time I reached Tombstone, I decided I'd explore the idea of opening a Benson saloon, provided Joe Campbell, Ned Nichols, and Til Walteree hadn't cheated me out of my profits in my absence.

The first thing I did in town was point Flash to my house. After I dismounted, I grabbed the sack with the tomcat, stepped to the door, opened it, untied the sack, and pulled the cat out.

I figured the cat'd be thankful, but he had an odd way of showing it. He clawed at my face, scratching me a dozen times before I threw him inside and slammed the door shut. I heard a terrible screech and then more commotion than I thought a cat and a thousand rodents could make. I decided to name the cat Satan for the way he had treated me and hoped that by the time I returned he'd been just as mean with the whole tribe of mice and rats.

Then I went over to the Stubborn Mule, half expecting to see the sign changed and my name replaced by Joe Campbell's, but everything was as I'd left it, except that Campbell had grown his beard back.

He and Walteree greeted me. "Looks like the Apaches didn't quite finish the job," Campbell said, eyeing my scratched face.

"You ought to see the Injuns," I replied.

Nichols got all nervous. "Apaches? They near?"

"No, Ned. Just go about your work."

Ned shook his head. "You just be real careful."

"There ain't no Apaches here, Ned."

"Maybe not, but it ain't Apaches I'm worried about." He pointed to a back corner where a poker game was in progress. "It's him I'm worried about, the pasty-faced fellow."

I turned around and took in a card game with four players. The fellow facing me, his back to the wall, looked like a gambler from the cut of his clothes. He had a narrow mustache, thin lips, and eyes as cold as a corpse. His pale skin, pimpled with sweat, gave him a sickly look. His fingers moved over the cards easily and, judging by the pile of money in front of him, successfully.

"He looks like a puny one to me. I know a tomcat that could take him for sure."

"I never seen a fellow that made me this nervous."

"Hell, Ned, you're scared of the dark. What about Wyatt Earp? He seemed a mean one."

Ned nodded. "But he didn't seem crazy mean."

"What do you mean?"

"This fellow don't seem afraid of dying."

"Everybody's afraid of dying," I said.

"Not him."

"Who is he?"

"Calls himself Doc Holliday."

Chapter Three

For once, Ned Nichols had reason to be nervous. Doc Holliday was the most dangerous man I ever knew. He was little more than a stick of dynamite surrounded by gaunt flesh and sunken eyes, a man with nothing to live for and nothing to die for. He looked so frail he couldn't have knocked a fart out of a bean-eating schoolboy, but I saw men twice his size back out of his way. He'd started out working in the Oriental with Wyatt but got in a dispute with Milt Joyce and shot the saloon owner in the hand, thereby ending his association with the Oriental. He made every sane man nervous. Nichols must've been the sanest because he was jumpier than a frog in a hot skillet.

"When he asks for whiskey," Nichols whispered, "I don't give him any but the good stuff."

We were losing money every time we sold him a drink, but that was cheaper than losing your life. Screwing up my courage, I walked over to his table just as he won a hand. His stare was colder than a banker's heart as he raked in his winnings and downed a jigger of whiskey. I saw the pearl handle of a holstered, nickel-plated revolver peeking from under his coat. He wore it butt forward on his left hip so that it angled toward his belly button, within easy reach of his right hand as he dealt cards. I would've taken on all the Earp brothers before I'd have challenged Doc Holliday.

Barely taking his eyes off me, he collected the cards

and shuffled them for the next hand. He coughed but didn't say a thing, just watched.

I was nervous as an itch come scratching time. "Don't mind me."

Holliday drawled, "You sound southern."

"Arkansas."

"A pity. Georgia is vastly better."

"General Sherman burned Georgia, but he was scared to torch Arkansas."

"Wasn't anything worth burning."

The men around the table laughed.

"Nor stealing," Doc finished, drawing another laugh. "There's room for another if you've got the money to burn."

"Us Arkansawyers don't have anything worth burning or stealing."

Holliday answered with a narrow grin and a hard stare. "You must be Lomax."

I nodded.

He eyed Satan's scratches on my face. "You been kissing a cactus?"

"A wildcat attacked me," I told him.

"Her name wasn't Kate, was it? Big Nose Kate?"

"Nope."

"Good." With that, Holliday began to toss cards around the table, manipulating them with nimble fingers. I knew he was cheating, but I couldn't catch him at it no matter how hard I tried. I figured I should kick him out of the saloon, but I had more brains than guts and decided it best to just leave him be.

I retreated from his table. Only after I reached the bar did I realize how nervous I had been—my knees felt like mush, and my palms were clammy. "Don't gall Holliday," I said.

"Don't worry," Nichols replied.

Campbell motioned me toward the end of the bar. "Let's go back to the office for a minute," he said, heading down the hall before I could answer.

I fell in line, passing a bedroom where Corina DeLure must've been giving some fellow a sad ride because he was sure moaning. I slipped into my small office behind Campbell, who closed and latched the door.

"What's this about, Joe?"

"Money," he whispered. "I figured you'd want your profits for the last two months." He went to the corner where he'd tossed an old pair of boots and picked one up, stuck his hand inside, and pulled out a wad of paper money.

"There's three hundred and sixty dollars here," he announced, handing it all to me.

"Shouldn't the take've been closer to six hundred?"

Campbell shrugged. "Sometimes less is more."

"Less ain't more when it comes to money."

"Business was down."

"Business is always down when you grow your beard, Joe. Shave it off tonight or don't come in tomorrow."

Campbell grumbled.

"No other saloon owner's paying you a dollar a day." I started counting the money.

He groaned, then forced a nod at me as he unlatched the door and departed, leaving the door open. I hurriedly totaled the money to make sure Campbell could add. Before I'd counted out two hundred dollars, I realized someone had joined me in the room. I spun around to find a black-haired woman with dark eyes, a wicked smile upon her painted lips, and a nose that was three sizes too big.

"Vell, vell, vant to take a poke for some of dat money?"

I'd never seen this woman before, but I'd seen plenty of her type. Her accent was thicker than Joe Campbell's skull, and I doubted she understood English any better than Satan the cat did. I figured she was from somewhere I'd never been and didn't care to go.

"Who hired *you*?"

"I don't know," she answered, looking back over her shoulder. "I vill get him for you."

"No, no. Who said you could work here?"

"Vork? Here? Yes, for ten dollars." She pointed across the hall. "The bed's still varm."

"No, no! Who said you could get customers from this saloon?"

"Vell, Doc said so."

I let out a slow breath. "What's your name?"

"Kate."

I shook my head. "You're Doc's woman?"

"Ven he vants me, yes. Ven he doesn't, I'm my own voman. Sleep vith men I vant, men who pay."

"I ain't sleeping with you, and I ain't paying you."

"Vhy not? You have the money."

"Don't want to make Doc mad."

She laughed. "Ven Doc's not mad, Doc's asleep."

"Get along now. Go!" I motioned for her to get out, then took her arm and pulled her to the door.

I had to admit she was a comely woman, save for the nose, and I had a good curiosity about how she treated a man. But I'd never considered suicide, which I figured I might be doing messing with Doc's woman, even if she was her own woman most of the time.

When she stepped into the hall, I released her arm and closed the door behind her, latching it quickly. I recounted the money, which came to three hundred and sixty dollars, just as Campbell had said. I pushed it down in my pocket, unlatched the door, and returned to the bar.

I could tell Campbell was still mad about me ordering him to shave. "Remember, Joe, less beard is more face."

He grumbled. Ned Nichols laughed.

As I stepped behind the bar, I heard Kate's husky voice. "Vant to join the game of poker? You have plenty of money, yes?"

I wanted to punch her big nose for announcing I was carrying a wad of money on me. If the wrong person heard it, my life would be worth about three hundred and sixty dollars.

Holliday called out, "Kate tells me you've got money to burn now."

"She's wrong," I answered.

"You calling my woman a liar?"

I gulped. Right then and there I decided that Doc

Holliday would find a reason to kill me if he ever wanted to. "I said she's foreign, hard to understand."

Holliday grinned. "You can have her, unless you'd rather go find another cactus to kiss."

"I'll pass."

Holliday nodded. "You're safer with thorns."

Kate punched his shoulder.

"See what I mean?" He brushed Kate aside and resumed dealing.

Still tired from my trip, I decided to go home before Kate found some other way to torment me. I told Nichols to see that Flash was stabled and fed.

When I got to my house, I rushed inside, shutting the door quickly to prevent Satan's escape. Looking about the parlor, I spotted a half-dozen dead mice, but not the cat. In the kitchen I found a dead rat and another dead mouse but still no Satan. I slipped into the bedroom, wondering if he'd found a hole in the floor or wall big enough to worm his way outside.

Deciding I wasn't going to find the cat anytime before morning, if at all, I took off my coat and dropped it on the mattress. Then I pulled the money from my pocket, poked my hand far enough under the bed to lift the floorboard where I kept my tin box, and slipped my latest profits inside. Just as I replaced the box and was about to back out, Satan attacked.

Screeching, the tomcat lunged for my butt, his claws slashing at my britches and digging into my soft flesh. I screamed and jerked my head up at the pain, bumping against the bed frame and collapsing on the floor as Satan worked over my behind.

I must've passed out then, because it was dark when I came to. I crawled out from under the bed, took off my clothes, and slipped under the bedcovers. Although I didn't hear many mice or rats that night, I didn't get a good sleep, either, not with my butt all cut up and bloody and my face still scratched and tender.

The sun was midmorning high when I got up. I managed to put on my clothes, including the pants with the seat Satan had shredded. I slipped into my coat, hop-

ing it'd cover my bottom, then headed outside, leaving
the door cracked in case Satan wanted to escape.

My behind was so sore, I decided to walk over to
Dr. George Goodfellow's office. Goodfellow, who had
been an army doctor, had settled in Tombstone because
he was interested in treating gunshot victims. He got
plenty of practice and saved several men with wounds
that were usually fatal.

I found him at his desk reading a thick medical
book. Rising, he greeted me and peered at my face. "One
of the saloon girls get mad at you?"

Shaking my head, I pointed to my butt. "That's
where it hurts."

He walked around behind me and lifted my coat.
He couldn't contain his chuckle. "She must've been a
feisty lady."

"It was a cat. A tomcat."

Goodfellow escorted me to the adjoining room and
put me on a table with a pillow for my head. After removing my britches and drawers, he boiled some water
and washed the dried blood off. Then he dabbed each
scratch with coal oil. The way it burned, he might just as
well have tossed a match to my backside. When he was
done with that, he put some salve on and treated my
face.

"That's a mean tomcat."

"Satan's his name."

"Can't say I've ever seen a cat around here before."

I grimaced as he dabbed coal oil on my cheek. "I
brought him back from Mesilla."

"As many rats and mice as there are hereabouts, a
fellow could make some money breeding and raising cats
for sale."

I'd considered raising cattle and even breeding
horses, but never running a cat outfit. "If they turned out
as mean as Satan, the cats'd be running Tombstone
within a year."

"Might be an improvement," Goodfellow replied,
"with all the mischief the townsite company is causing."

When he had finished with my face, he told me to
come back if I noticed any deep soreness after a couple

days. I paid him three dollars for his work, pulled my britches and boots back on, and headed for the door.

"Stay off your bottom as much as you can the next few days," he ordered.

Those were unnecessary instructions, I assured him.

On the way home my path crossed Doc Holliday's. The gambler tipped his hat, then spotted the back of my britches.

"Damn, Lomax, you been sleeping with a cactus? Kate might hurt you, but she won't leave any scars." His laugh erupted into a coughing spell.

"Just be glad I didn't come to you for treatment."

"I'm a dentist, not a doctor," he wheezed between coughs. I realized then why Holliday was so thin and pale—he had gambler's disease, consumption. Lungers had nothing to live for but death.

At my house I slipped inside and spotted Satan lounging in a corner, playing with a dead mouse. He looked up, hissed, and resumed toying with his mouse. I made it to the bedroom without him attacking, then napped a bit and went back out later to buy a new pair of britches.

A couple days later, after the pain had subsided, I decided to go to Benson to see about opening another saloon there, but my bottom was sore enough that rather than ride Flash I took the stage. That was a mistake.

The stage was full, but I was lucky—I squeezed inside the coach while a couple other passengers had to ride on top with the driver, Bud Philpot, and the guard, Bob Paul. Also on board was a strongbox holding some twenty-five thousand dollars in silver. We left Tombstone in the late afternoon and must've hit every bump on the road. My rear end was still tender, and I felt each jolt all the way from my tailbone to my brain.

It must've been rough on Bud Philpot, because we could hear him groaning from the driver's box. Seems he had been taken by bowel cramps and was not feeling good enough to control the team. We passed through what had been Watervale and wouldn't have stopped— because there was nothing there—except for Philpot's stomach pains. Anytime there was an unscheduled stop on a stage, everyone got nervous because of the threat of road agents. As Bud reined in the team, Bob Paul leaned down from the driver's box and eased our fears.

"Bud's not feeling well. Bowel problems," he announced. "I'm gonna drive and let him rest a little."

"Don't let Bud drop his problems on us," I answered, drawing a laugh from the other passengers crammed against me.

"Shame there ain't room for him to lie down inside the coach," Paul said, hoping a few folks would give up their seats and ride on top.

"We're paying passengers," announced the guy next to me. "He's getting paid to ride out top."

With my sore bottom, I knew I'd fight to the death before giving up my cushioned seat for a seat on top.

Hearing no takers, Paul switched places with Philpot and followed the trail northwest toward the San Pedro River and Contention, a respectable community with some mining companies. Paul was a better driver than Philpot; he hit only every other bump or hole in the road.

By the time we left Contention, it was turning dusk, that time of day when it's not dark but it's not light and everything is hard to make out. About a mile outside of Contention, I stuck my head out the window to try to see where we were before it got too dark to tell. We'd just crossed a dry wash and were starting up the other side when I saw what looked like a fellow with a mask over his face step into the road.

"Hold the stage!" he called out. Everyone in the coach stiffened, some grabbing for their wallets and shoving them in their boots or hiding them elsewhere.

Two more men emerged from the bushes ahead of us. I pulled my pistol free, ready to defend myself.

The stage slowed as it reached the top of the incline.

One of the bastards fired a shot, then another.

I heard a thud and a moan, then the blast of a shotgun from overhead. I stuck my gun out the window and fired just as a body fell from the top, forward of my window and the rear wheel. As the wheel rolled over him,

the coach tottered to the side for an instant before right-
ing itself.

The team bolted forward then, throwing my aim off.
I fired at two men as we passed but missed both of them.
They shot back, and the passengers around me shouted
as bullets whizzed by or thudded into the coach.

As the stage raced ahead, I heard more shots, then
the scream of a man up top. We swerved from side to
side on the trail, a couple times almost tilting over.

"The reins, I lost the reins!" Paul shouted.

Inside the coach everybody was yelling and panick-
ing. It didn't matter if we'd left the road agents behind if
we were going to overturn. I holstered my empty gun
and stuck my head out the window to judge if it would
be safer to jump from the coach or ride out the fall.

I caught a glimpse of Paul, who looked like he was
about to jump from the careening coach. Then I lost
sight of him, though I heard him shout from up front,
"Hold on, dammit, hold on!"

Gradually the stage slowed. When it finally stopped,
I flung open the door and leaped out. I spotted Paul sitting atop one of the rear horses, trying to drag in the
reins and straighten them. Quickly I drew my pistol and
loaded it again, glancing back down the road to see if the
robbers had given chase.

I didn't see anything, but I heard plenty: a woman
passenger sobbing, men cursing, horses stamping and
blowing, and my own heart pounding like a drum. I
stepped on the wheel and pulled myself into the driver's
seat, where I found the body of a passenger. Bud Philpot
had fallen off the stage.

A couple men crawled out of the coach, but Paul ordered them back. "Stay inside. As soon as I get the reins
sorted, we're riding on. I don't want them catching up
with us." He pointed at me. "Were you the one firing
back?"

"I emptied my revolver and didn't hit a one."

"That don't matter. You stay up top and ride shotgun."

I didn't argue.

Paul tossed me the reins, then jumped off the horse

and walked around the stage, checking the wheels to make sure none had been damaged. Then he climbed up into the driver's box and helped me lay out the dead passenger among the bags and trunks.

"Damn," Paul said. "If Bud hadn't gotten sick, I'd've been dead."

"I guess the cramps can kill a fellow," I answered.

Paul took his seat and bent down to retrieve the shotgun from the floorboard. He broke it open, dumped the hulls, and put in two fresh shells. Handing the gun to me, he asked, "Do you know how to use one of these?"

"I've used them before."

"With a scattergun your aim doesn't have to be perfect, just close." Paul patted the seat, then wiped his hand on his britches. "Sit down, and don't mind the blood."

No sooner had I settled into the seat than Paul picked up the reins and started us to rolling again.

We created quite a stir when we pulled into Benson. A crowd gathered to look at the body. Leaving the stagecoach with the lawmen, Paul grabbed my arm, and we went to the telegraph office. He sent a message to Wyatt Earp back in Tombstone instead of Sheriff Johnny Behan. I didn't understand.

"Why Wyatt?"

"He does work for the stage lines."

I took that to mean Wyatt had Wells Fargo connections, and Paul might well be one of their detectives.

"Why not Behan?"

"He's a crook."

When the telegrapher asked for payment, Paul waved him off. "Charge it to Wells Fargo." Then he took the shotgun from me and suggested we go back to the stage. "Could you identify any of the men?"

"Wasn't enough light, that and the masks."

"Bastards," Paul said. "I didn't get a good look at them, either. At least we know Wyatt'll be on their tail, him and his brothers. That ought to put the fear of God in them."

When we got back to the stage, folks swarmed

around us, yelling questions, wanting answers that even we didn't know. Paul got a telegram back that a posse had started out after the killers, but that was all we heard that night.

I stayed in Benson two more days, looking the place over, trying to decide if I could make a go of it with a saloon. There just wasn't enough mining activity or miners to make it work. The railroad passed through Benson, but it didn't look to me like the town would ever have more going for it than that. Once the railroad reached Tombstone—and it was halfway to Contention by then—Benson would have nothing on Tombstone.

After a couple nights in Benson, I returned to Tombstone on the stage. It was an uneventful ride, in large part because my behind wasn't sore any longer but also because we weren't attacked.

When we got into Tombstone, the town was abuzz with gossip about the attack. At first, for all the trouble it had caused me, I had regretted being on the stage. But then I realized that my presence eliminated my name from the list of suspects. Some said it was area ranchers named Clanton and McLaury and maybe a few of their friends: Luther King, who supposedly admitted to the Earps he had held the horses during the robbery; Harry Head; Jim Crane; and Billy Leonard, who was apparently a friend of Doc's. Some even whispered that the Earps and Holliday were the ones who'd robbed the stage and were trying to pin the blame on some innocent cowboys. Big Nose Kate got drunk and accused Doc of being involved, but she was mad at him for some slight and couldn't be trusted any more than any other lying son of a bitch in Tombstone. Doc was arrested for a couple days, then released. There were more lies floating around Tombstone than you'd hear at a convention of Republicans.

A couple days after I got back, Sheriff Johnny Behan and his deputy, Billy Breakenridge, returned with Luther King and threw him in jail, but they must've left the door unlocked, because within a day he escaped.

Toward the end of that March, about the time I was readying to return to New Mexico and try to convince

Rosalita to come to Tombstone, the Earps returned to town. I was the first person they sought out when they got back.

I was minding bar at the saloon when they rode up, tied their horses, and strode in. There were four of them—Wyatt, Morgan, Virgil, and a man I didn't recognize for a moment.

They sidled up to the bar, looking mean enough to jump naked into a barrel of knives. They'd been on the trail for several days, eaten little if any food, slept on hard ground, and didn't have a thing to show for their work, not even Luther King, who by then had probably ridden out of Arizona Territory.

Wyatt didn't as much as howdy me or call me by name. He got straight to the point. "Were you on the Benson stage?"

I licked my lips and nodded.

Wyatt pointed down the back hallway. "Then let's step to your office where we won't be heard."

"There's nobody else to wait bar."

Wyatt turned to face my customers. "Any of you gentlemen thirsty?"

They were too scared to admit it if they were.

"Fine for now, but if any of you touch Lomax's liquor, then I'll come around to collect your money."

"Lomax?" said the stranger accompanying the Earps. "You wouldn't be Henry Harrison Lomax of Cane Hill, Arkansas, would you?" He answered his question before I could and before I recognized him. "Well, I'll be damned if it isn't Lomax."

Then I realized I was staring at William Barclay Masterson, Bat to all his friends.

"You two know each other?" Wyatt asked.

"Damn right," Bat answered. "We hunted buffalo together in the Texas Panhandle. Lomax's a great Indian fighter. He must've killed a hundred Comanche at Adobe Walls."

I reached across the bar and shook Bat's hand. "Good to see you, Bat. You're not keeping as good company these days as you did at Adobe Walls."

Bat laughed. "Yeah, but they're safer than Comanche and don't smell nearly as bad as buffalo hunters."

"Then you've been staying upwind from Wyatt."

Wyatt didn't find that so funny, but Bat laughed. We exchanged stories as Wyatt herded us toward the back office. Once the door closed behind us, Wyatt interrupted our pleasantries. "There's lots of rumors going around Cochise County about the Benson stage robbery. What did you see?"

"Two, maybe three men try to stop the stage, then shoot the guard and a passenger."

Wyatt's squinty eyes narrowed even more. "Did you recognize any of the bandits?"

"Not a one."

Lifting his forefinger, Wyatt punched my chest and asked me another question. "You wouldn't be putting out any rumors, would you, that the robbers might be any Earps or Holliday?"

I shook my head.

"If I ever hear otherwise," Wyatt told me, "I'll see to it that you never tell another lie again."

"Come on, Wyatt," Bat protested. "Leave him be."

"Not if he's spreading rumors about us. He can harm our good names."

Good names? It was all I could do to keep from laughing.

"His word's straight."

"It better be straighter than his liquor," Morgan butted in.

"Go along, boys," Bat said. "Let me visit with Lomax. I can keep him straight. I'll catch up with you later."

The Earps left me and Bat alone. When he was sure they were gone, he took off his hat and wiped his forehead.

"Wyatt's not the same anytime he's around Doc Holliday. And being in the same town's too close. Holliday's nothing but trouble. You best stay away from him."

"I plan to, but if he's that bad, why're you hanging around?"

Bat shook his head. "I don't intend to. I'm leaving day after tomorrow. I don't know what all Holliday's mixed up in, but I bet it's more than he's letting on."

"I've got business in New Mexico Territory and was planning on leaving, too."

Grinning, Bat slapped me on the back. "We can ride partway together."

We left town two days later. Some folks said Wyatt scared me out of town, but I wanted to go see Rosalita in Fort Sumner. Bat and I had a lot of catching up to do on the trip. But he was smarter than me, because he never returned to Tombstone.

I did.

Chapter Four

I went to see Rosalita in April and then again in July. On the second trip I heard that two of the suspects in the Benson stage robbery—Billy Leonard and Harry Head—had been killed in New Mexico. Their luck was only slightly worse than mine, though. Rosalita changed her mind more often than the wind changed direction, and at the end of July she told me to return to Tombstone on the way to hell.

I followed her directions part of the way, and between Fort Sumner and Tombstone I stole every cat I could catch. It rained almost every day, and by the time I got back I had six wet gunnysacks, each with two mad cats inside, tied to my saddle. Flash stepped lively, worried those cats would get loose and cut us to shreds. My new cats were mean enough to take on any dog in town.

With so much rain, I was shocked to find that much of Allen Street had burned down in my absence. I learned later how it had happened. It seems one of my competitors at the Alhambra had gotten a bad barrel of whiskey and trundled it out under the wood awning in front of the place. A bartender who must've been dumber than Joe Campbell himself decided to see how much whiskey remained in the barrel, so he struck a match and held it over the hole in the top. He saw more than he wanted to when he dropped the match into the barrel and it exploded in flames. The fire burned down most of the commercial district, destroying sixty-six businesses, eateries, stores, and, most importantly, saloons. But what was bad for Tombstone was good for business at my saloon.

After making sure the Stubborn Mule was still standing unscathed, I rode to my house and found Satan, all fat and lazy, lounging on the front step. I'd locked the damn cat in the house, hoping he'd die of starvation or thirst, but the son of a bitch must've found a hole in the floor he could squeeze through. I never did find that hole, but from that day forward he was able to get in and out of the house as he pleased. He perked up when he heard the screeching from the sacks, like he was ready for a little female company. I dismounted, tied Flash, unfastened the gunnysacks, and dropped them in front of him.

Satan hissed and arched his back. Just to be on the safe side I jerked out my pistol; I wasn't going to let that cat scratch my behind again. He backed down when he saw the gun and started moving from sack to sack, sniffing at each. He settled on one that I took to have two females inside. When he screeched, they screeched back. Carefully I pushed Satan back with the point of my gun and slowly unknotted the twine.

The sack exploded as those two female cats flew out, all fangs and claws. They jumped for my face and began to scratch the hell out of me. I fell down spitting fur and would've been clawed to death if Satan hadn't intervened. That tomcat jumped into the fray and showed those females who was boss. He chased them off and left me on the ground, cursing as best I could with fur in my teeth and scratches on my cheek.

I took the other five sacks and tossed them in the shade of the house so the remaining ten cats wouldn't roast in the hot July sun. Then I walked over to Doc Goodfellow's office. He was patching up a stumpy cowboy with a big, dark bruise on his shin. The fellow was ugly enough to have been Joe Campbell's brother but too stupid to have been even a philosopher. If ugly wasn't his mother, she was damn sure related to him. His beard looked like it had been trimmed by the two cats that had just given me a close shave. His eyes were the same murky brown as his tobacco-stained teeth. Tiny shreds of tobacco were caught in his beard like he was saving them for hard times. By his clothes it looked as if he had already been through hard times. His britches were torn in a couple places, and his shirt was dirty enough I could've planted two or three rows of vegetables.

Goodfellow looked at me and shook his head. "Brought another herd of cats to Tombstone, did you?"

I nodded.

"Soon as I finish with Ike, I'll fix you up. A horse kicked him."

Ike grinned. "Maybe you ought to rustle cattle. They don't have claws." He chuckled.

I thought about kicking his leg just to let him know I didn't take that kind of insult, but I feared he might be friends with one of those cats and I'd be sliced to pieces by morning. I sat in a chair and waited as the doctor wrapped a bandage around his leg.

When the cowboy hobbled toward the door, he meowed like a damn cat, then laughed.

I nickered like a horse and stomped my boot twice on the floor and smiled. "Come by the Stubborn Mule sometime for a drink on the house, cowboy. Don't be afraid. The mule on the sign won't kick, and I'll give you the best stuff."

Ike grumbled something best left unsaid.

"You wouldn't be interested in buying a couple cats, would you? They'll help rid your place of mice and rats." By the look of his attire I thought a few rodents could be nesting in his clothes.

Ike growled. "I shoot rats when I see them."

"That could be suicide for you." He was so dumb he didn't understand the insult.

"Meow," he said again as he hobbled outside, leaving the door open.

Doc Goodfellow shook his head and moved to close the door.

I got up and sat on the examining table. "Who's that ass?"

"Ike Clanton. He calls himself a rancher. Most folks, myself included, figure he does more rustling and mischief than ranching. He runs around with the McLaury brothers, Curly Bill Brocius, and some of the other fine citizens of Cochise County."

I'd heard the names. "Sounds like the type of citizens I ought to sell some of my cats to."

Goodfellow examined me. "They didn't get your butt this time, did they?"

"No, I've learned to protect my better side."

He laughed and cleaned the wounds, then rubbed them with coal oil and salve.

"Put the word out I've cats to sell. They're tamed right nice."

"Looks like it," Goodfellow said as he finished doctoring me.

"Five dollars each or ten dollars a pair. Hell, Doc, they may even bring you some more business."

He tugged his ear. "I've plenty of business to get by."

I paid him for his services, then headed for the Stubborn Mule. It was still early afternoon, but the place was crowded and noisy because it was one of the few saloons still standing after the fire. Ned Nichols was jumping from customer to customer at the bar, trying to keep up with the orders.

"Where's Joe and Til? You look like you need some help."

Ned nodded. "They're resting. Since the fire we've been catching customers faster than we can string them. They'll be in tonight after six."

I smiled. "Business must've been good."

"Joe keeps up with that."

"I've got some chores to attend. Can you handle it yourself?"

Nichols shrugged. "As long as we don't run out of the good stuff. As much business as we've been doing, I fear we'll run dry on good liquor and Holliday'll shoot me."

"I'll take care of that." I turned toward the door and fought my way through the crowd to Holliday's table.

"Welcome back, Lomax. Care to sit at my table?"

"Actually, it's my table, Doc."

"Ooops." He chuckled. "I reckon it is." Then he

stared at me with those bloodshot eyes. "Well, shoot me for a billy goat, Lomax, but you're all scratched up. Have you been copulating with a cactus again? One of them big-busted saguaros?"

I denied the charge.

"Why, that's what the ladies are for. They must not've taught you that in Arkansas. Last time I hear you even got scratches on your butt. You need Kate to show you the difference between pecking a cactus and a woman. Kate can be your side girl if you want to keep sparking Miss Saguaro." Holliday laughed, then took a sip of fine liquor and started dealing.

"Don't shoot Ned if we run out of the good liquor, Doc. The way business has been, we're having trouble keeping your stock."

"You have my word, Lomax, one southerner to another."

I fought my way out of the saloon, then went home to free those damned cats. When I turned the corner, I saw a dozen people lined up at my place. A woman with two young girls pointed at me. "Are you the one with the cats for sale like Doc Goodfellow said?"

I nodded I was.

"I'd like two for my girls," she announced.

The others shouted that they wanted cats, too.

"There's not enough to go around," I answered.

"I'll pay ten dollars apiece," offered a thin man in a derby.

The woman with the two daughters sighed. "I heard they were five dollars apiece. I can't afford any more." Her girls, no more than seven and five, started to cry.

"The first two are five dollars apiece. The rest cost more."

"How do you explain that?" asked the man in the derby.

"Less is more," I told him.

"Huh?"

"The less cats there are, the more they cost."

The woman pulled ten dollars from her coin purse and pressed the bills in my hand. "There's your money. Where's the cats?"

I led her to the shade of the house. "Pick out a gun-nysack."

"Don't the girls get to see them first?" asked Momma.

"Not at five dollars each."

The two girls agreed on a sack. The oldest said, "This is like Christmas."

Of course she hadn't met the cats yet, so I figured she might change her mind once they came out clawing and scratching.

Their mother bent over to help them free their new pets.

"I wouldn't open that sack just yet, ma'am, and not outdoors."

Her fingers kept unknotting the twine. "Why not?"

"They might be wild."

She ignored me and pulled the sack open. Each girl reached inside, grabbed a cat, and pulled it out. Both cats seemed scared, but they didn't fight. The little girls held them close, petting their heads and gently stroking their fur.

I reached over to pet one, and the animal snarled and bit the tip of my finger. "Damn," I said.

The mother snorted indignantly. "Somebody needs to wash your mouth out with soap. Come along, girls. Don't listen to the vile words of that man." She turned about and marched away. The girls, though, only seemed interested in the cats in their arms.

After they departed, the others in the line paid me ten dollars apiece for the cats, the derby man taking two and everybody else one. I stepped back each time a gun-nysack was opened and pulled my hat down over my eyes, hoping none of the cats would recognize me. A couple cats were feisty, but none nearly as mean as Satan or the two that had escaped after attacking my face.

With ninety new dollars in my pocket, I went inside, hoping to get a little rest, but I couldn't sleep. Losing Rosalita had gotten me down in my boots. There was only one thing that could make matters better, and that was a bottle of whiskey. I was hoping Doc Holliday hadn't consumed all the good stuff and that I'd have a chance to get drunk and forget Rosalita.

When I returned to the Stubborn Mule, I found business had picked up even more, but Joe Campbell and Til Walteree had come in early to help Ned out. I pushed through the crowd for the back office, where the good whiskey was kept.

Holliday saw I was in a hurry. "Lomax," he called, "Miss Saguaro was in earlier looking for you." He laughed. Everyone looked at him like he was crazy.

I barged into the office and slammed the door behind me. Then I went to the corner where four cases of good whiskey were stacked. Three of them were empty, and the fourth had only three bottles left. I uncorked one and started in on it. Halfway through, Joe Campbell entered as meek as a mouse at a meeting of cats—mean, face-scratching cats.

"Lomax, you're back."

Holding up my bottle, I showed him how much I had downed. "More is less. More for me is less for Doc Holliday."

"You okay?"

"Sure, I'm okay. My girl doesn't want me, Holliday's drinking my good stuff dry, you're probably stealing my profits, and Satan's stalking me."

"Satan stalks us all," Campbell said, "but I didn't steal your money. It's all there. That's what I came to tell you."

"Get out of my sight until I sober up. Then you can pay me every cent I'm due."

He nodded and backed out of the room. I stayed and finished that bottle, then another one. No matter how much I drank, it was only a fraction of what Doc Holliday had been drinking uncut. Every time he took a drink of the good stuff, I lost money. The more I thought about it, the madder I got.

I'd had enough of him drinking my liquor and insulting me; it was time to do something about it. I stumbled a bit and my eyes were blurry, but I didn't care. I wasn't certain I could find my gun or if I even carried one, now that the Earps were enforcing the ordinance prohibiting guns, but that didn't matter, either. I would strangle the skinny runt.

I swaggered over to Doc's table and spit in his drink.

The other fellows at the table scooted their chairs back fast enough to catch up with yesterday. Walteree, hammering a spigot into a new keg of beer, froze. Ned Nichols took to shaking like a willow in a stiff breeze.

"I knew you cut your drinks, Lomax, but I thought you were more discreet than that."

"Go for your gun, Doc."

As soon as I said that, everybody jumped out of the way.

"You drunk fool," one of the cardplayers yelled, "that's Doc Holliday you're challenging!"

"He ain't a doc, he's a dentist. Call him Dent Holliday. Now, go for your gun, Dent."

"Why, I couldn't do that, Lomax," Holliday replied, too scared to get up from his chair.

"Why not? You a coward?" I went for my pistol.

"No. You're not wearing a gun."

I hit my thigh hard and came up holding a handful of air.

"You got a knife on you, Lomax?"

"No," I admitted.

Doc grinned. "I do."

He moved so fast I couldn't tell where he pulled that knife from, but it flashed like his wicked smile. He stood up. "Now I'm gonna cut your gizzard out and tie it around your neck."

He took a step toward me. I wasn't scared and thrust my chest out at him, grabbing an empty whiskey bottle by the neck and swinging it at the table edge. But I missed, and the bottle slid from my hand and shattered at my feet.

"I ain't got a gizzard."

"Well, Lomax, we're about to find out, aren't we?"

As Holliday inched toward me, I heard footsteps behind me and glanced around. But I never saw the mallet aimed for the side of my head. Walteree knocked me senseless, and I collapsed on the floor.

The next day I woke up in bed in the back room of the saloon, my brain pounding and my jaw throbbing. My mouth was dry except for the lingering taste of blood. I was bleary-eyed and uncertain I would live.

Ned Nichols walked in, and for a minute I thought he had a twin. But as my vision cleared, only one Ned stayed in focus.

"Water," I whispered.

"You're lucky to be alive," he observed. "If Til hadn't knocked you up 'side the jaw, you'd be wearing a coffin and six feet of dirt. You're lucky Joe Campbell had stepped out to the outhouse when it happened."

"How's that?" I croaked.

"He said we should've let Doc kill you so the saloon'd be ours."

"Are you gonna fetch me water or talk me to death, Ned?"

Nichols sneered. "You almost talked yourself to death last night." He disappeared out the door.

I felt my face. My right jaw had a knot the size of a hen egg beneath the ear, and it hurt when I talked. It hurt when I didn't talk.

Nichols returned with a tin cup of water. He helped me lift my head, then put the water to my lips. It was cool and good until it reached the back of my mouth, where it felt like I'd bit into a burning ember. I spit water. Nichols took the spray on the chest.

"That hurt?" he asked.

"Hell, yes, it hurts."

"Can't hurt as bad as if Doc had taken to carving on you with that knife. You spit in his drink and called him Dent."

"I was drunk."

"Snot-slinging drunk."

By then I was scared and knew I had to take the cure so I'd never get drunk again. "Ned," I said, "I want you to get me a glass and a bottle of whiskey."

"I can't let you drink again, Lomax, or Doc'll kill you."

"Do as I say. I'm leaving to take the cure."

"The cure for what?"

"For drinking."

"I didn't know there was one."

"You didn't grow up in the Ozarks, either."

"That's a fact." Ned left and returned in a bit with a full bottle and an empty glass for me.

"Now help me get on my boots and hat," I commanded.

He did. Then I ordered him to get Flash saddled. After he left, I collapsed back on the bed, my head a-spinning. I knew I should wait a day to take the cure, but that might be too late; I might get drunk around Doc Holliday again. After a short spell Nichols returned to tell me Flash was tied outside.

"Help me up and at him. Take the bottle and glass and put them in my saddlebag." Nichols got me through the saloon crowd and out to the street, packed my glass and bottle, and helped me into the saddle. The bright sun made me dizzy, but I had to follow through on this.

"Point me toward the San Pedro," I said.

"You're still whiskey-addled."

"I'm gonna be dead if I don't get the cure. Once you get Flash pointed toward the river, slap him."

No sooner was Flash aimed west than I heard Nichols's hand hit his rump. Flash took to jogging as I struggled to stay in the saddle for about eight miles of hell to the San Pedro. It took me about an hour to reach the river, but it seemed longer, my head aching so and my jaw throbbing. The river was up some from all the rain but had dropped enough to expose the muddy banks. I slid off Flash and stumbled in the mud, falling to my knees at water's edge.

I splashed my face, hoping to shake the liquor clabbered in my brain. Then I tried to focus my eyes on the water, praying I'd find what I was after, but the glare was blinding. So I pushed myself to my feet again and stumbled downstream, looking for any shallow pools that might have formed along the bank when the river fell. I found a couple small ones, then a larger pool maybe three feet across with a rock bottom and dozens of minnows swimming back and forth. Falling to my knees in the pool, I swatted at them, trying to catch one, but my aim was bad and my hand was slow. The minnows darted out of reach.

Desperate, I took off my hat and dragged it along the bottom, then lifted it up by the brim. Cursing at not catching a single minnow, again I pulled my hat like an awkward net through the water. When I held it up and squinted at the murky liquid slowly seeping through the felt, I spotted three minnows swimming crazily around.

"The cure!" I shouted, then howled because of the pain in my jaw.

Carefully I placed my overturned hat on a dry rock and staggered toward Flash. I fumbled the saddlebag open and pulled out the liquor bottle and the empty glass. As I shuffled back to my leaking felt hat, I bit the cork on the bottle with my front teeth and jerked it free despite the pain in my mouth. I spat the cork out, then fell to my knees beside my hat. The water was almost gone, and the three minnows were flopping about. After filling my glass with whiskey, I plucked up those slippery minnows and dropped them in, holding the glass to my eyes and waiting to make sure they were dead. They were lively for a moment, then sank to the bottom.

I wasn't the superstitious type and didn't believe in magic spells and things of that sort—unless they worked—but I knew for certain that downing a glass of liquor in which minnows had died was a sure Ozarks cure for drinking whiskey. I couldn't remember if the cure called for drinking just the whiskey or the whiskey *and* the minnows but decided to take no chances. Holding my nose with one hand and lifting the glass to my lips with the other, I dumped liquor and minnows down my throat.

The liquor was strong, the minnows were slicker than snot, and I almost threw up as soon as I swallowed them, but I managed to hold it all down because my life depended on it. I finished every damn drop. Then I grabbed the whiskey bottle by the neck and flung it as far as I could. It hit a slab of rock and shattered. I threw the empty glass away, too.

Then I waited there on my knees, hoping I never had another craving for whiskey within gunshot of Doc

Holliday. When I felt sure the minnows weren't going to come back up, I grabbed my wet hat and tugged it down on my head. Cool water dribbled down my face but did nothing to put out the fire in my aching head and throbbing jaw.

Pushing myself to my feet, I staggered upstream toward Flash, who was watching me like I was crazy. Maybe I was, but at least I wasn't a mule. I grabbed Flash's reins, took the saddle horn, shoved my foot in the stirrup, and pulled myself into the saddle. It took all my strength, but I somehow managed to settle into place and point Flash back toward Tombstone.

The sun was hot and hard on my eyes. When I finally reached Tombstone and rode down Allen Street, it seemed everyone was staring or pointing at me. I heard someone say that I was the idiot who had challenged Doc Holliday. Though I wasn't an idiot, I didn't care to stop and debate the issue. I just wanted to get home and rest. I'd been dead drunk before and knew the headache would go away, but I wasn't certain about the throbbing pain in my jaw.

When I reached my place, I slid off Flash and stumbled up the steps and inside. I made it to the bedroom and undressed without the tomcat assaulting me, then collapsed on the mattress. The sound of buzzing flies grated in my head. Occasionally one would land on my jaw, and I would groan from the touch. I tried to rest, but it was hard to make my jaw comfortable. Night finally came, and somehow I slept, my rest disturbed sporadically by Satan and another cat fighting and breeding outside for what seemed like half the night.

By morning my head had cleared, but my jaw seemed sorer than before. And my throat was dry. I wriggled my tongue, trying to coax out some moisture, but it brushed against a back tooth and sent pain shooting through my skull.

"Oouuch," I moaned. Carefully I stuck my finger in my mouth and touched the tooth. It gave and sent another bolt of pain through the side of my face. From the touch and the resulting pain I realized the tooth was cracked. I had to find a dentist.

Fighting the pain, I got up and dressed, then staggered outside toward Fourth and Fremont and the office of the dentist Gus Millard. But his door was locked, with a sign in the glass: GONE TO BISBEE. BACK TOMORROW.

Then I went to Allen Street and Seventh, where Milton L. Browne had a dentist's office. His office had burned down, and there was no sign telling where he might have moved. Now the pain was excruciating, as if someone was holding a hot poker to the back of my mouth. I was desperate. I knew of only one other dentist in Tombstone: Doc Holliday.

I didn't care if I was risking death to see him. The pain was so bad, death couldn't have been any worse.

I stumbled over to the Stubborn Mule, hoping he'd be playing poker at the back table, but he wasn't there, though a good crowd was. Behind the bar Joe Campbell talked to me between customers.

"Where's Holliday?" I asked.

He told me where Doc and Kate boarded. "You gonna try to kill him again?" He grinned. "Good luck."

I staggered out of the saloon and toward their abode. I wasn't sure I was at the right place until I knocked on the door and heard Big Nose Kate answer. "Who is it?"

"Lomax, Henry Harrison Lomax."

"Vat do you vant?"

"I want Doc."

There was silence for a minute.

"I want Doc!" I cried, desperate with pain.

The door swung open. Holliday stood there in his long johns, holding a gun in my nose.

"Come back to kill me?" he snarled.

"You just as well kill me before this tooth does."

Doc eyed me, and when he saw I wasn't armed, he lowered his pistol. "Need a tooth removed?" he asked, a wicked smile on his face.

I nodded.

He licked his lips. "I'd be glad to use my dentistry on you."

Chapter Five

As I entered the two-room adobe, Doc Holliday broke out in a fit of coughing and doubled over in his sweat-stained long johns. It was a deep, gouging cough. Even in my own pain I flinched at the sound. Kate, who wasn't wearing a stitch of clothing, handed him a cloth from beside the washbasin. He wiped his hand and mouth, and I saw a smear of blood when he tossed the cloth aside. My stomach felt queasy.

I turned my head and found myself staring at Big Nose Kate. I had to admit she was well equipped for her profession: dark sultry eyes, pouty lips, a fine bosom, a narrow waist, and broad hips. About the only imperfection was that large nose, hooked at the tip.

Holliday pointed to a table. "Would you, Kate?" he gasped, his eyes wild. She brought him a flask of whiskey, from which he drank heartily.

As he lowered the flask and capped it, he eyed me. "Every day starts this way, Lomax." He jiggled the flask and tossed it on the bed. "This may be whiskey to you, but it's medicine to me. It eases the pain. Consumption's a low, smoldering pain, unlike the flaring pain of your tooth. You'll live no matter what I do to you. I'll die no matter what anybody does to me."

Kate took his arm. "I vant you to stop saying such things."

"Ignoring it won't change it, Kate." He pushed her hands away and doubled over, coughing again. As he stumbled to the washbasin, he pointed to a chair by the window. I eased over and sat in it.

Holliday wiped his mouth, then glanced at Kate. "Dahling, why don't you put on some clothes. Lomax is in enough pain already."

"Vatever you vant." She picked up a nightgown.

"You have to admit, Lomax, she's better looking than Miss Saguaro." He hesitated, then lifted his finger to his lips. "Ooops. I forgot you're so touchy about your consort."

He was toying with me, reminding me of my threats against him in the saloon. Maybe he was going to kill me. That seemed preferable to the toothache. The agony was so great I wanted to grit my teeth, but that only made the pain worse.

From beside the washbasin Holliday picked up a small satchel, which he placed on the windowsill. He opened the bag and fished out some of the meanest-looking tools I'd ever seen. Some looked like pliers, others like tiny pry bars. One reminded me of a meat hook. I began to wonder if the pain in my mouth might not be as bad as the pain of getting it removed. I squirmed in my seat, especially when Holliday spoke.

"No other patient of mine ever spit in my whiskey," he said, his voice low and raspy. "You're either the bravest or the stupidest patient I ever had."

"Then shoot me and put me out of my misery."

"Not until I've fixed your teeth. Now, open up."

Soon as I opened my mouth, he grabbed my head and twisted it toward the light from the window. I groaned. When he leaned over my face, I thought I would pass out—not from the pain but from his breath.

I'd traveled the Texas Panhandle when it stank of rotting buffalo corpses, I'd gone on cattle drives with fellows who didn't bathe for months, I'd eaten Chinese food, and I'd once shaken the hand of a U.S. senator, but nothing in my life ever stank as bad as Doc Holliday's breath. I wanted to stick my head in a privy hole just to get a little fresh air. I wondered if I could grow gills and live underwater so I'd never risk getting this close to Doc again. It smelled as if his lungs were just rotting away with consumption. I was about to pass out when he moved back from my face and turned to the windowsill again.

"Looks like you've got a cracked wisdom tooth. It's gonna be hard to get to and painful to get out. What was that you were telling me the other night when you spit in my drink? Something about me drinking your liquor and ruining the good name of the Stubborn Mule?"

"I was drunk," I pleaded.

"So was I," he responded.

I was beginning to think I might've been better off if I'd waited for Milton Browne or Gus Millard to tend my tooth.

From his satchel Holliday pulled out a wooden wedge and an instrument that looked like an awl. "I need to probe the tooth to make sure I'm correct." He waved the awl in front of my nose.

"What's the doorstop for?"

"To keep you from biting my hand off. Now open."

Grimacing, I parted my lips.

"Now, relax."

As soon as I did, he shoved the wooden wedge in the left side of my mouth. "Good. Now tell me if this hurts."

He touched the tooth with the probe, and I screamed. "Aaaargh!"

"I didn't hear you," he replied, tapping the broken tooth again.

"Aaaargh, hammit!" I screamed, the wedge garbling my curse words. "Hamn you to hell, Hoc Holliday!"

"My, my, Lomax, are we no longer friends?" He jerked the wedge from my mouth. "I didn't understand you. What did you say?"

"How can you tell, Doc Holliday?" I lied.

"Tell what?"

"It's broke."

He shoved the wedge back in my mouth and struck the tooth with the tip of the probe.

I screamed again, but I didn't curse him.

"That's how. And I see the tooth's split down the middle."

He jerked the wedge out again and reached for the windowsill, then chuckled. Three or four men had gathered outside the window to see what the commotion was all about. "Move along, fellows. You're blocking my light."

"We'd best go," one said. "That's Doc Holliday."

"Who's the fool in the chair?" asked another.

"Looks like that fellow Lomax who spit in Holliday's whiskey," said the third. "Maybe we need to notify the undertaker."

Maybe I need to find another dentist, I thought, but Holliday was breathing in my face again, and I almost passed out from the smell. He waved a wooden-handled instrument that had an angled scoop at the end of a metal rod. "This is an elevator. I'm going to try to pry it beneath the crown and lift the tooth from the gum and jawbone."

The more he explained what he was about to do, the more dentistry sounded like hard-rock mining to me. I wondered when he was going to bring out the blasting powder.

He shoved the wedge back in my mouth and made a quick pry at the tooth. I screamed and stiffened in the chair, but he yanked the elevator out quickly. I tried to catch my breath.

"The tooth's split down the middle, and I can't pry it all up at once. If Walteree had hit you harder, he could've knocked the whole tooth out, and we wouldn't be having this problem."

If Doc Holliday hadn't been born, I wouldn't have been having the problem, either, but I didn't mention that. I wondered if a man could die from a broken tooth. I'd never known of anyone dying from cramped bowels, either, until the Benson stage robbery.

Holliday dropped the elevator on the windowsill and picked up the tool that looked like a bent meat hook with the curved claw mounted sideways on the bent bar. "This is a key extractor," he said, putting the handle in his right palm and holding the business end against the smallest finger on his left hand. As he twisted the handle, the hook tightened around his finger. "That's how I'm going to grip your tooth and twist it out. This should hold the whole tooth together and bring it out in one piece. Only problem is the roots in these back teeth. If they're straight, we may be able to get them out in one piece. If not, they may break." He seemed to enjoy telling me how those wicked tools could torture me.

He picked up another instrument and held it before my eyes. It looked like an awl with a threaded tip that came to a sharp point. "If I break off a root, I can't leave it in there. So I'll use this screw elevator to twist into the center of the root, then yank it out."

I shook my head to say I wasn't sure I wanted to go through with this, but he shoved the wedge deeper in my mouth.

"Sometimes even the strongest man passes out from the pain. That can be a blessing," he said.

That wouldn't've been as big a blessing as getting a whiff of fresh air.

He placed the screw elevator in my lap, shoved the key extractor in my mouth, and twisted it around my tooth.

All the earlier pain had merely been an introduction to the torture of that extractor. The metal twisted into the tooth and took hold tighter than a miser's grip on his last dollar. As Holliday twisted that extractor, I twisted in the seat, gasping at the fire that shot like molten lead through my jaw.

"Aaaaarrrrrggghhh!" I cried between the wedge on the left side of my mouth and the devil's finger on the right.

I bit into the wedge and felt my fingernails digging into the armrests on the chair. I screeched like a cat and bucked like a bronco. As if the pain wasn't bad enough, I heard a crunching noise and figured Holliday had just twisted my jaw in half. Then he pulled his hand free, and I saw a bloody tooth wedged in the key extractor. My jaw was aflame. My mouth tasted of blood.

"Damn," Holliday said, "one of the roots broke off." Dropping the key extractor in my lap, he grabbed the screw elevator and shoved it back in my mouth. He jabbed it a couple times into my gum, then hit something solid that sent pain shooting like lightning through my face and neck. He screwed the tool into the root as I thrashed about some more in the chair.

Again I heard a sick, crunching sound. He pulled the elevator out, holding it up to the light of the window.

"Got it!" he said, jerking the wedge from my jaw. "Let's just say I cut out your gizzard after all."

I shoved myself up from my chair, stuck my head out the window, and spit blood. When I pulled my head back in, I felt dizzy and weakened by the pounding pain. "It still hurts, dammit. You sure you got the right tooth?"

Holliday took the key extractor and loosened its grip on the thick tooth. It fell into two pieces in his palm. "I'm sure."

"I'm not." I fell into the chair. "The pain's still there."

"It'll be there for a couple more days."

I began to sag as Holliday went blurry.

"You're the first patient I ever had who didn't pass out from either the key extractor or the screw elevator."

He spoke too soon. He got blurrier and blurrier, and the room seemed suddenly warm and dark.

When I woke up later that afternoon in my own bed, I still had the taint of blood in my mouth—and a bit of a reputation. I learned later that after I passed out, Doc told folks I'd come to his room trying to make good on my earlier threat. He said we got in a terrible fistfight but that he'd finally knocked me out with a punch to the mouth, then had me carried home.

He praised me for settling our differences man-to-man rather than spreading vile rumors like the Clantons and McLaurys had, linking him to the Benson stage robbery. When a few upstanding citizens reported they had seen him pulling on my tooth, Holliday challenged anyone with a different story to discuss it with him. No one did. So Tombstone accepted Doc's account, whether anyone actually believed it or not.

At first his story didn't make a damn bit of sense to me. Everybody knew he could kill with his pistol, his knife, or his stare, but most doubted he could win a fistfight with anybody over six or under eighty years old. So

I decided he was just trying to build up his own reputation.

After a couple days the pain began to subside, and I felt about as good as a fellow could who'd taken the cure, lost his girl, been hit with a mallet, and had a tomcat stalking him. But one thing I'd learned about life since leaving home: Every time something goes bad, it creates a chance for something even worse to happen.

Her name was Hattie Ketcham. And Hattie came looking for me.

As word spread about my two encounters with Doc Holliday, people began to take notice of me. Business at the Stubborn Mule picked up because people thought I could keep order inside, even with Doc Holliday dealing cards.

It was about noon a week after Doc Holliday had pulled my wisdom tooth. I was resting in bed, enjoying the breeze blowing in the window, when I heard a rap on the door. Yawning, I got up, pulled on my britches, and ambled out to the parlor, keeping a wary eye out for Satan.

At the door was a fine-looking young lady with a covered basket on her arm. She stared at me, taking in my features and seeming impressed with my bare chest. Without saying a word, she reached for my chin and turned my face to the side so she could see the bruise along my right cheek. "Are you Lomax?"

"Me and my brothers."

"That where Doc Holliday slugged you?"

"That's what they say," I answered, not caring to contradict anything Holliday might have told folks.

Impressed, she offered me the basket. "This is for you."

"Why?"

She shrugged. "Because I felt like it."

After looking at her a moment, taking in her fine figure, her long dark hair, and her sky-blue eyes, I wondered what exactly she felt like. But I'd been around enough women over the years to know that generally the only reason they ever felt like doing something was because they had something up their sleeve. Or up their skirt.

She pushed the basket toward me, but I hesitated.

"It's not poisoned," she said.

I hadn't thought of that, but it put me to questioning even more why, of all the men in Tombstone, this woman had come to me.

"Go ahead, now, take it. When I come back for the basket, you can tell me how you liked my cooking."

No matter how bad her cooking might've been it was bound to be better than my usual fare. I took the basket and thought about inviting her inside but decided it improper, especially if someone was watching. I didn't know who this woman was or what she was after.

She eyed me like she was looking over livestock. "You got any more name than Lomax?"

"Henry," I answered.

"That'll do."

"It'll have to because that's what it is. What's your name?"

"Hattie."

"You got any more name than Hattie?"

"Not for now I don't." She turned and walked away. "I'll be back for my basket."

Watching the sway of her hips as she left, I had to admit she could make me forget Rosalita. She looked like a more decent type than Rosalita, too. When she had disappeared down the street, I stepped to the kitchen and set the basket on the table. Big mistake!

Apparently I'd disturbed Satan from his sleep. Hissing, the tomcat sprang to his feet and leaped for my pants, where he hung on with his claws. I grabbed him with both hands and pulled him off, but he wriggled away and lunged for my chest, his claws plowing furrows down my bare flesh before he slid down and landed at my feet. I kicked at him, but he scampered into the front room.

Looking at the scratches on my chest, I loudly cursed the cat again. It was a shame Hattie hadn't brought a basket of poisoned food so I could feed it all to Satan and watch him die.

I slammed the door to the parlor, then sat at the table and lifted the cloth cover from the basket. Inside was a loaf of bread still warm to the touch, a dish of apple butter, a couple slices of fried ham, some boiled potatoes, pickles, and two tomatoes.

Feeling right thankful, I tore off a hunk of bread and took a bite. It was fine bread, warm and moist. I smeared some apple butter on and gobbled it down. Then I attacked the ham and vegetables, tearing off more chunks of bread to go with it. It was as fine a meal as I'd ever eaten in my own house. By the time I was done, I felt like a new man, save for the fresh scratches on my chest and the ache in my right jaw.

After giving the food a little time to settle, I finished dressing, putting on my holster and gun in violation of the new city ordinance. Then I headed for the Stubborn Mule. Joe Campbell still owed me the saloon profits he'd saved while I was away in New Mexico.

When I walked in, Campbell was practically fighting off customers at the bar, there were so many. He looked like he hadn't shaved in a day or two.

"Dammit, Joe, keep the beard shaved or find another job."

He scowled. "You don't like change."

"Sure I like change, but I like folding money better."

"No, I mean change, new things."

"No, I mean change like the money you owe."

He jerked his thumb toward the hall. "It's in the office." Half the men at the bar looked at me like they'd gladly kill me for the money, no matter how small the amount.

Angered, I pushed my way through the crowd toward the office, making sure no one followed me but Campbell. He must've thought I doubted his honesty. I figured honesty was the one thing money couldn't buy—of course I always wanted enough money to see if that was true, but it just had a way of slipping through my fingers.

When we got to the unlocked office, Campbell

marched to the rolltop desk, lifted the cover, and pointed to a stack of bills and a pile of coins.

I gasped. It looked like a good fifteen hundred dollars or more. I no longer doubted his honesty, but I began to question his intelligence.

"You left money out where anybody could take it?"

"Nobody knew where it was."

"It wouldn't take much to find it."

Campbell pointed to the strongbox I'd bolted to the floor to keep my money in. "That's where someone'd look, not on the desk."

"You're crazy."

"I ain't neither. The safest place to hide something is where everybody can see it."

"That don't make any more sense than most of your gibberish. If that's true, why do we have banks? Why do banks have safes? Why do stages carry strongboxes? Hell, Bud Philpot died because bandits were looking for money where they knew it'd be."

"I thought you said Bud died of stomach cramps."

I sighed and decided I'd better start looking for the biggest piece of lumber in Cochise County to see if I could knock some sense into him. I thought about teaching Flash to tend bar.

"Joe, I don't know that you're ever gonna learn this business."

"It was my business before you stole it with crooked cards."

"They were your cards."

"It don't matter."

"You were trying to take my money. Maybe you're right, Joe, that more is less. The more money I have, the less you got."

Campbell grimaced.

"Joe, you're too stupid to ever have much money. You were tending bar in a tent when I found you. Your bar was a plank between two empty barrels. Now, look at this place. We've got a fine wood frame building, a mahogany bar, best backbar in Tombstone, fine paintings, and wall-to-wall customers."

"Only because Allen Street burned," he reminded me.

"We serve the best liquor in town."

"Until the customer's had too many to know the difference."

"If less is more, then wrong can be right," I reminded him.

"Then yours is mine," Campbell said.

"Huh?"

"If less is more and wrong is right, then yours can be mine."

"What are you talking about, Joe?"

He looked at me and then around the room. "One day this saloon'll be mine."

"Not unless I sell it to you, and I ain't selling it to you or anybody else."

Campbell started ranting. "Day is night and night is day. Hot is cold and cold is hot. Up is down and down is up."

"Speaking of up, Joe, why don't you just shut up?"

He scratched his head and started to speak.

I held my hand up. "In is out—you ever heard that one, Joe? Now that you're in this room, why don't you see if you can get out?"

"Huh?"

"Leave. Get your ass out of here. Go back and tend bar. Drunk is sober and sober is drunk. You get it?"

He was as confused as a bastard at a family reunion.

I grabbed his humped shoulder and twisted him around toward the door. "Now get to tending bar."

Campbell stepped toward the door, then turned to give me a bit of advice. "Don't leave that money out on the desk where some fellow can find it."

It was all I could do to keep from screaming. I hated mightily that I had taken the cure because I could have used a drink just then.

"Yours is mine, yours is mine," Campbell repeated on his way out.

I closed the door and counted the money. It totaled $1,647 plus coins. I kept wondering if this was all or if Campbell had been taking money from me, maybe paying himself two dollars a day in my absence. Sometimes I thought he was too dumb to steal, and at other times I thought he was too crazy not to. After I bundled up the money, I went back out and accosted him.

"Did you pay yourself and Nichols and Walteree in my absence?"

"I did. We were due our pay. You accusing me of stealing our pay from you?"

"I was just checking that you got your due." I figured he was due about a ton of brains, but I didn't know how I could fit them in his head. Maybe that was what the hump on his back was for. "I'll be back tonight, when it gets busier." I charged out the door and headed for home, planning to hide my money.

When I walked in, I knew right away something was wrong. I didn't see anything in the parlor. Then I stepped into the kitchen and found Satan sprawled out on the floor, lying so still he had to be dead. I stooped to grab his tail so I could throw him outside.

That's when the bastard came to life. He snarled and snapped and bit at my fingers, his fur standing on end, his back arched as he dared me to take a step toward him. Cursing, I backed away, and he stalked past me into the parlor. I hated that damn cat!

I went to the bedroom and shut the door so he couldn't slip in and ambush me. On hands and knees I slid under the bed far enough to lift the floorboard and fish out the tin. With the latest profits I had close to three thousand dollars, plus stock in several worthless mining properties.

After hiding the tin again, I stood up and stretched, then heard a knock on the door.

"Henry," said a voice as smooth as silk.

I thought it might be Hattie Ketcham, or possibly Satan throwing his voice to ambush me. Carefully I opened the bedroom door into the kitchen, looked both ways, then slipped through real quick. In the parlor I spotted Satan sharpening his claws against the wall. I walked to the door without turning my back to him.

"Henry? You home?"

As soon as I opened the door, Satan reclined on the

floor and stared lazily at Hattie Ketcham. I kept one eye on him and the other on her. She had a smile that would melt stone, and I sure enjoyed the cut of her figure in the gingham dress she was wearing.

"I came for my basket," she cooed.

I wasn't certain whether to let her in to take her chances with Satan or to keep her safely out of range. And losing a fight to a tomcat would certainly diminish the reputation I'd developed fighting Doc Holliday.

"May I come in?"

I stammered for the right thing to say.

"I take that as a yes?" She came in and shut the door, then seated herself in my rocking chair. "I can't stay long. Someone might see me."

I went to the kitchen to get her basket, cloth, and tin plate, never turning my back on Satan.

The cat was lounging in her lap when I returned, and Hattie was stroking his ugly fur. "What's her name?"

"It's a he. Satan's the name."

"Satan? What an ugly name."

"It suits him."

Satan purred as she stroked his back. I put the basket on the floor by Hattie's feet.

"You must think me a forward woman," she said, "bringing you food and inviting myself into your house."

"The food was good."

She smiled. "Thank you. If I'm too forward, forgive me, but do you have a lady you keep company with?"

"No more," I admitted.

"I'm sorry for you and for her. But happy for myself."

I scratched my head. "How's that?"

"You're a fine-looking man. And a brave one."

I could find nothing to argue about there.

"And I need a brave, strong man for a beau. Anybody who can stand up to Doc Holliday twice is right for me."

I strutted about the parlor for a moment, pleased she'd seen some of my stronger qualities.

"Fact is, I need a brave man to visit, have some fun with."

"Why's that?"

"It's my folks," she said. "Here I am almost twenty, and they'll have nothing to do with me seeing fellas. I'll wind up an old maid unless I find a strong man that won't back down to them."

I was beginning to see an advantage to having a reputation as a fighting kind of fellow. "I back down to no man."

"That's what I've heard," she replied. "I just want someone that'll take me out a few places, maybe to a dance on occasion, and have a little fun. My folks think fun is the same as sin. I'm like a caged bird that wants to fly. The last two fellas I've courted, my folks scared them away and threatened me."

I didn't know who her folks were and probably should've inquired more right then and there, but as long as she wasn't related to the Earps, Clantons, or McLaurys, I figured things would be okay.

"What'd you say your name was?"

"Hattie."

"You told me Hattie, but not your full name."

"Hattie Ketcham."

I wasn't familiar with any Ketchams in Tombstone, so I figured there wouldn't be any harm in courting her. "I don't know your family."

"And I can't introduce you. I have to slip out of the house to see men. We'll have to visit on the sly. They'll smother the life out of me until no man'll have me for a wife or anything else."

I stepped over and patted her on the shoulder. "No, you'll never have that problem, Hattie."

Satan lifted his paw and took a swipe at the fly of my pants.

I jumped back.

Hattie giggled.

Satan just purred.

When she finished giggling into her fist, she put Satan on the floor and grabbed the basket as she stood up. "Thank you, Henry, for treating me like a lady, even when I'm a bit forward, but I had a good feeling about you."

I was sure thinking about a good feeling of her.

"Night after tomorrow," she said, "there's a fandango in Charleston. I could slip out before dark, and we could ride over. Dance a few hours and come back. I'd like that."

She didn't waste any time asking for what she wanted. I wondered how long it would take me to get what I wanted, her being as forward as she was and all.

"I can rent a buggy, and we can do that. Where do you live?"

"I shouldn't tell you. If you passed by, even by accident, it'd upset my folks, and they might beat me."

My blood started boiling. I wasn't going to let that happen. I was the man who had stood face-to-face with Doc Holliday, even if I was drunk. I was the man who had gone to Doc Holliday's house to settle a score, even if that wasn't entirely true.

I wasn't going to let Hattie's family treat her badly. I just wasn't.

Boy, was I wrong!

Chapter Six

The next day I bought a new suit of clothes and new boots and made arrangements at the O.K. Corral to rent a buggy for the trip to Charleston. Then I went to see the lawyer Henry Guinn to discuss the legal papers I'd signed before visiting Rosalita.

Amelia Guinn greeted me at the door. "You didn't bring any of those saloon girls, did you?" As I entered, she poked her head outside to make sure I hadn't been accompanied by a female of ill repute.

"I didn't bring any last time, and I didn't bring any this time."

"I don't want Henry getting foolish or sinful ideas from them."

I stared at her in amazement. "Why would he ever stray from you? You're twice the woman he'd ever find in a saloon."

She smiled, putting the best face she could on so much ugly. She was so homely she must've slapped her feet each night to get them to go to bed with her. Of course she had to see her feet to slap them, and, as big as she was, I wasn't sure that was possible.

"Is it true what they say about you, Lomax?"

I crossed my arms over my chest and rocked on my heels. "You mean about me staring Doc Holliday down?"

"No, that you drive herds of cats to Tombstone."

"I've been known to bring a few cats to town."

"I'd sure like one next time you do. I'll pay a pretty penny."

It was hard to believe anything she touched could be pretty. "I got out of cat ranching. It was too dangerous."

"I'd pay anything for a cat. My husband's good for the money."

Him being a lawyer, I figured that someone else was good for the money once Guinn picked his pocket.

"I don't have any more cats for sale."

"Know where I could find one?"

"I know a saloon girl who's thinking about getting rid of hers. Want me to send her over?"

Amelia gave me a glare that could've frozen hell with enough left over to cool down Texas considerably. "Don't you even think about that. I don't want him coming within sight of a saloon girl."

As long as Amelia was at his side, Henry Guinn'd never see a saloon girl because she blocked the view. Angered at my suggestion, Amelia stomped into her husband's office, the whole house rattling with each footstep. She announced my name and stomped back out. I'd seen buffalo and cattle stampedes before, but neither scared me as much as her tonnage charging past.

Henry Guinn followed in her wake, unhooking his glasses from his ears with one hand and shaking my hand with the other. "How's Joe Campbell doing? It's been a while since I've seen him at church."

"We've been busy at the saloon, but Joe's quoting the Bible every day," I lied.

"I'm not surprised. He's a deep thinker."

"About as deep as an empty well."

Guinn motioned me into his office. "How's business?"

"Better than ever since Allen Street burned down," I replied.

"We were lucky the fire didn't reach us."

"Come by the Stubborn Mule sometime, and I'll give you free drinks to celebrate your luck."

Guinn shook his head. "I don't drink."

I didn't know how any man could live with Amelia

Guinn and not drink. "Come on by anyway. I bet one of
the saloon girls'd be glad to give you a ride in the sack.
On the house."

Guinn stepped back, waving his hands in front of
him. "Oh, my, my, no. That would be sinful."

I winked, then looked back over my shoulder to
make sure Amelia wasn't near. "Yeah, but wouldn't it be
fine for a change?"

"Oh, no, no, no, I couldn't do that."

"If you can't do it with Amelia, you could sure do it
with one of my girls. They'd raise your flag mighty high,
they would."

Guinn cleared his throat. "It's a despicable business
you're in, debauchery and drinking and gambling."

"Campbell's in it, too."

"He goes to church. I don't see you there."

He had a point I couldn't argue, but I always figured
God paid more attention to where a man's heart was
rather than where his butt was. My butt was seldom
planted in a church pew.

"I came on legal matters," I said.

"You should get to them before I am further insulted
and suggest you seek representation elsewhere." He
hooked his glasses back over his ears and stared at me all
bug-eyed, then motioned for me to take a seat. "I assume
your visit is about your lot and the disputed claim?"

"No, it's about those papers I signed before I made
those trips to New Mexico—the ones that give Joe
Campbell power of attorney in my absence."

"Those papers are still in good order now," he told
me.

"I want to destroy them."

"Well, sir, Mr. Lomax, that's not how we do things.
I'll need to draw up new papers, making null and void
the previous agreement. That can be handled easily."

"Then I'd like it done quickly. I don't want Joe
Campbell to have any reason to shoot me, and he's just
crazy enough to do it."

"Not Brother Campbell," Guinn replied. "He's a
fine man. God will provide for him."

Grinning, I nodded. "Then work up papers for God

to turn His affairs over to Joe if He can't carry on His business."

Guinn eyeballed me, clearly relishing the next bit of news. "I suppose you haven't received the papers yet, but the Gilded Age Mining Company has started proceedings to evict you from your house."

"What?" I almost spit out my teeth. "It's my house, dammit, bought and paid for with my money."

"Well, the law will determine that."

"Law? I got papers on the house and lot. I paid the money."

Guinn shook his head. "The title to the lot wasn't clear. The townsite company laid out the town without clear title to the land."

"Then let's kill them."

"That's against the law."

"So's stealing land a fellow's bought and paid for." I shoved my fingers in my pocket.

Guinn's eyes widened behind those thick lenses. He must've thought I was going for a gun. Pulling out a roll of money, I watched his expression change from mean to pleasant. "How much is it going to cost to fight the mining company?"

"You'll owe me ten dollars for working up new papers related to Joe Campbell's responsibilities and a hundred dollars to respond to the mining company's claims."

"A hundred dollars? That's robbery!"

"The mining company has plenty of money to throw at this matter. It will be expensive to fight them, maybe even cheaper for you to give up the lot and move your house to a new location."

"What?"

"It's on a stone foundation, isn't it?"

I nodded.

"It can be lifted off the foundation and carried to a new site. I've seen it done in disputes like this before."

"I like where I am."

"So does the mining company."

"The bastards."

Guinn wagged his finger at me. "No more of that

kind of talk in this house. Amelia's ears should not hear
such vile words."

I wanted to slug Henry Guinn in the nose, but I figured he'd just call the law and I'd be in more trouble. So
instead I pulled a hundred and ten dollars off my roll and
tossed the bills on the desk.

He jumped on that money like Satan on my face,
licking his lips as his fingers straightened the bills into a
neat pile.

"Now, that should get the mining company off my
back."

Guinn shrugged, still eyeing the money. "It might
cost more. You never know what tricks the company
might pull."

"A hundred dollars won't guarantee what's right?"

"That'll be for the judge to decide."

"Maybe I should just bribe the judge."

"That'd be illegal."

"So's stealing my house and lot."

"Not if the judge says otherwise."

I lifted my arms in exasperation. In every boom-
town I'd ever been in, I'd heard a clamor for the law to
come in and civilize the place. Only problem was, the
law was just as bad as the lawless, and the little man got
trampled by them both. It was fancy-pants lawyers with
fat-assed wives who got rich while the workingman was
sweating and working long hours to make a go of it. A
workingman made his money by the sweat of his brow,
but those damn lawyers and politicians made theirs by
putting ink on paper. "It's not fair."

Guinn just smiled at me. "That's the law."

I was mad enough to eat nails and spit tacks. Maybe
that son of a bitch Joe Campbell was right. Maybe more
was less. Maybe more law was actually less law. It
burned me to think about it. Without another word I got
up and strode out.

"Tell Joe we've missed him at church," Guinn called.

The thought of a lawyer in church riled me more. I
slammed the front door behind me and strode down the
street, figuring I'd need something to cool me off. I
looked at the sky and decided I might not have to wait

long, not with storm clouds building to the west. Lightning flashed through the dark clouds, followed by thunder rumbling like God was mining the sky. Though I'd already rented a buggy at the O.K. Corral, I wondered if it was wise to take a rig to Charleston the next night for the fandango, especially with as much rain as we'd already had since the Fourth of July.

Hattie came by my house just as I was returning from Guinn's office. "I can't stay long," she said as I opened the door for her.

The moment she walked in, Satan jumped down from my rocking chair and ran toward us. I prepared to defend myself, but the damn tomcat purred and rubbed against Hattie's leg. I suspected it was a trick but felt a little easier when Hattie picked him up and stroked his fur.

"How are you, fellow?" she asked. The tomcat just purred and looked at me like the truce was only temporary.

A clap of thunder rolled over the town, setting the windows to vibrating. "Hear that?" I asked.

"Thunder."

I nodded. "If we get much rain, I don't know that it's wise for us to take a buggy to Charleston for the dance."

Frowning, Hattie looked at me with those pretty blue eyes and batted her lashes until my knees were weak and my sap started rising.

"Maybe we could stay here. Go to the theater," I suggested.

"My folks don't like me seeing fellows. If someone told them I was seeing a man, they'd cause trouble, even for a brave man like yourself. I don't want that."

Thunder rolled over Tombstone again.

"We don't have to take a buggy," she went on. "I can ride a horse. I don't mind. We can get there faster on horses and won't have to worry about getting stuck or turning over."

"You might get mud on your dress."

"I'll go in riding clothes and change when I get there."

It just didn't seem wise to make the trip, not with the weather like it had been. "I don't know."

"Please. The desert's so pretty after all the rain." She gently tossed Satan to the floor and put her arms around me.

I threw a smug look at Satan. The fires of hell were burning in his eyes. "Okay," I said.

Hattie giggled, then planted a kiss on my cheek. "There's more where that came from," she said, "but I've got to go. I'll meet you here tomorrow afternoon about five o'clock. Then we can ride to Charleston, dance a couple hours, and no one'll know the difference."

I tried to exchange slobber with her, but she slipped out of my grip and escaped out the door. I couldn't wait to dance and maybe do something else in her arms the next night.

After she left, I walked out on my front step and looked to the west where the clouds were building. I figured we had an hour, maybe less before the rains hit, so I pulled the windows down in the house and hurried over to the O.K. Corral. I wanted to get a refund on my buggy and go over to John Dunbar's livery stable to rent a pair of saddle horses. Dunbar generally had better saddle mounts, though there wasn't much difference between the buggy animals at the two stables. John Montgomery at the O.K. Corral didn't charge as much as Dunbar for stabling an animal, so that's where I kept Flash.

I found Montgomery forking hay to a couple horses. He spotted me and cursed. "Dammit, Lomax, sounds like we're gonna get more rain."

"At least the town won't burn down again."

Montgomery laughed. "Didn't hurt your business, wiping out all those saloons on Allen Street. If you hadn't been in New Mexico Territory, I'd've sworn you were behind the fires. Everybody's always thought you were a fool for putting your saloon on Fremont Street, but I guess you had a gut feeling that Fremont wouldn't burn down."

"I had a feeling, yes, sir, I did," I lied.

He pitched more hay into the feed trough, then

pointed his pitchfork at the roof. "Damn roof's got so many leaks the water's getting my hay wet and ruining it. I'd just as well feed it to the animals so it doesn't go to waste. Flash is putting on weight with all the extra groceries, Lomax, and no charge to you."

"Obliged, John. Now, I need your help. I need to get my money back on that buggy for tomorrow night."

Montgomery tossed me a grin, thinking it was a joke.

"Really," I said.

Montgomery, who was friendly when you weren't talking about money, jammed the pitchfork into the rotting hay. "It's been a bad month, Lomax. I turned down another customer who wanted the buggy today because I was holding it for you. I can't let you have your money back."

"What?" I wondered if he'd been taking lessons from my lawyer.

"Dammit, Lomax, I've been feeding your damn mule extra fodder since you got back from New Mexico. Believe me, the mule needed it."

"The hay was gonna rot anyway."

"My buggy was gonna be rented anyway, but I saved it for you and sent the other fellow elsewhere. He even offered me more money."

"I can't help that."

Montgomery let out a long breath. "Money's been tight after the fire, folks rebuilding. The rains haven't helped things, Lomax. I just can't stand to lose the money. Your business hasn't been hurt by the fire; it's been better. But not mine."

The corral owner was correct about that, I had to admit. Even though I didn't like it, I appreciated the fact that Montgomery wasn't a lawyer, and even if he did cheat me out of a few dollars on the buggy rental, he couldn't take a pen to paper and cheat me out of any more.

"Okay, John, you've convinced me. Have the buggy ready tomorrow by four-thirty. And I'll want your two best saddle mounts to boot."

"You ain't spoofing me, are you, Lomax?"

"No, sir. I'll pay in advance again."

"Ten dollars, then."

I fished my money roll out of my pocket and peeled off ten dollars.

"I'm obliged for your understanding and your business, Lomax. Fact is, I had some debts to pay off, and I spent your money as soon as I got it. The fire and then the rain have hurt my business bad."

I shoved my money back in my pocket. We shot the breeze a little more, and Montgomery assured me he would give me the best mounts and rigs he had the next day. As I left the stable, I glanced to the west and saw the thunderheads churning toward Tombstone. "Looks like you'll lose more hay before the day's over," I called to Montgomery.

He cursed as I jogged off toward the Stubborn Mule. The storm clouds to the west finally blotted out the sun, and the streets turned dark and oddly quiet behind me, but up ahead there seemed to be a big commotion coming from somewhere.

The closer I got to the Stubborn Mule, the louder the noise got, and I realized the commotion meant business was booming and I was gonna get rich. I marched inside like I owned the place, grinning at the shoulder-to-shoulder crowd.

"Meow," somebody said as I squeezed between a couple cowboys. I caught a glimpse of Ike Clanton, mocking me. He hadn't gotten any better looking since I'd last seen him. I was glad I didn't have any mirrors on the wall. Ike was so ugly that if he'd looked in a mirror his reflection would've puked on the floor. "Played with any more kitties lately?" he called after me.

"Nope," I answered. "And I ain't been kicked trying to mate a mare, either."

"You son of a bitch!" he yelled. "It weren't a mare!"

"Then you deserved to get kicked if you were mating a stallion."

Ike lunged for me, but someone stepped between us. I pushed my way to the bar and squeezed around behind it. Joe Campbell, Ned Nichols, and Til Walteree were working as fast as they could to keep up with the business.

"What's going on, Joe?"

"Cowboys from all over are coming into town. They got cabin fever, I reckon. Rains didn't let them celebrate the Fourth of July. Rain's muddied up their work so, they just wanted to have some fun."

I figured there was nothing wrong with their fun as long as their money was good and they weren't gonna tear anything up. Ned Nichols, though, was scareder than a Methodist at a Baptist baptism. He sidled over to me and whispered in my ear.

"These fellows are rustlers, thieves. Some of them are supposed to be murderers."

"They look like drunks to me," I answered.

No sooner were the words out of my mouth than Ike Clanton shoved his way to the bar opposite me, planted his palms on the bar, and leaned over. "Who you calling drunk, cat poker?"

"All of you, stallion pecker."

Ike slapped the bar. "I ain't taking that kind of talk from no cat poker."

"You don't scare me," I answered, grabbing a mug and filling it with some of the turpentined whiskey. "I've seen meaner kitty cats."

Already red from so much liquor, Ike's face colored even more. He didn't flinch at a sudden clap of thunder that rattled the building and stopped all the other noise for a moment.

"You bastard," Ike said. "I'm gonna take you down."

The moment he lifted his hand off the bar, I was going to throw the liquor in his face and blind him for a minute. Just as it seemed he was about to make his move, a younger man shoved his way forward and grabbed his hand.

"Settle down, Ike. No cause to start fighting."

Ike shook his arm, trying to free himself from the young man's grip. "He accused me of screwing horses, Billy."

"Stallions," I corrected.

Ike swelled up like a bullfrog and would've burst if

the young fellow hadn't laughed nervously. "You don't know who this is, Ike."

"Don't matter, after what he said."

"He was just funning, that's all. This is H. H. Lomax, the man who spit in Doc Holliday's drink. He ain't scared of nobody, and he's faster than lightning. You gotta listen to me. I'm your brother."

That was the first time I laid eyes on Ike's brother, Billy Clanton. He was maybe nineteen, too young for gnarly whiskers like his brother's, but he had the same loutish look as Ike, just not as experienced. He must've been over six feet tall, at least four inches taller than his brother.

Ike, though, was better at giving advice than he was at taking it, and I held the glass of whiskey ready to blind him. He mumbled something I didn't understand.

Billy shook his arm nervously. "This is the man that stared down Doc Holliday."

Ike tugged his beard. "That don't scare me. Holliday's the runtiest thing I've ever seen."

"Not so loud," Billy protested. "Holliday's over in the corner playing poker."

"I don't care where the runt is, I ain't scared of him." Ike blustered and bellowed as Billy pulled him across the saloon. His place at the bar was taken by a slender man with a long face, receding hairline, and thick mustache. He had cold eyes and a soft voice that seemed more dangerous than Ike's bluster. And it was.

"I'll have a whiskey—and none of that thinned stuff your bartenders serve after a glass or two," he said.

I motioned for Ned Nichols to get a good bottle. Just as I did, a flash of lightning blazed outside, then exploded in a clap of thunder. Everyone, drunk or sober, seemed to catch his breath, then laugh nervously. When Ned stepped back to the bar, he was so jumpy the bottle shook as he poured a jiggerful, spilling a considerable amount on the bar. I had a feeling it was the customer more than the lightning that frightened him so. Then I realized we were out of good stuff.

The fellow took the jigger and tossed the whiskey down his gullet, then cat-quick grabbed the shaking whiskey bottle from Ned's hand. "I'll pour my own. Won't spill as much that way." He turned his hard gaze on me. "It true you stared down Doc Holliday?"

"That's what they say."

"You don't strike me as the type to stare down anything except widows and orphans."

"Argue with them, not me. I ain't going around saying it."

"Ike may blow a lot of hot air, but he's scared. Me? I'm not scared of you or Doc Holliday."

"I'll remember that, if you just tell me your name."

"Johnny Ringo," he said, turning away from the bar and carrying the whiskey bottle with him.

"Ned," I said, "go tell him to pay for that whiskey."

He began to shake like a dancing girl until I grabbed his arm.

"I's just kidding, Ned."

Ned blubbered, "I thought I was gonna have to quit or die."

"Quitting's easier."

I watched Johnny Ringo squeeze through the crowd, then grab the arm of Corina DeLure as she passed by. She laughed and put her arm in his, and they made their way to one of the back rooms.

A sudden cool breeze rushed through the windows, accompanied by another blast of thunder. Then the skies cut loose with a downpour. Tombstone had fine streets, especially if you liked dust or mud. The rest of the day was going to be mud.

I helped tend bar for an hour or more. Then business slowed down some, though the crowd remained. There was no place anyone could go without getting doused, and several of the fellows only allowed themselves one bath a year. They clumped together in groups away from the half-dozen or so leaks that had sprung in the roof. A couple fellows went around grabbing their buddies and tossing them out in the rain and mud, and everyone was having a grand time.

Some of the talk at the bar was about the poker game going on in the back corner. "Who's playing?" I asked.

"Doc Holliday, but Frank Stilwell and Pete Spencer are holding their own against him."

Stilwell and Spencer were a couple more fellows with bad reputations. Stilwell worked as a deputy sheriff on occasion but didn't do much else. A lot of folks had their suspicions the pair had been involved in several stage robberies around the county, but there was no proof in suspicions.

I ambled over to the poker game, grabbed a chair, and leaned up against the wall to Holliday's left. It was just the three of them playing, a couple other fellows having already been busted by Doc. I followed the game for a spell and couldn't understand why Doc didn't end it. He knew how to cheat with the best of them, but it was like he was gauging them.

Stilwell was a cocky fellow, always laughing loudly when he won. "I'm winning all your sugar, Holliday," he said as he pulled in a small pot.

Doc just grinned, as calm as a priest, never getting riled. I figured he had something other than a card up his sleeve, the way he let the game go on and on. When he was slow putting his ante on the table before a hand, Stilwell needled him.

"Sweeten the pot with a little more sugar, Holliday."

Doc held up a handful of bills. "Down south, Frank, we call this money. Sugar? Why, that's a name we call our fine ladies. Of course, you probably don't know much about ladies, now, do you?"

Stilwell lifted a handful of his own money. "I guess I can buy all your kind of sugar with my sugar, wouldn't you say, Holliday?"

"I wouldn't say much in conversation, except with a gentleman." Doc cocked his head and smiled. "That's why I have so little to discuss with you, Frank."

"You going to deal, Holliday, or chat?"

"Why, deal, of course, Frank. I's just trying to be sociable before I put all your sugar in my bowl."

Doc tossed cards around the table, and the game continued back and forth. Finally I got bored and returned to the bar.

Joe Campbell motioned for me to accompany him

down the hall to the office and storeroom. I followed, uncertain what he wanted. "We're running out of liquor. The good stuff's already gone."

"Well, let's piss in some jars and see if we can sell it. They're so drunk they wouldn't know the difference, and it'd run through their systems a lot quicker."

Campbell sighed in disgust.

I shook my finger at him. "Joe, I remember something you said the first time we met."

"The time you stole my saloon from me?"

"That's the time. You said, 'A man's got to follow his piss.' Well, I'd like to see if we can sell it."

Campbell shook his head. "It'll be days before we can get any more liquor."

"We'll order more from Tucson."

"Sure, but until the roads dry out and the creeks drop, there ain't gonna be any liquor getting into Tombstone."

Damn if Campbell wasn't right, for once. I wondered if there was any way, by his philosophy, that sober could be drunk. If not, a lot of cowboys and miners were going to be disappointed for a spell.

I returned to the bar and waited for the rain to end. It was an hour or more after dark when the clouds moved on. Outside, the streets were a quagmire and quiet except for cowboys trying to wade through the mud to find their horses.

By midnight the crowd had pretty much disappeared, except for a handful of men, Big Nose Kate, and Corina DeLure. Corina hadn't been worn out by all the activity, not even by Johnny Ringo, who'd gone back for seconds.

Doc Holliday finally got tired or bored and broke Stilwell and Spencer. "I guess you'll have no sugar for your coffee now, Frank."

Grumbling, Stilwell grabbed his hat and strode out the door, Spencer in his wake.

I ambled over and sat down opposite Holliday. He had a strange grin on his face like he still had something up his sleeve.

"They held out for a long time," I said.

"I let them win until I was ready to retire. Kate, it
seems, has an itch that only I can scratch." He looked at
me kind of odd. "Funny, isn't it, the many ways you can
identify a man. By his look, by the sound of his voice,
even by the words he uses." Laughing, he stood up, put
on his coat, grabbed his hat, and pinched Kate on the
rump. "Did you make any sugar tonight?" he asked as
they walked outside.

Chapter Seven

The next day I fretted like a yearling at steering time, anxious to meet Hattie and ride to Charleston for the fandango. By late afternoon, when I picked up the buggy and two horses, the clouds were building again to the west, and I feared we'd get caught in a downpour coming or going. There were draws to cross and always the chance of getting caught in a flash flood. I decided to suggest staying in Tombstone, maybe going to my house and visiting if she was afraid of being seen.

I wore my good clothes over to the O.K. Corral, which was a mistake because I muddied my boots, splattered my pants, and drew John Montgomery's curiosity. He opened the stable door as I walked up, eyed me up and down, and shook his head. "Who died?"

"Nobody you'd know," I replied. "You got my buggy hitched and my two horses saddled?"

Before he could answer, two men walked out leading fine-looking geldings. I'd seen them in my saloon the day before and in town on occasion, but I didn't know their names.

"I appreciate your business, boys," Montgomery said. "You're always welcome at the O.K. Corral."

They nodded. They were unmistakably brothers, their eyes gray and crisp, their brown hair wavy. Both wore trimmed mustaches and a little vee of whiskers beneath their lower lip.

"Lomax," Montgomery said, "do you know the McLaury brothers?"

"Can't say we've met."

"They're good customers." Montgomery pointed to the taller of the two. "That's Tom. He's the hardworking one."

Tom touched his finger to the brim of his hat, then extended his hand. As I shook it, I felt the calluses from his labors.

Montgomery pointed to the other one. "That's Frank."

"I'm the handsome one." Frank lifted his chin and eyed me but never lifted his hand when I swung mine toward him.

I dropped my arm to my side. "Pleased to meet you, too."

Frank lifted his trigger finger at me. "You're the one that said Ike's been poking horses."

"Stallions, I believe I said."

Tom snickered.

Frank shot him a quick glance, then strutted another step toward me. "Ike Clanton's a friend of ours."

"And a friend of several horses, it seems." I shouldn't have said that, but Frank McLaury had a swagger about him that I didn't like.

Tom seemed amused by the exchange. "Come on, Frank. You know Ike's always shooting his mouth off. Let it go."

Frank twisted to his horse, shoved his foot in the stirrup, and hauled himself into the saddle. His horse danced beneath him. "I don't take to funning, Lomax, not when people we don't even know are calling us and our friends rustlers, saying we're in with stage robbers, things like that. That's what the Earps have been saying, and I'm tired of it. We're just ranchers trying to make a decent living. If a man sets foot on our place and don't mean no trouble, we don't ask where he's been or what he's been doing. The Earps have eaten our food, and we didn't ask them how much pimping they'd been doing in Tombstone." He spat at my feet, jerked his horse around, and rode off.

Much more calmly, Tom McLaury mounted up. He offered a pleasant smile I took for an apology. "There's some truth in what Frank says, but he's just a mite edgy."

"No harm done." I touched the brim of my hat as Tom turned his horse down the street and rode after his brother. I watched them disappear around the corner, then turned to Montgomery. "They thieves or not?"

"Who isn't in Cochise County?"

Montgomery was beginning to sound a lot like Joe Campbell, but I had to admit I probably couldn't've sorted the crooks from the decent citizens, excepting the lawyers and politicians, of course. I knew what side of the street they walked on.

Montgomery tried to get me to tell him where I was going, what with the skies threatening, but I wasn't admitting anything to him that might get back to Hattie's folks. Giving up, he went inside and led out the buggy. I climbed into the seat and waited for him to bring out the two saddle horses, a bay and a chestnut gelding. They weren't the best-looking horses I'd ever seen, but it didn't matter since we'd be riding in the dark much of the way.

"Tie them to the back," I ordered.

He obliged me. "I hope you're not planning to take the buggy far, not with it threatening again."

"You should've thought of that when you wouldn't refund my money." I rattled the reins and sent the buggy to sloshing through the mud. At my house I tied the two horses out back and waited for Hattie Ketcham.

She arrived on schedule, wearing riding clothes and a hat and holding an umbrella in one hand and a canvas bag in the other. I could tell when I met her out front she was disappointed with the buggy.

"A buggy'll never make it," she said, stamping her foot.

"I paid in advance and couldn't get a refund."

"So we take a buggy and get stuck somewhere between here and Charleston?"

"No, I've got horses tied behind the house."

"You're smarter than I thought." She tossed me the

canvas bag, grabbed my arm, and cooed, "I've looked forward to this for days."

I pointed to the west. "Storm clouds are building. We won't get there and back without running into some rain."

"I don't care. I just want to have some fun and dance. I bet you're a good dancer."

Not caring to admit I wasn't, I nodded. "I can stumble around with the best of them." I looked to make sure no one was paying us any mind, then grabbed Hattie and carried her around back to the chestnut. As I put her foot in the stirrup and boosted her into the saddle, my hand brushed against her bottom. She didn't seem the least bit embarrassed by it. I was encouraged.

"We could stay dry inside my parlor and do a lot of talking," I offered.

"Why talk when we can dance?"

Why dance when there are other things we could be doing? I thought. "Okay." I secured her umbrella and bag to her saddle.

I untied our horses, handed her the reins, then mounted the bay. We rode southwest out of town, moving at a walk so as not to draw undue attention. After we descended the mesa, we nudged our horses into a lope and headed for Charleston, not quite eight miles away.

Charleston, a town that had sprung up beside the San Pedro River, was a hangout for rustlers, thieves, and murderers, which made it only slightly less respectable than Tombstone.

The well-traveled road was deeply rutted from use and slippery from the rain. We hadn't gone far when we passed an abandoned wagon stuck in the mire. We passed a half-dozen more, the teamsters having unhooked the horses and taken them back to Tombstone and leaving the wagons until the desert dried out.

"You'll never see it greener," Hattie called. "And smell that sweet sage—isn't it grand?"

"Not as grand as you," I said, figuring my comment might help with things later.

Hattie just giggled. "You're so sweet."

We rode at a lope a couple more miles. Then Hattie

leaned forward on her chestnut and slapped him on the neck. "Let's race!" she screamed, laughing as her horse pulled away from mine.

I kicked my bay's flank, and the horse charged forward. But it seemed clubfooted on the slick road, so I pulled back, reluctant to risk hurting the horse or myself. Hattie, though, tore full speed down the road, finally stopping and waiting for me when she saw I wasn't racing.

"What's the matter?" she cried when I rode up.

"My mount's a little gimpy," I replied.

Rattling her reins and directing her chestnut beside my bay, she shook her head. "You're just scared. I didn't figure you'd scare for anything if you stood up to Doc Holliday. My folks say he's the meanest man around. Only fellow that comes close to him is Johnny Ringo."

"Your folks know Holliday?"

"Nobody knows Doc Holliday, though my folks have been around him some. My uncle's as close a friend as he has in this world."

"Why come I've never heard of him? Wyatt Earp's the only fellow I've ever known to be friends with Doc Holliday."

"Yeah. He's my uncle."

"What?" I about choked. "You told me your name was Ketcham, Hattie Ketcham."

"It is," she said. "My mother was Bessie Ketcham before she married Jim Earp. He's my stepfather, actually, but as close to a father as I've got now."

Feeling dumber than a wagonload of manure, I dropped my chin and shook my head. I knew the Earps were particular about their women and most especially the young ones that hadn't been bedded aplenty.

"How old are you, Hattie?"

"Old enough to know what I want to do and how to do it."

"And how old would that be?"

"Going on twenty. You ain't turning yellow on me, are you?"

"It's just that there're more of the Earps than there is of me."

"All together, though, they aren't as handsome as you."

I'd make a fine-looking corpse when the Earps found out.

"You aren't mad at me, are you?" she cooed, then batted her eyelashes until I could practically hear them flapping.

When I glanced at her, my sap started rising, and I kept hoping I might get a little piece of heaven before her uncles sent me to hell. "How could I be mad at the cutest thing at the dance?"

"How can that be when we aren't even there yet?"

Before I could answer, she slapped her reins against the neck of her horse and cut loose with a shrill whistle. "Let's get there quick as we can."

The chestnut darted forward, slinging mud and muck on me and my bay. Deciding I was going to die anyway once the Earps found out about us, I dug my heels into the bay's flanks and gave chase. I could've passed her, but I lagged behind so I could watch the bounce of her bottom in the riding outfit. She laughed and giggled and taunted me all the way to Charleston.

We arrived before dark, both of us out of breath from the hard ride, and rode around town until we heard the music. As I dismounted, I looked to the west, where the clouds had turned as dark as my prospects for living once I got back to Tombstone. I helped Hattie from her horse, then tied both mounts to the hitchrack.

Hattie took down the bag with her dancing clothes, stepped up to me, and planted a kiss on my cheek. "We're gonna have a great time."

I had my doubts. To the west, occasional flashes of lightning split the sky, and thunder rolled toward us. There was no way we would get back without getting doused, and it was possible we might get cut off from Goose Flats if one of the draws flooded.

Hattie grabbed my arm and jerked me toward the door. I looked around a final time, counting three buggies, five wagons, and a couple dozen horses outside. I figured the weather had scared a lot of folks into staying home.

We walked inside just as a dance was ending. Everybody clapped and stomped their approval of the fiddle player, two men on guitar, and another on a harmonica. Besides the musicians, there were maybe forty other people, with probably twice as many men as women. I surveyed the room quickly, hoping I didn't see anybody I knew. Fortunately I didn't.

An old woman with a hitch in her gait and more wrinkles than gray hair welcomed us when the applause died down.

"Where can I change?" Hattie asked breathlessly.

The woman pointed to a corner where a couple quilts were clothespinned to a rope that had been strung wall to wall. "Behind the quilts. One of the women is nursing her baby back there, but she won't mind."

Hattie ran to change, leaving me with the old woman. "Come far?" she asked. "You're not from Charleston, are you?"

"Tombstone," I answered.

"You're loco to ride here in dangerous weather to dance."

"We heard you Charleston folk were nice and friendly. Guess we heard wrong."

"We're waterlogged," she said.

And wrinkled and ugly, I thought but didn't say, not caring to insult her or her hospitality.

No one except the old woman seemed interested in talking to me until Hattie Ketcham emerged from behind the quilts in her dancing dress. It was a dark blue, high-necked dress with a lacy collar, cuffs, and hem. She wore a sparkling necklace and a brooch pinned above her nice bosom.

No sooner had she reached my side than a dozen men crowded around, introducing themselves to her. She seemed pleased as punch with the attention, and I was beginning to wonder if she had been interested in me after all or had merely used me to get her to the dance.

But when the music started, she grabbed my hand and pulled me out on the dance floor. It had been a while since I had danced, so I was a bit rusty, brushing her toes every four or five steps, but I got warmed up af-

ter the second dance and didn't trample her toes more
than every seven or eight steps. She seemed so happy to
be dancing that she didn't mind, likely because she was
the best looker at the dance, maybe in all of Charleston.

After a dozen dances I was tired and wanted to sit
out a song, but as we walked toward a bench a dozen
cowboys surrounded her like chickens around a june
bug, all wanting a dance.

"Henry brought me, and I'm not dancing with another man unless he thinks it's okay."

"We could shoot him. Then he wouldn't object," one
of the fellows said.

"It's okay to dance with them a bit," I said.

Hattie smiled, the one who had suggested shooting
me smiled, and then I smiled.

It was almost an hour before she finished dancing
with each of the cowboys, and by then the thunder and
lightning were drawing closer. When she was done, she
came back and took a seat on the bench, taking my arm
and pulling me closer.

"My folks wouldn't like me dancing, not with so
many. Thanks for bringing me and letting me have some
fun." She leaned over and kissed me on the cheek. I
never saw so many jealous men.

"Maybe we ought to start back, see if we can beat
the rain," I suggested. "It must be close to midnight."

"Two more dances. Then we can go."

I hesitated.

"Please." She batted her eyelashes again, and I gave
in.

As soon as the music started, she grabbed my arm,
pulled me up, and had me dancing before my head
stopped spinning. The rain seemed to be holding off, and
I thought we just might be able to finish the next dance,
get her changed, and start back to Tombstone without
any trouble.

But I was wrong.

About the middle of the dance, a gunshot sounded
in the doorway. The music died, and the dancing
stopped. My first thought was that the Earps had trailed
me from Tombstone and planned to shoot me right there.

I was going to point out every other man she'd danced with so I wouldn't die alone.

But the fellow standing at the door was a stranger to me. He might have been six feet tall at the most, but a Mexican sombrero with a high crown made him look huge. Curly black hair spilled from beneath the hat. A black mustache accentuated the snarl on his lips. He wore ammunition belts crossed over his work shirt and twin gun belts with a holster on each hip. In his right hand he held a smoking pistol, in his left a half-empty bottle of whiskey.

He stared at us all, then lifted the bottle to his mouth, took a healthy swig, and cut loose a belch that echoed around the suddenly quiet hall. "Pardon my manners," he said. "I'm Curly Bill Brocius. Don't mind me—I just came to watch the dance." He laughed and waved his gun around. "So, why don't everybody start dancing again?"

That was the first time I saw Curly Bill. He had an odd reputation. He'd once shot a tin of water from a saloon owner's hand and killed his horse out in the street with the same bullet. He was supposed to be a decent, likable fellow with a good sense of humor when he wasn't drinking, but he drank a lot. I was beginning to think everybody in Arizona Territory was inbred with a whiskey bottle.

I figured Curly Bill'd want to dance with Hattie. If he did, I was probably as good as dead. He'd kill me if I tried to protect her, and the Earp brothers would kill me if I didn't. Suddenly I didn't feel like dancing any longer.

Curly Bill, though, was in a different mood. He pointed his gun toward the musicians. "Start playing. And everybody start dancing."

The musicians began another song, but they didn't have the same enthusiasm as before. Nor did the dancers. We moved awkwardly around the dance floor, everyone scared to turn their back on Curly Bill for fear he might plug them.

He waved his gun at the men standing around without partners. "You fellows pair off and start dancing, too."

They did as they were told, and pretty soon every-one was dancing. But for all our best efforts, Curly Bill just wasn't satisfied. He fired his gun in the air again. "I got an idea. Let's see you take off your clothes and dance. Now, that'll be fun."

The women gasped, the fellows looked at one an-other, and everyone hesitated.

Except Curly Bill. He fired his gun again, but this time over our heads instead of at the ceiling.

All of us dancers started removing our clothes.

Curly Bill pointed at the musicians. "You fellows, too."

By then several women were sobbing. A couple of the younger fellows were trying not to smirk, thinking it all funny. Everyone got down to their drawers and kind of hoped that was what Curly Bill had in mind. It wasn't.

"I want you buck naked, all of you!" he bellowed.

Well, I'd always been told that all men were created equal, but that was a lie. There was nothing equal about the men there, nor the women, either. Worried as I was about Curly Bill and his gun, I kept glancing at Hattie. She had a fine bosom and a set of hips that didn't disap-point me. I caught her peeking at my pistol, and I had trouble keeping it down after that.

"That's better," Curly Bill said, then waved the gun over his head. "Start the music again."

The musicians did as they were told as best they could, though the two pickers with instruments at their waist didn't miss as many notes as the fiddler and har-monica player. I think everybody was wanting a guitar to hide behind, though Hattie, being young and carefree, didn't seem nearly as concerned as the other women. She was a sight to behold, too, and all the cowboys couldn't help glance her way when they weren't checking out Curly Bill's aim.

While some of us had been dancing close when we were dressed, everybody was dancing at an arm's length once we were naked. The old woman who had greeted us at the door passed us on the arms of a young cowboy. She was wrinkled all the way to her toes and sagging a bit in the middle. He, too, was sagging, though I couldn't blame him.

The song seemed to go on forever. Curly Bill was swaying with the music and laughing at all the fun he was having. On the way to the dance I'd thought about how much I'd like to see Hattie shed of her clothes, and I guess I should've just gone up and thanked Curly Bill for providing me with that opportunity. But somehow I couldn't build up the nerve, not with him sucking on whiskey and looking for a reason to shoot someone. If he wanted a target, I was gonna suggest the old woman.

But Curly Bill never asked for my advice. He just kept sneering and leering at us. After a swig of liquor he'd draw his shirtsleeve across his lips, then grin like he was the only fellow in the room still clothed.

The fiddler finally tuckered out and pulled his bow away from the strings. The harmonica player dropped his harmonica from his lips and held it in front of his hips, covering what little pride he had left. The two guitar players, who'd been hiding behind their instruments, looked from one to the other, uncertain whether to keep on playing or just stop.

Curly Bill helped them decide when he tried to clap with the liquor bottle in one hand and the revolver in the other. "Fine music, fine dancing!" he called as he tried to applaud.

Of course we were all uncertain what to do, so we broke from our partners and tried to cover our assets as best we could with only two hands apiece. Some of us had more to cover than others.

Apparently Curly Bill did not feel we were giving the musicians and ourselves appropriate recognition. "Clap, dammit!"

For a moment I wasn't certain if he was admitting a certain medical problem or suggesting applause. Everyone else, though, sure thought he wanted a round of applause. They started clapping like they were beating a rug.

Curly Bill seemed to forget what the applause was about and bent over at the waist to take a bow. As he straightened up, he accidentally discharged his pistol into the floor. "Damn," he said, trying to steady himself. He kept blinking like he was having trouble focusing.

Several of the cowboys glanced at each other, like they were readying to jump him. But Curly Bill didn't give them the chance. When his eyes finally seemed to focus, he grinned widely and belched again. He took a swipe at his lips with his sleeve. "This is one dance you won't forget. Me, neither." Still grinning, he backed out the door and evaporated in the darkness.

As soon as he'd disappeared, everybody grabbed clothes, even if they weren't their own, to cover themselves, then swapped back and forth until they had the garb they came in. The women were sobbing, young men were catching a last glimpse of Hattie, and I was just trying to find my new suit before some fellow claimed it as his.

Once the younger men were dressed, they rushed out in a clump, talking about revenge on Curly Bill. I kept trying to hide Hattie's dress so I could look at her just a little bit longer. Clad in nothing but her drawers, she finally glanced my way and caught me.

I held up the dress. "I found it." I carried it over to her.

She had a wicked grin on her face. "This was more fun than I've had in a long time."

I nodded. "Nobody kept any secrets tonight."

Hattie giggled as she took the dress from me. Instead of putting it on, she marched to the corner and slipped into her riding clothes. Had she been modest, that's what she'd've done to begin with, but she seemed to have enjoyed the leering of the cowboys.

When she was done, we went back outside and mounted for the return trip, racing the clouds to see who would make it to town first. The clouds won, even though they must've snagged on a mountaintop and knocked the bottom out. They dumped enough water on us to float an ark. When we got back to Tombstone, we were drenched and cold.

I offered to take her to my house, build a fire, and generate some heat, but she thought she ought to get back home. I was disappointed, of course, having hoped to get a closer dance with what I'd seen, thanks to Curly Bill, at the fandango. Praying that none of the Earps was out on the street looking for her, I rode with her to her house. It was dark and seemed calm.

"Good," she said as she dismounted fifty feet from the place. "They must not've missed me." She took her bag of clothes and umbrella, which had done little good in the downpour, and stepped over to my horse. "I had fun, Henry. I'd like to see you again."

"I wouldn't mind seeing more of you, Hattie."

"Why, Henry, you saw about all of me there was to see."

"And I liked what I saw."

She handed me her reins, then grabbed my arm and pulled me down so she could kiss me on the cheek. Then she scurried toward the house, and I sat in the saddle watching as she climbed in the window of her bedroom. It seemed she had slipped in unnoticed, but as I turned the horses back toward home, I heard a loud voice I took to be Jim Earp's.

"Where the hell have you been, Hattie? We've been waiting for you."

I kicked my mount in the flank and trotted home, praying Hattie wouldn't mention my name in any of her discussions with her mother, her stepfather, or her uncles.

Chapter Eight

When I returned the horses and buggy to the O.K. Corral the next morning, John Montgomery eyed them closely. "Buggy ain't too bad, but you sure muddied up the saddle horses. Some say you were seen riding out of town with a young lady. Any truth to that, Lomax?"

"What kind of fool do you think I am?"

"How many kinds are there?"

I shrugged. I'd never given much thought to the question, although Joe Campbell probably had. "I must be the kind of fool that'd build a saloon on Fremont instead of Allen. I don't get the business they get on Allen, but we don't burn to the ground on Fremont."

"That's a pretty big fool right there."

"Yes, sir. I'm also the kind of fool that'd take his business elsewhere when a liveryman asks too many questions."

Montgomery gulped.

"Weren't no stages robbed last night, no shootings or thefts that would make it any concern of yours where I took your horses. They didn't get in any mischief, and neither did I. If you doubt that, then ask them."

Montgomery took my word for it and didn't ask any more nosy questions. He smiled. "Thanks for your business, Lomax."

"Take good care of Flash," I reminded him. "If I

104

hear any complaints from my mule, I'll take him elsewhere."

I walked out back of the O.K. Corral and turned on Fremont toward the Stubborn Mule, figuring to check on how business had gone while I was away in Charleston. When I walked in, Til Walteree was tending a half-full saloon, not bad for the middle of the morning.

Walteree nodded. "Howdy, boss. Where were you last night?"

"Home," I answered. "I didn't feel up to coming in."

He cocked his head at me, looking dumber than if he'd been born in Louisiana. "You weren't home last night, because I came looking for you. Knocked on the door. You never answered."

"I's feeling bad, Til, and must've been sawing logs awfully good when you came by."

Grimacing, Walteree shook his head. "No, sir. I slipped around to your bedroom, lifted the window, and crawled in."

"You what?"

"Just checking on you. You weren't in bed, you weren't in the house. I looked everywhere, even under the bed, but you were gone."

I fought to keep my calm. I didn't want anybody checking under my bed. If he saw the loose floorboard, he might find the tin with my money and valuable papers in it. I had to cover myself and quick. "I must've been in the outhouse, Til. My stomach was cramping so, and I know I made several trips there."

Walteree's face darkened. "I checked there, too. Unless you crawled in the pit, you weren't there. Now, there was a horse and buggy tied outside and tracks where two other horses had been out back. It didn't make sense to me, but I recognized the buggy as one of John Montgomery's rigs. I checked at the O.K. Corral. He said you'd taken the rig and two saddle horses."

Now I grimaced. "I was feeling so bad, Til, I thought I might try to ride the sickness out."

Running his fingers through his hair, Walteree eyed me like I was lying. "What was wrong with riding Flash?"

"I wanted an animal that could run."

"But why two?"

"One to run out of town and the other to run back in."

"But why the rig?"

"To carry me back if I couldn't stay in the saddle."

"Who followed you in the buggy?"

"Damn, Til, you're forgetting I'm boss. I'm the one who's supposed to be asking questions, like how was business last night?"

"We cleared close to a hundred and seventy-five dollars. Business has been up since Allen Street burned down. But where were you last night?"

"Til, what difference does it make?"

"I don't know," he replied. "You'd have to ask Wyatt Earp."

I coughed, choked, and just about spit out my teeth. The Earps must have known everything that went on in Cochise County, and Wyatt was likely looking to plug me with so many holes I'd whistle when the wind blew. "Wyatt was looking for me?"

Walteree nodded. "Seemed it was important."

"Did he say what it was about?"

"He just said he needed to have a word with you."

"About what?"

"He didn't say."

"Did he look mad?"

"He looked like he always does."

Wyatt always looked mad. "What time did he come by?"

Walteree scratched his chin. "Hard to say for certain, but it was before dark. Six or six-thirty, I'd say."

I was shaking. Wyatt must've known I had taken Hattie. I was surprised he hadn't ridden out after me, killed me on the trail, and left me for the buzzards. Maybe when Hattie got home, the Earp men had beaten a confession out of her. They'd know how I had danced naked with her and hadn't stood up to Curly Bill. About how I had taken her to Charleston in the face of floods and lightning. I had plenty to worry about.

All concerned, Walteree looked at me. "You okay?"

"It's the shakes. My fever must be breaking."

"You had a fever, too? Maybe I need to get you to Doc Goodfellow's office. Let him see you."

I thought of the Earps. "I may need Goodfellow later."

"You look like you could use a drink. You look so bad I'd give you some of the good stuff, if we had any, but we ain't had a shipment of liquor in a week on account of the muddy roads."

"I've taken the cure, Til."

"What cure?"

"For drunkenness. I drank whiskey with dead minnows in it."

Walteree gagged. "That's one of them Ozark superstitions, ain't it?"

"It's no worse than downing one of those water scorpions you bayou boys eat."

"You mean crawdaddies?"

"Whatever you call them, they ain't nothing but water bugs."

I was fearing Wyatt would chew me up and spit me out like them Louisiana boys did those crawdaddies. I was sure tempted to take a drink, but I decided I should stay sober so I could keep my wits.

Turning from the bar, I stumbled to the door. "I'll be back tonight if my sickness breaks, Til."

He called after me, "You take care of yourself. That fever must still be breaking, the way you're shaking."

I stepped outside and started for home. The sun was bright and glaring, and the water-soaked ground gave up vapors like Tombstone was venting hell. Over on Allen I could see and hear carpenters nailing up wooden frames to rebuild the mercantiles and saloons. Their work had been slowed by the unending rain. I looked at them too long, though—as I was wading across the mud of Fifth Street, I happened to see Wyatt Earp striding toward me from Fourth.

He must've seen me at the same time, because he waved his arm and called out my name.

Pretending not to see him, I cut north on Fifth Street. As soon as the buildings blocked his view of me,

I started running through the mud to the boardwalk, then hopped onto the walk, slinging mud over other pedestrians as I raced by. I had only one thought: Run home, grab my money and mining papers if Walteree hadn't stolen them, then slip back to the O.K. Corral, saddle Flash, and ride away.

The rear half of the block was mostly vacant except for a few scattered shacks and hovels, so I angled across the back, figuring Wyatt would stay on Fremont and miss me. Sloshing through the mud, I clung to the backs of the buildings facing Fremont and looked over my shoulder every minute for Wyatt Earp and his gun. I was looking in the wrong direction.

Just as I was about to dart between two buildings, Wyatt stepped in my path.

At that moment I sure wished Amelia Guinn was with me. I could've hidden for a week in the tent of her dress, and Earp would never've found me.

As it was, I had my wits to protect myself, but at that I felt only half prepared. My momma always told me not to lie, but she'd never stood face-to-face with Wyatt Earp after a night of being naked with his niece or stepniece or whatever the hell she was to him.

Wyatt shook his head. "You got reason to be nervous, Lomax?"

I wasn't sure if he was asking a question or making a statement, whether he was about to shoot me or just pull his gun and buffalo me up beside the head like he'd done so many fellows since coming to Tombstone. Give Wyatt a badge, and he started laying goose eggs on the side of men's heads.

"What r-reason would I have to be n-nervous?" I stammered, trying to keep my hand from trembling, my knees from knocking, and my heart from jumping out of my throat and running away.

"You've got law problems."

I gulped. There was no law against going to a dance, no law against riding out of Tombstone whenever I felt like it, even accompanied by his niece. But the more I thought about it, the more I felt like riding out of Tombstone right then.

Earp eyed my waist. "You're not carrying a gun."

"There's an ordinance against it."

"Then you best be prepared to arm yourself, because some folks may be coming after you."

The folks he was talking about had to be all the Earp clan, but why was he warning me? If Hattie Ketcham had called her family "the Earps" instead of "my folks," I might not have been in such a bind. "You mean you're coming after me?"

Wyatt looked at me like I had been chomping on locoweed for the better part of my life. "Whatever gave you that idea? We've heard some of the miners may be coming to move your house off the lot. And your lawyer needs to see you."

"It's my lot, bought and paid for, and why didn't the lawyer Guinn come tell me himself?"

"You know Amelia Guinn. She won't let him within a hundred feet of any saloon with fallen women."

I knew for a fact that was true.

"I tried to get the message to you at the Stubborn Mule last night, but no one could find you. You weren't out catting around with some saloon girl, were you?"

"She wasn't a saloon girl," I said without thinking. Then I tried to cover my tracks. "It was Amelia Guinn."

Wyatt laughed. "You ain't that stupid, even if you are from Arkansas."

I had a question for him. "Why are you doing me a favor, seeing as how we didn't get gee-haw too well the first time we met?"

"Sheriff Johnny Behan's behind the trouble with the lot jumping, and he double-crossed me. I intend to get even. Other thing is, after Doc wounded Milt Joyce at the Oriental, you let him deal cards at the Stubborn Mule instead of kicking him out."

"He set up table, and I didn't have the guts to kick him out."

Wyatt grinned. "No man alive's brave enough to spit in Doc's whiskey and then let Doc pull his tooth. It's either guts or stupidity."

I had to agree. How else would I've gotten hooked up with Hattie Ketcham? I figured I'd pressed my luck about as far as I could. "I best get over to Henry Guinn's place."

"Just watch out for your house." Wyatt touched the brim of his hat with his trigger finger and walked away.

I stood there catching my breath and hoping again he'd never find out that I'd been dancing with his niece. I began to think it would be healthier for me just to forget Hattie Ketcham, but a vision of her dancing the last dance kept coming back to me. After I calmed down, I turned around and headed toward my lawyer's office.

Amelia Guinn was just coming out as I stepped to the door. "No saloon girls," she growled.

"None followed me."

"See that none do."

I was not about to argue with her. She hoisted an umbrella like it was a turkey drumstick and opened it up.

I looked both ways down the street, then pointed at the sky. "Don't see any rain clouds. Looks clear to me."

She shook the umbrella. "This is for shade, not for rain. An umbrella has more than one use. But you're a saloon owner—what would you know about these things?"

Enough to figure out one more use for that damn umbrella, but I didn't think it wise to tell her, not with her outweighing me double.

Amelia looked at my boots, planted herself in the doorway, and shook her head. "You're not going in until you take off those muddy things. I'll not have you tracking up my house."

She had me over a barrel. It would've taken a twenty-mule team to drag her out of the way. I wrestled my boots off, my hands getting sticky with mud before I succeeded.

She looked at my socks, noting the holes in the toes, and huffed. "Why won't one of those saloon girls darn your socks for you?"

Shrugging and trying to shake the mud from my hands, I looked Amelia straight in the eye. "They spend more time mending what's wrong with a fellow's britches than his socks."

Amelia scowled.

I reminded her, "One of those saloon girls has a cat, and you don't."

"But I've got my decency."

As fat as she was, I sure hoped she kept it. A fellow could drown in the sweat that must've pooled on her body.

"Don't get any mud on my floor, you hear?"

"Yes, ma'am."

Nose held high, she waddled away. I knocked on the door, announced myself, and entered, stopping to grab a handful of Amelia's fine lace curtains and wipe my hands. I checked my socks to make sure I wasn't getting any mud on the floor like she requested, then closed the door.

Guinn looked up from his desk as I walked into his office. "I'm glad you finally came. I tried to reach you yesterday evening, but someone said they'd seen you riding out of town."

"They must've been seeing things. I was in town all night."

Guinn shrugged. "No matter. The mining company has filed to have your house removed from the lot. As your legal representative, I have made appropriate court responses to prevent them from throwing you off. However, rumors are going around that the mining company's raising miners to physically move your house off the lot. I'd heard they might even try something as early as this afternoon."

"It'd take a lot of them."

"They've plenty to do the job, no doubt." Guinn stared at me bug-eyed through his glasses. "I'm trying to protect you and your interests as best I can. I've written up some legal papers I need your signature on." He motioned for me to join him at his desk. "Now, there are three sets of papers for you to sign. The first, as you requested, removes any power of attorney from Joe Campbell in your absence." He dipped his pen in ink and offered it to me. "Read it and then sign it on the bottom."

It was two pages of highfalutin lawyer words that made less sense than tits on a boar. He had three copies for me to sign—one for me, one for him, and one to file at the courthouse.

"The second paper gives me power of attorney for you in the disposition of all issues related to maintaining your claim on your house lot. This also allows me to assume decisions for all related financial matters after any absence of yours of three months or longer from Cochise County."

To my way of thinking, when I had given him the hundred dollars earlier to handle my legal matters, I'd also given him the power of attorney. I figured the papers just sealed that arrangement. I signed it without reading the damn thing, confused by the words in just the first sentence.

"The third paper is basically the same as the second, except that it pertains to the lot at Fremont and Fifth where you have located the Stubborn Mule. This is a precautionary contract in case a similar problem develops with your saloon lot. The same three-month provision applies."

He dipped the pen in the inkwell for me again, and I signed without reading. Why I didn't read the papers more closely would come back to haunt me later, but at the time I figured I'd just have to hire another lawyer to explain them, and one lawyer was enough for any one man to have to pay.

When I finished inking the papers, Henry Guinn licked his lips like a fox in a henhouse. He was so slick he probably could've eaten a chicken without getting feathers in his mouth. He gave me my copy of each set of papers and told me to keep them in a safe place in case any questions ever arose over his handling of my business.

I did have one question, though not about that. "How'd you come to send Wyatt Earp for me?"

"I'm a Republican. He's a Republican. Ninety-nine percent of our problems in Cochise County would be resolved if there weren't any Democrats. Look around. Behan's a Democrat and as crooked as they come. The Clantons, the McLaurys, Curly Bill Brocius, and all the rustlers and stage robbers are Democrats."

"Most of them are southern boys," I said. "You got something against southern boys?"

"Not a thing, other than them being stubborn, loud, and ignorant."

"I'm from Arkansas."

Guinn just looked at me with those bug eyes.

I didn't care for him insulting the South. And I thought he'd overestimated the Republicans and underestimated the Democrats. To my way of thinking they were just skunks of different stripes. It didn't matter which one created a stink—the odor was usually the same.

"Where you from?"

"Illinois, the great state that sent Abraham Lincoln to the presidency."

"In Arkansas we've sent a lot of fellows to the gallows. They were mostly Republicans, though."

It took a moment for my words to catch up with Guinn. Like a lot of lawyers, he talked too fast and listened too slow.

"That, Lomax, is a slander upon the fine name of the Republican Party."

"I meant to insult them."

He groaned. "Stubborn, loud, and ignorant. That's all."

I turned around and started out of the office, but Guinn called after me.

"One thing I forgot to tell you, Lomax. You owe me fifty more dollars for legal work."

I spun around, my mouth as wide as his wife's hips. "Fifty dollars?" He could insult my southern heritage, but he wasn't too proud to take fifty dollars from a stubborn, loud, and ignorant Arkansawyer. I'd've got more pleasure handing my money over to a robber than to a lawyer, but much as I hated to admit it, I did need his fancy words on paper. "I don't have it on me. I'll get it to you tomorrow."

Guinn eyed me. "You're not losing money on the saloon, not with Allen Street burned down, are you?"

"Not unless your friend Joe Campbell's stealing it from me."

Guinn became indignant. "I will not have you speak that way about such a fine fellow as Joe Campbell. The meek like Joe Campbell will inherit the earth."

"Yeah, but they're so dumb they won't know what to do with it."

Guinn took to yammering.

I wondered if the punishment for killing a lawyer was the same as for killing a man, but then I reconsidered. I'd've hated to have Amelia Guinn chasing me all over Arizona Territory for making her a widow, because no other man would take her for a wife, unless of course Guinn left her rich—in which case I might consider it.

"I'll get you your money tomorrow."

I left, stopping by the window just long enough to grab the muddied panel of the lace curtain and rub the dirt in a little harder. After checking to see that I hadn't gotten any mud on the floor, I let myself out, found my boots on the porch, jerked them on, and started back for my place, hoping it was where I had left it.

Sure enough, everything looked just fine. The house was still on its foundation. But I sensed danger. Satan was lurking somewhere.

I slipped up to the front step, planted my foot softly on the wood, and tried to keep from making any noise as I turned the knob and opened the door. I eased inside, slowly shutting the door behind me. I moved to take a step, then froze. There on the floor was an envelope with my name written on it in a delicate hand. I was pleased. The letter had to be from Hattie. When I bent to pick it up, my pleasure ended.

That was when Satan attacked.

He charged from the kitchen and leaped with claws spread and teeth bared for my face. I lifted my hand and tried to swat him away, but he managed to swipe my cheek with one paw. I screamed as he came down biting and scratching at my leg. When I tried to straighten, I fell backward into the door instead. Luckily I managed to stay on my feet, or he would've scratched my eyes out and clawed me to shreds. Getting my balance, I kicked him as hard as I could.

"Meaaaarrgh!" he screeched as my boot lifted him

off the ground and flung him into the wall. He hit hard, then slid to the floor, still clawing and scratching. I drew back my foot to kick him again, but he scampered back into the kitchen, where he whined and whined.

I should've taken my boots off so I wouldn't track mud through the house, but this was my house, not Amelia Guinn's, and I needed the boots for protection should Satan attack again. When I was certain his whines were far enough away, I bent and snatched up the letter.

Keeping one eye on the kitchen door and the other on the envelope, I lifted the flap, pulled out the letter, and read it.

> Dearest Henry:
>   I enjoyed our time together last night. You were the handsomest man in the hall, both in and out of your suit. Isn't that naughty?
>   I can't remember having more fun. You are so brave to sneak out with me since you know what you would face if we were caught. That's what makes it so much fun.
>   I can't wait until we can get together again.
>   Lovingly, Hattie

Well, I was mighty pleased with myself on the one hand, thinking I might get to trot in her harness, but worried, too, what would happen if word got back to Wyatt that I was seeing his niece.

I folded the letter and slipped it into my pocket, then moved cautiously to the kitchen. I was getting tired of Satan ambushing me, and I had decided this was to be the final showdown. But when I went in, stomping my boots, Satan actually cowered in the corner. I swung my boot in his direction, slinging mud at him, and he whined.

The damn cat was scared of my boot. When I stepped toward him, he covered his head with his paws, then bolted toward the parlor when I took another step. I halfheartedly kicked at him again as he went by. I'd finally put the fear of God into Satan.

I went into my bedroom, anxious to see if Til

Walteree had found my hiding place beneath the floorboard. Getting down on my hands and knees, I scooted
under the bed far enough to lift the loose board and stick
my head underneath. My fingers quickly wrapped
around the box and lifted it out. I could tell by the
weight to it that nothing had been taken. I removed fifty
dollars to pay that thief Guinn, then pulled the legal papers from my pocket and shoved them and Hattie's letter
in. Quickly I slipped the tin box back and replaced the
floorboard.

When I pushed myself out from under the bed, I
saw Satan standing in the doorway. He seemed to have
regained some of his courage, but I pulled my boot off
and lobbed it at him. He screeched and scampered away.
I had finally discovered how to control the tomcat.

I bolted up, grabbed the boot, and followed him into
the kitchen, but he escaped into the front room. At the
parlor doorway I dropped the boot, then took the other
one off and tossed it beside its mate. Satan backed into
the corner and didn't even try to look past the boots,
much less sneak around them. He didn't bother me
again.

Before dark I went to the saloon and worked the
crowded bar. I didn't have the courage to deliver the fifty
dollars Guinn said I owed, not after soiling Amelia's lace
curtains. So I sent Joe Campbell out to deliver it.

"I want a receipt," I told him.

He nodded.

"It true you go to church with them?"

"Try to," Campbell replied. "It's good for the soul."

Figuring I'd confuse Campbell before sending him
on my errand, I asked him a question. "Does everybody
have a soul?"

"They do."

"What about cats—do they have a soul?"

Campbell scratched his head. "Nope."

"Just people?"

"Yep."

"Are their souls the same?" I asked.

"Nope, people are different."

"Are their souls like themselves?"

"I reckon. Why?"

"Nothing, really. I was just thinking Amelia Guinn must have the biggest soul in all of Tombstone."

Campbell grimaced. "That wasn't a very nice thing to say."

"Don't forget the receipt," I said.

Shaking his head, Campbell walked out the door. Business was jumping that night, though a bartender never knew for certain how good a night he'd had until the customers cleared out in the early morning. If nobody'd been killed, no fights had broken out, and no tables, chairs, glassware, or liquor had been destroyed, you generally came out okay.

Doc Holliday was in the corner at his usual table, cheating players out of their hard-earned money and coughing bits of his lungs into his handkerchief. Kate watched, slipping him a clean handkerchief occasionally. A couple times Holliday brushed his hand across his cheek, letting me know that he'd seen the results of my latest encounter with Satan. He'd probably start teasing me about dancing with Miss Saguaro or something, and I just hoped this time I didn't get drunk and spit in his whiskey. I hadn't had much of a hankering for liquor since I took the cure, but I was never sure how long the cure would hold.

Ned Nichols, Til Walteree, and I had steady work until Joe Campbell returned an hour later.

"Did it take lawyer Guinn that long to write out a receipt?" I asked.

"No, not at all. Me and Amelia just got to talking."

"About what?"

"About how she was gonna strangle you for getting mud on her curtains."

"Less is more," I reminded Campbell.

"Huh?"

"Less on the floor is more on the curtains."

Campbell shoved his hand in his pocket and pulled out a paper signed by Guinn for my receipt. He pressed it in my hand. "You shouldn't make fun of Amelia Guinn. She's a fine woman, she is."

"I couldn't agree more," I answered. "She's fine enough to make two, maybe even three women."

"You mock her left and right."

"Joe, she's so big, her left is right and her right is left."

"She's a fine, religious woman."

"She's got horns holding up her halo." I could tell Joe was angering, so I backed off.

He didn't speak to me the rest of the night, and it hurt my feelings enough that I took the night's profits and headed on home. Back at the house I lit a lamp, pulled off my boots, and watched Satan cower in the corner when I put them in the bedroom doorway, figuring to test if the boots would keep him out at night. I went to bed and woke up the next morning alive and without new scratches.

After dressing I went to the O.K. Corral and had Flash saddled up because I was tired of walking through the mud. Then I went to one of the mercantiles that were still standing and bought some peppermint candies to share with Hattie the next time we got together. About noon I stopped at an eatery for some lunch, paying little attention to the crowd at the far end of the street, which I took to be one of the periodic meetings of miners complaining about one thing or another. As I ate, I thought about Hattie and when she might get a message to me so we could meet.

After paying for lunch, I rode Flash home, taking my time. Outside my house I tied Flash and stepped inside, looking out for Satan. I didn't see him, but I did see that the damn cat had dragged some kind of cloth on the floor from somewhere.

I didn't recognize what it was for a moment. Then it hit me: It was a dress. I was confused for only an instant longer.

Beyond the kitchen I could see into the bedroom. There stood Hattie, leaning against the wall.

Naked!

I smiled.

She smiled.

I nodded.

She nodded. "Wanna dance?"

I jerked off my boots and dropped them by the door, then ripped off my shirt and threw it on the rocking chair, all the time moving toward her.

This was the moment I'd been waiting for.

She held out her arms for me to dance into.

I fumbled with my trousers, got them unbuttoned, and shucked them on the kitchen floor, then pulled off my socks and tossed them on the kitchen table, hopping closer and closer to her arms—and the other good parts.

At the bedroom door I managed to slip out of my long johns, and now I was as naked as she was. I fell into her arms and kissed her.

All I wanted was Hattie. I didn't care about anything else, not even the noise outside. She wanted me, too, and didn't seem to care about anything else.

Most of all I didn't care about Satan. In fact, I'd forgotten about him and left my boots by the front door. But as Hattie and I danced toward the bed, I remembered.

That's when he yowled and latched on to my bare butt with his razorlike claws.

Chapter Nine

Satan clawed at my buttocks.

Screaming, I pushed Hattie back and swatted at him, knocking him down my leg. His claws tore more trails of blood along my flesh, and as he landed at my feet, his teeth latched on to my ankle. I squealed and kicked him into the wall, but my bare foot didn't have quite the same authority as my boot. Satan came back snarling.

Now I'd had it with that renegade tomcat, threatening me and delaying my chance to finally warm the sheets with Hattie. I decided to shoot the son of a bitch. I bolted to the kitchen for my pistol, but he leaped in my path, and I halted like I'd been reined in hard.

Behind me I could hear Hattie tittering, but I was too scared to glance back at her for fear Satan would attack something more important than my behind. I feinted to the left, and Satan darted that way. Then I charged through the kitchen door, tripped over my drawers, and went sprawling on the hardwood floor. Stunned for a moment, I tightened up like a miser in front of the offering plate, expecting Satan's claws to dig in and cut me in more pieces than a politician slices the truth.

After a moment I managed to get to my hands and knees, shaking my head of the mud that had clogged up my brain. As my senses returned, I heard two noises that made me nervous.

"Here, Satan, come here, Satan," Hattie called.

That made me mad. She should've been whispering nice things in *my* ear instead of inviting the tomcat over.

In my anger I didn't pay any mind to the other noise, the growing clamor of a mob down the street. I didn't know who they were planning on lynching, but if Hattie hadn't been naked in the next room waiting to lift my spirits, I'd've gone out and suggested they hang old Satan.

Climbing to my feet, I staggered over to the apple crate where I hid my revolver and jerked it from among the few pots and pans I kept around. I checked the load—five bullets—and hoped that would be enough.

Ready to kill, I slunk toward the bedroom, then pulled back, thinking it wise to get reinforcements. So I retreated to the parlor and the boots that struck fear into Satan. I wrestled them on, figuring if my bullets didn't get him, I could stomp him to death. I just hoped I didn't lose a limb in the process.

Taking a deep breath, I started toward the bedroom again, slipping to the kitchen door to make sure Satan wasn't there waiting to jump on me. He wasn't. Encouraged, I eased toward the bedroom door, worried for a moment because Hattie had quit calling the cat. I hoped he hadn't killed her. That would've really made the Earps mad.

Gun in hand, boots on feet, grit in my craw, I eased toward the door, then jumped inside, swinging my gun across the room, looking for that damn cat. When I saw him, I cursed. Hattie, who had slipped into bed, sat with the sheet draped around her bosom and Satan in her lap, stroking his back.

"Stand back," I said. "He's a killer."

"No, he's not."

"Throw him on the floor so I can shoot him!"

"Don't you dare!" She was indignant.

"You wouldn't feel that way if he attacked *your* bottom."

She tittered again. "He was just protecting me."

"Problem is, he's protecting you when you're not around, and I've got the scars to prove it." I stepped toward the bed.

Satan tensed, the fur standing on his back. He'd seen my boots.

I inched closer, cocking my revolver just in case.

The cat jumped from Hattie's lap and scampered to the wall. I followed him with my revolver as he retreated, eyeing my boots the entire way. When he drew even with me, he jumped for the kitchen.

I released the hammer on the revolver and bent to place it on the floor. As I straightened, Hattie giggled and threw back the covers to show me what awaited. The sight made me forget about Satan's scratches.

When I fell on the bed beside her, she shoved playfully at me. "Aren't you gonna take your boots off?"

"Not as long as that tomcat and I are in the same house."

She tittered again. The sound was beginning to grow on me, though not as much as the sound outside. I reached for her but froze when all the commotion and yelling seemed to stop right outside my front door.

"This is the house!" one fellow yelled.

"Let's get it!" answered another.

The mob whistled and hollered.

Hattie quit tittering.

"What the hell?" I sat up in bed and looked out the window in time to see several men run past, carrying mining picks and shovels. Then I heard the sound of picks striking the stone foundation. I didn't know what the mob was doing, but I knew what the Earps would do if they found me with Hattie. I preferred to face the mob.

"Be quiet," I said between gritted teeth.

Her face paled. "What are we going to do?"

"Get dressed," I answered as a man poked his head through the open window. I flung the covers back over Hattie, hoping he couldn't identify her.

"He's got a naked girl in bed with him!" he shouted.

I dove for the floor and grabbed my pistol.

"He's wearing his boots and nothing else!"

A couple more curious fellows peeked in the window.

I shoved my pistol in the first man's nose. "Next bastard that sticks his head in my window's gonna have his brains scattered."

He ducked quicker than a Republican ducks responsibility.

Hattie was sobbing, and I was feeling pretty down myself. A couple bastards looked in the other window, so I flopped across the room and introduced them to the business end of my revolver. After chasing them off and making sure both windows were clear, I eased Hattie to the floor, still draped in the covers. "Put on your dress, quick," I whispered. "I'm not certain what they're up to, but you got to get out of here."

Hattie crawled about on her hands and knees, finding her drawers and dress and wrestling them on under the sheet.

I ran from the bedroom, through the kitchen, and into the parlor, picking up my clothes where I had strewn them. I jerked my long johns over my boots, ripping them at the ankle, then tried to pull my pants on, but they hung on the bootheels. So I yanked my britches free and fought my boots off, glancing around to make sure Satan wasn't sneaking up on me. The cat was nowhere to be seen. I wished he was a dog so I could loose him on the mob.

Quickly I pulled my britches back on, not even taking time to button them. Then I shoved my left foot in my right boot, yanked it off, and put it on the correct foot. I grabbed my other boot and wrestled it on the proper foot this time, probably only because I didn't have another one to choose from.

Outside I heard the chipping on the foundation stop. "Get the timbers!" yelled one man.

"Move the mule!" shouted another.

I had forgotten about Flash. The mule brayed, and then I heard a scream, followed by a string of profanity that would've made a bullwhacker blush.

"Damn mule kicked me!" a fellow howled.

"Get a shovel and I'll hit him between the eyes, teach him a few manners," added another.

I pulled on my shirt and grabbed my pistol. I wasn't going to let anybody attack Flash. Just as I jumped up,

I felt the house begin to wobble. I had to save Flash, but first I had to check on Hattie.

Dashing back in the bedroom, I found her cowering in the corner beneath the bedcovers.

"Are you dressed?"

"Save for my shoes. I can't find them."

"Don't show your face."

"But what are they doing?"

"They're trying to move my house off the lot."

I scrambled to the window and looked outside. The men had shoved timbers through the holes they had knocked in the foundation and were preparing to lift the house off its stone perimeter. There must've been a hundred men just on that side of the house. I didn't look out the other side but figured there were that many there as well.

My five bullets wouldn't go far, but there would be enough to take on the son of a bitch that had messed with my mule.

I charged to the front door, but the bastards at that end lifted the house, and I found myself running uphill. Then the fellows at the back hoisted their side, and I stumbled forward, running into the wall by the door. Though I was sober as a Baptist in the front pew, I was stumbling around like a drunk. I flung open the door and put a foot out for the front step, but it was gone.

I spotted the fellow who'd been threatening my mule, though, and he was lifting his shovel in the air to strike Flash right square between the eyes. Flash was kicking and dancing, trying to pull free from the hitching post.

As the house was being inched toward the street, I held on to the door, lifted my pistol, and fired at the shovel. My first shot missed, but the house stopped moving at the sound of the retort. My second shot hit the shovel blade and sent it flying from the hands of the fool aggravating Flash.

Everything went dead quiet for a moment. Then Sheriff Behan ran around to the front of the house. "Who fired those shots?"

"I did," I answered from the doorway, my unbuttoned pants beginning to slide down. I let go of the door-frame and grabbed them before they fell to my ankles. "I'll kill the son of a bitch that messes with my mule!"

Behan shook his head. "This is a legal matter of Cochise County. You're a squatter and have to move off this lot."

"I bought and paid for it!"

"The title's not clear."

I was down to three bullets, but I decided to keep one for Johnny Behan.

Turning his back to me, Behan marched around the house, yelling to the men to finish moving it.

"Do I own the street?" I yelled.

"Nope," Behan called back. "And once it's in the street, it becomes a town problem. Now move it, boys."

The house jerked forward again. I knew I was defeated. But then the Earp brothers appeared across the street, and I knew I was dead.

The miners moved the house another two or three feet, oblivious to the Earps. Virgil, being the town marshal, was in the lead. Wyatt and Morgan stood on either side of him, the sleeves on their gun hands rolled up. Virgil carried a shotgun. He held it up in the air and discharged it.

My house stopped in its tracks.

"What the hell's going on here?" Virgil demanded.

Behan stepped to the street. "It's a county matter, Marshal."

"It's a town matter if you move it into the street."

Behan pointed at me. "Lomax is a squatter on land owned by the Gilded Age Mining Company."

"That's for the courts to decide. Until they do, we're not gonna leave Lomax's place in the middle of a town street."

The sheriff took off his bowler and looked from Virgil to the gang of men holding my house in the air. Behan was always a good one to talk high and mighty until someone called his hand. Then he could become meek as a losing politician.

He might've pondered the situation all day, but Wyatt stepped forward. I'd heard there'd been bad blood between the two since Wyatt had started squiring Josephine Marcus about town. Behan apparently thought Josephine was his. It didn't seem to bother Wyatt that he already had a wife.

"Put your hat back on. The glare off your head is blinding me."

Behan didn't seem to find the remark too funny, but all the fellows holding up my house did. They laughed so much the house started vibrating.

"The law's getting impatient, Behan."

"I'm the law," Behan replied.

"So are we," Wyatt answered. "Maybe we should just settle this right here and see which law is right." Slowly, deliberately, Wyatt wriggled the fingers on his gun hand. He believed quick justice was better than slow justice. No doubt with Wyatt's way the matter would've been settled right there on the street, but Behan was slower to settle things and, most likely, slower to draw.

Wyatt could've stood there until he died and Behan would never've slapped leather. Finally Behan shook his head and replaced his hat. "Boys, put the house back on the foundation. We'll win in the courts and have the pleasure of moving it another day."

My house moved backward then, and the front step came into view. The fellows in front let their end down first, catching me unprepared. I grabbed for the doorframe but missed, then stumbled off the porch, my legs churning as I tried to catch my balance. I'd've stayed on my feet had my unbuttoned pants not slid down to my knees, but instead I tripped and lunged forward, my shoulder striking Behan right in the gut. As I tumbled with him, I lost my pistol.

The sheriff howled and fell over backward, cushioning my landing and losing his hat. He heaved for breath and called me a few choice names. I jumped up to my feet, pulled my britches up, and buttoned them quickly. Then I fetched my pistol where it had fallen by Flash. Behan stood up and dusted his coat and backside off, then picked up his hat, which had crumpled beneath him.

"Lomax, I'll have to take you in for assaulting a peace officer."

"What?" I yelled. "It's your own damn fault, you letting them move my house!"

"I'll need your gun." He held out his hand.

Virgil stepped toward Behan. "Seems this is a town matter, too, Behan. It's not your jurisdiction."

I was mighty pleased at having the Earps there to defend me, but mighty worried that they might step inside and find Hattie in my bedroom.

"You Earps don't run this town," Behan answered, still trying to work his hat back in shape.

Wyatt shook his head. "We'll all be blinded if you don't put that hat back on. Oh, yeah, Josie says hello."

Behan seethed at the mention of Josie, but he wasn't man enough to do anything about it. He slapped his hat on his head and spun around. "Come on, boys. The courts'll settle this our way."

Wyatt grinned. "Behan, there's not enough courts in the country to settle all the differences between you and me."

The sheriff marched away, the other mob members trickling after him. They were mostly miners, men with callused hands and callused brains.

I took a quick look at the house; it seemed to be sitting square on the foundation. Through the front door I caught a glimpse of Hattie and waved for her to hide. Luckily, all three Earps were busy watching the mob disperse, so I darted to the front door and into the kitchen, flushing Satan into the bedroom.

Hattie was shaking. "It's my uncles, isn't it?"

"Yes."

"What are we gonna do?"

"I don't know about you, but I'll die if they find you."

Her answer didn't comfort me. "Probably."

"Get in the back and get under the bed."

Hattie dashed into the bedroom, and I slammed the door behind her. I'd barely gotten into the parlor before Wyatt entered.

He cocked his head at me. "It true you had a naked young lady in your bed when all this commenced?"

"Where're Virgil and Morgan?"

"They're checking around the house, making sure nobody left a cigar or something that'll burn down your place. I wouldn't trust anybody that runs around with that son of a bitch Behan. They might burn your place down or back-shoot you. Morgan and Virgil'll make sure they won't do anything more for now."

I just hoped they didn't look through the bedroom windows like the fellows in the mob had.

"Who's back there?" Wyatt wanted to know.

I thought about telling him "Your wife," but since Mattie rhymed with Hattie I decided that might not be such a good idea. Then I thought I'd say it was Josie Marcus, but that would only make him mad. I didn't know how to answer *and* survive.

Wyatt nudged me in the side. "Who is it? Do we know her?"

About that time Virgil and Morgan came in, tugging their mustaches and grinning widely.

Virgil laughed. "There's a female hiding under your bed, Lomax. Now we know why your britches were around your ankles."

Morgan grinned. "We were worried about you, Lomax, thinking you hadn't had much companionship, the way you downed the sheriff."

The three of them took to laughing. Wyatt stepped toward the kitchen door. I stepped in front of him.

"Can't let you see her."

Wyatt shook his head. "Sure you can."

He pushed me away, but I slid back in front of him as he entered the kitchen. "Don't go in there."

"What's to stop us?" Morgan wanted to know.

"Satan!"

"I don't believe in the devil," answered Wyatt.

"Once you meet Satan you will."

He laughed and tried to step around me. I moved to stop him, but Virgil and Morgan grabbed my arms.

"This is a legal matter now," Wyatt said, laughing.

I began to panic. I had to come up with a lie. Or die. "She only came here to warn me about the mob. That's all, honest."

"Nothing to be ashamed of, Lomax. We're proud to see you've still got it to give to the women," Wyatt said.

"No, don't."

Wyatt laughed. "You're acting like you were poking our niece."

Virgil and Morgan laughed, too.

Then Wyatt slapped his knee. "It's Kate, isn't it? I thought you'd taken a liking to her. Wait'll I tell Doc."

"No, no!" I cried, struggling against Virgil and Morgan.

Wyatt put his hand on the doorknob and turned it slowly. "Nothing to fear, miss. We're just checking out the room."

I held my breath, figuring the three Earps would fill me with so much lead I'd assay out at a hundred dollars a ton.

"Don't!"

Wyatt pushed opened the door.

There was a terrible screech.

Satan shot past Wyatt, then ran between Virgil's legs.

Wyatt and Virgil both jumped and hollered. Morgan just laughed.

Wyatt barged into the bedroom, looked around, then bent and checked under the bed. "Nobody here. She must've crawled out the window." He sounded disappointed.

Virgil grinned. "I wish we'd gotten here in time to meet your girl."

Morgan agreed. "We could've had some fun telling folks you were riding a mare when the mob came."

I laughed, hoping Hattie had gotten so far away from my house that she could smell ocean breezes. "I'm obliged for all your help."

Wyatt grinned. "It was worth it just to watch Behan back down. He might slap a woman around, but he won't stand up to a man."

Morgan giggled. "And seeing Lomax try to mate him in the middle of the street was better than anything I've seen in a good while."

I thanked them for their good humor, their help in

saving my house, and their wanting to check on the safety of my girl. Then I thanked God they had not found Hattie.

As I escorted them to the front door, Virgil slapped my shoulder. "We were glad to help, Lomax."

Wyatt grinned. "When we figure out who it is, we'll let you know, and you can tell us if we're right." He and Virgil laughed and joined Morgan in the street.

If I'd had a cannon, I'd've blasted their tails clear over to Allen Street, but as it was I grinned as best I could, shut the door, and let out a deep breath. I'd faced death before, but never under odder circumstances.

I guess I should've let that be the final warning and quit trying to see Hattie, but it was hard on a man to see that much of a woman to no end. But besides Hattie, my greatest fear was that my tin box had been seen by one of those scoundrels and stolen while my house was off the foundation. I checked the parlor for Satan, then stepped into the kitchen, spotting him curled up in the woodbox eyeing me and my boots. I went into the bedroom, closed the door behind me, and, before scooting the bed back in place, got on my hands and knees and lifted the floorboard.

The box was gone!

My heart jumped into my throat. In a panic I groped around some before my hand finally touched the top of the tin. Apparently my house wasn't as square on the foundation as I'd thought. Then another fear hit me. Had someone found the box, emptied it, and replaced it as close to the original spot as possible?

I jerked the box out, unlatched it, and lifted the lid. To my relief the money was still there as well as the stock certificates, the legal papers, and the letter from Hattie. I considered destroying the letter but decided not to.

Carefully I planted the tin box back in place. Then I got up and looked around the house. What little furniture and belongings I had had all shifted. Some of the things in the kitchen had fallen over, and a lamp in the parlor had broken and spilled coal oil on the floor.

But for all the bad luck I'd had that afternoon, I guess I couldn't have asked for better luck now. My house was still sitting on its foundation, I had all my money and papers, and the Earps hadn't found out I had been with Hattie when all the trouble began.

I stayed around the house the rest of the afternoon, putting the furniture back in place and checking every so often that Satan wasn't sneaking up on me. An hour or so before dark I rode Flash to the Stubborn Mule. It was clouding up toward the west again, so I went to the mercantile and bought a new slicker and a hat cover so I wouldn't get soaking wet the next time Cochise County flooded.

When I arrived at the saloon, I tied Flash out front and went inside. It was another busy evening, a lot of activity, but the noise all stopped when I walked in. I'd seen that happen when Wyatt Earp walked into a saloon, but never me.

A few men clapped and cheered. "Who was she?" yelled one.

"Was she better than Behan?" called another.

I just grinned and held my head up proudly as I stepped toward the bar. Men I hardly knew were slapping me on the back, congratulating me. Even Corina DeLure and the other saloon girls smiled. Everyone seemed happy about my afternoon exploits, everyone except Joe Campbell.

When I stepped behind the bar with him, he had but one word for me. "Shameful."

I shrugged. "What are you talking about?"

"What you did today."

"Don't worry. It wasn't Amelia Guinn."

That remark angered him.

I took off my new slicker and hat and hung them behind the bar.

"Your carnal cravings are an abominable sin," Campbell said.

"Huh? My wood carvings? What did you say, Joe?"

"Your carnal cravings."

"What the hell's that?"

"You know, your lust."

"Damn, Joe. You're going to church and hanging around Henry and Amelia Guinn too much. It's bad for your mind. Remember, more sin is less, or more church is less, or something like that. Isn't that what you used to say?"

Campbell spit on the floor and walked to the other end of the bar. He had a mad on for certain. I rather enjoyed my notoriety, provided Hattie's name wasn't brought up. It wasn't.

I wandered around the saloon a spell, winding up at Doc Holliday's table. He was playing a couple strangers. He winked at me. "Who was your sugar—or can you divulge the fair maiden's name?" I shook my head, and Doc nodded. "A southern gentleman indeed, even if he is from the lesser state of Arkansas."

A half-drunk customer opposite Doc banged his fist on the table. "Are we gonna play or visit?"

"But, sir," Doc chided, "you could use the interlude to improve your play."

"The interwhat?"

"Lewd," Doc said. "Like Lomax's shameful conduct today, bedding a maiden. From the sound of it, Lomax, the house moved beneath you."

I grinned and moved on so the drunk cardplayer wouldn't start any trouble. Outside, a light shower began to fall, and distant bursts of lightning lit the night sky. During one brief flash I saw Flash standing sadly in the rain. I figured I ought to get him to the O.K. Corral and out of the weather, so I stepped behind the bar and reached for my new slicker and hat.

Joe Campbell sidled over to me. "You leaving?"

"I'll be back after I take Flash to the corral."

"How about I take Flash for you and call it a night?"

"Are my wood carvings still bothering you?"

Campbell nodded.

"Damn, Joe, you're working in a saloon where men buy drinks and women. If it's that bad, why don't you quit and go to work in a mercantile or find you a sewing circle with some other old ladies?"

"Religion's good for you."

"If it don't kill you, it is. I figure the Guinns and that pastor've been putting too many good thoughts in your mind."

"You want me to take your mule or not?"

"Sure," I said. "I plan to be here until closing time."

"I won't be back."

"Fine," I answered, shoving my rain gear toward him. "The rain'll be done with by the time I leave. You just as well wear these."

Campbell grabbed the hat and slicker and put them on, then strode out the door and rode away. Damn if religion hadn't taken a stupid man and made him even stupider. Fact was, I was glad to be shed of Joe Campbell, and I didn't pay much attention to the gunshot a few moments later down Fremont Street.

Shortly after that, a fellow burst into the saloon. "Lomax has been gutshot!" he yelled out.

Everybody stood up from their chairs, shouting.

I felt my gut, and it seemed okay. I waved at the fellow who'd brought in the news of my demise, and several other men pointed to me behind the bar.

The fellow at the door saw me, did a double take, then shook his head and scratched his chin.

"I'm fine," I announced.

"Maybe so, but whoever was riding your mule's been shot."

Chapter Ten

Men bolted out of the saloon, me with them. I was scared. Whoever had shot Joe Campbell might've thought it was me. Had the Earps found out about Hattie?

A circle of men had gathered around Campbell, who was lying in the mud in the middle of the street when I reached him.

"God help me," he groaned.

I wasn't sure God'd be able to do much for him. I squatted in the mud and looked at his belly oozing blood.

Doc Goodfellow was his best chance—maybe his only chance—to survive. "We've got to get him to the doctor!" I yelled.

Virgil Earp ran up. "What happened?"

"Joe Campbell was shot," I answered.

"Who'd want to shoot him?"

I shrugged nervously. "He was riding my mule and wearing my slicker."

"You men carry him to the doctor," Virgil ordered.

Til Walteree came up behind me. "Stable Flash for me," I told him.

"What about Joe?"

"I'll go to the doctor with him."

A half-dozen men helped me lift Campbell and carry him to Goodfellow's office. Goodfellow answered the door in his nightshirt.

"Bad one—gutshot," Virgil said. "I doubt he's got a chance."

Campbell groaned and bucked like he wasn't ready to leave dirty and muddy Tombstone for pearly gates and golden streets. That's what I've never understood about religion: If everybody's so ready to get to heaven, why do they fight and struggle to stay here on earth?

Goodfellow pointed to the examining table, and we carried Campbell over and dropped him. He cursed and screamed, not thanking us for getting him out of the rain, then thrashed on the table like he was being branded by a poker from hell.

"Lomax, you and the marshal hold him down," Goodfellow said. "The rest of you get out of here. It's not gonna be pretty."

After that comment I wished he had sent me out, too. He took a brown bottle from a cabinet, uncorked it, and poured some liquid on a sponge. As Virgil and I held Campbell down on the table, Goodfellow covered Campbell's nose and mouth with the sponge.

"The chloroform will put him out of his misery in a moment."

Campbell squirmed a bit, then relaxed and went limp.

Goodfellow turned to me. "Go in the kitchen, build a fire, and boil me a pot of water."

"Hell, Doc, he's gutshot, not giving birth."

Goodfellow clapped his hands. "Do what I say."

I knew not to argue. I ran into the small kitchen, put wood and kindling in the stove, and lit a match to the wood. As the fire took hold, I found two pots of water Goodfellow apparently kept ready for such emergencies. I set one on the stove and went back to check on Campbell.

"I've got water heating," I announced, then saw what the doctor was doing and almost passed out. Goodfellow had cut off Campbell's shirt and was slicing open his belly like you'd gut a deer.

As he worked, he talked to the marshal. "He was shot from behind. Bullet entered low on the left side and came out a couple inches above and to the right of the navel."

"If the bullet came out, why're you cutting him open?" I asked.

Goodfellow kept cutting. "Sometimes the bullet'll break into pieces or splinter a bone. Either way can be fatal."

Dropping his knife, the doctor probed Campbell's entrails with his finger, then began to pull them out and lay them on his belly. I was getting light-headed at the sight and at the thought that the bullet had probably been meant for me. I wondered who might have fired that shot. Was it over the town lot, or something else? Did the Earps know I had been with Hattie? If they did, Virgil sure wasn't showing his hand. Was it Amelia Guinn for me wiping mud on her curtains? Or was it just some coincidence?

I closed my eyes, trying to stay conscious. When I opened them, Goodfellow had a strand of Campbell's entrails in his hand and was sewing up a tear like an old lady would darn a sock.

He glanced at me. "You're a little pale, Lomax. Go check the water."

Catching my breath, I turned and retreated to the kitchen. The water was near boiling, so I picked up the other pot and set it atop the stove. Still light-headed, I leaned against the wall for a moment, then eased back toward the front room. Goodfellow had about twice as much gut out on Campbell's belly as when I had left. I didn't know how he was going to get it all back inside, but I kept my boots on in case he needed help stomping.

Goodfellow laughed, then held up a narrow splinter. "A piece of rib. I knew something other than bullet lead did some damage."

He showed the bone fragment to Virgil, then saw me and offered it to me. Out of instinct I took the bone, then dropped it when I realized what it was.

"It's not poison," Goodfellow said.

I nodded. "I know."

"How's the water?"

"One pot's boiling, and the second's starting."

"Bring the boiling water in here," he ordered.

I didn't question him, though I had no idea what he was going to do. I found a couple leather gloves and put them on, then grabbed the pot handle and toted the water to him.

Goodfellow pointed to a counter at his elbow. "Put it there." He gently fingered Campbell's entrails, looking for other tears to fix.

"What are you going to do with the water?" I asked.

"Once it's not too hot to the touch, I'm gonna wash his guts off, try to clean 'em so he'll live."

"I thought a gutshot man was as good as dead."

"I've saved more than I've lost by doing this."

Maybe God *was* looking after Joe Campbell, even if He was having Doc Goodfellow do all the dirty work.

I took off my leather glove and touched my finger to the water. "It's scalding hot."

"We'll have to wait," Goodfellow said, examining another stretch of entrails. "Good thing, too, because I just found another rip." He took his needle and thread and began to sew up more of him. By the time he was through, Joe was going to have more thread in him than a store-bought suit.

I touched the water again. It was still too hot.

Virgil Earp looked at me. "If this don't beat all, the doctor fingering his guts and then thinking he's gonna live."

"Can you get all those guts back inside?" I asked.

"Never failed yet. How's that water?"

It still seemed a mite hot. "Too hot to me."

Goodfellow reached over and dipped his finger in. "Close enough." He pointed to what looked like a ladle. "Fill it with water, Lomax, and bring it to me."

I did as I was told. He picked up a strand of gut. "Pour it over this."

I'd done a lot of odd chores in my life, but nothing like laundering Joe Campbell's guts. I hesitated.

"Go ahead," Goodfellow ordered.

Gritting my teeth, I slowly poured the water over his guts.

"Dump it on him as fast as you can," Goodfellow commanded.

I doused the strand of entrails.

"Good," he said. "But keep doing it."

As fast as I could, I filled the dipper with water, then dumped it on a new stretch. After I'd cleaned a section, Goodfellow would work it back into Campbell's belly. It didn't look as if he was ever going to get everything back in, but he kept at it and gradually made progress.

"Virgil," he ordered, "bring the other pot in here."

I pointed to the gloves, and Virgil grabbed them on his way to the kitchen. He returned shortly with the boiling water.

"It's still boiling," he said. "It'll need time to cool."

Goodfellow nodded, obviously proud of the work he'd done so far. "I think Joe'll pull through, though it'll take a few days before we know for sure."

"After seeing what you pulled out, Doc, I have my doubts."

The doctor nodded. "This is why I left the army for Tombstone. I knew I'd have plenty of chances to work on gunshot wounds."

"That's a sorry comment on Tombstone, isn't it?" Virgil said.

"But a good comment about medicine and how far it's come. Someday an injury like this will be nothing for a good surgeon to fix." He paused a moment to test the second pot of water, deciding it was still a bit too hot.

While he waited, he got a curved needle and some more thread. I'd seen him sew up the holes in the gut, but I wasn't sure I could watch him close up the opening in Campbell's flesh.

Goodfellow tested the water again and said it was cool enough. I dipped the ladle in and started washing off the last sections of gut. The doctor finally pressed all the entrails back inside and glanced at me and Virgil like he knew we'd never believed he could get them all back in place.

"Now, Lomax, pour water over the wound and over exposed gut."

Again I doused Campbell's guts, washing out the wound. I must've dumped a dozen dippers on him before Goodfellow told me that was enough.

Next the doctor closed the flaps of skin and began to stitch them together like a woman sewing cloth squares at a quilting bee. His stitching wouldn't've won any prizes from quilters, but when he was done, Campbell's gut was closed up tighter than a preacher's mind.

Virgil shook his head. "If I ain't seen all, then this is as close as I'll ever come to it."

Goodfellow rolled Campbell on his side, sewed up the hole where the bullet had entered, and rolled him over on his back again. "That's all we can do for now." He dipped his hands in what was left of the water. "If his wound doesn't take to festering, he should survive. It'll take a day or two to see, then three or four weeks before he can get around. I'll keep him until morning, but after that he'll need to stay in bed with someone to look after him." The doctor turned to me. "Will you be able to do that?"

Now, I had to admit I owed Joe Campbell for taking a bullet that was probably meant for me, but I didn't think I had to nursemaid him back to health. I sure didn't want to keep him at my house, and if I put him in the back room at the Stubborn Mule, he would scare away my girls and my business, moaning and groaning all night and day. As self-righteous as he was getting, I figured the church ought to put him up. Then I remembered that the Guinns had spoken highly of him.

"Doc, I think I know a place that'll be better than anything I could provide."

"Where?"

"Henry Guinn's." I darted out the door and down the street. Although the rain had stopped and the sky had cleared, the street was surprisingly quiet. Only then did I realize I'd spent more than three hours working on Campbell's innards.

It was late to be calling, I knew, but I had to inform the Guinns of Campbell's unfortunate encounter with a bullet. And I had to see if I could work them into enough of a lather that they'd care for him until he was on his feet. If he died, then he was their problem.

I raced to their house, pounded on the door, and announced myself. "Henry Guinn," I called, "this is H. H. Lomax! There's been trouble!" I could've walked right in, it not being the custom at the time to lock doors, but I hesitated. I didn't want to get any mud on Amelia Guinn's floor, and I didn't want to risk seeing her in her nightgown. That would've been enough to blind a fellow or at least stop his yeast from rising.

After enough commotion to awaken the dead, I finally heard a response from Henry Guinn. "Go away. I've got a gun."

He also had a buffalo for a wife, but that didn't cow me, either. "It's me, H. H. Lomax."

"He better not have a saloon girl with him!" yelled Amelia, as charming as ever. "And he better not get mud on anything of mine or I'll put a knife to him."

I didn't doubt her. "It's trouble, bad trouble. Joe Campbell's been shot."

Amelia screamed.

"My God!" Guinn exclaimed, opening the door. He stood in his nightshirt and nightcap, holding a small revolver. "Is he alive?"

"Doc Goodfellow laundered his guts, then sewed him up."

"Gutshot!" screamed Amelia, lumbering up behind her husband. It was dark so I couldn't see her, thank God, but I could hear her heaving breath and mumbling sobs. "Is he gonna live?"

"The doctor can't say for certain, but he needs someone to care for him. That may make a difference in whether he pulls through."

"We can do that," Amelia offered. "It's our Christian duty."

"So it is," Guinn answered.

"Let's go see him, give him comfort," Amelia said.

"Please get dressed," I said. "You might cause a stir on the streets in your nightclothes." Actually I feared she'd start a damn stampede, and then all of Cochise

County would be abandoned, the Stubborn Mule with it.

"Give us five minutes," Guinn said. "Then we'll be there to comfort Joe and pray that everything's right with his soul."

I figured they needed to pray that everything was right with his guts, but Guinn slammed the door in my face before I could say as much. I walked back to Doc Goodfellow's. Virgil Earp had left.

"Any luck?"

"The Guinns'll take care of him, I'm sure of it."

The doctor shook his head. "Before it's over, Amelia Guinn'll be telling me how to doctor him. That's one hardheaded woman. I don't know how Henry Guinn's been able to put up with her."

"He's probably afraid to leave."

"I don't blame him. That is a hard, jealous woman."

"Yep," I replied. "She'd put a scorpion in his pocket and then ask him for a match. And she doesn't like me too much. Seems I got a little mud in her house, and she won't let me forget it."

When we heard a rumble outside, we both knew to shut up. It was either a thunderstorm or Amelia Guinn approaching at a run.

The door swung open, and she shot in like water out of a burst dam. She was heaving for breath and sweating like a tallow candle. I didn't see Henry Guinn at first; it took him five minutes to walk around her and into view. She stomped in and headed straight for Joe Campbell, whose sewn-up belly was still showing. Pressing her hands together under her chins, all three of them, she began to pray.

"May the Great Physician heal Joe Campbell's wounds so he will survive to bring more glory to God, Amen."

"Amen," Henry Guinn said. "Who would shoot poor Joe Campbell, Doc?"

Goodfellow shrugged. "He was riding Lomax's mule and wearing Lomax's slicker when it happened. They may have been aiming for Lomax."

Amelia gave me a look that would've bored a hole

through an oak tree. "It's just terrible that a sinner like you is walking about while a kind, decent man carries a bullet in him."

"We both work the same saloon," I reminded her.

"But he doesn't consort with vile women, and he goes to church most Sundays."

"I don't consort with vile churchgoers." I could've sworn that steam rose out of her ears, but it might have been the vapor from her evaporating sweat.

Doc Goodfellow stepped between us. "This isn't helping Joe."

Amelia glared like she'd make a steer out of me if I ever got mud on her curtains again, then turned to the doctor, smiling like she was searching for a husband. "We'll do whatever we can to make Joe's last days pleasant."

"He's got a good chance to live, if he doesn't start to fester."

Amelia squinted at Campbell's belly, all cut and stitched. "I don't see how, not with all you've done to him."

Doc Goodfellow looked at me like he'd been slapped with a wet buffalo chip. "I tried to save him as best I could."

She grunted. "Only the Great Physician can save a life. It's all in His hands now." Her eyes filled. Between her sweat and her tears I figured we were going to have water up to our ankles before long.

Meekly Henry Guinn stepped forward. "Do we need to take him to our place for rest, Doctor? We'll take care of him for certain."

"He needs to stay here until he wakes up from the chloroform. After that, if he's not reporting any unusual pain, we'll carry him to your place. You might prepare a bed for him."

Amelia kept blubbering about how terrible it was that Joe Campbell had been shot and how Tombstone would've been better served if the assassin had shot me instead.

Goodfellow looked at her. "You best go home and

get a good night's rest. I'll let you know before we bring him over."

When the couple had left, Goodfellow shook his head. "Wheew. She's mean enough to suck eggs out of a widow woman's basket and cunning enough to hide the shells on her neighbor's porch."

"She keeps her stinger out all the way," I added.

Goodfellow looked from me to Campbell, then back again. "I'd rather be gutshot than meet up with her in the dark."

"It has its advantages, as long as you're not put up in her house to recover."

"Campbell won't mind it."

"I reckon not, if he lives," I replied. "If he dies, then hell won't seem so bad next to Amelia Guinn."

Goodfellow laughed and slapped me on the shoulder. "You may be right. Now, you head back home and rest. Thanks for your help." As I stepped to the door, he offered a final warning. "You best be careful. Someone may still be shooting for you."

Nodding, I said good-night and warily returned home. I made it without incident and walked inside. I was tempted not to light a lamp, but my other worry got the best of me. There could be an assassin hiding in the dark—or worse, Satan could be preparing to ambush me.

I lit the lamp and inspected the parlor, which was as I had left it except for another envelope that had been pushed under the door. I recognized Hattie's handwriting. Squatting down, I picked up the letter with my free hand, then went into the kitchen.

Satan stirred in the woodbox. I lifted my foot so he could see I was wearing my boots, and he settled back down as I marched by. In the bedroom I looked around to make sure no one was skulking in a corner or hiding under the bed. Then I shut the door, set the lamp down on the washstand, and opened Hattie's letter.

Dearest Henry:

I can't believe you-know-who didn't catch us in bed together yesterday. I'd never been in bed before when the whole house moved.

*I'm sorry about the scratches on your behind. I
had fun. Can't wait to see you again.*

                                                    Hattie

I blew out the light, undressed, and crawled into
bed, already dreaming of Hattie.

Awaking a little before noon the next day, I reread
her letter and then hid it in the tin box under the floorboard. I dressed and headed out again, stopping by the
saloon to make sure Til Walteree and Ned Nichols hadn't
burned down the place or driven off all my customers.
Business was good for the middle of the day.

From the saloon I figured to visit Henry Guinn and
see how I stood legally after Behan's attempt to move my
house. I knocked on the door. Fortunately Henry answered instead of his wife.

"What do you want?"

"Talk about my legal situation, what with Behan's
men trying to take over my plot."

"Your situation is not as important right now as Joe
Campbell's. We're preparing a bed for him. We'll have to
talk about this later."

The way I saw it, I was paying him money to look
out for my interests. I didn't figure Joe Campbell would
dole out anything for the care he would be receiving. But
I'd learned not to argue with a lawyer, especially not my
own.

I turned around and marched over to Doc Goodfellow's. When I walked in, I found him checking his patient. Joe Campbell saw me and snarled.

The doctor glanced over his shoulder at me. "I told
Campbell how much help you were last night, staying
here the whole time I worked on him."

Campbell shook his head. "Lomax is the reason I
got shot."

I stepped beside the doctor. "What do you mean?"

"Just before I was shot, I heard some son of a bitch
yell, 'I've got you now, Lomax!' That's the last I remember."

"Did the voice sound familiar?"

"I'd heard it before, but I couldn't place it. Maybe it'll come to me."

"You tell Virgil Earp?"

Doc Goodfellow answered for him. "Yes, Lomax, he did, but I need you to quit asking him questions. Joe needs to save his strength so he can recover."

Hell, I thought, I was just trying to learn enough to keep myself from getting shot. If I was shot, I wasn't certain anyone would take me in, save possibly Hattie, and that might be the end of me anyway.

Though I didn't feel I ought to be putting Campbell up at my place, I figured I ought to help carry him to the Guinns' so he could begin his term with Amelia. "You gonna need help getting him to the Guinns'?"

Goodfellow nodded.

"I'll get some others to help."

"Give me an hour."

"That's when I'll be back."

As I walked down the still-muddy streets of Tombstone, I felt like my back was a target. I studied every face I met, wondering if the man behind those eyes was the one who had hoped to kill me. My belly was jumping like it was full of bedsprings. I was relieved when I made it to the saloon, where business was strong and keeping Ned Nichols and Til Walteree busy behind the bar.

Several patrons pointed at me as I walked in.

Walteree motioned me over. "Lot of folks anxious to see you."

"Why?"

"They're making bets how long you'll live."

"What?"

"Word's out that Campbell was shot by accident and it was you the assassin was after. All sorts of speculating going on about who did it. Some say it was a couple of Behan's men who tried to move your place. A few think it was Ike Clanton, what with you riding him about mating with stallions. Frank McLaury's name came up once. So did Doc Holliday's, Johnny Ringo's, and Wyatt Earp's and his brothers'."

"Hell, why don't you add Amelia Guinn's name to the list? I got mud in her house. And Holliday was deal-

ing poker in my own saloon when the shooting occurred.
Doesn't anybody put any good sense to these rumors?"

Ned Nichols said, "A rumor ain't a rumor if it's the
truth."

He sounded like he'd been around Joe Campbell too
much.

"Nobody thinks it was Sheriff Behan, though. He's
not man enough for that," Nichols said.

A fellow has no idea of the number of potential enemies he has until he's been shot at. Then the enemies
tend to add up a lot faster than his friends. Some of these
boys were making Satan look downright friendly.

"I came to get a few volunteers to help move
Campbell from Doc Goodfellow's to the Guinn place,
where he can recover."

Before I could stop him, Walteree raised his voice
above the din. "Lomax needs help moving Joe Campbell's body."

"He ain't dead yet," I corrected, but nobody seemed
to care.

Two dozen volunteers sprang from their chairs, offering to help. I was impressed by their feelings for Joe
Campbell and turned to Walteree. "I guess a lot of these
men really liked Joe."

"Nope," he said. "They want to be around in case
you're shot at again."

I could only shake my head, as I hadn't been shot at
the first time. When the time was right, I led the crowd
down to Doc Goodfellow's, and we carried Campbell
over to the Guinn house. There were so many of us
Amelia couldn't keep us from tracking mud in her house.

She wished bad luck upon us. After that, my luck
doubled in Tombstone. I went from having no luck to
having no luck *and* bad luck.

Chapter Eleven

For the next three or four days I was as skittish as a horse beneath its first saddle. I couldn't shake the idea that someone was going to shoot me. I looked over my shoulders more times than an owl with its tail feathers afire. When I tried to visit Joe Campbell, Amelia looked at my boots and wouldn't let me in. She was madder than a she-bear with two cubs and a sore tit for all the mud the mob had tracked into her house.

"Joe don't want to see you," she said, crossing her hamlike arms across her ample bosom. "Another stray bullet meant for you might hit him." Of course I didn't see how any bullet fired into that house could ever get around her, but I didn't mention that.

All that time I was pining for Hattie but feared if I went out with her a stray bullet might hit her instead of me, which would mean we were both dead once the Earps found out.

The Stubborn Mule continued to do a good business while the other saloons were rebuilding. A lot of our customers had placed bets on where I'd get shot and hung around the saloon to collect on their bets in case I was. Back and gut were the leading choices, though I heard one fellow had bet on the groin. All bets on location were off, of course, if the assassin used a shotgun.

Virgil Earp came to see me two days after Campbell's shooting, wanting to know if anybody had reason to shoot me.

"I got mud on Amelia Guinn's curtains. Behan raised the mob against me. Could've been him or one of them."

"Not Behan. He'd have somebody else do his killing, but I don't think it was anybody in the mob. They were mostly miners, not the ones involved in all the robbing and killing in the county."

"Who would those be?"

"Hell, Curly Bill Brocius has robbed a couple stages, and Frank Stilwell's robbed so many all the stage horses recognize his voice and stop when he calls out. Johnny Ringo's involved, and so are the Clantons. The McLaurys may be, too. You didn't give them any reason to shoot at you, did you?"

I shrugged. "Not that I know of."

"Who was the woman you were bedding down when the mob interrupted?"

"Wouldn't be gentlemanly for me to name her."

Virgil shook his head. "Maybe not gentlemanly, but it would be smart, might help us finger Campbell's attacker and protect you. It wouldn't be Corina DeLure, would it? She's a working girl that's been sweet on Johnny Ringo from time to time."

"I can't say."

"Was she a married woman? You don't have some jealous husband after you, do you?"

"Virgil, I can't tell you more than I already have."

He shoved himself away from the bar. "I reckon your reasons are good enough, though none too smart."

I didn't know if he knew something about Hattie and was trying to smoke me out or if he was really fishing for any facts to help solve Joe Campbell's shooting.

One thing the conversation did do was keep me alert to Johnny Ringo, who'd taken to hanging around the Stubborn Mule even when he wasn't in the back bedding his favorite, Corina DeLure. Word had it he could outdrink and outshoot any man in Tombstone, save possibly Doc Holliday. Those similarities were probably what made the two such bad enemies, but there they were night after night in my saloon, Holliday dealing cards with his back to the wall in one corner and Ringo sitting in the other, drinking his whiskey and watching Corina DeLure work my customers until he was ready for her. Sometimes he'd drink so much liquor the vapors would've exploded if he'd lit a cigar. He enjoyed taunting me whenever I took a new bottle to his table.

"Have *you* placed any bets on where you'll get shot?" he asked. "You know, I could place a heavy bet on your right ear, then shoot it off and collect a pretty penny."

I slammed the bottle on the table. "The only thing you'll shoot off is your mouth."

Ringo took offense. He stood up and said, "That's big talk from a bottle washer."

The saloon went silent except for a lone voice across the room. "My, my, Johnny Ringo," said Holliday, "that wasn't a very pleasant thing to say to the proprietor of this fine establishment."

Doc Holliday stood up, and a path instantly cleared between him and Ringo.

"Ain't none of your concern, Holliday."

"I beg to differ, Johnny Ringo. You've interrupted my game and changed my luck."

Johnny Ringo grinned. Though he'd drunk a bottle of whiskey, his hand was as steady as his gaze. Holliday was as calm as ever. I never saw two more dangerous men face off without an ounce of fear between them, and I figured one of them would slap leather for sure.

Holliday smiled. "Of course, Johnny Ringo, you must remember that if a stray bullet strikes Lomax, we might lose our bets."

Ringo pursed his lips, then replied, "I'd hate to ruin everyone's fun. Maybe we can settle this after Lomax gets his."

Both men nodded agreement, but I didn't know whether to feel relieved or doomed. They took their seats, and my customers went back to drinking and having a good time.

With Campbell out and business still booming, I was forced to spend several nights sleeping in the back room when the girls had finished their shift and gone home. I always changed the sheets so they were clean and didn't smell of whiskey, tobacco, sweat, and lust. Come ten o'clock each morning, when we opened the saloon, I'd handle the bar until Ned Nichols or Til Walteree showed up, then run to the house.

About a week after Campbell was shot, I found another letter from Hattie. She said she was getting itchy to see me and suggested I meet her that night. I took favorably to the idea, and when I went back to the saloon later that afternoon, I had Ned Nichols go down to the O.K. Corral and rent a buggy. He was to leave it on Fifth Street so I could leave by the back door of the saloon, find it, and meet her.

Even though the saloon stayed busy, after dark I told Ned I was going to work in the office, checking the books and our liquor inventory. When Ned and Til weren't looking, I slipped out the back door, clung to the shadows as I snuck to Fifth Street, and climbed in the buggy. I steered the horse around and trotted off to meet Hattie, who was waiting in front of a darkened store a block from her house. She stepped to the buggy and threw what looked like a blanket on the floorboard.

Quickly she climbed up in the seat, put her arms around me, and gave me a quick kiss on the cheek. As I started the buggy rolling, my yeast was rising. I was anxious to put my dough in the oven, but we had no place to go, not with an assassin possibly watching my house and her folks staying at hers. And so many people were curious about who I'd been bedding when the mob attacked my house that I couldn't step into a hotel without immediately raising suspicions and a crowd.

"I've missed you," Hattie said, "but it's been fun hearing all the talk, people wondering about the mysterious woman you were with."

"It may be fun for you, but it's a mite scary for me. Your uncles are curious."

"But why are you scared? You're the man who stared down Doc Holliday. In fact, I hear you stood between him and Johnny Ringo at the saloon and prevented a gunfight between them."

"If you're found out, your folks'll just slap you

around a little. If they find out about me, they'll kill me, especially if they find out what we've been doing."

Hattie tittered. "Been doing? What have we done?"

Besides seeing each other naked, we hadn't done a thing. My yeast kept rising for the right reasons, but my dough kept falling for the wrong ones. "I don't guess we've done anything," I admitted.

Hattie toed the blanket by her feet. "I'd like that to change. I brought us something to lie on when we get out of town."

The night was dark, perfect for us to ride off the road a ways, spread her blanket, and spend a little time trading slobber. I drove the wagon far enough from town to be safe, but not so far that we couldn't hear the sounds of Tombstone. I tied the buggy and jumped down, scampering around to help Hattie to the ground. She took out the blanket and spread it on a clear spot. We just stood in each other's arms for a few minutes, glad to finally be close and alone. From somewhere in town I heard a couple gunshots, but that was nothing new. As far as I was concerned, there was about to be lots more fireworks on a blanket outside of town.

Hattie must've read my mind, because she pushed herself away from me and started to unbutton her blouse. I could just make out her fingers as they worked their way down, and it was all I could do to keep from breaking into a little jig. I was finally going to be able to bake my bread.

She pulled her blouse out from her skirt, and I was ready to dive in when I heard the strangest sound from Tombstone. My name was being called.

"Lomax, H. H. Lomax!" came a shrill cry through the still night air.

I shook my head, thinking it was only my imagination. Then the cry came again. And again. Each time it seemed like more men were picking up the call.

"What's happening?" Hattie wanted to know.

"I don't know, but it can wait."

"I'm not so sure," she said, beginning to button her blouse back up.

Soon my name was being shouted in unison by a

mob of men wandering the street. Shortly we saw four or five torches in the crowd.

"Lo-max! Lo-max!" the mob chanted.

Hattie tucked her blouse in her skirt, then grabbed the blanket. "Get me back to the house quick."

A moment before I had been practically drooling, and now my mouth had turned drier than an abolitionist's beer mug.

Hattie bounded to the buggy. "Come on, Henry. Let's go."

I ran around the buggy, jumped in, and started the horse in a tight circle back toward the road.

"Lo-max, Lo-max," chanted the crowd, "where are you?"

Damn, I thought. I wasn't going to need a conscience if this was the way people kept up with me in Tombstone.

"What do they want, Henry?"

Hitting the road, I straightened out the buggy. "I don't know. I guess they're trying to keep us decent."

The mob marched down Fremont Street toward us, then turned and went down Allen Street, moving away from us but still chanting my name.

"Lo-max! Lo-max!" they cried.

I just hoped no one took up the cry "Hattie! Hattie!" or I was as good as dead.

Though we weren't far from town, I drove as fast as I thought I could without attracting attention. As we neared Hattie's house, I saw a lamp burning in the parlor and knew her folks were up.

"Do they know you went out?"

"Not unless they checked my bedroom. I crawled out the window."

I hoped her luck would hold. Mine seemed to be going to hell.

"Let me out beside the house, and I can slip in the window without them knowing. I haven't been gone that long."

"I know."

Drawing the buggy up as close as I dared, I leaned over to kiss her, but she'd already jumped out, dragging the blanket behind her. She ran to her window and climbed in.

I thought everything had turned out okay, but then I heard a man's voice. "Where the hell you been?"

Almost instantly the lamp in the parlor was moved, and shortly I saw a glow in Hattie's window.

"What were you doing with that blanket? Seeing a fellow again?"

A man's head appeared out the window. For a moment I sat stunned, then lifted the reins and slapped them against the horse's rump. The animal trotted forward.

"Stop, you son of a bitch, stop!" called the man I took to be Jim Earp. But I ignored him. The last thing I heard was, "You're barely sixteen, Hattie, and behaving like a saloon girl."

Hattie'd lied to me, telling me she was almost twenty. I knew I shouldn't be seeing her again if she wasn't sixteen yet, but I just couldn't stop my yeast from rising. I raced down Fremont toward the Stubborn Mule, then turned my buggy on Third Street and headed toward the saloon from that direction, figuring to come in from behind the place on Fifth Street and sneak in the back without anybody realizing I'd gone anywhere.

Glancing toward Allen Street as I turned, I saw the tail end of the mob and heard them chanting my name. I raced ahead to Fifth, stopping close to the spot where the buggy had been parked before. After I tied the reins, I jumped from the seat, slipped around to the back of the saloon, let myself in, then eased into my office. Before I could sit down at my desk, Til Walteree burst in.

"Where you been, Lomax?"

"I stepped outside to take a leak."

Walteree cocked his head. "That ain't so."

"As long as I'm paying you fifty cents a day to tend bar it is."

He scratched his head. "I guess you're right." He backed out of the room and turned for the bar.

I decided to follow him. There were only about a third as many customers in the saloon as when I'd left. Doc Holliday was sitting in the corner, dealing poker to a single player. He glanced up from the pasteboards and grinned at me.

"Well, Henry Harrison Lomax, I see you've returned from the dead. A lot of your customers were worried when they heard gunshots. They thought you'd been assassinated. They wanted to find you."

"That was mighty kind of them."

Holliday shrugged. "They just wanted to see where you'd been shot. There's a lot of money riding on your well-being. As for me, I never thought you were shot. I figured you just might be trying to dip your wick in a little sugar. Remember, there's always Kate."

"I'll pass," I said. "I do fine without paying for it."

Holliday coughed. "I can tell." He returned to dealing poker.

Outside, the chanting grew louder. "Lo-max, Lo-max." A couple men rose from their tables, stepped out on the boardwalk, and whistled at the mob.

"Lomax is back!" yelled one of them.

"He got shot in the back?" asked someone in the mob. Several men cheered.

"No," replied another. "He wasn't shot. He just showed up again."

A groan went through the crowd.

The roving gang entered in clumps, one half-drunk man trying to bring his torch in with him until the others told him to throw it in the street with the others. They were all disappointed that I was still alive and whole.

Johnny Ringo was among them, along with Ike and Billy Clanton and Frank and Tom McLaury. As usual, Ringo had been drinking.

"We heard shots and figured you was a goner, Lomax," he said.

"I'll double my bet he gets it in the back," said Ike Clanton.

Holliday interrupted. "Gentlemen, getting it in the back is not what Lomax has been doing. He apparently had a rendezvous with his paramour."

"Pair of what?" shouted Frank McLaury. "More? How can he get a pair of more?"

"It's from the French," Johnny Ringo explained. "It means his lover."

Frank, who was cockier than a rooster with three peters, angled toward me. "He's too ugly to have a woman. Must be a heifer."

I shook my head. "I'm not the one walking in here with cow dumplings on my boots." I pointed at Frank's footwear, splattered nicely with cow dung.

Frank slammed his fist on the bar. "I don't take kindly to insults."

"Ain't an insult, Frank. It's the truth. That's cow droppings on your boots. Now, an insult would be me saying something like 'No wonder all the new livestock in Cochise County is ugly, if you're punching the cattle and Ike Clanton is punching the horses.' *That* would be an insult if I said it, but I didn't."

Several men laughed, but Frank failed to see the humor in my remark. "I'm the handsomest cowboy in Cochise County," he bragged.

"That's what I hear from the cows."

Frank got within striking distance and drew back his fist to hit me, but Tom McLaury grabbed his arm. "Come on, Frank, he was just funning you like you was funning him."

"That ain't funning, it's insulting, especially from a fellow who's so ugly his mother must've fed him with a slingshot."

"At least my kids don't say mooo," I reminded him.

Frank lunged for me, but Tom slowed him until a couple other men grabbed him. "Easy, Frank," said Tom.

As for me, I'd been waiting so long to get my bread baked, I was edgy and confident I could use a good fight. I lifted my arms and doubled my fists. "Let him go," I barked. "I'm ready to fight him and anybody else who thinks he can take me."

Deep down I didn't figure they'd let him go, but they did. Frank McLaury charged me like an enraged bull. I jumped aside when he got within reach and stuck my boot out. He tripped, ran headlong into the bar, and fell to the floor, where he lay sprawled and stunned for a moment.

As he pushed himself up, shaking his head, I positioned myself. When he turned around, I plowed one fist into his teeth, the other into his nose. He spewed blood, howled, and swung wildly at me, missing each time. Fending off a couple blows to my head with my left hand, I punched him in the gut with my right.

Frank gasped, then doubled forward. I grabbed his head and flung it toward the ground just as I jerked my knee up. His face flattened against my leg before he collapsed on the floor.

"I'll be damned," said Johnny Ringo.

I spun around to him, getting angrier by the moment. "You want some of these, Ringo?" I challenged, holding up my fists.

He shook his head and backed away just as Tom McLaury came forward. I thought he was about to attack me, but he bent to check his brother. With a sigh he grabbed Frank by the arms and dragged him outside.

"Anybody else want to take me on?"

The saloon was suddenly dead quiet. I actually saw fear in the eyes of the men within punching distance. They backed away, shaking their heads. I gained a measure of respect from those men that night.

"Any other questions?" I asked the crowd. The men looked away and started minding their own business again.

After the last customer left that night, I closed up the saloon and told Til Walteree to take the buggy with him and return it to the corral the next day. I stayed the night at the saloon, not even bothering to change sheets before falling into bed and going to sleep.

The next morning I opened at the regular time. After Ned Nichols showed up, around noon, I left him in charge and went to the house to clean up and get ready for another night. I boiled water in the kitchen, poured it in a washtub, then shaved and took a bath. Satan was circling the washtub, but I left a boot on either side, and the cat kept his distance.

I was running out of clean clothes, so I put on the suit I'd worn to the dance in Charleston. Then I gathered my dirty duds, stuffed them in a canvas war bag, and started for Hop Town, the Chinese section on the west end of Tombstone.

To my surprise, I ran into Hattie Earp. Her cheek was bruised, and she had a scared look about her. She looked both ways down the street before falling in beside me.

"What happened?"

"Don't look at me," she commanded. "Just walk and listen."

"Shoot."

"My pa hit me, says he'll skin whoever's been taking me out at night. My uncles've been saying the same thing."

I gulped.

"If they find out, Henry, no telling what they'll do. They can be so mean sometimes."

I grimaced. Whipping Frank McLaury was one thing, but taking on the whole Earp family was another. "Maybe I can throw them off the trail, get them to pestering someone else."

"Be careful," she warned. "I know you're not afraid. I heard what you did to Frank McLaury last night. You've stood up to Doc Holliday, too, but my uncles can be mean. I know."

I didn't doubt her. "I'll be careful, and I'll stand my ground."

She nodded. "I knew you were brave enough to stand up to them. They can't run my life."

I had a question for her. "Hattie, how old are you?"

"Going on twenty."

"How close to twenty are you?"

"Just four."

"Four days, four weeks, four months, or four years?"

"Years," she said defiantly, turning and marching away.

I kept going to Hop Town. There must've been a half-dozen laundries there, and it seemed as if a representative of each one saw me coming with my bag of clothes. They jumped on me like white on rice and implored me to give them my business. I never heard so much chin music in all my life. Their English wasn't worth a damn, though it was better than my Chinese. I felt as popular as the only whore in a mining camp.

"Do raundry, best price," said one.

"No, no, me do raundry best," said another.

"Iron crothes, too, for free," offered another.

They were arguing and gesturing and shouting. I thought about yanking their pigtails to get a little quiet, but their customs were so backward I figured they'd take it as a sign I wanted them to make more noise. They made me so many offers I couldn't understand that I was as confused as a woodpecker in a petrified forest.

"I want my damn clothes washed!" I shouted. They went silent.

Then the littlest fellow among them slipped between a pair of his competitors and grabbed my sack of clothes.

"Me do crothes. Just speak your name."

"Lomax," I said. "H. H. Lomax."

Instantly all the laundrymen fell to their knees.

At first I thought they'd decided I was some sort of god to worship, but that didn't explain why they were all looking over their shoulders. "What's the matter?"

The one with my laundry stood up first, but ever so slowly. The others rose one by one and backed away, pointing and snickering in Chinese.

"What's the matter?"

"We careful in case mean man shoot at you, Romax," answered the one with my laundry.

"It's Lomax. What mean man?"

"Whoever shoot you, Romax," he answered. "We not be in way."

"It's Lomax. What do you mean you don't want to be in the way?"

"Of shot. Don't want to be in way of shot. Might affect betting."

"Betting? What are you talking about?"

"Where you get shot. We make bets. Most bet backshot. Some gutshot."

I couldn't believe the little sons of bitches were betting on where I'd get shot, but I shouldn't've been surprised. Everyone else in Tombstone was.

They began to chatter again, and then to laugh. Another laundryman stepped up to me. "Romax, who woman you sreep with?"

"Sreep with?"

This brazen Chinaman nodded, then made a circle with the forefinger and thumb of his left hand and pushed his right index finger back and forth in the circle. "Sreep with?"

They all nodded.

"You betting on that, too?"

"Just curious," he answered.

I'd never seen such bad manners. I'd've whipped the lot of them if I hadn't needed my clothes washed and ironed. I turned to the one who was handling my laundry. "When ready?"

"Tomorrow," he said, "if you stay rucky and no get shot, Romax."

"Romax rucky." I stormed back toward the Stubborn Mule with a lot on my mind. Seemed like everybody in Cochise County was betting on where I'd get shot or wondering who I was bedding down. And if it wasn't the assassin that got me, it'd be the Earps for fooling with Hattie.

It was getting mighty hot in Tombstone, and I tried desperately to think of something to throw the Earps off my trail. They were like drought in the Southwest—inevitable. I considered selling the Stubborn Mule and opening a saloon over in Bisbee. That would put a few miles between me and Tombstone and the Earps. Selling out, though, would probably take a little time, and in the interim I had to throw the Earps off my track. The best way to do that was to start a rumor about someone else slipping out with Hattie.

There were a lot of men in Tombstone who would've loved the chance to go out with her, but I wanted one I didn't like. I didn't have to think much past the previous night and Frank McLaury.

When I got back to the Stubborn Mule, I asked Ned Nichols and Til Walteree if they'd heard any stories about Hattie Ketcham Earp skipping out with anyone. They said no, though they'd heard about a set-to between her and Jim Earp after he caught her coming in the window after going out with a fellow.

"The name I heard is Frank McLaury," I said.

Both men leaned toward me. I knew they would put some stock in this rumor, but I didn't want to overdo it.

"I don't know that I believe that, but it could explain why the Earps and the McLaury bunch don't get along together."

Walteree and Nichols began to chew on that like a cow chews cud.

"Now, don't you mention that to anybody," I said. "I don't want to harm the name of that innocent young lady, though Frank McLaury's name can lie in the mud forever."

I figured they'd wait a few minutes before they started spreading the word, but I had to be certain that the rumor got around from a couple angles to give it more weight. I didn't mention it again that day, but the next day when I returned to get my laundry, I thought I'd spread a little manure in Hop Town.

"Romax rucky not shot," my laundryman said when I showed up at his shack.

"Not as rucky as Frank McRaury," I said. "If the Earps ever catch him out with Hattie Ketcham, there'll be the devil to pay."

The Chinaman nodded as he handed me my bag of clothes. "Rucky Romax," he said.

I paid him, then issued a warning. "Don't talk to anyone about Hattie and her fellow. It could mean trouble."

"No talkee," he replied.

The moment I stepped out the door, I heard plenty of Chinese chin music. I didn't know what he was saying, but I had my suspicions.

I dropped off the laundry at my house and stopped by the Stubborn Mule about midafternoon. Corina DeLure and Big Nose Kate were sitting at a table, ignoring the customers.

"What's the matter, ladies? Have you lost your charms?"

"No," said Corina. "We're bored."

"I thought that *was* you ladies' job—to be bored."

"I don't understand," Kate replied.

"For a few days it was fun waiting for you to get shot," Corina informed me.

"Yes," Kate agreed, "but no more."

I sighed. "I've had fun not being shot at."

"But you didn't bet," Corina pointed out.

"Where'd you think I'd get shot?" I asked her.

"Head."

That was a comforting thought. I turned to Kate.

"Ass."

"Why?"

"It just seemed right."

I'd taken about all the insults I could stand from them. "Well, ladies," I said, "let me share some excitement with you."

"You pay like everyone else," Corina said.

"No, not that. Let's go for a little walk."

"Vhere?" Kate wanted to know. "Doc vill be here in a little bit."

"To see Joe Campbell, see how he's recovering."

"It beats staying here," Corina said.

"It'd boost Joe's spirits to see you fine ladies."

I assisted them from their chairs, and we stepped out the door. "By the way," I asked, "has either of you ever met Amelia Guinn?"

They shook their heads.

"You'll just love her."

Chapter Twelve

The three of us marched to Henry Guinn's place. I couldn't help but smile with Corina DeLure on one arm, Big Nose Kate on the other, and Amelia Guinn not suspecting their approach. I figured to see a catfight bigger than Satan himself could create once those three got in the same room. I had to give Amelia the weight advantage, but she hadn't had the fighting experience that Kate and Corina had had dealing with drunks, young bucks, and assorted other men with less than honorable intentions. Of course Amelia would have religion on her side and, as fat as she was, that was a damn big side.

When we stepped up on the porch, I checked my boots to make sure I had a little mud on them. I knocked on the door a couple times before Henry Guinn himself opened it and looked at us through his thick spectacles. His eyes widening, he glanced over his shoulder, nervous as a pig in a slaughterhouse.

"You can't come in," he whispered, "not with those women."

Glancing at Corina and Kate, I could see the hurt on their faces. I leaned toward Henry. "Sure I can, and them, too."

"No." He spoke so low I could barely hear him.

"Joe met these ladies at a church social."

"We're real social," Corina offered.

Guinn started to shut the door, but I slipped my

boot inside. "They want to wish Joe Campbell well, and if they don't get to, they just might start sending little letters to your house, telling you how much they enjoyed your company the other night."

Guinn vehemently shook his head. "No, no, that would be terrible."

"It would," I agreed, "especially if poor little Amelia found out. It would break her heart. And your neck."

I'd never seen a man turn pale quicker than Henry Guinn. He was white as a man can be and still draw a breath.

"They might even start a ruckus right now."

Henry Guinn pulled the door open. "I'll go to my office. Say you let yourself in."

"Thank you, lover," said Kate.

Guinn went from white to red faster than a bottle of good whiskey goes from full to empty. He pointed toward the rear of the house as he backed into his office.

Leaving the front door open in case Amelia charged us like the cavalry, we walked quietly through the parlor toward the sound of her voice. We came to a door and saw Joe Campbell propped up in bed facing us. Amelia sat with her back to the door, reading the Bible.

When Campbell saw us, his eyes widened.

"Joe," called Corina, not waiting for an introduction, "how the hell are you?"

Before I could teach her some manners, she moved to the bedside opposite Amelia.

Kate stepped beside Amelia, nodding to her, then studying Campbell. "You look vell."

His lip trembling, Campbell looked from Kate to Amelia.

Amelia slammed her Bible shut and stood up. She spun around as fast as she could sling that much fat in a circle and glared. "How dare you bring these ... these harlots into my house!"

"They're friends of Joe's and just came to wish him well. They miss him," I offered.

"It's not what it sounds like," Campbell tried to explain.

"How dare you call me a harlot, you ugly sow?" shot back Corina.

"That's what you are, both of you."

I figured I should try to calm things down, so I asked Campbell a philosophical question. "Joe, if more is less and right is wrong, can a harlot be a virgin?"

Campbell was too scared to answer.

Kate didn't seem to care what Amelia said or did, but Corina wasn't going to give up.

"And what's a harlot?" Corina wanted to know.

If she hadn't figured it out by then, I didn't know how many years she'd survive in the business, but she decided to answer her own question and show she was smarter than she seemed. "It's a woman who spends some time in a bedroom with a man that's not her husband." She pointed her finger at Amelia's ample bosom. "Like you."

Amelia sputtered at the accusation. "I'm not a harlot. A harlot has carnal relations."

Corina twisted her head like she'd been hit by fifty pounds of dumb. "What's a carnival got to do with it?"

"You ignorant harlot."

"Harlot? What's a harlot? It's a woman that takes money from a man for sleeping with her. You ever sleep with that skinny runt of a husband up front?"

"How dare you? Get out, both of you!"

Corina didn't let go. "That's what you're doing. You're sleeping with that mousy man, and he puts a roof over your head, clothes on your back, money in your pocket, and food in your belly. From the size of you, you make a better living at it than I do."

Amelia sniffed. "We're married."

"You make your living on your backside, no different than me."

"It ain't sin."

"Ha!" Corina answered. "Only difference is I don't limit my charms to one man."

"And that's why you're a harlot."

Corina placed her hand on the bed beside Campbell's legs and leaned toward Amelia. "You could make a fortune if you just got your fellas to pay you by the pound."

Amelia screamed and lunged across the bed, clawing at her. Campbell yelled in pain as she splatted across his thighs and belly. I figured the impact probably split his gut open and I was gonna have to help Doc Goodfellow sew him up again, but Amelia wasn't thinking anything except how she was going to show Corina the light by scratching her eyeballs out.

Poor Campbell was moaning whenever he could gasp a breath. I wanted to ask him if more weight was less or light was heavy, but he wouldn't have heard, not with all the screaming going on between Amelia and Corina. I'd've figured Amelia had the bigger set of lungs, having more room to keep them in her ample frame, but Corina had a powerful set and held her own.

Amelia gave up on trying to crawl over the bed and rip out Corina's pagan heart. Instead she hoisted her skirt to charge around. I stepped back in horror. There was no way I could stop her from killing poor little Corina right then and there.

Joe Campbell couldn't stop her, either. He was gasping for breath and flinging back his covers to see if the hem on his belly had come undone.

Corina was as good as dead, I figured, but before Amelia could charge her, Big Nose Kate made a suggestion. "I vouldn't do dat."

There was something persuasive about her Hungarian accent—or maybe it was the derringer she pressed against Amelia's ear.

If the meek shall inherit the earth, as Henry Guinn had told me, then Amelia could've received the deed right then and there—though it would probably have been only a quitclaim deed and not worth a thing. She turned gentler than a shy lamb.

"Ve came to visit vith Joe Campbell. Ve can't talk vith you making all dis noise. Little gun only make a little noise, but plenty to make quiet from a fat girl."

I'd always thought Amelia was so religious she'd relish the chance to meet her Maker, but she wasn't as religious as I thought—or hoped. Even though she could've inherited the earth at that moment, I figured she'd've settled for just enough land to get her out of range of Kate's little peashooter.

With the gun still in her ear, Amelia eased back toward her chair, knowing she'd be the first to hear the shot if Kate's finger slipped. Calmly she sat down, barely breathing.

"I vant you to start again, like ve just came in da room." Kate wriggled the gun like she was prying wax from Amelia's ear.

Amelia flinched and scrunched her face.

"I vant you to act friendly to us during dis visit."

Amelia nodded weakly.

"Dat is good. My name is Kate, Big Nose Kate. My friend is Corina DeLure." She lowered the gun.

Taking a deep breath, Amelia wiped away a band of perspiration from her upper lip and smiled as best she could, but I've seen chickens with better grins. Her wide eyes were still focused on the derringer. She opened her lips, but nothing came out.

Kate tried to give her a few English lessons. "Say velcome."

Amelia hesitated.

Kate waved the gun at her nose.

"Welcome."

"I vant to hear our names. Velcome."

"Welcome, Lomax and Corina and Big."

Kate grimaced and shook her head. "I vant you to call me Kate, not Big and not Nose. Velcome us again."

Amelia nodded slowly. "Welcome, Lomax and Corina and Kate."

"Say something how glad you are to see us."

"I'm so glad you came to visit Joe Campbell."

"Dat's good," Kate said. "Now, I vant you to start reading again."

I'd never seen Amelia so willing to listen to someone else's suggestions. She started reading Scriptures, though her smile was so stiff that if she'd sneezed her face would've shattered into a thousand pieces.

Corina and Joe Campbell began to talk about how

things were at the Stubborn Mule and how glad she was he hadn't been killed.

"Is it true they yanked your guts out, then shoved them all back in?" she wanted to know.

Campbell shrugged carefully, still in pain from Amelia's collapse upon him. Kate asked him a few questions but mostly worked on improving Amelia's manners, if not her religion.

I decided it was time to slip up front and see Henry Guinn about selling my saloon. I smiled at Kate. "You girls just continue your chat while I visit Henry."

Kate nodded. "Vhatever you say, Lomax. Ve vill just be chatting."

For once, Amelia didn't insult me or ask me to take off my boots. I retreated toward the front, opened the door to Guinn's office without knocking, and found him pacing back and forth in front of his desk. He looked as nervous as a barefoot man in a bramble patch.

"Is Amelia okay?"

I stroked my chin and nodded. "They had a rough start of it, Amelia and the girls, but they're friends now. Amelia's reading the Bible to them, trying to convert them. And Joe, he seemed to be better after your wife got through with him in bed."

Guinn's eyes widened, and his jaw dropped wide enough for livestock to have escaped from his mouth.

"I couldn't believe it, either," I admitted, "but you just never know about women and when they get the urge. If I's you, I'd keep an eye on them, because I'd hate for the preacher to hear about them."

Guinn flinched.

"Now, don't get me wrong, I wouldn't go telling the preacher nothing unless I got drunk and happened to let it slip, but you don't have to worry because I've taken the cure and given up drinking."

The lawyer threw up his arms. "She wasn't—you know—*with* him, was she?"

"It was hard to tell with those big thighs of hers, but it's like my pa used to tell me. Even a blind hog occasionally finds an erection—or was it acorn?"

Confused, Guinn moved to his chair, sat down, and

placed his head in his palms. "Amelia, Amelia," he kept repeating.

"I didn't come here to talk about Amelia," I informed him. "I want to sell my house and saloon. I'm thinking about moving out."

Guinn frowned. "Can't do it," he said, his voice quivering.

"What do you mean I can't do it?"

"Well, you can, but since both lots are still disputed, there's no way you can sell, since you don't have clear title."

"But I bought it. I have the papers."

"The papers you have are good once the original title to the land is undisputed. It'll be a while before that's settled."

"I can't wait," I answered. "I could get shot."

"I know," Guinn said. "I bet on the chest."

Even my son-of-a-bitch lawyer was betting on me getting killed. "That's terrible."

"It does go against the Good Book, but I figured I might just as well sin over something I was interested in."

"Doesn't it go against the law?" I asked.

"No, not at all, as long as no one pulls the trigger. After that, the party that committed the crime has a legal problem, but all us who bet on your injury have done nothing wrong."

"How much did you bet?"

Guinn took pride in his answer. "Fifty dollars."

I about spit out my teeth. "Fifty dollars?"

"Yes, sir." Guinn nodded vigorously. "Seems you're quite a popular fellow, all the stories about you spitting in folks' drinks, cutting it with tobacco juice, pouring in coal oil, rattlesnake poison, anything you can find."

"The Allen Street saloons, they're the ones that do that. Not us respectable Fremont Street saloons."

"That's not what Joe Campbell says. He says it's all true, and that you spread stories about the other saloons."

I shook my head, astounded at the vile rumors. "Joe

must've been out of his head when he said that. Getting shot's been tough on him."

"He told me all this before he was shot. Said he always felt it was dishonest. And I couldn't agree more. A man reaps what he sows. Dishonesty begets dishonesty."

I'd always thought dishonesty begat lawyers. It struck me that a lawyer giving a lecture on honesty was about as odd as a teetotaler railing about the evils of liquor. How would he know if he'd never tried it?

Guinn kept lecturing me, but I held up my hand to cut him off. "Just tell me once everything's clear on my lots so I can sell them."

"Oh, I'll tell you, once you settle up what you owe me."

"What?"

"Fifty dollars."

"I'm not covering your bet," I insisted. "How come I owe you?"

"I've put in more time and effort protecting your lots than anybody else's in town. I'm due that money."

"I don't have fifty dollars on me, unless, of course, you want me to invite one of the girls up here to give you fifty dollars' worth of—you know—entertainment."

He shook his head and waved his arms. "No, no, just the money."

I left Henry and went down the hall, expecting to hear more blubbering and threats, but what I heard was one of the girls sobbing and Amelia reading the Bible with a little more confidence than when I had left. I feared she had stepped on the toes of Corina or Kate and the pain was more than they could stand. I paused outside the door and listened to Amelia:

"'He, that being often reproved hardeneth his neck, shall suddenly be destroyed, and that without remedy. When the righteous are in authority, the people rejoice; but when the wicked beareth rule, the people mourn. Whoso loveth wisdom rejoiceth his father: but he that keepeth company with harlots spendeth his substance.'"

At the mention of harlots a great wail arose. I recognized Corina's whining. When I stepped inside, Amelia was hugging her and patting her tenderly on the back.

"That's okay, honey. You've seen the evil of your ways, and you can repent. God will take care of you. God will wash the stains of your sins away, and you can be cleansed of sin forever."

I looked at Kate. She shrugged and rolled her eyes. She was still holding the derringer, but she didn't seem to know what to do with it.

Joe Campbell lay smugly in bed, his arms folded across his chest and a so-there look on his face. "God works in mysterious ways, Lomax," he said.

At the mention of my name, Amelia spun around and came toward me, tears in her eyes. Before I could stop her, she flung her arms around me, grabbed my head, and shoved it toward her shoulder. I'd never been in an avalanche, but when she smothered me with her ampleness I had an idea what the terror must be like.

"God bless you, Lomax. You brought a precious lamb to God."

I'd brought two whores to see a bartender.

"Truly, God does work in mysterious ways."

I scratched my head and must've looked like I'd come up five cards short of a full deck. It was getting hot inside Amelia's suffocating grasp. I tried to wrestle my way out.

Then Corina came over, ripped me free from Amelia, and threw her arms around me, thanking me all the more. As if that wasn't enough, Amelia hugged us both. It was the closest a living man could get to heaven and hell at the same time.

I squirmed free and edged quickly to the door, motioning to Kate to join me before she was overtaken with religion, too.

"Vhat happened vith Corina?" Kate wanted to know.

"You tell me," I replied, pulling her down the hall.

Amelia followed us. "You can come back, Kate, and we can read the Bible again, and you can talk to Joe."

"I vouldn't vant to do no such," she answered.

"Come to church Sunday," Amelia offered.

"I'll be dere," Kate said.

"Lomax can come, too, if he's still around." She smiled. "I bet he'd be gutshot."

Even the self-righteous Amelia had bet on where I'd get shot. I turned to Kate. "Did you wager I'd get shot?"

"No, I only vager on sure things. Doc talked about vagering on a spot and den shooting you dere."

Kate wasn't making me feel any better as we left the house and walked over to the Stubborn Mule. We'd no more than stepped in the door than Johnny Ringo was up and coming our way.

"Where's Corina?" he demanded. "Someone said you'd left with her and Kate. Now that you've had them both, I want her."

I grimaced. "I don't know when she'll be coming back, Johnny. She's got some new yearnings."

Kate held her derringer out to Ringo. "You might vant to shoot her vhen she comes back."

"*If* she comes back." I smirked.

Ringo frowned. "What do you mean?"

"She's changed, you might say. Turned religious on you."

Ringo laughed, thinking it was all a big joke. When he didn't take Kate up on the loan of her derringer, she tucked it back wherever she kept it and sidled over to Doc's table.

"Well, well, dahling," he said, "have you been sharing your charms with Lomax?"

"I saved vhat you vant for you."

Holliday shrugged and started dealing again. "I don't feel up to it today."

"But I vant you later."

"Not today, not until I say."

Kate, who could get madder than a preacher in a saloon, stormed across the room and started flirting with every customer—save Ringo—trying to get them all to go with her to the back room. No man was going to take a poke at Big Nose Kate. Messing with her could be about as healthy as putting a gun to your temple and pulling the trigger. Guns weren't always loaded, but Doc generally was, which was what made him so dangerous.

Til Walteree and Ned Nichols wanted to know how Joe Campbell was doing. I told them his religion and Amelia Guinn were carrying him through. When I further informed them that Corina DeLure might have found religion, they hooted and hollered and carried on like I couldn't pull their legs without tickling their feet.

"It's true," I kept repeating.

"If she's given up that line of work, Johnny Ringo's gonna be a mite upset," Ned Nichols said. He glanced across the saloon and suddenly got as nervous as a sober politician on election day.

After dark, Corina DeLure returned. She'd changed into a black dress with a high neck, long sleeves, and every button buttoned. She looked like she was in mourning.

Johnny Ringo stood up and called, "Over here, Corina."

She ignored him and headed straight for the bar and me.

Ringo shoved his chair back from the table and elbowed his way through the crowd. "Woman, I was talking to you. I'm ready."

Corina turned and looked at him for a moment. "I'm not."

"Then get ready, quick, while the back room's available."

"I can't," she said. "I'm quitting this."

"No, you're not."

"Yes, I am," she said. "And I owe it all to Lomax."

I could've done without the credit. Johnny Ringo was as unpredictable as the weather and twice as dangerous.

I shrugged. "It was that damned Amelia Guinn."

"Isn't she wonderful?" Corina cooed.

"You and her almost scratched each other's eyes out."

"But then she started reading, and I listened."

"That was a mistake," Ringo interjected.

"And I saw that my sins were many."

Ringo looked bewildered. "That wasn't sin—that was fun."

Corina shook her head. "I'm not doing that again, not unless you want to get married. Then we can have carnival relations."

Ringo's eyes widened with disbelief. "Carnival relations?"

I shrugged. "I thought you were an educated man."

Ringo lifted his hat and ran his fingers through his thinning hair. "Give me a bottle of your best liquor, but none with mule piss in it."

I took a bottle from the backbar. Ringo grabbed it and retreated to his table, shaking his head.

Corina came to me and started to say something, but Frank McLaury appeared from nowhere and grabbed her arm. "How about me? Ringo's not as handsome as me."

"I'm giving it up." She jerked her arm from his grasp. "No man's gonna put his hands on me again unless he's my husband."

"I'll be your husband for an hour," McLaury offered.

She refused his generosity, then turned to me. "I wanted to thank you for helping me find my way, Lomax."

Frank whistled shrilly, and the saloon quieted. "Corina," he yelled, "wants to thank Lomax for helping her find religion and leave her profession!"

Several men booed.

"I say we string him up!" Frank yelled.

"No, no," called Ike Clanton from across the room. "Let's shoot him so we can settle all bets."

The majority of my customers clapped in agreement.

Corina grabbed my arm across the bar and pulled me toward her. "Please go with me to the back room."

"Whoa," Frank called. "She won't have any of us, but she's taking Lomax."

The men hissed again.

I hesitated to leave the bar, but Corina's eyes pleaded like her words never could.

"Sure." I walked with her to the back room and closed and latched the door behind us. When I turned to her, she had tears in her eyes.

"I want to thank you for what you did," she said again.

Shrugging, I admitted, "Whatever it was, it wasn't what I intended."

She hugged me. It was a genuine hug, not the false kind she shared with paying men. "I always knew it wasn't right, but a woman doesn't have many other choices in this world."

I'd never thought about it, but I guess she was right. There was cooking and maybe running an eatery or a boardinghouse; the Chinese did the laundry, and my kind did just about everything else.

"How you gonna make a living?"

"I don't know," she said, "but I'll survive."

"Well, don't count on scraps from Amelia Guinn's table."

She hugged me tighter, like we were brother and sister. I felt proud of what I'd done, even if I hadn't done anything. Then I heard a commotion outside the door.

"Open up, Lomax, open up!" It was Johnny Ringo. "She's my girl, and I intend to have her."

"She's giving it up, Johnny," I called, thinking we were safe behind the closed door.

The first shot startled us.

Corina screamed.

I flinched, then shoved her on the bed as the second shot exploded through the door. I rolled her over, and we both fell on the floor. Then I crawled to the window and pried it open so she could get out.

"Hurry!" I cried. She scrambled to the window and clambered outside.

As soon as she was out, I stuck my leg through and was about to escape when another bullet shattered the wooden door. A sharp pain shot through my butt. I fell to the floor and landed on my hip, sending another jolt of pain running through me. I screamed, certain I was going to die.

The door burst open, and Johnny Ringo ran in, his gun still smoking.

"She got away!" Ringo screamed, then looked at me. "Lomax's shot! He's down!"

A cheer erupted as my customers stampeded into the room.

"We can settle our bets!" yelled one man.

I tried to get to my feet, but my right leg felt useless.

"Don't kill him," Ringo said, as a couple men pulled me over on my side.

"Damn," said one. "It struck low."

A groan went through the crowd. I figured I'd bleed to death or get shot by some mad bettor before I got to a doctor.

"Get a doctor," I pleaded.

Nobody paid any attention until the room exploded with another gunshot. I saw Ringo's gun pointed skyward and still smoking. "Let's get him to Doc Goodfellow. If he doesn't die, we can do another round of bets."

Another great cheer arose. Several men picked me up and carried me out of the room, down the hall, through the saloon, and out on the street.

Word must have spread like wildfire through Tombstone, because a mob was already waiting at the doctor's office. The noise had roused him, and he was at the door almost as soon as we reached his place. He let in the six or so guys who were carrying me and pointed them toward the table.

When they dropped me on my back, pain shot through my entire right side. I knew it was a sure sign of my impending death. I screamed. Doc Goodfellow shooed the men out of the office.

"We just want to know where he was shot."

"I'm sure you do," Goodfellow called as he locked the door. He scurried back to me, shaking his head. "You have about the worst luck of any man in Cochise County, save Joe Campbell. Where were you hit?"

"In the back, low," I managed between gritted teeth.

Goodfellow rolled me over. "I think I see the problem."

"Am I gonna live?"

"I figure so." He unbuttoned my britches and carefully pulled them down.

I cried out in pain. "I'm not gonna die, am I?"

"Oh, you're gonna die, all right."

I bit my tongue.

"But not tonight. It's not a bullet wound. The bullet must've shattered some wood. You got a splinter the size of my thumb in your behind. It'll take me a spell to get it all out, but I want to tell all your friends so they can quit worrying."

Goodfellow stepped to the door, unlatched it, and went outside. The crowd went silent except for one man. "Where'd the bullet hit him?"

"Wasn't a bullet," Goodfellow said. "It was a splinter in the ass."

The crowd groaned.

"Looks like all bets are still on!" shouted Johnny Ringo.

Chapter Thirteen

After Doc Goodfellow removed the splinter and patched up my behind, it took a few days before I could use my sitter for what it was intended. Once I was better, I decided to look into opening a new saloon in Bisbee.

The Stubborn Mule was making good money, but things were getting tight for me. I wondered if I would be able to escape Tombstone with my life. The rumors began to circulate about Hattie seeing Frank McLaury. A lot of men believed the rumors, and that galled Frank.

About three days after Doc Goodfellow treated my butt, I had reason to fear that those rumors would lead to a lot of killing. The McLaurys, the Clantons, Johnny Ringo, and even Curly Bill Brocius came to the Stubborn Mule to drink and play cards, though they did more drinking than anything else. The more they drank, the more they talked. The more they talked, the more they drank.

Ned Nichols was the first to get nervous, but he was always nervous. Anytime someone farted, Nichols checked to see if he had been hit by a bullet. But when Til Walteree came to me, I knew things were getting serious.

"You better do something, Lomax," he said. "They're talking trouble if I ever heard it. Frank, particularly, is mad, mouthing off about Doc Holliday spreading rumors."

Then and there I made a decision. As soon as the shooting started, I was going to hide behind something that wouldn't splinter and send a sliver of wood into my butt. "Nobody's foolish enough to mess with Holliday," I said.

"You were," Walteree reminded me.

"I'd been drinking."

Walteree pointed at their two tables. "So have they."

The words were no sooner out of his mouth than Curly Bill stood up from his table. "What are you pointing at, barkeep?"

Walteree gulped. "I was saying ya'll needed more liquor."

"You think we're too dumb to tell you when we're thirsty?"

Fact was, I didn't think all of them put together were smart enough to spit downwind, but I didn't think it wise to tell them that, not when there was a lot of money riding on where I'd get shot. I ignored Curly Bill, but he wouldn't let the question go unanswered.

"Lomax, you son of a bitch, you've gotten our business since the Allen Street saloons burned down, but they're starting to reopen, and we'll take our business elsewhere," he informed me.

"Anytime you happen to pass my saloon, Curly, I'd sure appreciate it," I replied.

He didn't understand my answer. "That's better."

No sooner had Curly sat down than Frank McLaury stood up. "That was a damn insult."

Once again I had to explain to Frank what an insult was. "No, Frank, that was an invitation to pass by anytime. An insult would've been if I'd said you smell like you want to be left alone."

Frank studied me real hard, then licked his lips. "You packing a gun, Lomax?"

"Nope," I admitted. "It's against the town ordinance."

"Then heel yourself. I'm not taking any more insults, ordinance be damned."

"I didn't insult you. I's just telling you what an insult was."

"We're gonna settle this once and for all, you always

insulting us cowboys like we're dumber than a sackload of turds."

"Yeah," said Ike Clanton, standing up beside Frank. "Telling us we're poking livestock and such."

"Sit down, Ike. I'm gonna kill him."

Frank was so drunk I could've shot him in the head and he'd've had to sober up to die.

Behind me Ned Nichols took off his apron and threw it on the bar. "I'm not feeling well, Lomax. Maybe I'll see you tomorrow." He scurried out the door, with several customers following him.

Frank blustered on. "You're a coward, Lomax, just like the Earps. You talk, but you ain't got the guts God gave a sick chicken."

Out of the corner of my eye I saw Doc Holliday perk up at his card table and throw in his hand. "Settle up with each other," he said to the two men at his table. "This game's over." Doc didn't take kindly to someone insulting the Earps, Wyatt being probably his only real friend in all the world.

"Get yourself a gun, Lomax," Frank instructed me again.

A couple fellows offered me theirs, but I waved them away, figuring the moment I put one on Frank'd plug me. And when he did, he'd probably win his bet on where I'd get shot.

Then Doc called across the room, "Here, Lomax. Care to use one of my guns?"

I didn't answer for a moment, gauging Frank's reaction to Doc's generous offer.

"This ain't your affair, Holliday," he answered.

"Why, Frank McLaury," Holliday replied, "I can't believe you'd deny me a chance to keep you out of jail."

"Huh?" Frank grunted.

"If you shoot Lomax unarmed, for certain you'd go to jail for murder. That's where the Earps'd put you, and you know it."

"The Earps are vermin."

Doc rose slowly from his chair. "Why, Frank McLaury, that wasn't a very nice thing to say about friends of mine. I just don't know that I should tolerate such blasphemy."

"Blast your ass to hell, Holliday. This is between me and Lomax. I've got a bone to pick with you, too, but not just now."

I edged toward a shotgun I kept behind the bar to settle friendly little disputes.

"Why, Frank McLaury, if you've a bone to pick with me, why not pick it now, when you've got the whole skeleton to choose from?" Holliday was smiling, but he had his fighting face on.

Frank was drunk, but not so drunk that he didn't see the hardness in Holliday's eyes. "I don't like the rumors you've been spreading."

"What rumors, Frank McLaury?"

"That I've been seeing Hattie Ketcham."

"Why, Frank McLaury, I cannot believe that you would ever think I would blaspheme such a decent young woman as her."

"Blas-what?"

"Blaspheme, Frank McLaury. It means insult. Lomax said it best, Frank McLaury, when he said you smell like you want to be left alone. That's an insult or a blaspheme."

"I ain't been seeing Hattie Ketcham."

Holliday shook his head. "Somebody has been, and when the Earps find out who, they may just teach him a few manners."

I swallowed hard.

"And," Holliday continued, "if I find out who's been spreading those rumors about her, I'll kill him myself."

I swallowed harder.

Tom McLaury grabbed his brother's gun arm. "Come on, Frank. There's nothing here worth fighting about."

Though Holliday stood alone across the room from the six cowboys, they were afraid of him.

"It's just not worth tangling with him," Tom pleaded.

Frank jerked his arm from his brother's hand. "Stop spreading lies about me, Holliday, or there'll be hell to pay."

Slowly Doc Holliday shook his head. "I told you, Frank McLaury, that I did not darken her pretty name by linking it to yours."

"It ain't just that. Somebody's been spreading lies that me and Tom've been rustling cattle, robbing stages. It ain't true."

"Maybe if you'd quit hanging out with the likes of Ike Clanton and Curly Bill Brocius, those stories would quit spreading."

Frank shook his head in anger. "A man can choose his friends."

"And he can live with the consequences. The Earps are my friends. You bastards've been spreading stories I robbed the Benson stage and killed Bud Philpot to cover the tracks of some of your thieving friends."

No sooner were the words out of Holliday's mouth than Ike Clanton, his brother Billy, and Curly Bill Brocius rose to their feet.

You never heard such a scraping of chairs and a stamping of boots as my customers flew for cover.

Only Johnny Ringo among the cowboys remained seated.

Slowly I reached for my shotgun, raised it bar-top high, and leveled the barrel at the group facing Doc Holliday.

Suddenly emboldened, Frank taunted him. "Care to draw, now that you aren't playing cards?"

"Why, Frank McLaury, you *are* a brave man, with so many backing your play."

Frank lifted his arms and doubled his fists. "Okay, then, Holliday, let's settle it like men. Bare knuckles."

"Why, Frank McLaury, that's like playing chess—it takes so much time to decide the outcome. I'd prefer to settle it quicker and for good, so I can get back to my cards without you interrupting again."

Frank lowered his fists. "You won't fight, Holliday, because you couldn't whip a crippled kitten."

With as fearless a gesture as I ever saw, Holliday nodded to the other cowboys. "You in, Johnny Ringo, or sitting out this hand?"

"I'm keeping an eye on Lomax," he answered. "If

the shooting starts, I want to plug him and collect my bets."

I bumped the shotgun so it'd cut him in half if he so much as looked at me crooked.

Holliday gave Frank a thin smile. "Make your play, Frank McLaury."

I didn't figure it would be a second before there'd be more holes in my saloon than I could plug with a wagonload of corks, but the cowboys hesitated. They had cold feet no matter how hot the weather.

The tension was broken by a clatter of boots on the wooden walk outside. Virgil Earp burst into the saloon, his marshal's badge shining on his chest.

"Easy, all of you," he said. "We don't want any trouble."

"Trouble's coming, Virgil," Holliday said. "You're only delaying it if you stop this."

"It's my job," Virgil answered. "Now, Ike, Frank, Tom, all of you, just clear out and sober up. When your heads are clear, you'll know this was all over nothing. You're violating the gun ordinance. If you get out now, I won't arrest you."

Holliday spoke up. "They called you Earps liars, Virgil."

Virgil clenched his jaw for a moment, then shook his head. He never took his eyes off the cowboys. "Don't matter the cause, even if it is family. My job is to stop trouble."

"You got a skunk by the tail, Virgil, until we settle this matter with them."

"Shut up, Doc," Virgil ordered, "or I'll throw you in jail for being armed. Now, you fellows get out of here and sleep it off. This is the law talking, not Virgil Earp."

Ringo, who'd barely moved a muscle during the encounter, nodded. "We'll get you Earps and Holliday, too, after Lomax gets his. A lot of us have good money riding on him."

Virgil didn't answer. Doc looked mean as a bulldog after a bowlful of gunpowder.

Ringo rose slowly from his chair and grabbed Frank by the arm, pulling him toward the door. Tom McLaury jumped toward his brother, staying between him and Holliday to screen trouble. Snickering, Curly Bill motioned for the two Clantons to leave and followed his compadres out the door.

We heard the men mount up and gallop away. A couple of them pulled their guns and shot in the air. Everyone in the saloon ducked by instinct, everyone but Holliday. He stood there straightening the lapels on his coat. Virgil Earp stepped outside to make sure the cowboys weren't shooting at anything except the moon.

Feeling a mite queasy, I lowered the shotgun and propped it against the backbar. Johnny Ringo wanted to shoot me because Corina DeLure had turned to religion. The Earps would probably shoot me if they ever found out I had been seeing Hattie. And Doc Holliday would likely shoot me if he learned it was me spreading the rumors about Hattie Ketcham and Frank McLaury. Figuring I should try to stay on Doc's good side, I went to his table.

"You need something, Doc?"

"A bottle of your best."

I hollered for Walteree. "Bring Doc a bottle of our best."

Holliday eased back into his chair. "It's headed to no good," he said, as much to himself as to me. "Virgil should've let me settle it with as many as I could take."

"You think Hattie's really been seeing Frank McLaury?"

He shrugged. "She's smarter than that. What I don't like is somebody trying to ruin her good name by saying that she is."

"I can't believe that, either," I said, trying to keep my voice from cracking. "What'd you do to a man like that, Doc?"

"I'd shoot him."

"He'd deserve it," I answered, my voice none too confident.

Walteree approached with the bottle. I grabbed it from him and plopped it down in front of Doc, but it fell over and almost rolled off the table.

With his catlike reflexes Holliday caught it. "Why,

Lomax, you're as nervous as if you'd been spreading those ill-founded rumors about Hattie yourself." He laughed.

"The bottle's on the house." I escaped to the bar, where I planted my hands on the counter to steady myself before my mushy knees gave way.

Walteree didn't make me feel any better when he said, "I'd sure hate to be the fool that's spreading rumors or the one that's slipping around with her. Those fellows are in more danger than the Clantons and McLaurys."

The way Walteree was talking, I figured I might just as well go down to the undertaker and get measured for a wooden box in which to spend the rest of time. If anything told me I ought to look at other options, that encounter was it. A saloon in Bisbee was sounding better all the time.

By the time I left that night, carrying more of my nightly profits with me, I was looking over my shoulder every other step. If I wasn't scared on the way home, I was plenty scared when I slipped inside, closed the door, and lit the lamp. Besides Satan, sitting in the corner staring at me, there was another letter from Hattie.

My hands trembled as I picked it up and opened it. I read it and caught my breath.

> Henry:
>   I've missed you. I was worried when I heard you got shot but was afraid to go see you. Then I heard you were shot while consorting with a saloon girl. That angered me. I want an explanation.
>   Hattie

In my life not only had I handled dynamite, I'd been stabbed, almost hanged, shot at by more men than I cared to remember, and attacked by the meanest tomcat God ever let walk on the earth. But nothing scared me more than Hattie's letter. A woman was the most dangerous animal on earth and an Earp woman the most dangerous of that breed. I knew right then I needed to get to Bisbee and check out opportunities there. Then I wondered if Bisbee would be far enough away from the Earps. If not, it was at least a start in the right direction.

I carried the lamp into the bedroom and shut the door so Satan couldn't follow me in. Then I got under the bed and took out my tin lunchbox. I put Hattie's letter in with the others and took out enough money to make more than seven hundred dollars when added to the night's profits.

The next day I decided to go to Bisbee for sure. With that much money I thought it safer to ride the stage than to go alone on Flash. Too, my butt was still sore. The Sandy Bob Stage, named for its operator, Sandy Bob Crouch, made an evening run to Bisbee, so I would have to wait all day to make the trip. The whole town seemed on edge.

On the way to the Stubborn Mule late that morning, I had the misfortune of running into Hattie Ketcham. There was fire in her eyes and anger in her step when she saw me. She angled across the street, intersected my path at the corner, and fell in beside me, not looking at me but talking in a low, husky voice.

"Did you get my letter?"

I allowed I had.

"I want an explanation."

I'd decided I didn't want anything to do with Hattie anymore. "Nothing to explain."

"What?" she said, her voice a growl. "You either tell me or I'll tell my folks it was you I'd been sneaking out with, that you'd been naked with me and tried to attack me again." Her words dripped venom.

The last thing I wanted was her telling her folks anything about me.

"Were you with a saloon girl?"

"I was, and she was thanking me."

"Just how was she thanking you?"

"I took her to see Amelia Guinn, the lawyer's wife. She's real religious, Amelia is, and she helped Corina find God."

"You think I'm gonna believe that?"

I kept walking toward the saloon. "Her name is

Corina DeLure. She's worked my saloon for a couple years. Johnny Ringo likes her, thinks she's his girl."

"And so you went with her, and he found out and shot you because he found you in bed with her?"

"No, she thanked me for helping her, turning her away from the trade. She was scared of Ringo, and he broke in on us. I helped her out the window so she could escape."

Hattie seemed to pull in her horns a bit.

I figured I might just as well lay it on thick. "I took a bullet trying to protect her," I said.

"I heard it was a splinter in the butt." Hattie eyed me like she was uncertain whether or not to believe me. "Maybe I was wrong."

"We need to split up so no one gets suspicious."

She seemed to soften. "Can we see each other again soon?"

"Sure," I lied, "but not tonight. I'm shorthanded at the saloon, with Joe Campbell still out. It'll be a couple days." I didn't want to get within gunshot of her again.

"You're not seeing someone else, lying to me, are you?"

"No. Why would I lie to the prettiest girl in Tombstone?"

Hattie seemed flattered, but I wanted to get rid of her as fast as I could. My momma taught me not to lie, and I generally followed her advice, except when my tail got caught in a crack. But Momma'd never taught me much about dealing with women. Even though I had sisters, that hadn't prepared me for women.

"We best split up," I said, "before people take notice."

Hattie smiled. The venom had turned to sugar, but I knew the sugar wouldn't last.

At the next corner I turned toward the Stubborn Mule, and she kept walking. I found Ned Nichols and Til Walteree at the saloon taking care of things as usual. What surprised me was Doc Holliday. He wasn't at his accustomed table in the corner.

"Where's Doc?" I asked.

Til Walteree shrugged. "He came in an hour ago.

Said he wouldn't be in today. Ned said he saw him riding out of town right after noon. Morgan Earp was with him."

"Good. Maybe the sons of bitches are gone for good."

Walteree grinned. "I'll tell him you said so."

"Hell, he'll probably wind up killing me anyway."

"That's how I feel about him all the time," said Nichols.

I shrugged. "With Doc out, you boys can probably handle business tonight."

Walteree winked. "So you and your lady friend can get together. Who is she? Is it Big Nose Kate?"

"You think I'm crazy? Hell, no. I'm riding the Sandy Bob Stage to Bisbee tonight. I may buy into a saloon in Bisbee."

Walteree shook his head. "All they mine in Bisbee is copper. There's more future in Tombstone and silver."

There might have been a better future in Tombstone and in silver, but not for me, not with Hattie on a string I couldn't cut. "Nope, the future's in copper. You boys just take care of business the next couple of days until I return."

"We've never let you down," said Nichols.

From the saloon I went over to Henry Guinn's to see if he had resolved any of the legal problems with my property.

Amelia Guinn answered the door, holding her nose in the air like she was better than me. "Corina DeLure's been attending church since your visit."

"I need to see your husband."

"He told me to tell you he hasn't settled anything yet on your land problems."

"I'd like him to tell me that himself, since I'm paying him enough to keep you in groceries for a few days."

"No, sir. Until you change your heathen ways, he says you're to deal with me."

"Heathen? Hell, woman, he's the lawyer, not me."

She folded her ham-hock arms across her ample bosom and just stood there, daring me to try to get past her. "Henry says to tell you that you owe him another hundred dollars."

"Last time I was here it was just fifty dollars."

"Well, it's gone up another fifty."

"Are you eating that many groceries?"

Amelia must've been hungry, because she didn't think that was funny.

"How about if I give you a cat instead of a hundred dollars? You said you wanted a cat."

"We want the hundred dollars."

Even though I had more than seven hundred dollars on me, I was through throwing my money down a rat hole. "Things've been tight. I don't know how long it will take me to get that kind of money."

Amelia shook her jowly face, and I thought the fat would never stop trembling. "While Allen Street was burnt down, you should've made a lot of money."

"The saloons are opening back up. Things'll get tighter."

"Then you better take on another job," Amelia laughed, "or my husband'll wind up owning your saloon."

"He'll have more chances for saloon girls then."

Amelia didn't seem threatened anymore. "You saw what the word of God can do to a saloon girl. Corina DeLure'll become a fine citizen in spite of her sinful past. But that's the miracle of salvation."

"You've got a lot more work to do on Big Nose Kate."

"If she understood English better, she'd've been converted like Corina."

"Well, Amelia, you're always welcome at the Stubborn Mule if you or your husband want to try to convert her or any of the other girls. Of course, we may have to knock out a wall to get you inside, but you just let me know you're coming and I'll be glad to accommodate you."

She sniffed, then shut the door in my face.

I turned around and went back to my house, relieved to find that Hattie hadn't left me a letter. I took a nap until late afternoon, then went downtown to a new eatery and ate a good meal before the night ride to Bisbee.

I was at Sandy Bob's a good half hour before the stage arrived. I paid for a round-trip fare. Behind the counter I saw a green strongbox, padlocked, and knew the stage would be carrying a little money in addition to what I had on me.

The stage left right at six-thirty. The seat and the road were hard on my butt, but I managed okay. It was just me and two other passengers, neither being much of a talker, which suited me just fine. Though we carried a strongbox, we didn't carry a shotgun guard, just a driver. The stage line must've thought the lack of a guard would fool any robbers.

They were wrong. About halfway to Bisbee we rounded a bend, and the horses seemed to falter.

"Hold on!" came a cry from the side of the road.

The driver was no fool. He drew up the reins and brought the stage to a halt.

"Throw down the strongbox!" called a voice that seemed vaguely familiar.

I was sure glad the stage was carrying a strongbox, because I didn't figure the robbers would search the passengers, too. But I was wrong.

After the strongbox clunked to the ground, I heard the same voice say, "Everybody in the coach out." The door opened, and a man with a mask stood there pointing a gun at us.

I was the first one out, and I got close enough to the robber to get a whiff of his breath, even through the bandanna over his face. I swallowed hard. Only one man I'd ever encountered had breath that bad.

That man had pulled my wisdom tooth.

That man was Doc Holliday.

Chapter Fourteen

"Raise your hands and keep them in the air," the robber growled. He sounded like he was trying to disguise his voice.

If the robber recognized me, he gave no sign as he ushered the other two passengers out. He wore his hat low over his eyes so I couldn't see anything but a narrow slit between the brim and the top of his mask. His duster gave him a little more body, but even so he seemed skinny enough to be Doc Holliday.

The robber motioned to us with a nickel-plated revolver like the one Doc carried. "Stretch your hands for the moon, and let's see if you're carrying any sugar." He coughed slightly.

When he said "sugar," I thought back to Doc Holliday beating Frank Stilwell at poker. After cleaning Frank out, Doc had mentioned to me how you could identify a man in different ways, including the words he used. I believed this was Doc Holliday robbing the stage and trying to lay a trail that would point to Frank Stilwell.

If the robber was Doc, and if his breath didn't knock me out first, I figured I could easily overpower him. If it wasn't Doc, I might wind up dead, which was probably going to happen to me in Tombstone anyway. It seemed that no matter what I did, I always came out about even.

My thoughts of jumping the robber ended when another masked man with a shotgun stepped around the back of the stage.

"Driver," called the second robber, "throw down the mail sack, then come empty out the boot."

"It's just baggage," the driver replied.

"Do as I say." He waved the shotgun at the driver.

No fool, the driver tossed down the mail sack, marched around to the back, untied the leather cover, pulled all the baggage from the boot, and dumped it on the road.

Meanwhile, the robber with the pistol went through the pockets of the first passenger, taking his pocket watch, a pocketknife, and a few bills and coins. "That all the sugar you got?"

The voice sure sounded like Doc's, but the bandanna muffled it enough that I couldn't be completely certain.

Moving to the next man, the robber went through his pockets but found little of value. "You ought to carry more sugar with you when you travel," he said. "You never know when you many need to spend it."

Then he came to me. What my eyes couldn't confirm in the darkness, my nose did. Judging by his rotten breath, he had to be Holliday. He smelled like decaying flesh, just as I remembered from when I'd had my tooth removed.

The robber searched my coat pockets, my left britches pocket, then my right, where I kept my roll of seven hundred dollars. He pulled out the money roll and whistled softly through his mask.

"I've found a full bowl of sugar."

The shotgun-toting robber—who I suspected was Morgan Earp, though I didn't feel nearly as certain of his identity—grunted.

After the driver finished emptying the boot, the shotgun bandit shoved him toward us passengers.

"That's it," he said. "Unless you want to stay and visit, you best get on the stage and head to Bisbee."

"Wait," the pistol bandit said, waving his gun at the other. "Check the driver's seat. Maybe there's more sugar there."

The man with the shotgun climbed aboard, inspected the seat and floorboard, and tossed down a second mail sack. "You forgot something, driver."

"A little more sugar," said the one I was sure was Doc.

The driver grunted. "Can we go now?"

The near robber waved his revolver toward the coach. "Get in and get going. And don't look back, or we'll kill you all."

If that man was Doc, I had no doubt he meant every word he said. Shaking, we scrambled back in the stage and pulled the door to. We'd barely gotten into our seats before the anxious driver shook the reins and the stage lurched forward.

I was mad enough to bite a bullet in half. It seemed I couldn't ride a stage without someone being robbed or killed. And I'd lost seven hundred dollars and a chance, at least for a while, of buying a new saloon in Bisbee.

It was probably midnight or a little before when we finally felt we'd put enough distance between us and the robbers. When we arrived in Bisbee, the driver put out the word that the robber was Frank Stilwell because Frank was known to call money sugar. As for me, I kept my mouth shut about Doc and Morgan, because if I was right, that'd give them one more reason to kill me.

I didn't have enough sugar to stay in a hotel, so I slept on the wooden walk outside the stage office. Next day I killed time waiting for the Tombstone stage to leave by walking the town. I'll be damned if I didn't run into Frank Stilwell himself, coming out of a boot shop just as I was walking by. I almost bumped into him.

"Beg your pardon," he said, looking up at me, then grinning. "Well, hell, Lomax, if I'd known it was you I'd've just kept walking."

"Robbed any stages lately?"

He laughed easily, not like a man who'd committed a crime. "I get blamed for every robbery in Cochise County, you know that."

"The Sandy Bob Stage was robbed last night."

"That's what I heard, but do you think I'd be hanging around town putting new heels on my boots if I'd done it? The old ones were worn out." He pointed to his boots. "The heels've got a different feel to them. What are you doing here in Bisbee?"

That was my chance. I stepped closer to him, looked both ways down the walk, like I had a secret I didn't want anyone to hear, and leaned close enough to smell his breath. "I'm looking at buying a saloon here in Bisbee." His breath didn't smell good, but it didn't smell near as bad as that of the robber. I backed away.

Stilwell nodded. "It's a good idea, hedge your bets on a copper town. Me and Pete Spencer, we went in on a livery stable here."

"The same Pete Spencer that lives in Tombstone?"

He nodded. "We rode over yesterday to check on our stable. We'll ride back tomorrow or the day after."

"I'm heading back on the stage today."

"Surely it won't get robbed after last night."

I shrugged. "It don't matter now. I was on last night's."

"I'll be damned. Did they get any of your sugar?"

Licking my lips, I nodded again. "Enough to have bought me a saloon in Bisbee."

Stilwell shook his head. "Sorry to hear that. You need any money for a meal or the like?" He stuck his hand in his pocket and pulled out a pouch. I waited to see if he had a big roll of money, but the pouch was too small and the bills he pulled out were well worn and greasy.

"I'll get by," I answered.

"You sure?"

"Yep."

"Well, take care of yourself, and better luck on the way back."

We parted, and I headed back to the stage station and waited in the shade for an hour until the stage left for Tombstone. Having no money, the return trip presented me with little worry. We made it through the Mule Mountains, then were stopped by a posse come down from Tombstone to investigate the stage holdup.

It was an odd mix of men: Wyatt and Morgan Earp and two of their allies as well as two of Johnny Behan's deputies. Wyatt asked our stage driver if he'd heard anything that might identify the robbers. The driver responded that one of them sounded like Frank Stilwell, the way he spoke of sugar, then mentioned that one of the previous night's passengers was in the coach.

Reluctant to answer questions, I sank back into the corner. The possemen eased their horses closer to the coach.

"Who was on the stage?" Wyatt asked as he leaned over and looked inside. "Lomax, what the hell are you doing here?" He seemed surprised.

"It was me," I admitted.

Morgan Earp rode up on the other side and looked in. "What can you tell us?"

For a moment I thought his voice sounded vaguely like that of the second robber, but there was no way I could suggest that.

Wyatt cleared his throat, and I knew I should pay attention to him rather than Morgan. "What happened?"

"Two men stopped us between eleven and midnight. One carried a nickel-plated revolver, the other a shotgun." I looked at Morgan's horse and saw a shotgun of the Wells Fargo type in a saddle boot. I wondered if Doc and Morgan had robbed the stage, then ridden back to Tombstone. They were drinking pals, so it was possible, but I don't know that Doc would've invited Morgan along for a robbery without Wyatt knowing. I was as confused as a kid who dropped his gum in the chicken house.

Morgan yawned widely, like he'd lost more sleep than normal, then asked, "Any idea who the men were?"

He seemed a bit nervous at his own question, or maybe I was just imagining it. "It was too dark to tell."

"Can you describe them?" Wyatt asked.

I shook my head. "I paid more attention to their guns. One carried a nickel-plated revolver, and the other carried a shotgun like Morgan's toting on his horse."

Wyatt shook his head. "At least nobody was killed. We better ride." He rattled the reins and moved away from the coach. "Let them run, driver, and we'll see if we can catch the bastards."

The driver whistled, and we started again for Tombstone.

When we arrived, my bottom was plenty sore, and as soon as I got off the stage, I headed straight for my house. I cursed when I found another letter from Hattie under the door. Satan was nowhere to be seen. Figuring I was safe for a minute, I opened Hattie's letter.

Dearest Henry:
   I'm sorry I got angry. The thought of you being with that woman bothers me still. I hope one day soon we can get together again when no one's around.
                                                        Hattie

I went to the bedroom and double-checked to make sure Satan wasn't about, then crawled under the bed to add Hattie's latest letter to my collection. No sooner had I lifted the loose floorboard than I heard a terrible, familiar screech. A ball of clawed fur flew from beneath the floor and attacked my face.

Screaming, I jerked my head up and hit it on a bed slat. I saw stars before my face smashed to the floor, knocking Satan off and me out. In a while, as I began to shake the haze from my head, I remembered what I had been doing and finished retrieving the tin box. I put in Hattie's latest letter and made a rough count of my money. I still had close to five thousand dollars. As I replaced it under the floor, I knew I probably should take it all and slip out of town in the night, but I was worried someone would rob me again. I figured the best I could do was just lie low, avoid Hattie, and not anger Doc Holliday.

When I went over to the Stubborn Mule the next day, I was surprised to find Joe Campbell behind the bar. Doc Holliday was at his accustomed table, though by himself. I nodded to him, then went over to Campbell, who looked so pale and puny I thought he was a ghost.

"Glad to see you, Joe. You're looking good."

"I'm still weak. I'm only working a little bit at a time until I get my strength back."

"Yeah, poking Amelia Guinn'd drain even a strong man, much less one that's been gutshot."

"That's a bad thing to say."

"Bad is good—isn't that what you'd say, Joe?"

Campbell scratched his head.

"Less is more, remember saying that? A man's gotta follow his piss?"

Campbell just shrugged.

I was beginning to think he'd been shot in the head rather than the gut.

"I ain't cutting your liquor anymore," he informed me.

"At a dollar a day you will, Joe."

"Not unless you give me a dollar a day for each day I missed with your bullet in my gut."

"How'd you know it was my bullet? I ain't been shot at since, save when Ringo was mad at Corina. Maybe they were after you."

"If I told some of the fellows who drink here what you put in their liquor or that you piss in their beer, they'd take their business elsewhere after they worked you over."

I had to admit, Campbell had a point. "Okay, you can stay for a dollar a day."

"No," Campbell answered. "I'll take a dollar a day for those days I missed, but I want two dollars a day from now on."

"Doesn't that go against your beliefs, Joe?"

"What beliefs?"

"That less is more."

Campbell rolled his eyes. "What are you talking about?"

Damn if Joe Campbell hadn't changed. But what man wouldn't after being cooped up in the same house with Amelia Guinn for days? I'd about had it with him and would've thrown him out on the street, save that was kind of hard to do to a man whose guts I'd washed and who threatened to spread rumors about how I'd cut my liquor stock. I didn't know where he picked up such ideas. I figured he could do me less harm at two dollars a day, plus back pay, than he could with me not paying him a thing and him driving me out of business.

"You can stay, Joe, on one condition."

"What's that?"

"You quit talking religion in the saloon."

"We got freedom of religion in this country. It says so in the Constitution."

I didn't know much about the Constitution, but I figured I wasn't dealing with a fellow who needed a wheelbarrow to tote his brains.

"No, sir, you're wrong."

"Huh?"

"The Constitution applies to the states. We're not a state, just a territory. You think the president and the Congress would want all the rustlers, thieves, and murderers in Arizona Territory as citizens?"

Campbell scratched his head. "I hadn't thought about that. I'll have to ask Henry Guinn."

"What would he know? He's just a lawyer."

That confused Campbell aplenty. He shook his head and walked away, grabbing an empty mug from the bar.

I could've spent the rest of my life slapping him across the head with a chunk of firewood and never knocked enough sense in him to come in out of the rain.

When I turned around, I saw Doc Holliday eyeing me closely. My flesh began to squirm like a barrelful of snakes. He was giving me that same hard stare I'd seen beneath the hat brim during the stage robbery.

"Why, Lomax, now that your bartender's back, we've time to visit."

Doc wasn't the type to just talk, but I wasn't the type to turn down a conversation with a man I couldn't outgun. I walked over to his table, taking deep breaths and trying to keep my knees from buckling. "I never thought you much of a talker, Doc."

He grinned and tweaked the end of his mustache. "You might say I'm just interested in keeping up with the news. Like the robbery of the Sandy Bob Stage. It true you were on it?"

Hell, he shouldn't've had to ask, but I figured he was just trying to make himself look as innocent as a choirboy in Amelia Guinn's church. I nodded. "It's true."

"You lose anything?"

"Close to seven hundred dollars."

Holliday shook his head. "Sorry to hear that."

I bet he was. That was enough money to keep him in liquor for two or three days, unless he bought drinks for Johnny Ringo. Between them they could waste more liquor than a temperance woman with a hatchet. "It's a damn shame. I was going to buy me another saloon in Bisbee."

"It true Frank Stilwell was one of the robbers?"

Now, I hadn't mentioned Frank Stilwell in any of my discussions, and as far as I knew, all those who considered Stilwell the robber were out chasing him. Maybe word had gotten back to Tombstone, but I had my doubts. One thing I didn't have doubts about, though, was Stilwell's breath. It wasn't as rotten as Doc's, and Doc's was rotten enough to knock a fly off a gut wagon.

"I can't say for certain, Doc. It was dark, and the robber was masked. I couldn't have identified the robber even if it was you."

Doc's tongue flicked at the corner of his lips. "Too bad. It's a shame we can't rid this territory of all the bad men and make everybody as pious as Joe Campbell over there and Corina DeLure, wherever the hell she is."

"It is a shame, Doc."

"Good thing is, I figure Wyatt and Morgan'll catch up with Stilwell and bring him to justice, provided Sheriff Behan doesn't interfere. We all know he runs around with the Clantons and McLaurys and that bunch. Stilwell's as much a part of that gang as Johnny Ringo is. They're behind all these robberies."

I wasn't about to argue with him. "You're probably right, but that won't get me back my money."

"Seven hundred dollars, was it?"

"Close to it."

Doc picked up the cards and began to shuffle them. "Sometimes after a run of bad luck a fellow needs to play a few hands of cards. His luck is bound to change."

"After the robbery, Doc, I'm broke."

"No matter," he replied. "I'll stake you for a few hands."

I sat down at the table opposite him, figuring I'd play along rather than antagonize him. "Deal."

Holliday reached into his pocket and pulled out a roll of money. I knew it was mine. "We need to ante first." He peeled off a hundred dollars. "Here's my ante."

I held up my hand. "I don't have that kind of money to gamble with."

Shaking his head, he said, "I'm staking you. Here's your ante." He peeled off another hundred.

Before I could say anything, he shoved the money roll back in his pocket, picked up the cards, and dealt them snake-quick across the table.

I picked up my hand and had two pair, aces over jacks. Not having any money, I stood pat on the bet and asked for a single card. Holliday dealt me another ace, giving me a full house.

Holliday took four cards, then looked at me and folded. "See how quickly your luck can change?"

I hesitated to drag in the pot.

"Take it. It's yours."

"Don't you want to see my hand?"

Holliday grinned. "From the way you drew and the look on your face, I'd say it was a full house, aces over jacks."

"Close enough," I answered as I dragged in the money and shoved it in my pocket.

"See, Lomax, how quickly your luck can change?" he repeated. "Let's just hope it doesn't change again."

There was a threat in his voice, as sure as I was two hundred dollars richer than I had been a few minutes before. Even so, I was still five hundred dollars poorer, thanks to Doc, than I had been before the stage ride to Bisbee.

Holliday grabbed my cards and mixed the deck again, then dealt himself a hand of solitary. I slowly pushed my chair back from the table, knowing that the card game had been Doc's way of telling me to keep my mouth shut.

My hand quivered as I rubbed my chin. I returned to the bar, telling Campbell and Til Walteree I'd be back after dark. On mushy knees I headed to my house, figuring to take a nap so I could work all night and keep an eye on Joe Campbell, now that I was going to be paying him double.

When I got home, I found Satan in the front room toying with a dead mouse he had caught. By the look in his yellow eyes I knew he'd rather've been toying with me, so I shut the kitchen door and then the door into the bedroom. I decided to hang on to the two hundred dollars I'd won from Doc—which was really mine—instead of putting it in my hiding place.

I laid down and took a nap, arising in time to take a bite of supper at one of the eateries, then walk down Allen Street to look at all the new saloons before heading for Fremont and the Stubborn Mule. The new saloons were attracting a crowd, and it showed when I arrived at my place. There were only half the customers of recent nights.

As I walked in, I heard Joe Campbell talking like a newborn preacher. "Drunkenness is a sin unto the Lord," he proclaimed as he poured a whiskey for an unfamiliar customer. When he saw me, he closed his mouth tighter than a miser's wallet.

I stepped up to the bar. "Evening, Joe."

He nodded.

I pointed back to the office. "Why don't you join me for a few minutes?"

"We're kinda busy."

I looked around at the half-full room. "Til and Ned can handle it."

Campbell grimaced and followed me down the hall. As I passed the bedroom, I saw through the half-open door one of our women rutting with one of our customers. I paused.

"Look at that, would you, Joe?"

Lifting his nose in the air, Campbell stood there like he'd never thought about having a woman. Of course, spending all that time with Amelia Guinn would've turned any man's mind against women. "Sinful lechery," he said.

I moved on and opened the door to the office, holding it for Campbell to enter ahead of me. I followed him in and closed the door. "Maybe we need to get one thing straight," I said, pointing my finger at his nose. I was madder than a wet hen, and he must've sensed it because his eyes widened like he was facing death. "If you're gonna work in my saloon and sell my liquor, you best not be preaching against it or against gambling or against whoring or against any other sin my customers want to perform short of murder."

"I wasn't preaching, just stating the truth."

"The truth is false, and more is less!" I shouted back.

"Huh?"

"Dammit, Joe, you're the one that started spouting all this philosophy when I first won the saloon. Don't you understand? More preaching is less business."

Campbell scratched his chin. "I don't know."

"You say you're against me cutting the liquor because that's not honest, don't you, Joe?"

He nodded.

"I was just following what you're preaching, don't you see?"

Of course he didn't. "It's dishonest, putting water and everything else you do in the whiskey."

I sighed and shook my head. "No. You preach against drunkenness, but I'm more religious than you because I'm doing something about it."

"How?"

"Cutting the liquor."

"Huh?"

"The more I cut, the less actual liquor they drink, and the less drunk they get. That's why I do it, Joe. Can't you see?"

Though Campbell nodded, my explanation probably made too much sense for his muddled mind.

"If you want to make two dollars a day, you quit preaching in the saloon. Let fellows spend their money how they want to. If they decide to gamble, let them gamble. If they want to drink, let them drink. If they want women, let them have women, as long as they spend their money in the Stubborn Mule. Do you understand?"

He nodded. I nodded. We both seemed to agree, but I didn't think we both understood.

"I reckon I should get back to work," he mumbled.

That seemed like a good idea, so I motioned toward the door. As he turned and left, I could only stand there wondering where all of this was going to lead.

I followed Campbell back into the saloon and shook my head as I took in the room. The crowd had dwindled from earlier, and from the street I could hear part of the reason: A couple of the rebuilt saloons had added pianos and men who could almost play them. Even bad music was better than none. I wondered if I should get a piano and try to boost business or if I should start spreading rumors about the saloons that had pianos.

I stood behind the bar and watched the crowd dwindle. Doc, at his accustomed place, was dealing cards to two broke cowboys and letting them win enough to stay in the game and ease the boredom. Big Nose Kate flitted about, occasionally stopping at Doc's side.

"Vhy don't you finish dese two and come to bed vith me?"

"Get away, Kate. I'm in a game."

"If you vanted, you could end the game."

"I don't want to."

"I vant a man," she said.

"Then find one."

"I vant you."

"I don't want you, not now."

Kate's eyes flashed with anger. "I vill have me a man." She threw out her chest, held her nose in the air, and marched from table to table, offering her wares to every customer in the saloon. "If you vant me, I am free dis time."

Now, Kate wasn't a bad-looking woman, but no man in the saloon would dare bed down Doc Holliday's woman while he was in the next room. Finding no takers, Kate returned to Holliday. "Nobody vants me. Dey're afraid of you."

Bored with the game but exasperated with Kate, Holliday looked up and scanned the room, then pointed to me. "Give Lomax a ride. The poor fellow lost almost seven hundred dollars in the Sandy Bob Stage robbery. Why don't you treat him?"

Kate looked my way and grinned.

"No," I said, holding up my arm. I figured this might be a ploy to give Doc an excuse to kill me. He'd force me to go with her, then come in and shoot me for soiling his woman.

Kate sauntered across the room. "You vant me?"

"No," I repeated.

Doc gave me a hard, cold stare. "My woman not good enough for you?"

"No," I said, wondering if Doc might kill me for *not* going with Kate. Either way I could die.

Kate slipped behind the bar, pushing Joe Campbell out of the way, then grabbed my arm and pulled me down the hall. I resisted enough to defend my honor, but I had to admit my sap was rising.

The men in the saloon cheered, probably relieved that someone else would be bedding Doc's woman.

Kate jerked me into the bedroom and slammed the door. As she undressed, she got better looking by the moment. She started working on my clothes and then on me, and I had to admit she knew her business, even when she was giving it away.

But those few moments of pleasure were the beginning of the end of my stay in Tombstone.

Chapter Fifteen

The next day my life in Tombstone started going downhill fast. I figured the trouble would come from Doc Holliday—and ultimately it did—but it was Hattie Ketcham who got things rolling.

I found another note from Hattie under my door. If I'd known how hot she was, I'd have picked it up with tongs. As it was, I was more worried about Satan than about anything Hattie might say, but the tomcat was out of sight.

After lighting a lamp, I opened the envelope and pulled out the letter.

Henry:
   Don't lie to me this time, you son of a bitch. I heard you slept with Big Nose Kate, and you're not gonna deny it like the last time I found out you were sleeping with a whore. I'm tired of keeping our little secret. I'm gonna tell you-know-who. If I do, your life won't be worth a bucket of warm spit. If you don't want anyone to find out, then I want a hundred dollars to keep quiet. If I don't get it, I'll start spreading the word with you-know-who first. It hurts me that you would sleep with that sow. I thought you were brave enough to stand up for me, but you're just another coward.

Hattie

The "you-know-who" of her letter was either Doc or Wyatt. Although I'd been in binds before, not one seemed this tight. I must've stared at the wall for ten minutes before I snapped out of my trance. I didn't know what to do. Events were closing around me like a noose. I had a strong hankering for a drink, but the cure helped me hold off. The last time I'd drunk enough to forget my problems, I'd spit in Doc Holliday's drink. Now he might be coming after me for defaming Hattie Ketcham.

I slid the letter back in the envelope and was tempted to burn it, but I figured I might need proof later of the kind of shrew she was. So I took it into the bedroom and hid it with the others.

There wasn't much I could do to defend myself against Hattie and her vicious tongue. I could've given her Satan, but that seemed a dirty thing to do to the tomcat. Too scared to leave the house, I went to bed but had a restless night and was awakened midmorning by a knock on the door.

I pulled on my pants and stumbled to the parlor, opening the door without thinking to ask who it was. As it swung open, I saw Doc Holliday standing there, a sadistic grin on his face.

"You're not in the middle of somebody, er, something, are you?"

"Not since the other night," I answered, then realized that might not be the right thing to say. I wondered if he knew about Hattie.

"Kate's left town."

"Sorry to hear that."

Holliday nodded. "I wanted to be the first to tell you. I'm gonna start working another saloon."

I grimaced. "You can't believe those rumors about me cutting whiskey. They're not true, not a one of them."

"That's not why I'm leaving. It's Joe Campbell."

I rolled my eyes and looked at the ceiling. "What's Joe doing?"

"He's driving your business away. When you're not around, he's always mouthing off about the sins of liquor, gambling, and women. I admire a good sermon, but a lecture doesn't suit my taste."

"Joe hasn't been the same since he was gutshot. I guess I owed it to him to let him keep his job."

"Then you best not leave him on the job alone, or he'll scare away all your business."

"You should stay, Doc," I offered, trying to make it sound like I really wanted him in the Stubborn Mule.

"Once a reputation starts for a place, it won't change, and business'll dry up quicker than an old maid's tears."

"I've been trying to sell out, start anew in Bisbee, but the lawyer Guinn says I don't have clear title. He's trying to get that straight."

Holliday rubbed his chin. "Campbell's a running mate with the Guinns. I wouldn't trust Henry Guinn as far as I could throw his wife."

"He *is* a lawyer, that's right."

"That's enough. They cause more pain in this world than dentists." He gave me a sly grin. "Or gamblers."

I laughed nervously as Holliday walked away. I watched him disappear around the corner, then shut the door and went back to my room to finish dressing. When I was done with everything but my boots, I heard the faintest noise behind me and spun around to see Satan creeping up on me. I jumped over the bed and grabbed my boots before the tomcat had a chance to spring. He shook his head and stalked into the kitchen as I put on my boots. I walked confidently out of the house.

As soon as I stepped outside, my confidence melted like a block of ice in the sun. Standing across the street, her arms folded across her chest, was Hattie Ketcham, wearing a scowl as mean as any I'd ever seen on an Indian. She looked so angry I'd've pitied Satan alone in the same room with her.

When I turned down the street, she started in the same direction, angling to cut me off. I should've known never to get tied up with an Earp woman, but I'd let things other than my brain make that decision. I stopped and waited for her.

Hattie was spitting fire. "You get my note?"

I nodded.

"I can't believe you would sleep with that woman. I can't stand her. I can barely tolerate Doc Holliday."

"He speaks highly of you."

"Just because he wants to kill whoever spread those rumors about me seeing Frank McLaury doesn't mean I care for him. He's nothing but a snake."

Talk about the pot calling the kettle black. Hattie had a forked tongue as long as any I'd ever seen on a snake. "We all think highly of you, Hattie."

"Don't be blowing smoke at me, Henry Lomax, not after what you did to me."

"What'd I do to you?"

"Humiliate me, you son of a bitch."

"How, dammit?"

"By sleeping with Big Nose Kate."

"It was an accident."

She rolled her eyes. "You expect me to believe that?"

"I don't expect you'd believe anything I told you."

"Well, you can believe this," she said, crossing her arms over her bosom. "I want a hundred dollars, and I want it quick. If I don't get it, I intend to tell Holliday that you were spreading those rumors to throw my folks off your tracks and that you bedded me down like a common harlot."

The way I figured it, Hattie wasn't much more than just that. In fact, she was probably worse, since she was taking money and giving me nothing in return, save more worries and fears.

Hattie stood there glaring at me.

I shoved my hand in my pocket, pulled out my money roll, and counted out a hundred dollars, half of what Holliday'd let me win the day before. When she held out her open palm, I shoved the money into it. "That should keep you quiet, Hattie."

"For now," she replied, then turned around and walked off.

I was beginning to wonder if she wasn't more dangerous than her crazy uncles. Now I was more than ready to get out of Tombstone. All I wanted was to sell my house before somebody tried to move it off the lot again and my saloon before Joe Campbell drove away all the business. But first I had to see if Henry Guinn had resolved all my legal problems.

I walked across town to his house and knocked on the door. My worst fears came true when Amelia Guinn answered.

"You bring the hundred dollars you owe?"

I fished my money roll—what was left of it—out of my pocket and held it before her eyes. Licking her lips like she was looking at a side of roasting meat, she reached for it.

I jerked my hand away. "Not until I get to see Henry."

"He says you're to do all your dealing through me now."

I shook my head. "Not any longer. I deal with him, or you don't get any pay."

She glared at me. "Just a minute." She closed the door and in a couple minutes returned with Guinn.

"What do you want, Lomax?"

"I want to sell out and leave town."

He crossed his arms over his skinny chest. "I'm not giving you any legal advice until you pay the hundred dollars you owe."

"Owe for what? I haven't seen any results in weeks."

"The law takes time."

I offered him the hundred dollars, but Amelia snapped it from my hand quicker than a hiccup.

"It'll take six, maybe eight weeks to get it all resolved. I've got to get information from the territorial capital."

"I need to sell out and move now."

Amelia stepped between us, blocking my view, and started lecturing me. "You've been tempting him with saloon girls and other carnal pleasures. I'm here to protect him and make sure he walks in the path of righteousness. God punishes those who dwell in iniquity."

"Hell, woman, if I could just sell my property, I'd be glad to move to Iniquity, wherever the hell it is."

Amelia looked like I had slapped her with two pounds of raw liver.

"Don't use that kind of language in front of my wife," Henry Guinn barked.

"Hell, lawyer, I wouldn't if I had a chance to meet with you in private, but there's not a chance in hell of that, now, is there?"

Both Guinns gasped. "I'll let you know when I've news on your property," Henry snarled, "or when I need payment for services rendered."

"I ain't seen any services rendered."

They slammed the door in my face.

I started back down the street, afraid to go home for fear of finding another of Hattie's letters under my door, afraid to go to the saloon where my dwindling customers were probably being driven off by Joe Campbell's preaching, afraid to leave town and lose the money I'd invested, and afraid to stay in town for fear of getting shot.

When I arrived at the Stubborn Mule, I found it empty except for Joe Campbell, Ned Nichols, and Til Walteree behind the bar and Johnny Ringo at a table all by himself. He had only three empty bottles and a half-full fourth for company.

Nodding to Ringo, I advanced on the bar. "What's the problem? Why no customers?"

Campbell ignored me. Nichols and Walteree looked at him, then shrugged.

"Are you driving customers off with your preaching?"

Campbell turned his back to me.

"For the two dollars a day I'm paying you, I deserve an answer."

I got an answer, but not from Campbell. Nichols and Walteree simultaneously shouted, "Two dollars a day!"

"That's four times more than we make!" Walteree said.

"And he's driving all your business away," Nichols added.

"Preaching again?" I wanted to know.

"When you're not around, that's all he does, preach to folks about how they shouldn't be drinking, chasing skirts, or betting on cards," Walteree said.

"I don't like it when the place is empty," I started. Before I could finish, a voice from behind me interrupted.

"I like it empty," Ringo blurted.

"That's because it's not costing you money."

Ringo took a swig from his bottle, then slammed it on the table as he stood up. "No, I like it because there won't be any witnesses when I kill you."

At that moment the lack of customers didn't seem quite as pressing as Ringo's comment. "Why'd you want to do that, Ringo?"

"You ruined Corina DeLure." He stared hard at me. "She gave it all up, doesn't take men anymore."

I shrugged. "I didn't make her do that."

"Sure you did," Ringo answered. "You're the one who saw that she got religion."

"Amelia Guinn's at fault, Ringo. Kill her. She makes a bigger target."

Ringo laughed. "It's you I want. You stole Corina away."

"I never touched her."

"Maybe not her body, but her mind, Lomax. You got into her mind, ruined her with religion." Ringo pointed his finger at me. "I'm gonna plant a hole in you big enough to drive an ore wagon through."

"Hell," I answered, "why don't you shoot one wide enough for Amelia Guinn to walk through while you're at it?"

"This time I'll get the right man. No mistake like before."

I figured he was thinking back to when he shot through the door and put a splinter in my tail.

"Why don't you marry Corina?" I offered.

Ringo jerked his gun from his holster in a blink. "Don't be talking about me marrying a whore." He was so drunk I thought he was about to start crying.

Damn if he wasn't a strange one, wanting to have Corina for his pleasure but not for a wife because of her profession.

"Like I told Campbell, shut up," Ringo said. "I don't want you preaching to me about fallen women." He stood there a moment like he couldn't remember what he was doing. He looked at his gun, then lifted the barrel to his head and pushed up the brim of his hat. Again he stared at the pistol, as bewildered as a sheep at its first shearing. "Why've I got this out?"

"You were going to shoot Lomax," Campbell reminded him.

Ringo pointed his gun at me.

"Why, Joe, you lying son of a bitch," I protested. "He was gonna shoot you for all the preaching you've been doing."

Ringo turned his gun on Campbell.

Ned Nichols pulled off his apron and bolted for the end of the bar. "I don't feel too good. I'm going home."

Ringo swung his gun for Nichols.

Nichols almost passed out and went to hell on the spot.

Confused, Ringo said, "I wasn't going to shoot you, was I?"

Nichols shook his head faster than a turpentined cat. "Don't shoot me," he begged. "I didn't do nothing. I never poured tobacco juice in your drinks or any of those other things."

"That was always Campbell who did those things," I replied.

"No, it wasn't!" Campbell shouted.

Ringo held up his gun for quiet, then with his free hand pinched the bridge of his nose. "Just who was it I was going to shoot?" he asked, looking from Nichols to Walteree to Campbell and finally to me.

As addled as he was, I never figured he'd remember whom I might offer as his intended victim. "Doc Holliday," I suggested.

A smile wormed its way across Ringo's face. He nodded, then spun around toward Doc's usual table, cocked his pistol, and paused, moving his head from side to side like he was looking for Holliday. He turned back to me. "He's not here."

"He said he wanted to meet you in front of the Allen Street saloon."

Ringo holstered his gun, staring at me like he was having a hard time focusing. "Which one?"

"All of them."

He turned around and started for the door. "I'm gonna kill that son of a bitch."

"Why, that's just what he called you," I said.

Ringo growled, burst out the door, and marched away.

No sooner was he out the door than Walteree laughed. Campbell scowled at me like he was disappointed I hadn't been shot. Nichols stood there shaking.

"Ned, why don't you head on home and clean out your britches?"

"I wasn't that scared."

"Could've fooled me."

Ned left anyway. With no customers, I put Walteree and Campbell to sweeping the floor, dumping and polishing spittoons, cleaning glasses, and doing other chores we hadn't had time to do when business was booming. It hadn't been fifteen minutes after Ringo left that we heard some shots on Allen Street.

"Wonder if Ringo plugged Holliday?" I laughed.

"Nothing good comes out of a lie," Campbell said.

"What are you talking about?"

"You telling Ringo that he had planned to kill Holliday."

I snorted. "Hell, Ringo had so much liquor in him he'll never remember a thing that was said."

"Dying's not right."

"Neither's scaring business away, which is what you've been doing with your preaching."

"Yeah," echoed Walteree. "And you're making four times as much money as me."

"If one of you goes," I informed Campbell, "it'll be you."

He shook his head. "I'll bring the Stubborn Mule to its knees with all the stories I can spread about what you do to liquor."

"Can't do any more harm than your preaching's done already."

Campbell didn't say much else, just took to rubbing

a spittoon so hard I figured he'd wear a hole in it within the hour.

Ned Nichols returned thirty minutes later, reporting that Ringo had fired a few shots on Allen Street after failing to find Holliday anywhere. By nightfall we had the cleanest saloon in Tombstone—and nary a customer. I didn't think things could get any worse.

But the next day Wyatt Earp and his posse returned to Tombstone.

I was on Allen Street when they rode by. Frank Stilwell and Pete Spencer were both under arrest for the Sandy Bob Stage robbery. That night, Ike and Billy Clanton, Tom and Frank McLaury, Johnny Ringo, and Curly Bill Brocius came into the Stubborn Mule, all hot and lathered over the arrest.

Ike Clanton stepped up to the bar and asked for two bottles of whiskey.

"Whiskey's the devil's drink," Campbell said.

"Then invite the horny bastard to join us," Clanton answered as Campbell set a couple bottles on the bar.

"No, I mean that too much drink is sinful."

Clanton lunged across the bar and grabbed Campbell by the shirt, then pulled him until they were nose to nose. "I don't want to hear any more of your preaching, bartender, or I'll plug you with so many holes old Satan himself won't know whether you're a man or a sponge, you understand?"

Campbell lost a touch of religion real fast. "I understand."

Ike released him, then slid down off the bar, grabbed the bottles, and took them to the two tables where the other men had taken a load off their feet. He put a bottle on each table, and the men passed it around, sharing it without benefit of glasses.

"Those bastard Earps shouldn't've arrested Frank and Pete," Frank McLaury said. "And I think less of Frank and Pete, giving up without a fight."

"Why should they fight if they're innocent?" Tom asked. "We know they're innocent."

I knew they were, too, but I wasn't about to mention

it to this crowd. I didn't need any more enemies than I already had.

"It's us against the Earps," Clanton said. "We've got the sheriff on our side, so he'll back any play we make."

"The Earps are tough," Brocius said. "Don't forget that, or you'll wake up one morning and be dead by sunset."

Ringo grinned. "I can take any of them."

"One at a time," Brocius said, "but not all at once."

"And Holliday—I want to take him," Ringo said, then turned in his chair toward me. "Lomax, you're a son of a bitch for sending me out yesterday to kill Holliday."

"What are you talking about, Ringo?"

"You know what he's talking about," Campbell interjected. "I told you lying leads to no good."

I shrugged like I was confused, but Ringo didn't buy it. "You sent me out to shoot Holliday and thought I'd get killed or not remember."

"You'd been drinking," I reminded him. "You probably don't remember correctly."

"Sure he does," Campbell said. "What he said's exactly what happened. Lying always leads to no good."

I figured I was going to have to shoot Campbell to get him to shut up, but Walteree grabbed his arm and pulled him toward the back, leaving me and Ned Nichols to attend to the Clanton crowd.

Curly Bill Brocius slapped Ringo on the back. "Come on, Johnny. We can kill Lomax any day, easy as shooting sheep in a pen. How we gonna handle the Earps?"

"And Holliday," Ringo added.

"And Holliday," Brocius said.

Clanton slammed his fist against the table. "We just meet them and shoot it out."

"Hell, Ike, they're a steely-eyed bunch that'd have you wetting your britches before the shooting even started," Curly Bill said. "I say we shoot them in the dark. Less chance of being seen and being shot at night."

Frank protested, "I want them to know who killed them."

"Hell, Frank," said Curly Bill, "it don't matter what they know once they're dead."

The Clanton crowd were the only customers we had all night. I sent Campbell home before he got me shot. A few men came in after word got out on the street that he had left, but Ringo and Brocius made it plain they weren't interested in any strangers being within earshot of their big talk.

It was well after midnight when the Clanton bunch got up to leave. Curly Bill walked over to the bar and slammed the two empty whiskey bottles down. "It true you refill these with piss when they're empty, then sell them to drunks?"

I denied it adamantly, though I was glad Campbell wasn't around to counter my claim. "Not a word of truth in that."

Brocius grunted. "That's not what I hear about town."

"Just my competitors trying to take away my business."

"It's funny what you can hear around town," Brocius said, "but you know something I don't want to hear?"

I shook my head.

"I don't want to hear a thing about this conversation tonight. If you tell your buddy Holliday or the Earps, I'll come looking for you—because I know what you look like."

"Well, why shouldn't you?"

"I mean I know what *all* of you looks like."

"What are you saying?"

"Don't you remember the dance in Charleston? I seen you dancing naked with that Hattie Earp girl. Just because I'd had a few to drink doesn't mean I lost my memory, Lomax. All the other fellows were sure drooping while they danced, but your little pistol stood at attention like nothing I'd ever seen." Brocius laughed. "You should've seen him, boys. I bet the Earps'd love to have seen him dancing with Hattie. Of course I don't know how close he danced with her after the dance, but his pistol was sure primed and loaded."

Brocius could've probably shot me and done less

damage than by recalling the dance. "You must've confused me with someone else."

"Hell no, Lomax. I might've been drunk, but I wasn't blind. It's you that was catting about with the Earp girl. Probably even you that was spreading those rumors about Hattie running with Frank McLaury."

For an ignorant son of a bitch, Brocius was mighty good at figuring things out. I laughed as best I could, but it came out more a nervous cackle.

Brocius grinned. "Wait till I spread word you've been seeing Hattie. It'll start a new round of betting on where you'll get shot." Laughing, he backed out the door with the others, save Frank McLaury.

Frank spat on the floor. "I wouldn't go near one of the Earp women ever." He stormed outside.

Walteree rubbed his chin, then chuckled. "That true?"

"No, not a word of it."

"It was back during all the rains, wasn't it? Didn't you rent a buggy on one of those stormy nights? Did you rent it so you could take Hattie to Charleston?"

"No, Til, that's an absolute falsehood. I never took a buggy to Charleston." That was the truth—Hattie and I had ridden horses from the O.K. Corral.

"Damn, Lomax, you're either brave or stupid, seeing Hattie Ketcham. I heard the Earps slapped her around pretty good after she came back from a night out."

"I don't know a thing about that."

Til started to laughing and pounding the bar. He was laughing so hard I feared he was going to split a gut. I'd seen enough of my barkeeps' guts. "Now I know who she was."

"What are you talking about?"

"The girl you were in the sack with when the mob started to move your house."

"What?"

"Hattie Ketcham. You were in bed oiling your pistol, I suspect." He laughed. "You got your hands full of her, and then Behan and his miners try to move your house. When the Earps show up to protect your place, you don't know whether to be grateful or worried."

"It ain't true, none of it," I said, "but those are the kind of rumors that could get a fellow killed."

Walteree nodded. "That's a fact, whether my speculation is true or not. I'd hate to be walking around town worrying about someone spreading those tales, especially when folks are taking bets on where you'll get shot when that day finally comes."

I sighed. "What would it take for you to keep it under your hat?"

Walteree grinned. "I reckon two dollars a day for tending bar."

"That's a steep price."

"Not too steep for Joe Campbell. You rather see your business or yourself buried?" For a barkeep, Walteree had a way with words.

"I reckon I'd as soon see that I survive my business."

"You're not dumb for an Arkansawyer."

"Is everybody in Louisiana as crooked as you?"

"Everybody except the politicians. They're worse. Is it a deal? Two dollars a day?"

Walteree had me over a whiskey barrel. I couldn't bargain with him because I had no chips to throw on the table. He was as confident as a Louisiana Democrat on election day.

"Don't guess I have a choice. It's two dollars a day for you, provided you don't tell Ned Nichols. I can't have him wanting two dollars a day."

"He's too frightened to ask for a raise."

"With business as slow as it is, I can't afford to pay but one man wages that high."

Walteree crossed his arms over his apron. "I guess the only thing to do is to let go the man who's been costing you your business."

I could only nod. I was going to have to fire Joe Campbell and live with the consequences.

Chapter Sixteen

The next morning, when I returned to the Stubborn Mule to let Joe Campbell go, I ran into Hattie Ketcham, her arms crossed again, her foot tapping on the boardwalk.

"There you are, you son of a bitch."

I tipped my hat to her. "Good morning, Miss Ketcham."

She scowled. "The price has gone up."

"What are you talking about?"

"I'm talking about me keeping quiet and you keeping alive. Word's going around we were seen dancing naked in Charleston."

I wondered if Til Walteree or Curly Bill and his friends had been spreading that rumor. "I seem to recall you thinking it fun."

"We'd still be having fun if you hadn't taken up with Big Nose Kate. And don't tell me it was to talk religion. I fell for that with Corina DeLure."

"I hear Kate's left town for a convent."

Hattie held out her hand. "A hundred dollars."

"I gave you a hundred dollars last time."

"I want a hundred more, or I'll tell Doc you're the one spreading rumors about me and Frank McLaury. If he doesn't kill you, my uncles will when I tell them what you did to me."

"I didn't do anything."

"I want the money today!"

"I'm broke."

"Then you'd better find it."

"Or what?"

"Or I'll tell Doc." She held out her hand like she expected me to give her the money right there.

"I've stood up to Doc Holliday. I'm not scared of him or any of your badge-toting uncles," I lied.

She looked as disappointed as a coyote with a bleached bone. Then her face flushed with anger. "You're a dead man, Henry Lomax."

"Good. Then I won't have to look at your mule face."

Hattie slapped me, lifted her skirt, and stormed away.

I stood there rubbing my cheek, wondering if she had been bluffing or if she really was going to tell Holliday. I waited until she disappeared down the street before I resumed my march to the Stubborn Mule.

At the saloon I found Joe Campbell speaking of the evils of drink to my solitary customer, who didn't linger for a second drink. Campbell's face fell when he realized I'd overheard his lecturing.

I walked behind the bar and slapped him on the shoulder. "You know, Joe, over the years I've listened to a lot of your philosophy, but I think you were wiser before you were gutshot than now."

Campbell shoved a finger beneath his collar and loosened it.

"You've made many profound comments, Joe, like more is less."

"Huh?"

"Like more preaching is less business."

"I'm not preaching."

"What's good for the soul is bad for business."

"I didn't say that, never."

"Like dry is wet. A customer's mouth stays dry as long as the bottle stays wet."

"I didn't say that, either."

"Like down is up. Business is down when preaching is up."

Campbell shrugged. "I didn't say that."

"If you didn't, it's only because you didn't have time to think it up, not with all the time you're spending preaching. Every time you open your mouth, Joe, you take money out of my pocket, the same pocket that pays you two dollars a day."

"I'll start rumors about your saloon," Campbell threatened.

With a sweep of my arm I invited him to look around the room. "Your rumors can't hurt business any more than this."

It didn't take him long to count zero customers.

"Good-bye is hello, Joe. Good-bye to you is hello to new customers. I'm letting you go."

"You can't do that."

"It's my saloon, even if it is empty."

"We had an agreement."

"Agreements are made to be broken."

"I'll get a lawyer."

"Good. Get Henry Guinn. He's draining my money faster than I can make it now that you've scared off all my business."

"You'll be sorry."

"I'll be sorry until you get your ugly face out of my saloon."

Bewildered, Campbell stared at me. "What'll I do?"

"I don't care."

"I took a bullet for you."

"I laundered your guts to save you, and what do I get in return? You drive away all my business."

Campbell clenched his fists. "I'll get even with you for this."

"Hell, Campbell, get in line. Every son of a bitch in Tombstone's got something against me. Why shouldn't you?"

His lip quivering, Campbell jerked off his apron and threw it at me. "I bet you'll get shot in the head, Lomax."

"Even if I *was* head-shot, I'd still have more brains than you."

Campbell turned and stomped toward the door.

"Why don't you follow your piss, Joe?"

He barged outside. I knew I had to start rebuilding

my business so I could sell it and move to Bisbee. I sent Til Walteree around town that afternoon to announce that Joe Campbell was no longer tending bar at the Stubborn Mule. I hoped to get all my customers back, though I knew it would be tough with all the new Allen Street saloons.

Just after dark that night, Doc Holliday came in looking meaner than a mule on a sawdust diet. I hoped he wanted to deal cards at the Stubborn Mule again but feared he'd been listening to the rumors. "Howdy, Doc. You want your table back now that Joe Campbell's gone?"

"Lomax, you lousy son of a bitch."

Hattie hadn't wasted any time going to Doc. "I never cut your drinks, Doc, I don't care what rumors Joe Campbell's started," I replied, trying to throw him off the trail.

"The hell with Joe Campbell. Hattie Ketcham told me you were spreading some vile rumors about her seeing Frank McLaury."

I gulped.

"I told you I'd kill whoever's spreading those rumors, and I'm a man of my word." His hand plunged toward his waist. I expected him to pull his nickel-plated revolver, but he went for his britches pocket instead. When he jerked his hand free, he held a twenty-dollar gold piece and slapped it on the bar.

"Drinks all around," I suggested.

"No, dammit. Here's twenty dollars that says you get it in the back." He grinned. "Once I tell Wyatt and his brothers, it won't be just me looking for you." Doc turned to head for the door.

"Hold it," I called. "You spilled your sugar on the bar."

Holliday stopped dead in his tracks and spun about.

"You seem to forget, Doc, that I know a few things about you and your stealing sugar—and not just at card games, either."

Holliday tried to stare me down. "If you start any more rumors, I'll get you tonight when you walk home."

"Why should I worry about you, Doc? Every man in

Tombstone's talking about shooting me to settle all the bets."

"The difference," said Holliday, "is that I'll do more than talk. I'll settle it." He turned and walked away.

That's when I saw Til Walteree standing at the door. He watched Holliday pass, then ran to the bar.

"You're braver than I thought, Lomax. You stood up to Doc Holliday, and you weren't drunk this time. Think you can get out of this alive?"

"I've seen better men than me die."

Walteree scratched his head. "You're beginning to sound a bit like Joe Campbell."

"How's that?"

"You don't make any sense." He laughed.

Nothing made sense in Tombstone, except trouble. I had so many enemies now I couldn't count them, but Doc Holliday had suddenly risen to the top of the list. I figured he'd get me or have one of the Earps do it. I couldn't cover my back all the time or beat all of them at gunplay, but I could at least take Doc Holliday down with me if I turned him in for robbing the Sandy Bob Stage. But if I took my accusations to the law, which law was it to be? I couldn't go to the Earps, even though Virgil was the town marshal and Wyatt was rumored to be carrying the badge of a deputy marshal. Johnny Behan was probably more crooked than all the Earps put together, but he was on the side of the Clantons and McLaurys, who didn't seem to care much for me, either.

The law was crooked on both sides, but having no other choice, I went to see Sheriff Johnny Behan. I caught him in his office the next evening. He wasn't at all pleased to see me.

"We'll get your house off that lot yet," he said. "And I'd as soon you got out of my office now. You've gotten in bed with the Earps. Let them watch out for you."

"I've got some information to pass along, if you can keep a secret."

"There's nothing a friend of the Earps could know that would interest me."

"Not even if he knew who robbed the Sandy Bob Stage?"

Behan leaned over his desk and motioned to a chair. "Have a seat, Lomax. It's good to see you. How's the family?"

"I don't have a family."

"Oh. Now, what was it you were saying?"

"I wasn't saying anything, and I won't until I'm certain you won't tell where you got this information."

Behan grinned and ran his fingers through his thinning hair. "Lomax, you know you can trust me. Now, what was it you wanted to tell me?"

"Nothing, if you can't promise me you'll keep my name out of it."

"You have my word," he said.

I knew his word wasn't worth the paper it wasn't written on, but I was desperate. "It's about the Sandy Bob Stage robbery."

"Go on."

"I don't think Frank Stilwell did it."

Behan leaned forward again. "That's what Frank says. Who did?"

I looked to make certain nobody was around. "Doc Holliday for sure, maybe Morgan Earp with him."

Behan clapped his hands. "What makes you think so?"

"The robber's breath. It smelled like rotting flesh. It was the breath of a lunger, bad enough to make a maggot faint."

"How do you know Frank's breath won't do the same?"

"I ran into him in Bisbee the next day. It's not the same."

Behan grinned, then stroked his mustache. "Stilwell's trial's coming up soon. Would you testify to what you've told me?"

"What kind of fool do you think I am? I told you I wanted this kept quiet."

Behan nodded. "Then why you telling me?"

"Holliday's been threatening me, and if something happens to me, I want him to pay."

"Hell, Lomax, you fool, if something happens to you,

there won't be anyone to testify against him. He'll get you, and you'll get nothing except a grave."

"I'll be a dead man for sure if I testify. I've nothing to gain from it."

Behan licked his lips and rubbed his hands together. "You might gain peace of mind with Holliday off the street. You might even save your life. I have pull with the mining company, Lomax, and if you were to testify against Holliday, for a few dollars I'd see that all claims against your house lot and even your saloon were dropped. That would save you a lot of money that's now going to Henry Guinn."

I didn't like the idea of giving my money to a lawyer, who'd taken no oath to be honest and obey the law, but I disliked even more giving it to a crooked sheriff who *had* taken that oath. Anyway, why did Behan need the money? He was the tax collector for Cochise County, and the law allowed him to keep ten percent of everything he brought in. Some said his share exceeded forty thousand dollars a year.

"Business is down right now," I said.

"When business picks up, you let me know, and we can clear your titles. It'll make things simpler for all of us, Lomax."

"Not only do you have to keep things simpler, Sheriff, you've got to keep them quiet. I'll testify as long as you don't tell anyone before the day you want me to appear in court."

Behan nodded solemnly. "The trial'll be in Tucson, anyway, and I know how to keep things quiet until the time's right."

"I'm counting on it."

Behan got up and escorted me to the door, slapping me on the back. "Lot of folks've been wondering where you're gonna get shot."

"Where'd you bet?"

"I figured the shoulder, but don't you worry. I'll tell Johnny Ringo not to go hunting for you. He's still mad about Corina DeLure getting religion, blames it all on you."

"I'd appreciate a good word with Ringo."

Behan nodded as he opened the door. "I'll tell him he might get blood on his new boots."

"He's had blood on his boots before."

"These are new ones, though, and he's mighty proud of them. They're tooled with his initials across the side."

I didn't care about Ringo's boots. "Just remember: Don't mention this conversation to anyone."

"What conversation?" Behan laughed.

I slipped out of his office and into the dark, wondering if Doc Holliday or one of the Earps was drawing a bead on my back that any moment would send me to hell. After a decent evening of business, I went home with two dollars' profit, fought off Satan on my way to bed, and caught a good night's sleep.

Next morning, when I got to the saloon, Til Walteree could hardly contain himself. Making sure no customers were within hearing range, he whispered a question. "It true what you said about Holliday?"

"What are you talking about?"

"That he robbed the Sandy Bob Stage?"

I about swallowed my tongue. "Where'd you hear such nonsense?"

"That's what Sheriff Behan's telling folks."

"That son of a bitch."

"You're the one pointing a finger at Holliday. Word is that you said Morgan Earp was involved, too."

"I don't know how those kinds of rumors get started."

"A couple folks say they saw you at Behan's office. Fact is, Wyatt Earp was by here this morning looking for you, saying he had a few questions to ask in regards to the Sandy Bob Stage robbery."

"He didn't mention anything about Hattie, did he?"

"Not to me."

My life was beginning to sound like some of Joe Campbell's philosophy: Your friends are your enemies, and your enemies are your friends. I should never've opened my mouth about Doc Holliday and the Sandy Bob Stage.

Word was, charges had been dropped against Pete

Spencer in the Sandy Bob Stage robbery, but Frank
Stilwell was going on trial in Tucson for the crime. I figured that would get most of the Earps and the Clanton
crowd out of Tombstone for a while. I didn't realize it
would take me away, too.

As I was leaving the house the next morning, I happened to see a flash of movement to my side and saw
Wyatt Earp charging for me. Without a word he grabbed
my arm and shoved some papers in my hand. "That's a
subpoena. You're to appear in federal court day after tomorrow in Tucson to testify in the trial of Frank Stilwell."

"I don't know a thing."

"That's not what you've been telling Behan, Lomax."

"It was dark. I couldn't identify a thing."

"Wasn't so dark you couldn't smell a man's breath,
now, was it?"

"What are you talking about?"

"You know damn well what I'm talking about—you
saying Doc Holliday and Morg were involved in the
Sandy Bob Stage robbery. I never heard a more despicable lie. You better hope Frank Stilwell's convicted. And
you better not point a finger at Doc, or you'll be pushing
up daisies." He jerked his hand from my arm. "If you
don't show in Tucson, I'll have a warrant issued for your
arrest. It'll give me the right to shoot you on sight."

"You'd like that, wouldn't you?"

"I can't deny that, after all the lies you've been
spreading about Doc and all the dishonor you've brought
our family."

"What are you talking about?"

"Hattie—that's what I'm talking about."

I gulped.

"I've heard the rumors about you and her dancing
naked, about you bedding her when me, Morg, and Virgil
came to your aid, and about you taking her away from
town and ravishing her." Wyatt tapped the badge on his
chest. "This is all that keeps me from killing you right
now. Doc's sworn to kill you for spreading rumors she
was seeing Frank McLaury. That's plenty bad enough,
but the other things you did to her have set my blood to
boiling. I'd shoot you now, but the Clantons and

McLaurys have been threatening us. Once we take care of them, you'll be an easy bug to squash."

"Maybe they didn't like it when their friends were arrested by your posse for a robbery Doc and Morgan committed. I figure they think you'll do the same to them, arrest them for crimes they didn't do."

"Stilwell and Spencer've robbed enough stages. It don't matter which one we arrest them for, just as long as we take care of them." Wyatt poked my chest with his forefinger. "You just remember what you better not say in Tucson, or you'll be in deeper than you are now."

I nodded. What else could I do? Wyatt turned and walked away.

The next day I rode Flash to Contention, where the railroad had finally reached, and caught the train for Tucson. I took a room that night, then went to the courthouse the following day. Wyatt was there, and though I didn't see them, I heard Doc Holliday and Morgan Earp were in town to do some gambling. Though that was the story, I knew the two wanted to be nearby in case my testimony implicated them.

The next day I waited in the courthouse to be called as a witness. I testified after the stage driver, another passenger, and a fellow from Bisbee who claimed to have overheard Stilwell and Spencer talking about where to hide the money.

When I was called to the stand, I took the oath and settled into the hard chair. Stilwell, his lawyer at his side, sat in chains in front of the judge. The prosecutor, a tall slender man with bushy sideburns, sat at a desk in front of me.

After the preliminaries, the federal attorney asked me all sorts of questions about the robbery, including how much money I'd lost, how well I could see in the dark, and if I knew who the robber was. I told him that although I had my suspicions, I couldn't be certain. Wyatt Earp, sitting among the spectators, leaned forward in his seat and tapped his fingers on the butt of his pistol, as if to remind me of his threats.

Now, I'd been known in my life to stretch the truth a time or two, but those were times when I hadn't been under oath. I might not've been much of a churchgoing person, but my momma taught me to believe in God and never to violate a promise made on the Holy Bible.

The prosecutor clutched his lapel with one hand and pointed to Stilwell with the other. "Is this man the robber?"

"I can't be certain, because it was dark, but I have my doubts."

The prosecutor glanced quickly at Earp as if this wasn't what he expected to hear. I bet Wyatt hadn't expected it, either.

"Like I said, it was dark. I couldn't see much."

"Then you must not've gotten very close to him."

"No, sir, I got close enough to smell his breath. It smelled worse than a gut wagon in the summer sun."

"But, Mr. Lomax, how can you identify a man by the odor of his breath?"

"I ran into Stilwell the next day in Bisbee, coming out of a boot shop. I got close enough to smell his breath, and it wasn't the same."

"But it could've been Stilwell. Maybe his breath had improved overnight."

"Maybe," I said, "but likely not."

"No further questions," the prosecutor said.

The judge turned to Stilwell's lawyer. "Your turn."

Stilwell shifted in his chair, his chains rattling as his attorney, a short stocky man with thinning hair, rose.

"What's your business, Mr. Lomax?"

"I run a saloon, the Stubborn Mule, in Tombstone."

"Would it be fair to say you smell the breath of a lot of men over the course of a day, week, month, and year?"

"I reckon."

"What did the robber's breath remind you of?"

"A lunger."

"What's that?"

"A man eaten by consumption."

"You certain?"

I nodded. "Yes, sir."

"How do you know?"

"Consumption's common around saloons. I've even heard it called gambler's disease."

"Do you know if Frank Stilwell has consumption?"

"I don't."

"Could you tell if you caught a whiff of his breath?"

"Probably," I answered.

"Objection!" yelled the prosecutor. "The witness is not a doctor and has never been a doctor. Dispensing liquor is not the same thing as dispensing medicine, no matter what the witness thinks of his profession."

"It's more honest than being a lawyer."

The judge banged the gavel and reprimanded me. "The witness will refrain from giving his opinion unless asked. The objection is sustained."

"Very well," said Stilwell's lawyer. "We have a doctor to call to confirm Mr. Stilwell's health."

"Continue," said the judge.

"Now, then, Mr. Lomax, do you know anybody who has consumption among your regular associates?"

"I do."

"Objection," said the government attorney. "The question is irrelevant."

"No, Your Honor, the question is pertinent, if you will allow me to continue."

"Go ahead," the judge answered.

"Who among your regular associates might have consumption?"

I stared at Wyatt Earp. His lips tightened, and he shook his head. But I had taken an oath. "Doc Holliday," I said.

"Could this Dr. Holliday have been the robber?"

"Objection!" cried the prosecutor. "On trial is Frank Stilwell."

"Sustained," said the judge.

"Very well," said Stilwell's attorney. "Could Frank Stilwell have been the robber?"

"I don't think so," I responded.

"Now, Mr. Lomax, it was dark the night of the robbery, was it not?"

"It was."

"How were the men dressed?"

"Dusters, masks, and hats turned low over their faces."

"You could not identify them by their appearance, then?"

"I couldn't, no, sir."

"How did everyone come to identify them?"

"One of them used the word 'sugar' several times. It was a word Frank Stilwell was known to use when he talked about money."

"Did the robber use the word once, twice, how many times?"

"Several," I replied. "It seemed he was saying it enough so we couldn't help but notice."

"Are you telling me, Mr. Lomax, it was as if the robber was trying to lay a false trail?"

"That was how I took it."

"Do you have any idea, Mr. Lomax, who the robber was?"

"I do."

"Was it Frank Stilwell?"

"Not in my mind, it wasn't."

"No further questions, Your Honor."

The judge dismissed me, and the prosecution called another witness as I was walking out the door. I could see Wyatt chomping at the bit to get at me—and it wasn't to congratulate me for telling the truth.

With Holliday and Morgan Earp in town as well as Wyatt, I knew I could run into trouble at any minute, so I went to a gun shop and bought a new Winchester .44-40 and two boxes of ammunition. If trouble came, I would shoot back. I returned to my hotel, planning on a good night's sleep and riding the train back toward Tombstone in the morning.

As soon as I stepped in the door, I saw Doc Holliday and the two Earps sitting in the lobby waiting for me. I started to retreat but realized I was safer in the hotel instead of outside, where they could hunt me down.

"Why, Henry Harrison Lomax, what a pleasant surprise to see you here in Tucson," Holliday drawled.

"You going hunting?" Wyatt asked, pointed at my new rifle.

"I never know when I'm gonna run into varmints on the way back to Tombstone."

Wyatt smiled. "Did you hear the verdict, by chance?"

I shook my head. "Didn't hear a thing."

"Frank Stilwell got off," Holliday said, "largely, I'm told, because of your testimony about me."

"I was under oath."

"You're gonna be underground," Morgan interjected.

Doc lifted his hand to calm him. "Well, Henry Harrison Lomax, now I have several reasons to kill you—spreading all those rumors about Hattie and now besmirching my good name. Wyatt told me all."

"You can't believe everything you hear."

"Even if it's under oath," Doc challenged.

The three men rose to their feet. Wyatt grinned. "We just wanted you to know we'll finish our business with you back in Tombstone, if you've got the guts to return."

"Threats and big talk haven't stopped me yet."

"My gun will," Holliday said, "when I see you in Tombstone again."

The trio marched past me and out the door.

A white-faced clerk lifted his head from behind the counter. "Was that Wyatt Earp and Doc Holliday?"

"It was," I replied.

"Mister, you must be some kind of fool."

I retired to my room, propped a chair under the doorknob, and went to bed. I stayed in Tucson an extra day so as not to be on the same train as the Earps and Holliday. It gave me a little time to think about my future, which didn't seem too bright.

The next day, when I got on the train, I found Frank Stilwell aboard. He patted the seat and invited me to join him, as we had a lot to talk about. I was trying to figure out how to stay alive once I got back, so I wasn't in the mood for talking, but when Stilwell told me he was going to be met at the Contention station by Ike Clanton and the boys, I wondered if I'd even make it as far as Tombstone.

Chapter Seventeen

Ike and Billy Clanton, Frank and Tom McLaury, and Curly Bill Brocius were waiting at the Contention station. Frank Stilwell bounded down the aisle and out the car onto the platform. His friends slapped him on the back and congratulated him.

"You've got the damnedest luck," Ike bellowed, "getting tried for the only holdup in Cochise County you didn't have a hand in!"

"I owe it all to Lomax." Stilwell grinned and turned around like he expected to find me behind him.

I had remained on the train, watching through the window.

"Come on out, Lomax!" he called. "No one's planning to shoot you."

Toting my new Winchester, I stepped out of the passenger car and onto the platform.

Frank McLaury shook his fist at me. "I didn't promise not to shoot him. He's the son of a bitch spreading rumors I was seeing one of the Earp sows."

"Good to see you again, Frank," I said.

Stilwell grabbed my hand and pumped it. "You fellas leave Lomax alone. This son of a bitch testified that Doc Holliday pulled off the robbery. I'd always heard he wasn't afraid of Doc."

Ike mumbled that he was still mad about me suggesting he was sleeping with horses. If it was true, of course, it must've been blind horses, as ugly as he was.

Though they all hated me, save possibly Stilwell, I knew they hated Holliday and the Earps even more. "I ran into Wyatt, Morgan, and Doc in Tucson," I said. "If I was you boys, I'd look out. They told me that when they got back to Tombstone, they were gonna kill you one by one until Cochise County was a safe place for decent people to live."

"Hell," yelled Ike, "let's just head to Tombstone and kill them first!" He was gesturing so wildly I decided a few monkeys must've swung from the low branches of his family tree.

The men moved toward their horses, but I lingered, uncertain if it would be safer to ride back to Tombstone with them or ride out alone later. Stilwell motioned for me to join them.

"I've got to get my mule. You fellas go on."

"We ain't got nothing against you," Stilwell said.

"Like hell we don't," Ike protested. "He says I poke horses."

"And he's been saying I was interested in Hattie Earp," Frank McLaury added. "Let's draw straws to see who kills him."

"You don't want to harm a hair on his head," Stilwell cautioned.

"Why the hell not?" Ike demanded.

I was feeling pretty good about Stilwell and thinking we'd become good friends. Then he answered.

"Kill Lomax and you'll have to face Ringo!" All the bastards laughed.

Frank McLaury nodded. "Ringo's still mad about you giving Corina DeLure religion."

Stilwell added, "He wants the pleasure of killing you."

Ike slapped at his holster like he was going for his gun, then jerked his hand up and pointed his trigger finger at me. "Bang," he said. "Nobody can beat Ringo at gunplay, not even Doc Holliday. I'd hate to be in your boots."

I had to admit my boots were feeling a bit uncomfortable right then. Seemed like everyone I knew was out to kill me. Doc Holliday and Frank McLaury wanted me for spreading rumors about Hattie. Wyatt Earp was mad I had testified against Holliday. Morgan would go along with whatever Doc or Wyatt wanted. Johnny Ringo was mad about Corina's conversion. Ike Clanton was sure he could beat me in a gunfight. Joe Campbell wanted me dead for firing him. Amelia Guinn wanted me dead for tracking her floor with mud. Her husband probably wanted me dead so he could steal my lots.

"You riding with us or not, Lomax?" Stilwell asked.

"Where's Ringo?"

All the men laughed.

"Probably on one of his drinking sprees. He gets sad and likes to be alone," Tom McLaury said.

"Yeah," Ike broke in, "so he doesn't kill someone."

They all laughed again.

"Come on, Lomax, ride with us," Frank said. "Ringo wouldn't do anything to you with so many witnesses around."

"We'll meet you at the edge of town after you get your mule," Stilwell said.

They laughed and carried on as they strode down the platform and to the hitching rails along the street. I shook my head and turned toward the livery stable. After paying the liveryman for tending and saddling Flash, I mounted up and rode to the edge of town, feeling like a worm going to a meeting of sparrows. I joined the boys, and as we started for Tombstone, I tried to let Flash fall in behind the others, but Stilwell asked me to ride with him in the middle of the procession.

"That way," Ike reassured me, "we can shoot you where we want. There's a lot of money riding on where you get shot. I originally bet the back, but now I'm saying the balls."

"At least I got a pair."

Ike swelled up like a bullfrog. "I can still get it up."

"That's what I hear—" I paused.

Ike's chest swelled even larger.

"—from the cows," I finished.

"You bastard." He looked around at the others. "Where'd the rest of you bet he'd get it?"

"Chest," said Tom McLaury.

"Ass," said Frank McLaury.

"Back," said Stilwell.

"Me, too," said Billy Clanton.

Ike laughed and spit a wad of tobacco juice past Flash's nose. At least I thought it was tobacco juice. Ike's innards could've been so backed up it was something else, and he'd never've known the difference.

Flash jerked his head up. He didn't like Ike's manners. I could take their insults, but I didn't take kindly to them bothering my mule. If those sons of bitches were going to give me and Flash a hard time, I might just as well fight back, the safest way I knew how. I'd blame the Earps.

"It true, Ike, you eat bullshit stew?"

"Why, you son of a bitch!" Ike shot back.

I held up my hand. "That's what Wyatt was saying about you."

"That bastard."

I nodded. "Shame of it is, that's not all he's said about you Clantons." I pointed at Billy. "He said Billy's so dumb he couldn't blow his nose with a crate of dynamite."

Billy exploded with cuss words hot enough to fry bacon.

Knowing Frank McLaury was proud of his looks, I turned to him next. "I know we ain't real friendly, but I wanted you to know what Doc Holliday's been saying behind your back. Doc says you're so ugly you wrinkle his clothes and curl his tie every time you walk by. You're so ugly your ma used to borrow a baby to take to church, he says."

Frank looked like he wanted to shoot me, but all he fired off was some colorful language related to acts that I believed impossible for a man to do to himself. He and Ike started yammering about what bastards the Earps were. Although I tended to agree, I figured I'd be doing Arizona Territory a favor if I got the Earps and the Clantons to kill each other off.

"The Earps are saying all of you are rustlers, thieves, and robbers," I went on. "Now, I don't believe it for a minute, but that's what they've been saying."

"Those bastards," Ike kept muttering.

All agreed they had to stop the Earps from saying those things. By the time we reached Tombstone, I'd stoked a big enough fire that I prayed the whole town didn't burn down when we rode in, though another fire along Allen Street would've been okay.

"I'm tired of the lies," Frank McLaury said. "It's time we put a stop to it."

Ike added, "They ain't nothing but Yankee trash that's got a hard lesson coming."

I figured the fellows would want a little liquor to wash the trail dust from their throats, so I decided to show them my hospitality. "Boys, let's go to the saloon, and you can have all the drinks you want on me. It's the least I can do for you guarding me on the way back to town."

Those rustlers whooped and hollered, which didn't please me none because I was hoping to sneak into town without the Earps and Doc Holliday knowing about it. But Ike in particular was carrying on so much they might just as well've sent a brass band to the edge of town to welcome me and pin a target on my back.

I guess the risk was worth it, though, to get the fellows to drinking. A little liquor can do a lot for a man's courage, if not for his judgment, and I wanted to do everything I could to help them settle their differences with the Earps and Doc before any of them shot me to collect bets.

We rode up to the Stubborn Mule, dismounted, and tied our animals. I led the delegation inside. Til Walteree glanced up from the bar and gave me a nervous grin. "Lomax, I need to talk with you."

"Til, we can talk, but first I need you to give my friends here drinks all around. You keep their throats wet and their money in their pockets. It's all on me."

Walteree set bottles and glasses on the bar in front of the men. Ike Clanton, of course, picked up a bottle, pulled the plug out with his teeth, spit it into a spittoon, and began to suck on the liquor. The other fellows took glasses and poured whiskey, sloshing it on the bar. I didn't care how big a mess they made as long as they got drunk and brave.

After the fellows started drinking, Walteree pulled me over to the corner. "Three days ago Johnny Ringo was here looking for you, saying he was ready to kill you."

I gulped.

"But I ain't seen him since," Walteree said.

"That's good news."

"Not really, because yesterday Doc Holliday was in looking for you. He had blood in his eye." Walteree tugged at his ear. "He told me he wanted to know when you got back in town, because he planned to settle up, too. Threatened me and Ned if we didn't find him and tell him as soon as you arrived."

I looked around the saloon. "Where's Ned?"

"His nerves got him. He left town on the morning stage. Didn't care where he was going, long as it wasn't to a grave."

"You gonna tell?"

"I can't, being the only one here to work the bar. Unless you want to spell me." He grinned.

I shook my head. "Maybe another time. How's business?"

"It's picking up. We took in almost eighty dollars while you were gone." He shoved his hand in his pocket and pulled out a wad of bills for me. I pushed his hand away.

"Keep it, in case you have to pay for my funeral."

"I'll give you the best funeral eighty dollars can buy, if you will me your saloon."

"Hell, Til, take whatever you can get as long as you keep Clanton and his friends full of liquor."

"I thought you didn't like them."

"I don't, but when you've got as many enemies as I do, you've got to play them against each other."

The rustlers moved to a pair of back tables, drinking my liquor and cursing the Earps and Holliday. It did my heart good to hear all the vile things they were saying.

Walteree looked at me. "If I was you, I wouldn't go anywhere 'less I was armed."

"I bought a new Winchester in Tucson."

"Hell, you may need a cannon, as many enemies as you have."

He got no argument from me. I was about as well liked in Tombstone as a losing politician. "I'll take Flash to the O.K. Corral, then head home and stay off the street."

Walteree shook his head, all nervous again. "Don't. Big Nose Kate's left town, and Doc's taken to boarding at a place on the other side of the corral. If I's you, I'd go straight home and lay low."

I nodded. "Maybe things'll get better tomorrow." I looked at the rustlers, drinking and talking big. "Maybe they'll take care of the Earps tonight."

"It'll take more than them. Ike talks big, but he's all blow and no show. You stay home tonight, and I'll come by in the morning and bring you some breakfast. Maybe then we'll know how you stand."

"Thanks, Walteree."

"It's the least I can do for a dead man."

His parting comment didn't give me much confidence, but I had pretty much come to the end of the trail in a box canyon. I couldn't see any way out.

I left the saloon, untied Flash, jerked the Winchester from beneath the saddle, and led the mule to my house, tying him out back and out of sight from the street. Easing around to the front, I opened the door and jumped inside. No sooner was the door closed than Satan charged at me from the corner. I drew back my boot to kick his furry butt clear to Tucson, but he stopped and retreated.

The house was cool, so I lit a fire in the kitchen stove and waited and waited and waited, being careful not to stand in front of a window for too long. Near dark I grew hungry and found a few potatoes, which I fried and ate. I never lit a lamp and finally retired to bed.

Sometime after midnight somebody fired a bullet through my bedroom window. It hit the wall over my head. I figured it was just a shot to get me to show my head at the window so the assassin could finish me off. I rolled out of bed onto the floor, then pulled the mattress atop me as I waited for another shot. But nothing came, so I dragged the mattress to the corner and finished the night sleeping on the floor with my rifle at my side.

About midmorning Til Walteree showed up with some biscuits and bacon wrapped in a bar towel. He looked a mite pale, like he was scared.

"Bad night," he announced, offering me the food.

I took the towel and nodded. "Someone took a potshot through the window. Missed my head by inches."

"Your free drinks did some damage."

I started eating. "How's that?"

"Morgan and Doc ran into Ike Clanton at the Occidental Lunch Room before midnight. Then Wyatt showed up, and they all had words. Ike turned tail and left, just like I said he would."

I was disappointed that my liquor hadn't made Ike a braver man. Maybe I needed to buy a stronger brand. "You didn't give Ike and his boys anything but the good stuff after I left, did you?"

Walteree looked embarrassed. "I switched them to the cut liquor after a while."

"Dammit, the good stuff would've made them braver." I was beginning to feel I had wasted all that liquor, cut and uncut, for no better result than that.

"But," Walteree went on, "I hear Ike has been carrying a rifle about this morning, looking for Holliday and the Earps, and I know for a fact he came in the saloon asking if I'd seen them. He said he had something to give them. I took that to mean a few bullets."

"Good," I said.

"Word is, Doc learned you were in town last night and said he was going to find you this morning. It didn't sound like he was interested in playing cards."

I swallowed some bacon and biscuit. "Doc probably ain't up yet."

"But he'll get up sometime, Lomax, and when he does, I wouldn't want to be you."

"You're forgetting I spit in his drink."

"You're forgetting you were drunk that night."

"I'd've killed him then if you hadn't clobbered me."

Walteree shook his head like he didn't believe me.

"Way I figure it, Lomax, you got two choices. You can leave Tombstone and maybe live, or you can stay around and die. You're about as popular as a temperance woman in a beer hall."

I figured I had a third choice. Rather than wait for Doc to find me, I could search for him, maybe shoot him in the back. I had a new rifle and two cartons of cartridges.

"Where's Doc boarding now?"

"Up Fremont here, just beyond Fly's Studio. Why?"

"I might go visit him."

"You're a damn fool if you do."

"What've I got to lose, 'cept my life? And most folks are betting I've already lost that."

Walteree reached out and shook my hand. "Good luck, Lomax. You're either the bravest or stupidest fellow I've ever been around."

"You're forgetting Joe Campbell. He's the stupidest."

Walteree grinned, then patted his pocket. "I've still got the money for your funeral." He turned for the door like he never expected to see me again, outside of a coffin.

After he left, I felt a craving for a drink or two or three. The cure was wearing off. I needed something to screw up my courage to ambush Doc Holliday.

I figured the longer I stayed around the house, the greater the chance Doc would come looking for me there. I quickly finished dressing, put on my coat, slipped the two cartons of bullets in the pocket, grabbed my Winchester, and left to see if I could bushwhack Holliday.

After taking a deep breath, I cradled my rifle in the crook of my left arm and circled the house to Flash. I needed to get him to the O.K. Corral for water and fodder. I untied him and cautiously led him down the street.

Though I didn't know it at the time, it turned out that my liquor had had more of an effect than Walteree had led me to believe. Fact was, about the time he and I were talking, Virgil Earp had slapped Ike Clanton up 'side the head with his revolver and taken him to court, where he was fined twenty-five dollars for carrying his

Winchester inside town limits in violation of the town ordinance.

On the way out of court, Wyatt Earp had run into Tom McLaury and slapped him across the face with his hand. When McLaury said he didn't care for such friendliness, Wyatt slapped him with his gun. Since the Earps had relieved them of their guns, Ike and Tom went to a gun shop and bought new weapons, deciding they had been slapped by the Earps for the last time.

But I didn't know all that at the time, because I was too busy looking out for my own hide. It was about noon when I got Flash to the O.K. Corral.

John Montgomery stared at my rifle. "You looking for trouble?"

"No, Doc Holliday."

"Same difference. I hear he's looking for you."

"My gun'll shoot farther than his."

"But will it shoot faster or straighter? That's what matters."

I shrugged. "Where's he boarding now?"

"At Fly's Boardinghouse on Fremont. You can go through the back of the corral," he offered.

"Obliged."

"Is someone gonna take care of your funeral?"

"I've given money to Til Walteree."

Montgomery nodded. "Money'll change hands if you're hit."

"But there's none in it for me."

"Unless you get lucky and kill Holliday. Then you'll have a reputation. A lot of men'll come looking for you, wanting to kill the man who killed Doc Holliday."

I stepped past him into the stable, then through the pens into the open area between the back of the corral and the back of Bauer's Butcher Shop, Papago's Store, and the assay office. There I paused and looked toward Fourth Street and Spangenberg's Gun Shop, making sure Doc wasn't around before I slipped over to Fly's Boardinghouse and stepped inside. Camillius Fly's wife was there, and I asked if Doc Holliday was around.

"He left a while ago," she said. "You're Lomax, aren't you?"

I couldn't deny it. "I'll catch him later."

"He's been looking for you," she said. "I'm surprised you haven't been shot before now. I bet shoulder."

I crept around town, hoping to catch Doc unawares and plug him. I spent a good two hours looking but never caught sight of him, though I did glimpse the three Earps.

After much thinking I decided to hide out behind the O.K. Corral and try to ambush Doc from there. I leaned up against the corner of Papago's Store, from where I could see men passing on both Fremont Street and Fourth Street in front of Spangenberg's Gun Shop.

I'd been there maybe twenty minutes when I saw Frank McLaury and Billy Clanton ride up and dismount, tying their horses outside. As soon as their feet hit the ground, the gun shop door opened, and Tom McLaury and Ike Clanton stepped outside. The four men greeted each other, then strode inside. Ike was jawing so loudly I could hear him calling the Earps the biggest sons of bitches in North America.

When they disappeared inside, Frank McLaury's horse pulled its reins from the hitching post and stepped up on the walk, actually nudging the door open with its head.

According to town ordinances, horses weren't allowed on the sidewalks, but it wasn't all that rare for them to step up there. I wouldn't have thought much of it except that I noticed Wyatt Earp approaching. He saw the horse, seemed to recognize it, and strode toward it, taking the reins and jerking it toward the street.

No sooner had he touched the reins than the door to the gun shop opened, and the McLaurys and Billy Clanton emerged. Frank grabbed the reins from Wyatt.

"You'll have to keep the horse off the sidewalk," Wyatt barked.

Frank backed the gelding into the street. "Why do you Earps keep pestering us, spreading lies about us?" he wanted to know.

"You keep breaking the law, Frank. No other reason."

Frank growled as he tied the reins around the hitching rail and stepped back up on the boardwalk. "We're not going to take any more of this from you."

Wyatt shook his head. "Sure you are, Frank. Once you leave the shop with your new guns, it'll be my job to relieve you of them. There's an ordinance against carrying guns within the town limits." Steady as an oak tree, never flinching, he stood facing the three men.

Tom McLaury shoved Billy Clanton back inside, then grabbed his brother's arm and pulled him in as well.

Displaying the ultimate contempt, Wyatt turned his back to the door and stood for a moment staring across the street. That's when he saw me.

"Lomax," he called, "Doc's been looking for you."

I know he saw the gun, but I didn't linger.

"Doc says he wants to settle up his debt!" Earp yelled.

I shook my head and slipped alongside Papago's Store toward Fremont. Wyatt had given away my hiding place and would probably tell Doc where to find me. At the front of Papago's I looked both ways down Fremont, then scurried across the street like a bug hiding from the light. I took up a position between two buildings directly across from Fly's Boardinghouse, figuring the best thing to do was just wait and try to get off a shot at Holliday when he returned home, even if it meant staying there all night. Squatting behind a rain barrel, I watched the boardinghouse and the open lot beside it.

I waited. I figured if Doc gave up looking for me and took to playing poker, I might be there all night, but it wasn't half an hour before I had something to watch across the street.

The two Clantons and the two McLaurys appeared on Fremont, Frank and Billy leading their horses, and stopped at the boardinghouse. Ike and Tom went in. After a minute or two they returned to the street and motioned for Frank and Billy to lead their horses onto the vacant lot between Fly's and another house.

Like me, they all seemed nervous. They'd been there ten, maybe fifteen minutes when Sheriff Johnny Behan showed up, gesturing wildly to the Clantons and

McLaurys. Suddenly Ike pointed back down the street, and Behan spun around, dropping his hands to his belt and kneading them like he was scared.

Though I was scared, too, I poked my head out—and felt my knees turn mushy. Marching toward me were the three Earps and Doc Holliday. I'd never seen men look so mean and single-minded as those four did that afternoon. They could've faced the hordes of hell and come out with nothing less than a draw. I should've pulled my head back and gotten out of sight, but I just couldn't take my eyes off those mean men. They were wearing coats that hid their guns, but I glimpsed a shotgun under Holliday's. I gulped.

"I won't have any fighting!" Behan cried to Ike, his voice shaking. "Give me your firearms or leave town now!"

The Earps kept coming.

"They'll have no trouble from us, Johnny," Ike answered. "We're going to leave town."

Ike was as big a coward as ever turned tail and ran. The Earps and Holliday drew closer.

Behan abandoned the McLaurys and Clantons and scurried down the street. "I'll stop them!" he said, approaching the Earp party in front of Bauer's Butcher Shop. "Gentlemen, I'm sheriff of Cochise County, and I'm not going to allow any trouble." He was almost pleading.

The Earps stared toward the boardinghouse and brushed past him. Behan fell in step. "For God's sake don't go down there, or you'll get murdered!" he cried.

"I'm going to disarm them," Virgil announced, his voice hard.

"I've already disarmed them," Behan lied.

"Join 'em, Behan, or get out of the way," Wyatt called.

The sheriff got out of the way, and the Earps and Doc kept walking. I ducked behind the rain barrel and looked back at the Clantons and McLaurys, who were waiting nervously. For what seemed like an eternity, all of Tombstone stilled.

When the Earp group reached the vacant lot, I heard Morgan say, "Let them have it."

"Okay," Doc answered.

The four men turned toward the cowboys lined up in the vacant lot. Wyatt, Virgil, Morgan, and Doc stood with their backs to me, facing Ike Clanton, Frank McLaury, Tom McLaury, and Billy Clanton.

Wyatt called out to them, "You sons of bitches have been looking for a fight, and now you can have it!"

"Throw up your hands!" Virgil yelled. "We're going to disarm you, and there won't be any trouble."

Tom McLaury threw open his coat. "I've got nothing!"

"You sons of bitches out to make a fight?"

"No!" cried Billy Clanton. "I don't want to fight!"

There was another pause as they eyed one another. I feared no one would start shooting and give me an opportunity to kill Holliday. I'd never have a better chance than then to defend myself—but only if they'd start shooting. If they didn't, it might be Doc who ended up with the chance to shoot *me* in the back.

I lifted my Winchester to my shoulder, determined to settle my differences with Doc now even if the Earps and Clantons weren't about to resolve theirs.

Nobody moved.

I couldn't wait. Hands shaking, I leveled my Winchester at Holliday's back.

"No, I don't mean that!" cried Virgil Earp.

I didn't know if he was talking to the Clantons or his brothers and Doc. Or, God help me, if he had seen me drawing a bead on Doc. My hand quivered.

Holliday flinched, too, at Virgil's cry.

That's when I pulled the trigger. Instantly the street thundered with other gunshots.

Chapter Eighteen

I don't know how I missed Doc Holliday. Maybe I was so nervous my aim was bad. After all, I'd never before shot a man in the back, at least never when I was sober. Maybe Doc moved just as I fired. Maybe when he lifted his arm I hit his coat beneath the armpit. All I know is, I missed the son of a bitch.

The next thing I saw was Doc's hand with his nickel-plated pistol appearing from under his coat. The moment he fired, not a second after my shot, all hell broke loose.

The best I could tell, Doc fired the first shot and Morgan the next—after mine, of course.

Instantly Frank McLaury, who was still holding his horse, stumbled toward the street, grabbing for his gut and then his gun as he cursed Holliday. Billy Clanton took Morgan's bullet in the chest, grunted, and fell back against the side of the adjacent house, then slid down the weathered wood, leaving a smear of blood.

I guess I should've shot at Holliday again, but with my luck I'd've probably shot myself in the leg.

After the first shots there was a brief pause, maybe a couple seconds. Then Ike Clanton shot off his mouth. Though his brother was down and struggling to get up and draw his gun, Ike ran toward Wyatt Earp, swatting at his hand and screaming, "Don't shoot! Don't shoot! I'm unarmed!"

"Go to fighting," yelled Wyatt, "or get out of here!"

Coward that he was, Ike ran inside Fly's Boarding-house, abandoning the other three.

As he skedaddled, Wyatt fired, then Virgil. Holliday threw up his shotgun from under his long coat and shot at Tom McLaury, who was proclaiming he was unarmed. Tom stumbled backward, cursing and screaming as he grabbed his chest. Now both McLaurys and Billy Clanton were suffering from bad cases of lead poisoning—but they were as game as any men who ever trod this earth.

Still on his feet, Tom McLaury staggered past the Earps and down the street, crying for somebody to give him a gun. Billy Clanton, though he was hit bad, managed to pull his gun free and fire. He hit Virgil in the leg, knocking him down for a moment, but Virgil staggered back up and fired at Tom.

Billy Clanton, though, wasn't through. He shot at Morgan Earp.

"I'm hit!" Morgan yelled as he fell to the ground. But killing an Earp was harder than sweeping sunshine off the porch. Morgan pushed himself back up, apparently only dazed, and started shooting at Frank McLaury, even though Tom was closer.

Wyatt and Virgil kept firing at Billy Clanton, trying to kill him for sure, but Billy had more grit than a tubful of sand. Though he kept falling over, he fired anyway, winding up on his back, propped up with his right elbow and steadying his pistol left-handed on his bent left knee, still aiming at the Earps.

Frank McLaury's terrified horse finally jerked the reins from Frank's grip and galloped down the street. Frank stood with one hand over his bloody gut wound and the other aiming a pistol between Morgan and Holliday.

"I got you now," he said as he swung the pistol toward Holliday.

"You're damned if you do," Holliday answered just as Frank fired.

The bullet hit Doc on the hip, half spinning him around. "I'm shot!" he hollered, but he never left his feet. Instead he swung his gun around, took aim at

Frank, who was firing at Morgan, and squeezed the trigger.

Frank took a head wound from Doc or Morgan, who'd fired simultaneously.

Then the street was silent, though I could've sworn I heard a click as the hammer of Billy Clanton's gun fell on an empty hull. The whole thing had taken half a minute, little more, and everybody who had stood to fight the Earps was dead or dying.

Somebody ran to Billy Clanton and tried to jerk the revolver from his hand.

"Give me more cartridges," Billy pleaded. When no one did, he had nothing to live for, and the pain set in. He rolled and thrashed in the street until a couple fellows picked him up and carried him into a nearby house.

Frank McLaury was still breathing when Doc Holliday charged him. "That son of a bitch shot me, and I mean to kill him."

A couple men grabbed Holliday and pulled him away, assuring him that Frank was almost dead.

At first I was worried that someone might see me with the rifle and realize I had started all the shooting, but several other men came out onto the street carrying pistols and rifles. I joined them, passing by Frank McLaury, who by then was dead, lying half in the dusty street and half on the boardwalk.

Holliday was limping about a bit, and I hoped he had been hit, but it turned out Frank McLaury's bullet had glanced off his holster and not penetrated the cloth of his pants, much less the skin of his leg.

As a crowd began to gather, Holliday walked up to me, eyed the Winchester in my hands, then stared at me hard. Before I could say anything, he jerked up his pistol, pointed it at my chest, and pulled the trigger.

I figured I was a dead man, but the hammer of his nickel-plated gun fell on an empty chamber. The sound echoed through my quaking brain.

"Lomax, you're a lucky man. Your luck won't last the next time we meet."

I caught my breath, wondering if he'd known he was out of bullets when he pulled the trigger or if he had actually planned to kill me in front of so many witnesses. "No, you're the lucky man."

"A gambler makes his own luck." He turned and limped away.

Wyatt, who was luckier than a gambler, didn't have a scratch on him, though several bullets had punctured his overcoat. In all his years out West, I never heard of Wyatt ever getting touched by lead, though a lot thought he deserved a dose of his own medicine.

Sheriff Johnny Behan was one of those. No sooner had the crowds filled the street—making it safe from the possibility of more killing—than he marched out of Fly's Boardinghouse, where he had cowered like a child.

"I'll have to arrest you and your men," he announced to Wyatt.

"I won't be arrested, but I'll stand for what I've done. I won't leave town."

Behan shook his head. "That's not acceptable."

Wyatt pointed his finger at the sheriff. "Behan, you lied. You said they had been disarmed."

"No, I said I'd tried to disarm them."

"You'll not try to disarm or arrest me or my brothers." Wyatt turned to tend to the others. Morgan's and Virgil's weeping wives helped load them into a wagon a few sympathizers had brought up. The wagon carried them to Virgil's home, where I heard they forted up, uncertain of the mood of the town.

I retreated to the Stubborn Mule, shaken by what I had witnessed. I'd seen fights before—been in them on occasion—but never had I seen such a stand. When I got to the saloon, I marched up to the bar and placed my Winchester atop it. "Give me a bottle of whiskey," I ordered Til Walteree. The cure had been broken.

"You see the gunplay?" he asked as he brought me the whiskey.

I nodded, uncorked the bottle, and took a deep swig. There weren't enough minnows in the San Pedro River to keep me from drinking, not after that gunfight. The men who had killed the McLaurys and Billy Clanton weren't too happy with me, either, and I figured I'd be facing them myself in a matter of days.

Although I didn't know it at the time, the gunfight actually saved my life. Town sentiment was stacked against the Earps. Most folks seemed to know they had started the fracas and that one of their victims had been unarmed. That meant that the Earps and Holliday—the real snake in the dirty laundry—had to be on their best behavior until after the courts decided whether to charge them with murder.

I went through that whiskey bottle quicker than the pearly gates slam shut before a horse thief. It puts a man to thinking when men he has ridden with one day are dead by sundown the following day. There'd been a lot of talk, and I'd done my share of spreading rumors to protect my own hide, but the suddenness of the gunfight had shocked everyone: three men killed so quickly. The whole town felt vulnerable. Maybe that was why so many turned out for the funeral the next day.

The undertaker had done a fine job with the dead men, scrubbing their faces of the dirt that usually covered them and rouging their cheeks to give them the color that death had taken away. The three bodies were dressed in black suits and starched shirts and placed in polished black coffins trimmed in silver. Above the coffins in the undertaker's parlor hung a hand-lettered sign: MURDERED IN THE STREETS OF TOMBSTONE.

Come late afternoon, the bodies were loaded into two glass-sided hearses, Billy Clanton riding alone in the first and the two brothers riding together in the second. A group of musicians played a death march as the hearses crawled down Allen Street. The sidewalks were lined with the curious, most taking off their hats to offer their respects and many falling in behind the hearses and the band. I joined the procession to the cemetery, where two graves had been dug. The coffins were unloaded and toted to the graves, Billy Clanton to be buried in one, the McLaurys to be buried together in the other.

Many fine words were showered on the deceased, words nice enough to move grown men to tears. The McLaurys and Billy Clanton would've been proud had they not been dead. Then fireworks were shot off, and I could've sworn I saw the three bodies flinch as if the explosions were more shots from the guns of the Earps and Doc Holliday.

Ike Clanton was there, all somber and sober. Last I'd seen of him, he was running out on his brother and friends, but he sure got brave standing in a crowd with no Earps present. As I looked around, I realized that Curly Bill Brocius and Johnny Ringo were nowhere to be seen. It struck me as odd that those two fellows had not attended the funeral of their fellow rustlers and thieves. Maybe they were too grief-stricken to show themselves—or, knowing them, maybe they were out looting the McLaury and Clanton ranches.

Fact was, the funeral was barely over before men started talking about the absence of Brocius and Ringo. Some speculated they were drunk and had slept through the ceremony; others said they were planning to avenge the deaths as soon as they could get a good shot at the backs of the Earps or Holliday. Then there were rumors that Brocius and Ringo had set up the Clantons and McLaurys to be killed, and that Ike Clanton had told the Earps of the involvement of Brocius and Ringo in a couple stage robberies. There was also talk that the Earps had been involved with the Clantons and McLaurys in robbing stages by tipping them off when large shipments were going through.

One man I overheard said, "This's nothing but a bunch of stage robbers fighting among themselves."

That seemed about as likely as anything else.

I drifted with the crowd back to town, went to the Stubborn Mule, and tended bar, spelling Walteree for a while. For drinking men, the crowd that day was a solemn one.

When Walteree returned, he stuck his hand in his pocket and fished out the eighty dollars I'd left him for my funeral. "Here's your money back. I couldn't have afforded to put on as fine a show as the McLaurys and Billy Clanton got."

I shrugged. "They had more friends."

Walteree grinned. "It's a shame Joe Campbell isn't here to share his wisdom about death."

"Death is life," I said. "That's probably what he'd

say. But I could shoot holes in that faster than an Earp can plug a McLaury. Now the lawyers'll get involved to try and sort all this out, and things'll only get worse."

"A town can't become law-abiding without lawyers."

"Too much law is no different than no law," I replied.

"You're sounding like Joe Campbell."

"You're sounding like you might need to look for another job that pays you two dollars a day, Til."

He shook his head. "I'm satisfied here. You should be, too, now that business's picked up."

I had to admit I was pleased with the gradual increase in business, which I attributed to the departure of Joe Campbell. Despite the bigger crowd, the saloon emptied out early that night, and Walteree and I closed down and went our separate ways.

The gunfight had set Tombstone folks against one another. What had started as the killing of three grew into the killing of many.

I was on edge because somebody planted a foolish rumor that I'd tried to back-shoot Doc Holliday when the fight began. I don't know who would've started that rumor, because I thought I had hidden pretty well.

I felt a little better when Wyatt and Holliday were taken into custody. When bond was set at ten thousand dollars apiece, I figured they'd be cooling their heels in the jail for a good spell. I was wrong. Many of the men who ran businesses, and even Wyatt's lawyer, contributed more than the twenty thousand dollars necessary to get the two out. That was when I realized that the dividing line in Tombstone was between upstanding townfolk who wanted to make the place as respectable as themselves and the cowboys who lived outside of town and preferred to drink and gamble in a place as wild as themselves.

Two days after the shooting, I had the misfortune to run into Hattie Ketcham on the street. As soon as she saw me, she raised her stinger, ready to attack. She spit at my boots.

"You bastard, you're the cause of this, my uncles getting shot."

"Hell, you never liked them anyway. You only

courted me because I was brave enough to stand up to them."

"You aren't brave. You tried to shoot Doc Holliday in the back during the gunplay. That's true, isn't it?"

"The Earps wouldn't know the truth if it walked up and slapped them up 'side the head with an anvil."

"They're the law."

"I thought Behan was the law. He's the sheriff."

"You bastard. I'll see you dead yet!"

Then she started bawling and pounding her fists against her hips. I figured the only explanation was that she really loved me and was sorry about the trouble her lies and deceit had caused. Well, a woman's tears can melt a man faster than a campfire'll melt candle wax. I took a step forward, offering to comfort her. "So you still have feelings for me?"

Her tears disappeared faster than a roll of money in front of a lawyer. "Feelings for you? Hell, yes. I want to see you die."

I was as confused as a fireman in hell. "I thought you couldn't bear to see me die."

"I can't see you die, dammit, because my folks are pulling out of Tombstone, and I won't be around after tomorrow."

"You know where you're going?"

She shrugged.

"Then go to hell, Hattie." I spun around and left her cursing at me.

Getting Hattie out of Tombstone was the best thing that came out of the shoot-out. She left with Jim Earp and her mother a day or so later.

Five days after the gunfight, Justice of the Peace Wells Spicer opened the hearing to determine if the Earps and Doc Holliday should be bound over to the grand jury for murder. The courtroom in the Gird Block Building was crowded that afternoon when the session was gaveled to order at three o'clock.

Sheriff Johnny Behan had told me to be there to answer questions if I was called. I squeezed into the courtroom and plopped down on a bench, only to find I was

sitting next to Joe Campbell. On the other side of him sat
the lawyer Henry Guinn.

When Campbell realized I'd pulled into the stall beside him, he held his nose up in the air like he was too
good to be seen with a saloon owner. I ignored him for
a moment and leaned forward to address Henry Guinn.
"What's the status on the title to my land?"

Guinn didn't even look my way. "Joe, please inform
Mr. Lomax that the legal work is proceeding and that he
owes me another hundred and twenty-five dollars."

Campbell turned to me. "The legal work is proceeding and you owe another—"

"I heard him, Joe. I ain't deaf. Now, you tell the son
of a bitch that as much money as I've been paying him,
I deserve a direct answer from a man who'll look me in
the eye."

Joe turned to Guinn. "He says as much money as
he's been—"

"I heard him, Joe, but a man who would tell lies
about me to my kind wife deserves no better. The very
idea that I would take up with saloon girls is repulsive."

"You could have two or three for the same tonnage
as your wife," I offered, but the lawyer Guinn didn't
think that very funny.

"She's a decent woman," Campbell said huffily.

"She's meaner than a grizzly with a sore tooth and
just about as big," I responded. "I'd hate to be her husband if he ever slipped his marriage harness."

"That," said Henry Guinn, speaking directly to me
for the first time in weeks, "would never happen."

"If it did, no telling what she'd do to you."

"I have no more to say to you until you pay me another hundred and twenty-five dollars."

"Damn, what are you doing with all that money?
Burning it for firewood or paying freighters to haul in
food for Amelia?"

Guinn elbowed Campbell. "Tell him land transac-
tions are more expensive to straighten out when they're
done wrong than if he'd seen a good lawyer first."

I elbowed Campbell harder. "Tell Henry I didn't
know there *were* any good lawyers. Lawyers is what in-

terfered with my property in the first place. They're all greedy."

The lawyer Guinn butted in again. "Tell Lomax that avarice has nothing to do with it."

"Avarice has nothing to do with it."

"Who the hell is Avarice?" I wanted to know.

"I don't guess I've met him," Campbell admitted.

Guinn groaned.

"Are you still slapping people around with religion, Joe?" I asked. "Folks at the Stubborn Mule are glad to see you've gone on, though they think staying with a lawyer's a step down from preaching."

Guinn stomped his feet, slapped his thighs, and stood up. "We do not have to take this, Joe."

"All you have to take is my hundred and twenty-five dollars."

Guinn cleared his throat. "Let's find another seat where the company's better."

Joe Campbell was on his feet and on Guinn's tail faster than a hungry calf behind his momma at suckling time.

I pointed to the lawyers taking their places at the front of the court. "You might go up there among your own kind."

No sooner had they gotten up than three men squeezed into their places. They were rough-looking fellows who, judging by their aroma, hadn't bathed in a few months, but even so the smell was better than that of the lawyer.

I turned my attention to the lawyers up front. Thomas Fitch, a Republican with connections and a former member of the territorial legislature, was Wyatt Earp's lawyer. T. J. Drum was there to look out for Holliday's interests. The prosecutors were Lyttleton Price and Ben Goodrich, who, like Henry Guinn, neither drank nor gambled. I never could understand why so many lawyers never enjoyed some of the pleasures in life. I wondered if Goodrich had a fat wife, too, and if maybe there was something about fat women that I just didn't appreciate, other than shade in summer and warmth in winter.

When Judge Spicer entered, the room hushed and the proceedings began. The lawyers spoke their usual folderol, trying to make everyone else think they were smarter than they actually were, and then the hearing got under way.

Dr. H. M. Matthews, who served as the county coroner, testified first. Lawyers on both sides questioned him, and they all pretty much agreed that three men were dead and those three men had died of gunshot wounds and their names were Billy Clanton, Tom McLaury, and Frank McLaury.

Now, in my mind, you didn't have to be a doctor—or a lawyer, for that matter—to figure all that out. Half the folks in Tombstone could've testified to that without the title of lawyer or doctor in front of their names. Just establishing that three men were dead and who they were took the rest of the afternoon. When Judge Spicer adjourned the hearing until the next morning, we didn't know any more about who was at fault than we had right after the smoke had cleared. We did learn that Frank McLaury was wearing a pair of buckskin pants over another pair of pants. He'd've been better off wearing an iron shirt and hat.

The hearing resumed the next morning. We heard more testimony from folks who had been involved in the coroner's inquest or had had the misfortune to be on the street and witness part of the battle. As the days went on, I came to realize I was the only one other than the participants themselves who had seen the entire battle; everyone else had decided it wiser to hide than watch. But the more folks testified, the more I began to wonder if we'd been at the same gunfight.

We heard ten days of testimony before I was called to the stand. After placing my hand on the Bible and swearing to tell the truth, I took my seat by the judge's bench. I was nervous. Sitting at a table facing me were Wyatt Earp and Doc Holliday, scowling like they figured on teaching me some manners if they didn't like what I said. But they weren't near as intimidating as their lawyers.

The prosecutors started by asking me a few questions about what I was doing out on the street carrying my Winchester when it was against town ordinances.

"Trying to protect myself," I answered.

"Who would want to harm you?"

I pointed to Doc Holliday and Wyatt Earp. "They'd threatened to kill me. I was just making sure I had a chance if I ran into them."

"And why were they threatening to kill you?" Lyttleton Price wanted to know.

There were several reasons, but only one that mattered. "I testified in Tucson that I didn't think Frank Stilwell robbed the Bisbee stage."

"Why should they want to kill you for that?"

"Stilwell's who they pinned the robbery on."

"You were on that stage, were you not?"

"Yes, sir."

"And why didn't you think it was Frank Stilwell?"

"Because the robber was skinny and seemed to have consumption."

"Are you a doctor?"

"No, but I've been close enough to lungers to know the smell."

"The smell?"

"His breath," I replied.

"Are you saying the robber was Doc Holliday?"

"I'm saying the robber had lunger breath. I couldn't be certain who it was, but it was a lunger."

"Could it've been Holliday?"

"I reckon."

"So you thought they were out to kill you."

"Yes, and I got nervous when the four of them came down the street. I couldn't be certain they weren't after me."

"What'd you do?"

"I hid behind a barrel between two buildings facing Fly's Boardinghouse."

"So you saw the whole thing?"

"From start to finish."

"You alone among all the witnesses saw it all?"

"I reckon."

"Who fired the first shots?"

Now, I had sworn to tell the truth, and I guess I'd've had to admit to firing my rifle off had he asked me who fired the first *shot,* but he said *shots.* It threw me for a moment. "It was a nickel-plated pistol, so it had to be Doc Holliday, then Morgan Earp."

Wyatt's eyes narrowed. I wasn't making any better friends with the Earps, but maybe if I testified good enough the whole lot of them would be spending a little time in prison.

The prosecutors asked me to recall the sequence of events. I did it as best I could, although I began to realize how your mind could play tricks on you and how you could make a mistake without meaning to. I went through the thing step by step, answering all questions and trying to help the judge understand what dangerous sons of bitches the Earps and Holliday were.

The more I told the story, the more comfortable I got, especially when the questions focused on what happened rather than on why I was there to begin with. I felt certain I'd blackened the name of the Earps enough that they'd be in prison for a good while.

I was especially confident when the lawyer brought up my encounter with Doc Holliday.

"Did you run into Doc Holliday moments after the gunfight?"

"I did."

"And how did Holliday greet you?"

"He lifted his revolver and pointed it at my chest."

"Then what happened?"

"He pulled the trigger."

"How did you survive?"

"His gun was empty."

"What did he say after that?"

"He said I was a lucky man, but that my luck would run out the next time I got close to him."

"Did you take that as a threat?"

"Coming from Doc Holliday, most certainly. No sane man would take it any other way."

"Then what happened?"

"Doc just walked away. I didn't go near him again."

The prosecuting attorney ended his questions and

thanked me for my honesty. Glad that somebody had stated that for the record, I pushed myself up from the chair.

"Hold on, Mr. Lomax," said Judge Spicer. "You have to undergo cross-examination."

I knew I was in trouble when Wyatt Earp's lawyer stood up and sauntered over to me.

Chapter Nineteen

Even before he asked his first question, I decided the name Tom Fitch was just another way of saying son of a bitch. Earp's lawyer was a cocky, strutting fellow. He strode up opposite me, grabbed the lapels of his coat, and stared at me as if I was a criminal like his client.

"Tell me, Mr. Lomax: After you testified in Tucson at the Frank Stilwell trial, did you return by train to Contention?"

"I did."

"And with whom did you ride on that train?"

"All the passengers, the engineer, the fireman, the brakeman, the conductor."

The spectators laughed, as did Fitch.

"I see you're a literalist," he said.

"No need to go insulting me."

Fitch grinned again. "Let me rephrase the question. Who was the one person you sat with on the train?"

"Frank Stilwell," I admitted.

"And after you arrived in Contention, who'd you ride back to Tombstone with?"

I sighed. "Frank Stilwell and some others."

"Just who were those others?"

"The Clantons, the McLaurys."

Fitch rubbed his chin. "So you were good friends with the Clantons and McLaurys, were you not?"

"No, I was not."

The lawyer grimaced, then pointed his finger at me. "Odd behavior, then, Mr. Lomax, if you ride into Tombstone with men you don't like."

"Some of them had threatened to kill me."

"Who?"

"Ike Clanton and Frank McLaury."

Fitch laughed. "Now, let me get this straight. My client, Wyatt Earp, and his brothers, as well as Doc Holliday and Ike Clanton and Frank McLaury, all threatened to kill you. Is that right?"

I nodded.

"The judge can't hear you."

"Yes, that's true."

"How is it that everybody is out to shoot you?"

"I make friends easily, I guess."

The spectators laughed again, but Fitch bore into me with his eyes.

"Could it be that you've been known to cut their drinks with tobacco drippings, among other things?"

I didn't care to answer that question, so I tried to switch trails. "Several men were looking for an excuse to shoot me to settle their bets."

"Bets? On what?"

"Bets on where I'd get shot."

"What are you talking about?"

"When my bartender Joe Campbell was shot, a lot of men thought he'd taken a bullet intended for me. Everybody started betting on whether I'd take it in the back, the gut, the chest, the arm, the head, or such."

"Mr. Lomax, do you expect me and the other fine citizens of Tombstone gathered here today to believe such nonsense?"

"It's the truth."

"The truth is what we are here to determine, Mr. Lomax, and I don't believe you are being straight with your answers. Now, answer this: On the way from Contention to Tombstone, did you ever mention the Earps to all your companions, who, according to you, were not your friends?"

"Their names came up a time or two."

"And when they did, did you say anything that might be considered derogatory?"

I paused to think. I was under oath and knew the smartest thing might have been to lie, but I just couldn't. "A few times, yes."

"Like what?"

"Like they were dirty sons of bitches. But I didn't take that for derogatory, just the truth."

The spectators laughed, but the judge gaveled them down and turned to me. "Mr. Lomax, you will refrain from using vulgar language in this court."

I knew I had to consider what the judge wanted if I was to get what I wanted—the Earps and Holliday in prison for a few years. "Yes, sir," I replied contritely.

Fitch continued. "Now, then, Mr. Lomax, on that ride back to town, did you ever mention to your friends—or is it enemies?—that the Earps had threatened to kill them?"

"I don't recall specifically."

"Were you trying to stir up trouble?"

"No."

"Were you trying to protect your own hide, Mr. Lomax?"

"What are you talking about?"

"Well, sir, you've as much as said you have no friends in Tombstone, at least among the combatants, several of whom had threatened to kill you, according to your story. Is it possible you were trying to fan the flames of animosity between them so that maybe the men who had scores to settle with you might kill each other off?"

Fitch was a damn smart lawyer to be able to figure all that out. I was faced with a tough choice: Should I lie under oath or tell the truth? I stalled. "Repeat the question?"

"Were you trying to turn the Clantons and Mc-Laurys against the Earps?"

Before I could answer, the prosecutor jumped to his feet. "Objection! This line of questioning is not pertinent to the facts of the shooting."

"Sustained," said the judge. "Continue."

Fitch nodded, took a deep breath, and let it out slowly. "The day of the murders, were you—"

"Objection!" screamed the prosecutor again. "The object of this hearing is to determine whether or not it was murder."

"Sustained."

Fitch grimaced, then bit his lip a moment. "The day of the shooting, you were carrying a gun around. What kind of gun was it?"

"A Winchester forty-four-forty."

"Why?"

"To protect myself."

"From what?"

"Doc Holliday."

"Were you planning to kill Doc, perhaps ambush him?"

"I intended to protect myself."

"Were you not in cahoots with the Clantons and McLaurys on a devious scheme you worked out on the way back to Tombstone from Contention?"

"No."

"Wasn't it your plan to stir things up so the Earps would come after the Clantons and McLaurys and you'd be there with your Winchester ready to shoot them in the back?"

"No. I had no intention of shooting the Earps in the back." That was the truth; I had planned to shoot Doc Holliday in the back.

Fitch shook his head like he didn't believe me. "When the shooting started, did you fire at the Earps or Holliday?"

I'd shot before the shooting started, so I could answer his question without lying. "When the shooting started, I didn't fire my gun."

"Why? Were you a coward who couldn't follow through with his plan?"

The prosecutor stood up. "Objection."

"Sustained," said the judge. "Stick to the facts of the case."

I knew where Fitch could stick the facts as far as I was concerned, but I didn't think the judge needed my advice. From that point on, Fitch tried to shake my account of what had happened in the gunfight. But I stuck to my story.

"How is it, Mr. Lomax, that while everybody is seeking cover when the gunfire starts, you're watching the whole proceedings without so much as ducking?"

"I was partially hidden, I guess."

"You're either the bravest or the stupidest man in Tombstone, wouldn't you say?"

"Objection!" cried Price.

"Sustained," said Spicer.

"From where did you see the fight?"

"Across the street."

"Were the backs of the Earp party toward you when the shooting started?"

"Yes."

"Mr. Lomax," he continued, "I want you to understand that whoever fired the first shot in this unfortunate battle carries the blame for three deaths upon his shoulders."

I wondered if he knew I had fired the initial shot or if he was just trying to shift the blame from the Earp party to the Clantons and McLaurys.

"Now, Mr. Lomax, think very carefully. Who shot first, the Earp party or the Clanton party?"

"The Earps," I replied truthfully.

"Who among them?"

"The nickel-plated revolver fired first, so it had to be Doc Holliday. Then Morgan Earp got a shot off before any of the McLaurys or Clantons had a chance to fire."

Fitch grinned, making me feel a mite uneasy. I'd accused his clients of starting it all, but he didn't seem at all concerned.

"Is your eyesight good, Mr. Lomax?"

"Pretty near as good as I need."

"What were the Earps and Mr. Holliday wearing that day?"

"Clothes. What else?"

"But what did they have on over their clothes?"

"Long coats."

"Can you see through coats?"

I couldn't help but scratch my head. "Huh?"

"Can you see through coats? Like the long coats the Earp brothers and Doc Holliday were wearing?"

"No, of course not."

"Then how is it you can be behind the Earp brothers and still see who fired the first shot?"

"I saw it."

"You're across Fremont Street. It's eighty feet wide, the widest street in Tombstone."

"I know that."

"You're eighty feet away, and the men you accuse of firing first are wearing long coats. You can see their backs. And that's it."

"I saw when they drew. I heard the shots and saw the smoke."

"How can you be sure? Didn't the Earps block your view of Billy Clanton and the McLaurys?"

"Somewhat."

"Then you can't be certain of anything, now, can you, Mr. Lomax?"

"Sure I can."

Fitch turned around in disgust and walked back toward Wyatt Earp and Doc Holliday. "No wonder you don't have any friends in Tombstone."

"Objection!" cried the prosecutor.

"Strike that comment from the record. Are you through with your questioning, Mr. Fitch?"

"Yes, Your Honor."

"You may step down, Mr. Lomax."

I stood up, but my knees were shaky. Among the spectators I saw Henry Guinn and Joe Campbell snickering. I wanted to go over and slap them across the head, but I didn't figure that would impress the judge.

After me, Ike Clanton began his testimony. He was all dressed up in coat and tie and looked clean enough to be buried. It was the only time I ever saw him without a little tobacco in his mouth. He was told to identify himself.

"My name is Joseph Isaac Clanton. I reside four miles above Charleston on the San Pedro and am a stock raiser and cattle dealer."

And a murderer, thief, coward, and liar, I thought. I'd've had more respect for him if he'd said he was a rustler.

The prosecutor asked him where he'd been on October twenty-sixth. Clanton replied he'd been on the streets of Tombstone. He was asked if he knew the Earps and Doc Holliday. Scowling at Wyatt and Doc, he said he did.

"Did you know Frank and Tom McLaury and Billy Clanton?"

Hell, Billy was his brother, and everybody in Tombstone knew the Clantons and McLaurys ran together. These damn lawyers sure spent a lot of time plowing the same field.

"Yes, sir," replied Ike.

"Are they alive?"

"They're dead. They died on October twenty-six, murdered on Fremont Street between Third and Fourth."

"Did they die a natural death or a violent death?"

"A violent death. They were killed."

I figured everybody in the courtroom was going to die before they got around to the nub of the matter. The lawyer asked Ike to recount the events leading up to the fight, starting with when he arrived in Tombstone.

"I came into town the twenty-fifth of October, riding with Tom McLaury."

"Did you ride in with Frank McLaury, Billy Clanton, Frank Stilwell, H. H. Lomax, or anybody else that day?"

Ike looked for me in the crowd, held up his jaw, and shook his head. "I did not."

The lying son of a bitch. I wanted to stand up right then and tell him what I thought of that, but I bit my tongue, figuring I had more to fear from the Earps and Holliday than from Ike.

Then Ike testified about the gunfight itself, saying he and Tom McLaury hadn't been armed, that Morgan had shot Billy Clanton from two or three feet away when Billy's hands were in the air, and that Doc had shot Frank McLaury. Ike described the gunfight at length, favoring his side of things, until the session was adjourned for the day.

When court resumed the next day, the prosecutors questioned Ike about his relationship with Wyatt Earp before the gunfight. Ike told a curious story about Wyatt approaching him after the Benson stage robbery in which Bud Philpot had been killed. Wyatt offered Ike six thousand dollars if he would tell him where the three suspects—Billy Leonard, Harry Head, and Jim Crane—could be found and killed.

"When I asked Wyatt why he wasn't interested in bringing them in to trial, he told me they knew that Morgan Earp and Doc Holliday had been involved in the robbery."

"Why was Wyatt so worried that such word would get out?" asked Fitch.

"Wyatt was planning on running for sheriff of Cochise County and feared rumors like that would harm his chances."

"Is that why he never ran?"

"I never understood why he didn't, being as Head, Leonard, and Crane were all killed before the election. I guess you'd have to ask Wyatt."

During four days of testimony Clanton answered every question, some over and over again. By the time he was through, I had to agree the Earps and Holliday were about the biggest sons of bitches in Cochise County, save for Ike himself.

Three weeks after the gunfight, Wyatt Earp took the stand. The courtroom was packed. Tensions were still running high in town. Morgan and Virgil were still recovering at home from their wounds; word had it their women were carrying guns to defend themselves and their home in the event that attempts were made on their husbands' lives.

Right off, Wyatt's attorney asked him to offer his explanation of the events leading up to the gunfight. Wyatt countered Ike's testimony, saying he had indeed gone to Ike and Frank McLaury to seek their help in catching Head, Leonard, and Crane because he did plan to run for sheriff. He said he had offered Ike and Frank the reward of thirty-six hundred dollars for their capture, not their death, and that the only explanation for Ike remembering six thousand was that his arithmetic was as bad as his memory. Wyatt said he had promised to keep that offer secret and would have to this day were he not under oath to tell the truth.

"Ike Clanton lied that I said Morgan and Doc Holliday had anything to do with any stage robbery. It had nothing to do with me not running for sheriff. Johnny Behan told me if I wouldn't run, he would hire me after he was elected. He never did."

After Head, Leonard, and Crane wound up getting killed anyway, Wyatt said Ike and Frank McLaury began to get nervous that Curly Bill Brocius and Johnny Ringo might find out they had dealt with the Earps and come looking for them.

"After that," Wyatt told the court, "the Clantons and McLaurys started spreading rumors about us and our family, saying our wives were women of bad repute, that Frank was sparking my niece Hattie, and that Morgan and Doc had been involved in stage robberies. If that wasn't enough, they started threatening us. When we heard four of them were waiting for us around the back of the O.K. Corral with guns, we figured we best arrest them and bring them in before they back-shot us.

"I was tired of the threats from Ike Clanton and his gang. I believed they intended to assassinate us if they had a chance. I decided if I had to fight them, I wanted to face them in the open."

Wyatt then described his encounter with the Clantons and McLaurys at the gun shop when Frank's horse had stepped up on the sidewalk. Then he told about walking with Virgil, Morgan, and Doc to confront the Clanton gang. He dismissed Sheriff Johnny Behan's comments that the men had been disarmed as a further ploy to get him, his brothers, and Holliday killed. When efforts to disarm them failed, Wyatt said, the shooting had begun.

Then he started to lie. "Frank McLaury and Billy Clanton drew their pistols," he testified, "and I drew mine. The first two shots were fired by me and Billy Clanton, though I can't say which of us fired first. I shot for Frank McLaury, who was a dangerous man and a good shot by reputation. Virgil fired the next shot. After that everybody started firing except Ike Clanton. He ran by, grabbed my arm, and screamed, 'Don't shoot! Don't shoot! I'm unarmed!' I shoved him aside and never shot at him since I believed he was unarmed. Then I commenced to shooting at Billy Clanton and Frank McLaury."

By his words Wyatt confirmed for me that Morgan and Doc had been involved in the stage holdups. Those two had the sorriest reputations among the Earp party, both being heavy drinkers and hotheads. I knew they'd started the gunfight—not counting my first shot—and Wyatt was trying to cover their tracks.

Wyatt's attorney introduced as evidence a letter signed by more than sixty upstanding citizens of Dodge City, Kansas, vouching for Wyatt's character. It sure made me doubt the wisdom of folks in Kansas. I'd always thought people in Missouri were dumber, but that letter made me reconsider.

Wyatt held his own during cross-examination and was dismissed after a full day on the stand.

Three days later, Virgil Earp, still nursing his wound, came to the court and swore he would tell the truth. But like Wyatt he lied, saying that Billy Clanton and Frank McLaury had drawn first and commenced the battle. After he testified, a half-dozen other witnesses took the stand and gave their recollections of the bits of the story they knew.

The hearings ended the next to the last day of November. Judge Spicer gave his ruling the following afternoon.

The courtroom was hushed as Spicer read his decision. He started by noting the eminent legal talent employed by both sides in the matter, and I almost puked right there. As far as I was concerned, folks on both sides had lied so much they'd be provided a special place in hell, with the lawyers at the head of the line.

Spicer said the conflicting accounts—a lawyer's way of saying a lot of folks were lying—forced him to make his decision based on those facts that people could agree on. He pointed the initial blame at Ike Clanton for run-

ning at the mouth that morning and challenging the
Earps and Holliday to a showdown. Though Virgil Earp
was the marshal and it was within his authority as marshal to arrest Ike and the others who had joined him, he
had used poor judgment in allowing his brothers and
Holliday to accompany him. Even so, Virgil could not be
held accountable for that, as he had asked Sheriff Behan
for assistance earlier and been refused, and consequently
Spicer could find no criminal wrongdoing in Virgil's actions. He was merely trying to do his job and protect his
life.

As to the events at the battle itself, Spicer said the
weight of evidence corroborated the testimony of Wyatt
and Virgil Earp and the killings could not be viewed as
murder because the Earp party, acting within the lawful
jurisdiction of their office, faced the Clanton party with
the intent to arrest rather than kill. Further, Spicer said,
the fact that Ike Clanton, the instigator of so much of the
difficulty, was not shot when he proclaimed he was unarmed stood solidly in line with the Earps' account.

Finally Spicer looked at the court and gave his final
decision. "I conclude that the defendants, in the dis-
charge of their official business, were fully justified in
committing these homicides. There being no sufficient
cause to find the defendants guilty of the offense of
which they have been accused, I order them released."

The defendants jumped up and clapped, their lawyers slapping them on the back. As puny as Holliday was,
I thought his lawyer was going to kill him before he
stopped.

As for me, I was in more danger now than I had
been on October 26.

All of Tombstone was nervous, and tensions were
heightened by the approach of the city elections, scheduled for January third. Rumor was, the Earps didn't know
how to read the feelings against them, so none of them
were running for Virgil's position as marshal. Instead
they backed a former deputy marshal and a sympathetic
candidate for mayor. After the election and swearing-in,
the candidate they had backed would resign as marshal,
and the sympathetic mayor would appoint one of the

Earps in his place. If that happened, the Earps and even Doc Holliday would be able to justify all their future killings as enforcing the law.

Six days before the election, somebody ambushed Virgil Earp as he was coming out of the Oriental Saloon just before midnight. Some said as many as twenty shots were fired, though I don't know how they would know unless they were firing them. Virgil took a bullet in the left arm and one in the side. He lived, though Doc Goodfellow told him he'd have to amputate the arm. Virgil refused to allow it, so the doctor was forced to remove the elbow joint and the shattered bone around it. Virgil kept his left arm, but it was useless.

I felt a little better about things after the ambush, knowing there was one less Earp around to pester me and that some folks in Tombstone were no better shots ambushing a man than I was when I had aimed at Doc Holliday.

Rumor had it that Ike Clanton and Frank Stilwell had been behind the ambush. I figured the shooting might create a little sympathy for the Earp faction in the town election, but I was wrong. The voters turned against them and rejected their candidates.

I was breathing a little easier over things, thinking I could keep my business going and stay out of trouble in Tombstone now that the Earps had lost their badges.

I was wrong again.

No sooner were the election results announced than the U.S. marshal for Arizona Territory wired Tombstone and offered a deputy marshal appointment to Wyatt Earp. When Wyatt accepted the appointment, I knew I had better clear out of Tombstone for a while, because he planned to clear up the bad men of Cochise County. I didn't count myself among them, but I doubted that Wyatt would agree. I figured I'd get shot "accidentally" by one of the Earps, and everyone'd be able to settle their bets—provided the Earps didn't kill every man and male child in Cochise County first.

"I wouldn't want to be in your boots," Til Walteree told me. "You planning on leaving town?"

I was, but I didn't want to tell anyone, not even Til. "They can't run me out of town."

He just nodded and went about wiping down the bar.

Three days after the election, I marched over to the O.K. Corral and settled my bill for Flash.

John Montgomery eyed me suspiciously. "Clearing out, are you, now that Wyatt's got a badge?"

"Nope, I just remembered it was time to pay up."

"Sure, Lomax. You're scared, and you know it."

"Maybe, but I'm not leaving." I dug into my pocket and pulled out a wad of profits from the Stubborn Mule. Montgomery about tripped over his jaw at the sight of so much money. "There's more profit in filling whiskey glasses for men than water troughs for horses and mules," I said, peeling off enough bills to pay for Flash's care for six months. "That convince you I'm staying?"

Montgomery grabbed the money. "Whatever you say, Lomax. I always knew you were as brave as the best of them."

I still had a good chunk of money, so I marched over to Henry Guinn's place and knocked on the door. Joe Campbell opened it.

"You look like you've lost weight, Joe," I said. "You having trouble wrestling food from that sow Amelia come slop time?"

The door swung open farther, and there stood Amelia herself, ample arms over ample bosom.

"Afternoon, ma'am. You're looking as bountiful as ever," I said, taking off my hat before she could knock it off.

"Did you say bountiful or beautiful?" Campbell wanted to know.

"Beautiful, of course."

"Tell him he's a liar," Amelia said to Joe.

"You're a liar," Campbell repeated.

"I'm here to talk to your husband on my land problem."

"I'm not talking to you," Amelia said. "You've got to talk to me through Mr. Campbell."

"Hell, you sure are getting uppity."

"Tell him not to use that kind of language around me."

"Don't use that kind of language around her," Campbell said.

"I know. I heard her to begin with." I slapped my hat back on my head and wished I had something big enough to hit her with. Only problem was, she was so big that even if I did hit her it would probably take her a couple days to realize it. "I want to know the status on my legal work."

"He wants to check what's been done on his legal work," Campbell repeated.

"Tell him I'll ask."

"She'll ask."

Amelia waddled off into her husband's room while I stood waiting.

I talked to Campbell. "Religion's been your downfall, Joe. Once you got religion, you went to hell."

"I wish you wouldn't use that type of language around me."

"How about around Amelia? I bet there ain't a word big enough to go around Amelia." I laughed, but Campbell didn't, or if he did I didn't hear it for the rumble of Amelia waddling back across the parlor floor.

She stopped behind Campbell, all out of breath from the exertion. "Tell the iniquitous saloon owner that nothing's changed other than his bill."

"Nothing's changed other than your bill."

"It was a hundred and twenty-five dollars when the Earp hearing started."

"Tell him it's two hundred and ten dollars now," she said, grinning greedily.

"It's two hundred and ten dollars now," Campbell echoed.

"Damn! Has the cost of groceries gone up that much?"

"Has the cost of groceries gone up that much?" Campbell asked.

She punched him on the shoulder. "That's an insult."

"That's an insult," Campbell told me.

"Maybe it is," I replied, "but it didn't cost you a thing. I'll get back to you when I've got the money."

I returned to the Stubborn Mule and made Til Walteree promise to take care of business for me, since I would have to be careful now that the Earps were wearing badges again.

"You *are* leaving town, aren't you?"

"I can't say."

"I won't tell."

I left the saloon and walked over to the Bird Cage Theater, which had just opened after Christmas and featured a bar and gambling tables in front of the stage. I went in, had a drink, and when no one was looking slipped backstage and stole a wig and fake beard they were using in some play.

Then I returned home and kicked Satan across the parlor for good measure. I got under my bed and took the money from the tin box but not the legal papers or Hattie Ketcham's letters. Altogether I had six or seven thousand dollars in profits from the Stubborn Mule.

I packed the money on me and in my valise, then waited until dark. Wearing the wig and fake beard, I went to catch the stage. Luckily, none of the Earps were around, nor Johnny Ringo, Curly Bill, or any of the others who had threatened to kill me.

The stage took me to Contention, where I caught the train. Even though it was winter, I headed up north, figuring to get as far away from Tombstone and the Earps as I could. I wasn't certain whether I'd return or not, but if I did, it wouldn't be for a while, not until the trouble blew over.

I was right.

Chapter Twenty

By the time I stopped heading north by train, stage, and horse, I was in the Dakotas. I lost most of my money on gambling and liquor and was feeling low about that. About the time winter was ending and the land was greening, I decided to return to Cane Hill and visit my momma for the first time since I had left my Arkansas home right after the War Between the States.

I caught a Missouri River steamboat and rode the spring thaw toward home. I still had about five hundred dollars on me when I got on the steamboat, but I lost most of it to the gamblers on board. And when I tried to win it back, the gamblers—all decent fellows when I was losing—got mad that I had an extra card up my sleeve and threw me into the river outside of St. Joseph, Missouri. An old acquaintance there gave me enough money to buy a new suit and to ride the train all the way into Fayetteville, just a few miles from Cane Hill.

When I left Cane Hill, I wasn't sure where I was going, and I wound up in Texas for a spell. I thought about visiting two of my brothers who'd settled there—Jim, a rancher, and Andy, a Texas Ranger. But I figured Jim'd want to put me to work and Andy'd probably want to arrest me for showing up. Too, Texas had a certain smell about it. Texans seemed to have about as much manure on the outside of their boots as on the inside, and there were a lot of cattle in Texas.

By the time July rolled around, I'd had about enough of the heat and the smell and figured I might as well head back to Arizona and try to pick up my life and my profits in Tombstone. Arizona would be as hot as Texas, but at least it wouldn't stink as much. I'd done odd jobs and had enough money to buy a train ticket back and then maybe a broken-down horse and possibly a gun to defend myself.

I started back for Arizona, uncertain what I'd find. From the news accounts I occasionally picked up, it seemed things there had gone to hell—along with several men.

After Virgil was shot, Wyatt, as deputy marshal, had gone in search of his ambushers, who included Ike Clanton and a half-dozen others. Sheriff Johnny Behan had raised his own posse to arrest and protect his buddies from Wyatt and his men. So all these posses were riding around Cochise County looking for each other.

The kettle had heated up in the middle of March, when Morgan Earp was shot in the back while playing pool in Robert Hatch's saloon on Allen Street. He might've lived if he'd given his business to the Stubborn Mule, because I never had a killing in my saloon.

There were a lot of suspects in the killing, including Sheriff Behan, but the suspicion finally rested on Ike Clanton, Frank Stilwell, Curly Bill Brocius, and Pete Spencer. Wyatt and Doc Holliday plugged Stilwell a day or two later at the train station in Tucson. Later, at a place called Iron Springs, Wyatt and Doc ran into Curly Bill Brocius and his gang, and Wyatt killed Curly Bill.

The more men that I heard were dead, the better I felt about my return. If Behan, Wyatt, Ike, Doc, and Ringo could just get together and shoot it out, I could live in peace in Tombstone, provided Hattie Ketcham never showed up again.

Even so, I figured it best to approach the town cautiously. Rather than ride the train to Benson and on to Contention, I figured I'd get off at San Simon, northeast of Tombstone. Then I'd make my way south to Galeyville, in the Chiricahuas, and on west across the mountains. That way I'd avoid the main roads between Tombstone and Bisbee or Benson.

When I got off the train at San Simon, I was looking at a dusty town that looked deader than Frank Stilwell and Curly Bill. There were only a dozen or so buildings, and everybody must've been inside taking an afternoon siesta. As hot as it was, I didn't blame them.

Inside the small station the agent eyed me like he was expecting a better class of passenger. He was a skinny, quiet fellow with a nervous habit of licking his lips. He wore a green eyeshade and garters on his shirtsleeves.

"Where can a fellow buy a horse and gun?" I asked.

He licked his lips, then popped a sleeve garter. "Not much for sale around here."

"All I need's a mount, a gun, and some ammunition."

The agent snorted. "That's all anybody needs around these parts. Water isn't nearly as scarce as horses, guns, and bullets. There's an adobe down the road with a clapboard sign out front that says 'Buy and Trade.' An old Mexican's got some broken-down animals in the corral out back and a few things inside."

I thanked the agent and made my way outside and down the street to the small adobe. The building was cool and dark, lit only by the shafts of sunlight slipping in through the windows. Before my eyes could adjust to the dimness, the proprietor was beside me.

"*Buenos días, señor,*" he said.

He was a small man, brown as a bean, wearing a loose shirt, white baggy pants with a rope for a belt, and sandals.

"I need a few things—a dependable horse to get me to Tombstone, a decent gun for protection, and a few supplies."

The old man pointed me toward the back corner. "I keep my guns there."

I walked over to a small glass case and looked at his selection of firearms. Immediately I saw the gun I wanted, because it was the only one he had. "Let me look at that one," I said.

It was a battered .45-caliber Colt revolver with a serial number I would never forget: 222. I checked the six-shot cylinder and saw that it was empty, then lifted it toward the far wall and cocked the hammer. I barely touched the trigger, and the hammer fell on an empty chamber. The trigger seemed a mite sensitive, but I didn't figure that would be a problem. "What are you asking?"

"Twenty dollars."

"Too high. I'll give you thirteen dollars if you throw in a holster and some ammunition."

The Mexican reached toward a peg behind the gun counter and pulled down a gun belt with three bullets in the cartridge loops.

"Throw in the ammunition and you've got a deal on the pistol," I said.

He pointed to the three bullets in the gun belt. "There is the ammunition. No more have I."

"Three bullets? That's all?"

He shrugged. "Men will sell me their guns before they sell their bullets. You are lucky to get three. Everyone saves bullets for the Earp gang or Sheriff Behan's posse."

I tucked the pistol in my britches and slapped the gun belt around my waist. It would do. "I'll take it." I pushed the three bullets out and pulled the gun from my britches, ready to load it.

"Don't do that."

"Do what?"

"Load the gun inside."

"Why not?"

"No loaded guns in the store."

I shrugged. It seemed kind of stupid to me, but I didn't argue with him. I still had some other purchases to make.

"I want a canteen and seven dollars' worth of grub."

The old man stepped to a small table, where he picked up a gunnysack and filled it with a few supplies.

When he brought me the sack, I asked, "You got any animals that'll get me to Tombstone?"

"I have three horses and a donkey." He motioned for me to follow him outside. When we emerged into the bright sunshine, I was blinded for a moment. I followed him out to a small corral behind his store and shook my head. There wasn't much there, only a donkey and three old nags that couldn't have broken wind without tuckering out.

"That's the best you got?"

"Those are the best-looking horses for sale in San Simon."

"I've seen dogs that could carry me farther."

The horses must've heard us talking, because they hung their heads. I figured I could die of old age and get my own tombstone with my name chiseled on it before any of these horses could get me to Tombstone and my saloon. "Nope. Those horses wouldn't make a good meal for a buzzard. I'll take the donkey."

"Twenty-five dollars."

I pulled out my money roll and paid him. He smiled. Then I pulled out the revolver to load it, but the old man must've thought I was going to rob him.

"No, no! Don't shoot!"

I waved him off and loaded the three bullets in the cylinder and spun it around, noting that it stopped on a live round. Then I shoved the gun hard into its holster.

That was a mistake.

Kaboom! went the pistol.

I about jumped out of my boots, which was a good thing because the bullet dug into the ground right beside my foot, kicking up the hard pack.

The Mexican trembled like I had threatened him. All I'd done was load the revolver and almost shoot my foot off. I don't know why he should've been any scareder than me, because the bullet had come closer to my flesh than to his.

"Ooops," I said sheepishly. I changed the subject. "You got a saddle and bridle?"

He shook his head. "Just a hackamore and rope." He pointed to a fence post. "Take and ride away, fast."

I was a bit hurt that the old man seemed so anxious to get rid of me, especially after I'd given him such good business, but I swallowed my pride and marched to the fence post, where I grabbed the leather halter and eased over to the donkey. He was a small animal, not at all skittish at my approach. I patted him on the neck, then slipped the halter over his head and led him to the gate. Without a saddle I had nothing to tie my canteen and gunnysack to, so I looped a length of rope around the donkey's chest and tied my supplies to it.

When I was ready, the old man unlatched and swung open the gate. The donkey didn't seem to think nearly as highly of me when I was on his back as when I was standing beside him. My feet were about six inches from dragging on the ground, and I was sitting on the gnarliest backbone I'd ever encountered. I wasn't sure I could stand the pain all the way to Tombstone. But I knew Flash was awaiting me there. If Til Walteree had been honest in my absence, a good fortune was awaiting me as well.

As I rode past the rail station, the agent watched from the platform. He nodded and licked his lips. "You bought the revolver, didn't you?"

"How'd you know?"

"I heard it go off. That's a dangerous gun. Two men are in the cemetery because of it."

"It must bring good luck to its owner."

"Hell, fellow, it was the owners the damned thing killed. Seems it went off when they were handling it. Shot one of them in the leg, and he bled to death. The other man tried using it as a hammer to crack a walnut. It went off and gutshot him. He lived in misery for about three days, then up and died. I'd get rid of that gun, if I was you."

"You ain't me."

The agent snorted. "Then when you pass the graveyard, I'd pick out a plot where you'd like to be buried."

I thanked him for his concern and rode across the Southern Pacific Railroad tracks and on south to Galeyville, which was known as a rustler hideout. There was a chance I would run into Johnny Ringo or Ike Clanton or some of the others who had ridden with me in Tombstone, but if I made it to Galeyville, I could get information there on their whereabouts and steer clear of them the rest of the way.

Galeyville was about seventeen miles south of San Simon. The trip shouldn't have taken but three hours or so, but my donkey didn't seem all that pleased with my company. If I'd found a tortoise and hitched him up, I'd've gotten to Galeyville about as fast. The damn donkey seemed to enjoy stepping close to cactus and brushing my legs against the thorns, and when I'd curse and jerk on the halter, he just kept plodding along. I began to feel like a pincushion.

Unfortunately, slow as my donkey was, he wasn't slow enough to delay my arrival in Galeyville until after dark. There were maybe a dozen men on the trail that passed for a street, and they all had a hard look about them. They seemed too dumb to know right from wrong and mean enough to have preferred wrong anyway. I eyed them closely but didn't recognize a one. They all took to whooping and hollering and making fun of me.

"Hey," called one, "a donkey and a jackass just rode into town."

I tipped my hat and would've drawn my gun and plugged him if I hadn't been afraid it would go off and shoot me or the donkey.

A couple fellows started braying. It didn't hurt my feelings—by then I didn't *have* any feelings, my tailbone being so numb from rubbing against the donkey's knobby backbone that I didn't know if I could stand up once I dismounted.

Galeyville wasn't much of a town. Besides a saloon and a store, there were a few cabins and a hut where a blacksmith made running irons for the rustlers.

I drew up by the store and tied my donkey, then stumbled inside, my legs being so sore. The owner was a lazy fellow with a cigarette hanging out the corner of his mouth.

"Fine-looking animal you rode into town," he declared.

"He takes after you," I said.

The storekeeper must not've felt much like funning, because he pulled a double-barreled shotgun and pointed it at my gut. "Is that so?"

"Is what so?"

"That your donkey takes after me."

"Now, where'd you ever hear something like that?"

"I thought from you, but maybe I was mistaken."

"Must've been."

He lowered his shotgun.

"You happen to have a blanket and some bullets?"

"Got a couple of blankets, but no bullets. Bullets are hard to stock these days, what with so many prowling about for trouble."

"Oh, yeah? Who?"

"Ike Clanton's still running about. Some say Johnny Ringo's in the area, though I don't know about that. I ain't seen any of the Earp gang, but word's going around Ringo's challenged Wyatt to show his ugly face so they can settle their differences once and for all. But blankets, I got blankets."

He carried his shotgun over to a table and held up three of the dirtiest blankets I'd ever seen.

"Those aren't new, are they?"

"Nope," he said, "but their owners won't come looking for them. They're dead. You can have them all for a dollar apiece."

Figuring there weren't enough blankets in all of Arizona Territory to pad the donkey's back, I got out my money roll, peeled off three dollars, and took the blankets from the storekeeper. Outside, I draped them over the donkey's back. I was tempted to go to the saloon and have a drink or two to wash the dirt from my throat, but that was before I heard one of the ruffians on the street speak.

"That looks like the fellow who used to own the Stubborn Mule in Tombstone."

I still owned the Stubborn Mule, but I didn't care to debate the issue or linger in Galeyville. I mounted up and rode out of town, listening to the cowboys mock me and my donkey. A couple miles down the road I stopped to spend the night, and in the cool air I was glad for the three blankets, even if one had three bullet holes and bloodstains on it.

The next morning I woke up cold and stiff and continued across the Chiricahuas. About noon I reached

Rustlers' Park, where cowboys often gathered to exchange stolen stock, then started back down the mountains. The trip was hard on my donkey, so I spent the night at the foot of the mountains.

After resuming my journey about midmorning the next day, I came to Turkey Creek Canyon and turned down it toward Tombstone, still about forty miles away. I was growing more and more relaxed by the minute, thinking how smart I was to take the back trails. That was when I came upon a giant blackjack oak on Turkey Creek and encountered one of the men I least wanted to run into in all Cochise County.

It was Johnny Ringo. And he'd been drinking.

All I had on my side was my wits, my hair-trigger pistol, and my donkey. I didn't think it would be enough.

At first I didn't see Johnny Ringo. He was resting in the shade of the oak. Me and my mule were within thirty feet of him when he jumped from behind the tree and drew his revolver with his right hand. In his left he carried a bottle.

I figured I was about to be robbed. When I saw who it was, I figured I was about to be killed.

Even Johnny seemed stunned for a moment. He squinted at me, then rubbed his eyes, almost poking them out with the neck of the whiskey bottle. "Well, I'll be damned. If it ain't H. H. Lomax, you son of a bitch."

"Good to see you, too, Ringo."

He waved his gun at me. "Get down, and let's talk a spell."

"That's okay. You look like you're busy."

"You look dead," he said. "And you will be if you don't do what I tell you."

I climbed off the donkey's back and stepped gingerly on the ground, avoiding any sudden movement that might give Ringo an excuse to shoot me.

"Has anyone ever told you what a horse is? You're always riding a mule or a donkey. A mule's a damn plow animal. A donkey's what Mexicans ride. A horse is what a man rides. Aren't you a man?"

"I reckon I am."

Ringo nodded. "Probably the most hated man in Co-

chise County. Ike hates you. Doc hates you. The Earps hate
you. Your bartender hates you. Behan hates you. I hear
even your own lawyer and his fat wife hate you. I damn
sure hate you after what you did to Corina DeLure. You
must be the only man in Cochise County everybody hates.
Did you ever think of that?"

I admitted I hadn't given it a thought.

"But Corina—why'd you turn her to religion? She
was a fine one, the best I was ever with." Ringo's eyes
began to water. He was so drunk he was turning sappy as
a maple tree. "And you ruined her." He began to sob.

I wasn't feeling too healthy right then, not with him
holding his shaky finger on the trigger of a gun pointed
at my heart.

"Amelia Guinn's the one that turned her to religion."

"You're lying, Lomax. And I intend to kill you for
what you did to Corina. Did you know she's left Tombstone, even found a fellow that would marry her? That
wouldn't've happened if you hadn't gotten in the middle
of things."

It seemed like I was always in the middle of things.
I was getting tired of nothing ever working out just right.

Behind Ringo I saw his horse grazing in the grass
along the creek and wondered if I could make a run past
Ringo, jump in the saddle, and get away without being
shot. But even drunk, Ringo would've been as good a
gunman as I ever saw, short of possibly Doc Holliday or
Billy the Kid. I knew I could never make it, but it beat
standing there and being shot like a dog.

With his gun steady on my chest, he lifted the bottle
to his lips and drained what was left of the liquor. Then
he drew back his arm and flung the bottle as far as he
could, following its arc with his revolver like he planned
to shoot it in the air.

"Pow!" he said, as if he had pulled the trigger. He
lowered the gun and pointed it at my chest again. "I figure this is my lucky day."

"How's that, Ringo?"

"I get to kill the two sons of bitches I hate most in
this whole rotten world. You and Wyatt Earp."

"Wyatt's around?"

Ringo nodded. "We're gonna settle it all. Both of you'll be dead when it's all over."

"You talk big, Ringo, but you ain't killed me yet."

"No, dammit, but I've tried. I put a splinter in your ass and would've killed you before if I hadn't shot Joe Campbell instead."

"So you're the bastard that shot Joe Campbell?"

He nodded. "Behan wanted you off that town lot and paid me to shoot you. I didn't count on Campbell riding your mule, because you're the only idiot in Tombstone that would be caught on a mule."

"If you want to kill the son of a bitch that turned Corina to religion, then you best shoot yourself."

"Huh?"

"Corina got lonesome to see how Joe was recovering. When she went with me to see him, Amelia Guinn turned her to religion. If you hadn't shot Joe Campbell, she'd still be sleeping with you."

"Liar!" roared Ringo. "Get ready to die, you son of a bitch! I'm gonna put a hole in you I can drive an ore wagon through!"

Gulping, I decided I'd pushed him too far, but it was too late. I was prepared to die. I had no other choice.

"I'm giving you a fair chance, you son of a bitch," Ringo said, then shoved his pistol back in his holster. "Whenever you're ready, go for your gun."

I knew I couldn't beat him, so I bluffed. I moved my gaze from his eyes to a spot across the creek, trying to act like I'd seen something. "Wyatt," I said, then whistled.

Ringo just rolled his eyes and spit at my feet. "How dumb do you think I am, Lomax, to fall for a trick like that?"

"Hell, you were dumb enough to fall for Corina DeLure."

Ringo didn't think that was a bit funny. "Look, you son of a bitch, whenever you think you can beat me, go for your gun."

"We'll be standing here till hell freezes over."

"So you're a coward. No wonder everyone in Cochise County hates your guts."

That was when I decided to make my move.

Quick as I could I went for my gun, but before I touched the grips, Ringo jerked his own gun free and pointed it at my face. He cocked the hammer, then laughed. "It ain't fair, is it, me being so fast and you being so slow."

I figured I was about as close to death as I'd ever be without climbing inside a coffin. There wouldn't be anyone around to scrub and clean me like the undertakers had the McLaurys and Billy Clanton. The buzzards'd probably eat me and scatter my bones in every direction.

Ringo, though, wanted to play with me like Satan played with a wounded mouse. I guess the liquor made him think he could outshoot me any way he wanted.

"I believe I could draw water from a rock faster than you could draw your gun," he told me. He pointed to a spot on the ground in front of him. "I'm gonna put my gun down in front of me. You do the same. When you say so, we both dive for them and see who comes up the winner."

I swallowed hard, but my throat was drying up.

Ringo just laughed like he knew he'd win. It was the last time he ever laughed. "Take your gun out easy and hold it by the trigger guard," he commanded.

Slowly I pinched the butt of my revolver between my thumb and forefinger. My whole arm trembled. When the gun had cleared the holster, I held it with my left hand until I could pinch the trigger guard. "Let me check my load."

"Hell, Lomax, you're not as dumb as I thought. Check it," Ringo taunted. He started to squat, ready to place his gun on the ground.

I had only two bullets. I knew I wasn't fast enough to beat him, but with that hair trigger I might be able to jerk up the gun, and it would go off without me pulling the trigger. I turned the cylinder and left it on a live round, then crouched slightly, my hands trembling as my gun hovered above a pair of rocks by my side.

Ringo grinned. "You're about to die."

My throat was so dry I couldn't even swallow. I almost gagged on my nerves.

"Once our guns are on the ground," Ringo said, "we both stand up and wait."

"For what?"

"For one of us to make the first move."

We eyed each other like circling dogs.

He lowered his gun even closer to the ground.

My hands shook.

Ringo smirked. "You got to put it down sometime. If you don't, I'll kill you anyway."

I nodded and tried to say something, but my words couldn't get past my dry throat.

"You're a coward, Lomax."

I was beginning to believe that myself, the way my hand was shaking. Then the gun slipped from between my fingers and landed on the rocks.

The jolt discharged the gun.

In that instant I knew Ringo was going to kill me.

Chapter Twenty-one

I'd roamed the West long enough to have been around a few of the luckiest shots in history. I was at Adobe Walls when Billy Dixon made his famous long shot and knocked a Comanche chief off his horse atop a hill three-quarters of a mile away. Just the year before I'd been in Fort Sumner when Pat Garrett killed Billy the Kid with a shot in the dark.

But nowhere had I ever witnessed a luckier shot than when my gun slipped from between my fingers and landed on those rocks.

I glanced up at Ringo, expecting him to have his gun cocked and pointed at me. But he was flying backward like he was trying to dodge my bullet, his gun dropped on the ground at his feet. He fell hard, but I was sure he'd scramble back up, grab his gun, and shoot me.

I should've gone for his gun myself, but I was just as stunned as Ringo. Or at least I thought I was. I hesitated a moment, then lunged for his pistol, figuring mine was too touchy to grab. I cocked the gun, ready to show him who was in charge, as I stood up and laughed. "How's that for fast, Ringo?"

The son of a bitch must've been scared, because he didn't answer. He didn't move even when I kicked his boot. Wanting to show him how it felt to fear death, I stuck the gun in his face. But Ringo was beyond feeling. In fact, he was as dead a man as I'd ever seen. The bullet from my pistol had hit him in the right forehead and killed him without even knocking off his hat. I wondered, had Doc Goodfellow been around, whether he'd've tried to wash Ringo's brains.

All those years I'd wandered the West, I'd wanted to make a name for myself so people would look at me in awe and stay out of my way. Now I'd killed one of the fastest gunmen around, and nobody'd believe me if I told them I'd done it.

I glanced about, checking to make sure no one had seen the gunfight—which was what I took to telling myself it had been, rather than the luckiest accident in the history of the West. I didn't know what to do next, other than what anybody else'd do after committing a crime—run. But I was torn between running to make sure no one knew I'd killed Ringo and doing something to make sure everyone knew.

I shoved Ringo's pistol in my holster, then decided to steal something that everyone knew was Ringo's in case I had to prove my claim. I'd take his boots, the ones with *JR* hand-tooled on the sides.

Bending over him, I wrestled the boots free. As many cattle as Ringo was supposed to have rustled and as many stages as he was reported to have robbed, I would've guessed he'd been able to afford socks, but his feet were wrapped in torn-up strips of undershirts. I carried the boots over to my donkey and shoved them in the gunnysack with my supplies.

Then the thought hit me that Wyatt Earp might be heading here to find Ringo. I wanted to scare him, so I dragged Ringo over to the blackjack oak, sat him down on a knee-high rock, and propped him up against the tree.

I went back to retrieve my gun, then pulled enough cartridges from Ringo's belt to fill all but one of the empty cylinders. I left the hammer on the hull that had killed Ringo, then wrapped his fingers around the gun like he was waiting to shoot someone. After removing all but two of the remaining cartridges from the loops in his cartridge belt, I slid them in my own belt. His .45-caliber Winchester rifle with an octagonal barrel was propped against the tree next to him. I reached for it, then figured I shouldn't take too much that might make it obvious I'd killed him. I still couldn't decide whether it was best to pretend I knew nothing about the shooting or to claim full credit for it.

After looking around a final time to make sure no one had slipped up on me, I started toward my donkey, then stopped, deciding I could make better time on Ringo's horse. But rather than move my supplies over to the horse and risk someone riding up on me, I tied the donkey behind him, unhobbled him, then mounted up and rode toward Tombstone.

About two miles down the trail I figured I'd put enough distance between Ringo and myself—though I knew he wouldn't be following me—and it would be safe to transfer the supplies. But after I dismounted, it hit me that a lot of folks knew Ringo's horse. That could lead to trouble, someone either thinking I stole it or connecting me with his killing. I untied the donkey and slapped the bay on the rump. He darted away, and I climbed aboard the donkey and resumed my journey down Turkey Creek.

For a fellow with such bad luck, I'd had pretty good luck when I needed it. I was beginning to think I'd become a pretty fair shootist—killing Johnny Ringo and all—but wasn't sure it would do me much good. Some reputations are better to have than others.

I got to thinking so much about what a tough gunman I was that I didn't notice the approaching rider until it was too late to hide. There was something familiar about the way he sat in the saddle; he had the tall, lanky look of one of the Earp brothers.

The man was Wyatt, just as sure as Johnny Ringo was dead and drawing flies. He must've recognized me about the same time, because the white of his teeth suddenly showed beneath his drooping mustache. He brushed his duster back so it caught behind the butt of his pistol, then drew up his chestnut mount and waited for me to reach him.

"How the hell are you, Lomax?"

"Been better," I admitted.

"You're about to be dead." Wyatt cocked his head.

I knew more about poker than gunfighting, so I knew I had to bluff my way out of this new run of bad luck. "That's what Johnny Ringo told me."

Wyatt nodded. "We're supposed to meet at the blackjack oak on Turkey Creek."

"You'll find him waiting, but he won't be hard to beat."

"What are you talking about?"

"He's dead, Wyatt."

Wyatt smirked. "Yeah, and I suppose you shot him. No man in the territory save me can beat him, now that Doc's in Colorado."

"And me."

Laughing, Wyatt pulled back the duster so I could see the deputy marshal badge pinned to his chest.

"Shot him in the head."

"You're a coward, Lomax. Everybody knows that."

"I spit in Doc Holliday's drink."

"You were drunk."

"No one else is brave enough to do it, drunk or sober."

"Stupid enough, Lomax—that's what it's called."

I shook my head. "You don't want any of me, Wyatt."

Earp laughed. "I don't want any more of your lip. You ain't been nothing but trouble for the Earps. You called us the Puke brothers, you ruined Hattie Ketcham, you spread lies about Doc robbing the stages, and you probably pissed in our beer at the saloon."

He was pretty near right on all charges, but not being under oath, I denied it. "Not a word of that's true, save maybe about the piss."

"You son of a bitch."

"If you're thirsty and've got a mug, I'll pour you a beer right now. Of course, it'll be warm."

Wyatt almost gagged as he dismounted. "Get off that donkey, or I'll blow you off." He was getting close to exploding, so I slid off my mount.

"I killed Ringo on the draw, and I'll kill you on the

draw, Earp. Any man that can outdraw Ringo can out-shoot you."

Wyatt laughed.

I shook my head. "I was the only one to hear the last laugh Johnny Ringo ever had on this earth."

Wyatt's eyes narrowed as his lips tightened. I didn't know if my talk was giving him second thoughts or making him madder, but he stared at me for a long time.

"You've got a fine horse, Wyatt. If you want to ride into Turkey Creek Canyon and see for yourself, you can do that and still catch me before I go too many miles on this donkey."

I'd never seen such uncertainty in Wyatt's eyes. I wriggled the fingers on my right hand, limbering them up like I was getting ready to fight.

"You're lying, Lomax. There ain't nothing you've ever been involved in that ain't a lie."

Shaking my head, I pointed a finger at him. "Talk about lying, you and I know Frank Stilwell and Pete Spencer weren't involved in the Bisbee stage robbery. It was Doc and Morgan."

"Don't you be talking like that about Morg when he's not here to defend his good name."

"You lied on the witness stand. It was Doc and Morgan who shot at the McLaurys and Clantons first," I told him, failing to mention my single shot.

Wyatt eyed me. "I'll kill you for spreading rumors like that."

I shook my head. "I'll never mention them again if you ride away from here."

"You ain't bluffing me, Lomax. Ringo'd sooner shoot himself than let you shoot him."

"I'll show you something that will prove he's dead."

"There ain't an ounce of truth in anything you say."

I lifted my hand toward the gunnysack tied to my mule. "I'm gonna get something out of here."

"If you pull out a gun, I'll shoot you."

"When I pull out what I'm after, you'll be afraid to."

Wyatt gave me the evil eye as I unknotted the top of the gunnysack and shoved my hand inside. I slowly pulled out one of Johnny Ringo's boots and tossed it to him. He caught it with his left hand, his right moving to the grips of his revolver in case I tried to draw on him. I didn't make any sudden motions.

His gaze bouncing between the boot in his hand and the gun at my waist, Wyatt whistled. "Ringo's boot."

"The other one's in the gunnysack." I pulled it out and tossed it over.

He stood shaking his head. "I don't believe this."

I spread my feet and wriggled my right hand by my side. "It was me and him," I lied, "standing from me to you. He went for his gun, and I beat him."

"No."

"You care to try me, so I can make a believer out of you?"

Wyatt eyed me closely.

As I stood under his gaze, I tried to give the meanest, hardest stare I could. "The deal still stands, Wyatt. You get on your horse and ride up the trail. You may find Ringo's bay a couple miles back. A couple miles beyond that, you'll find Ringo sitting where I left him. There's a bullet hole in his forehead and a Colt in his hand. I'll start riding for Tombstone. If Ringo's not there, you can catch up with me, and we'll shoot it out, just like Ringo and I did."

Wyatt shook his head. "Why didn't you take Ringo's horse?"

"A man could get hung for stealing a horse."

"But not for killing."

I nodded. "You ought to know that, Wyatt."

Wyatt obviously didn't care for that comment and opened his mouth to say something, but I held up my hand and stopped him.

"If we go our own ways, Wyatt, you can claim you killed Ringo, and I'll never say otherwise. You've got a reputation as a shootist already. Men'll leave you alone. A reputation like that will only make more trouble for me."

Wyatt liked that idea. "I can keep the boots."

"Sure."

"And you won't be spreading rumors about Doc or Morg being involved in the Bisbee stage robbery?"

"You leave me alone, I leave the good name of your

dead brother alone. As for Doc, I hope I never run into him again. He'll do enough bad for his name as it is."

After what seemed like an eternity, Wyatt nodded. "What's in it for you, Lomax?"

"I can get back to Tombstone, take up running the Stubborn Mule, and lead a normal life."

"There's no normal life in Tombstone," Wyatt answered as he backed up to his horse.

"It beats being on the run."

Wyatt agreed. He packed Ringo's boots in his saddlebags and looked at me. "You're a hard one to figure out, Lomax."

"Just trying to make a go of it, like most folks."

He grabbed his saddle horn, put his foot in the stirrup, and pulled himself up in the saddle.

"Sure you don't want to stay around for a beer? I feel one coming on."

"Damn, Lomax. No wonder everybody hates you."

"That's what Ringo said before I killed him."

Wyatt shook his head, jerked the reins on his horse, and galloped toward Turkey Creek.

That was the last I ever saw of Wyatt Earp, though I heard years later that he claimed to have cleaned up Cochise County and killed Johnny Ringo. I always wondered, though, what he did with Ringo's boots.

After Wyatt Earp rode out of my life, I made water, got on my donkey, and started for Tombstone. With the way my luck had been running that day, I figured every five or six miles I'd run into another enemy I'd made in Cochise County. Maybe Ike Clanton or Johnny Behan would be next. But I didn't encounter a single person.

After those two days astride the donkey's knobby back and a couple nights sleeping on the hard ground, I was ready to get back to Tombstone and spend a night on my feather mattress. Too, with all the money the Stubborn Mule had no doubt made in my absence, I could afford the fanciest woman in town to rub my back—or anything else that was stiff.

When I finally came within sight of the mineworks around Tombstone, I had to admit it felt good to be back. I figured my only problems would be that damn tomcat

Satan and Henry Guinn and his wife. Well, I was wrong. I had more problems awaiting me than a dog has fleas.

As I approached, I pointed the donkey away from the trail and skirted the edge of town. Not caring to be seen for a while so I could collapse on my bed and catch up on my sleep, I dismounted and tugged my hat low over my head.

When I got near my house, I looked down the street and realized something was different. Real different. My house was still there, but what was left of it was charred timbers. Some son of a bitch had burned the place down, my feather mattress with it. All that was standing was the blackened bedsprings, warped bedstead, ruined stove, and charred wood that had once been my home. I was angered by the sight and wondered who had done it. Maybe it was the mining company, deciding it was easier to burn than to move. Maybe it was some of the Earp faction or the Clanton faction. Maybe a bolt of lightning had hit it.

Fearing the same thing had happened to the Stubborn Mule, I jumped on my donkey and charged down the street. I was relieved to see the saloon still standing. I could sleep in the bedroom there if one of the girls wasn't occupied.

But as I neared the building and got a better look, I stopped cold. The sign had been changed. Instead of the Stubborn Mule, my saloon had been renamed the Stallion Mare, evidently to save money on the sign painter. Joe Campbell's name had been painted over mine next to the word *Proprietor*. With a name that made as little sense as Stallion Mare, it made sense that Joe Campbell was responsible.

I tied my donkey to the hitchrack and stormed inside. Joe Campbell was standing behind the bar, his arms crossed, rocking on his heels and smiling like he owned the damned place. When he saw me, he turned whiter than fresh milk.

"Lo-Lo-Lomax," he sputtered, "you're back."

Every customer in the saloon went silent.

"Damn right. And I don't remember rehiring you

before I left. So gather up your things and get. Where's Til Walteree?"

"I fired him."

"You what?"

"I fired him. This ain't your saloon anymore."

"What do you mean it ain't my saloon? I didn't sell it."

"No, Henry Guinn did."

"How could he?"

"He's a lawyer."

"You're a liar!" I shouted.

"What's right is wrong, and what's wrong is right," Campbell taunted.

I'd had enough of his damn double-talk, so I jerked out my revolver and fired at him. He ducked. Customers scattered. "Right's not wrong, and wrong's not right!" I screamed. "I'm gonna show you a hit's not a miss and a miss is not a hit!" I fired into the bar.

Joe Campbell started praying for deliverance. I was planning on delivering a dozen or so bullets to his ugly carcass. No man was going to steal my saloon with me just standing by and letting him.

"What happened to all your religion, Joe?" I yelled.

He mumbled his prayers faster than a murderer with his neck in a noose and his feet on the trapdoor.

"Amelia Guinn ruined you with all her Bible reading."

"I took a gutshot for you."

After Ringo's confession I had to admit he was right, but I didn't figure it wise to share that. I raced to the bar and jumped around the end in time to see Campbell scurrying on hands and knees around the other end. I fired a shot into the plank floor.

"He got me!" Campbell screamed. "I'm dying!"

I dashed along the bar as Campbell staggered to his feet and bolted toward the door, a big splinter from the plank floor stuck in his butt. I knew the feeling. I could've plugged him then but held up for fear I might hit a bystander. Instead I fired a shot into the ceiling, then another as I rounded the bar and took out after Campbell, who was stumbling along the boardwalk, pulling at the stake in his behind. I fired at his feet. He fell down, cowering on the walk.

I charged toward him, grabbed his arm, and spun him over. That must've sent the wooden splinter plowing deeper into his buttocks, because he screamed louder. By then I was so furious I put the gun to his nose and snapped the trigger. The hammer clicked on an empty chamber, which probably saved my life, not to mention Campbell's.

Even though my gun was empty, Campbell fell still. He'd passed out from fright. About then I heard someone yelling for me to drop the gun and turn around.

I half obeyed, turning around with the revolver in my hand.

Johnny Behan was standing there. He lifted his gun and fired.

Stung by his bullet, I dropped my own gun and fell to the ground, grabbing at my shoulder. My shirtsleeve was sticky with blood right where my arm became my shoulder.

"It's H. H. Lomax!" a spectator yelled. "He's been shot!"

Several men rushed between me and Behan, one kicking my gun away and the rest gathering around me. I thought they were trying to protect me and that I had more friends than Ringo or Earp believed, but they ripped at my shirt and tore the cloth off my arm.

"He was hit in the arm!" cried one.

"No, it was the shoulder!"

"There's bets to be settled!" someone else yelled.

It was only a flesh wound, but I was getting a little drowsy, and my head was spinning. The last thing I remember was several men fighting around me.

When I awoke, I was in a bed, and at first I thought I'd been dreaming about finding my house burned down and my saloon taken from me. But when I twisted over, I saw the bars of the county jail standing between me and freedom.

My arm and shoulder burned from the bullet wound. I reached to touch it and felt a jolt of pain up my arm. Only my weakness kept my anger from exploding.

My house had been burned to the ground, my saloon had been stolen, and I was the one behind bars. The law was crookeder than a thousand miles of mountain road.

Across the room from my cell napped the son of a bitch who was supposed to be keeping law in Cochise County. Johnny Behan was propped back in his chair with his feet on his desk, snoring heavily. If I'd had a gun, I'd've shot him right there. As long as I was going to be in jail for something I didn't deserve, I figured I should at least do something that would give me pleasure during my stay.

"Sheriff!" I screamed.

Behan must've thought Wyatt Earp had come back to get him. He awoke with a start. As he reached for the gun at his side, the chair tipped backward, and he lost his balance. Windmilling his arms, he flung the gun halfway across the room. I covered my head in case the thing went off, but it merely bounced off the floor toward the door.

The sheriff tumbled over on his back and slammed into the floor. Still uncertain what had startled him, he clambered to his hands and knees and cowered behind the desk for a moment, but not hearing shots or breaking glass, he lifted his head up over the desk and stared in my direction.

"Lomax? Was that noise you?"

"What noise?"

"That yell."

I shook my head. "Sounded like Wyatt Earp to me."

Turning pale, Behan crawled to the door and retrieved his gun. His hand shook as he held it.

"Maybe I was just hearing things," I said.

Behan didn't know whether to believe me or not. He crept back around the desk and pointed the gun at the door for a couple minutes.

"Maybe I was wrong," I admitted, "about it sounding like Wyatt."

The sheriff grumbled at me, still uncertain whether I could be trusted. After about ten minutes he got up, holstered his gun, and strode over to my jail cell. I was hoping he'd come within reach so I could strangle him, but the fine sheriff didn't seem to trust me.

"Why you so jumpy, Sheriff?"

"They've found Johnny Ringo dead, near the Chiricahuas."

"That a fact? Is that why I'm in jail?"

Behan laughed. "Lomax, you ain't brave enough to kill that renegade tomcat of yours, much less Johnny Ringo."

"Who you reckon done it?"

The sheriff scratched his head. "I don't know."

"Me neither," I said, trying to sound anything but convincing. I turned away from Behan.

"What do you mean? You know something, don't you?"

I shrugged. "Nothing but hearsay. Nothing that would stand up in a court of law."

Behan came closer to the cell, grabbed a couple of iron bars, and shook them. "What are you hiding from me, Lomax?"

Glancing over my shoulder, I shrugged. "Nothing."

He didn't believe me. "I can make your stay here more tolerable, Lomax, if you tell me what's going on."

"I don't know."

"Looks like you'll be behind bars for a spell, Lomax. You never should've returned to Tombstone."

"And if I was you, Behan, I'd never leave Tombstone."

"What do you mean?"

"Nothing, unless you do what you can to get me out of jail." Bargaining with Behan was like dealing with the devil, but a man can't pick his friends when he's behind bars.

"I'll do what I can. What is it you're keeping from me?"

I shrugged. "I don't know if it's true or not, but I ran into a couple fellows on the trail into town, and they said Wyatt Earp had returned from Colorado."

Behan grimaced and shook his head. "I was afraid of that."

"There's more," I said.

His jaw tightened.

"He was carrying a list of names he showed these fellows."

"Yeah," Behan grunted.

"Ringo's name was at the top of the list, Ike Clanton's was second, and . . ." I decided to let him sweat a bit longer.

"And what? Whose name was third on the list?"

"Yours, Sheriff, yours."

He jerked his hands away and stalked across the room. "Damn. Won't Wyatt ever give up Cochise County?"

"Not until you and Ike are dead, I reckon."

Behan cursed. "The son of a bitch stole my woman, and now he wants my hide."

"Fact is, Sheriff, if you were to let me out, I might put in a good word for you with Wyatt if I ever ran into him."

Behan started laughing. "Wyatt hates you as much as me. Your name's probably fourth on his list. You're safer in jail than anywhere else, and you may be here for a while."

"For what?"

"Disorderly conduct, carrying a gun, and the attempted murder of Joe Campbell."

"Not a bullet of mine hit him. I was shooting in the wall or the floor or the ceiling."

"No lead hit him, but Doc Goodfellow had to dig a wooden stake out of his rear."

"It wasn't nothing more than a splinter. Anyway, he stole my saloon."

Behan shook his head. "He didn't steal your saloon. The Stubborn Mule was auctioned off after you failed to pay your debts."

"What are you talking about, Sheriff? I left Til Walteree in charge, and he was good about paying my liquor suppliers and everybody else. I even paid six months in advance for the care of Flash at the O.K. Corral."

"Maybe so, Lomax, but you didn't pay everybody you owed."

Trying to figure who I could've owed money, I pinched the bridge of my nose. I hadn't left with any gambling debts. "Who said I owed them money?"

"Your lawyer, Henry Guinn."

"What!" I grabbed the jail bars and could've pried them apart if I'd tried. I remembered something about the two hundred and ten dollars Amelia had claimed I owed. But I was good for it. The money could've been taken out of the saloon profits, if only Guinn had asked Til Walteree for it. "That ain't right."

"You've only yourself to blame," Behan said. "You signed the papers yourself."

"What papers?"

"The papers with Henry Guinn. First there was a power of attorney for Joe Campbell, which was rescinded after you and Joe had a falling out. Then there's the subsequent papers you signed for Henry Guinn to handle the disputed claim on your house lot. The papers allowed Guinn to auction off any and all of your property to settle any debt to him that was three months overdue."

"The son of a bitch could've sold the house. It would've brought more than enough to pay the debt."

Behan grinned. "Odd thing, Lomax—the house burned before the scheduled auction. He had no choice but to sell the Stubborn Mule."

"Who burned the house, dammit?"

"Does seem a bit of a coincidence, now, doesn't it, but you wouldn't mean to accuse Henry Guinn, would you? He's just a lawyer trying to follow the letter of the law."

"You think so? There's more honor in a gang of rustlers than there is in a convention of lawyers."

"The papers are on file in the courthouse. You can see them for yourself."

The mention of papers jogged my memory. I recalled having a set of the papers in the tin box I'd kept hidden under the floor of my house. If they hadn't been destroyed during the fire, I'd check them once I got out of jail. "It's robbery."

"No," Behan answered, "it's the law."

"The law's not got a right to steal."

"You signed the papers. You should've understood what everything said before you signed."

"I read over them, but there were a lot of highfalu- tin lawyer words, words that don't make much sense to regular hands."

"I bet you understand them now." Behan laughed.

"There's a lot of things I understand now, like not all skunks have a stripe down their back. How long will I be in jail?"

"Twenty days."

"How's that?"

"I figure you'll be fined twenty-five dollars for the charges against you. You only had twenty dollars on you. You'll still owe the county five dollars. The judge credits you twenty-five cents a day for every day you're in jail. You'll be here twenty days."

I took a deep breath. "I've got one request."

"What's that?"

"Why don't you invite Henry Guinn to see me? I'd sure like to have a little visit with him."

Chapter Twenty-two

The next morning Sheriff Johnny Behan and three deputies hauled me out of my jail cell to take me before Judge Wells Spicer, who had presided over the hearing into the Clanton and McLaury deaths. With as many deputies as Behan invited along, you'd've thought I was the meanest man in the territory. When I stepped out of the jail, I was surprised by a jeering crowd waving fists and wearing scowls like I'd cut their beer with something other than water. One man was even brandishing a hemp rope with a noose knotted at the end of it.

Behan took me by the arm and led me behind two deputies with carbines who plowed through the crowd. The third deputy trailed with a Winchester.

"I didn't realize Joe Campbell was so popular," I told Behan.

"He's not."

"Then what've they got against me?"

"You were shot."

"Hell, I was the one that was shot, not them."

"It's not that you were shot, but where you were shot. There's a lot of money riding on it. We need to settle this issue before the whole town explodes, or someone else is likely to shoot you again."

The sheriff led me into the courtroom, which was packed with more folks than attended any day of the Earp-Holliday hearing. They were noisy as a roomful of

schoolboys, but not nearly as smart. To my way of thinking they were a bloodthirsty lot, even though I knew
most of them and had even cut their drinks on occasion.
They didn't seem at all indebted to me for all the favors
I'd done for them over the years, especially when Allen
Street had burned down and my saloon was the only respectable one left in Tombstone.

A couple men growled at me, and one of them even
broke between the deputies and cursed in my face. I
clasped and lifted my manacled hands, then brought
them down across his face, bloodying his nose and
knocking him out. He crumpled to the floor.

My act of self-defense put the crowd to hissing and
chanting. "Shoot him! Shoot him!" they cried in unison.

Behan jerked me on down the aisle and chewed me
out. "Why'd you do that? They want your blood."

"Why're they so interested in a disorderly conduct
hearing?"

"This is more than a disorderly conduct hearing."

"What are you talking about?"

Behan ignored me.

I was beginning to wonder if somebody might have
seen me kill Johnny Ringo and told Behan. It was the
only thing that made sense, though I didn't think Ringo
had that many friends.

The lawmen hauled me up before the court bench
and sat me down at a table to wait on the judge.

Behan turned around to face the crowd and told
them it was time to quiet down so the judge could settle
all the legal issues at hand. "He ain't coming until you
get quiet."

His words didn't make much of a dent in the din.
The crowd kept yammering.

"Quiet!" Behan called without result. Then he
stepped on a chair and up on the table where I sat and
glared at the crowd, but he couldn't cow them the way
Wyatt Earp did. "If you don't shut up," he called, "I'll
have to clear the courtroom!"

"That'll only make matters worse," answered one
man in the front row, "until we get this settled."

"Then hush up, dammit!" Behan called.

The crowd gradually settled down, though there were still occasional disturbances at the back door as people tried to squeeze past deputies into the already packed room.

When the judge walked in, he was accompanied by another Winchester-toting deputy. Spicer looked over the crowd, shook his head, and took a seat behind the bench. A murmur rippled through the spectators until Spicer clobbered the bench with his gavel.

"Silence!" he commanded. "This is a court of law, not a circus. Anyone creating a disturbance will be removed from the court." Then he looked down at me. "Good to see you, Mr. Lomax. Sorry to see your wound."

"Thank you, Your Honor." I started to feel a little better about being in Spicer's court. He actually seemed sympathetic.

"I bet you'd get shot in the back."

The crowd chuckled, but I didn't find it that amusing. An uneasy feeling settled in my stomach. I still didn't know what I was doing in Spicer's court.

The judge started his legal talk. "We are assembled here today, Mr. Lomax, to determine two matters. First, in the matter of the charges of disorderly conduct, carrying a weapon, and attempted murder, we will determine whether you should be put to trial or whether, admitting guilt, you are then fined and permitted to leave jail. The second matter is examining the situation that led to your wounding and the facts as they relate to your future safety and the safety of Tombstone's law-abiding inhabitants. Now, as to the first matter, Mr. Lomax, you have been charged with disorderly conduct, carrying a weapon, and attempted murder. You may address those matters yourself, or, if you prefer, you can retain a lawyer to speak in your behalf."

I looked to Behan, then the judge. A lawyer had caused much of my trouble to begin with. "I prefer to make my own statements."

"Very well. Please stand."

Taking a deep breath, I rose and stood before the judge, who peered down at me intently.

"I'd been away from Tombstone six months. When I

returned, I found my saloon, the Stubborn Mule, had been swindled from me by Joe Campbell, a bartender I had fired."

"Mr. Lomax," Spicer interrupted, "swindling is a matter for the law to determine. It does not address the charge before you."

"Well, Judge, it does," I pleaded, "because Henry Guinn, who I thought was helping me settle some problems with the title to the lots of my house and saloon, came up with a way to sell my saloon out from under me to Joe Campbell. It just ain't right."

"Mr. Lomax, what's right and what's the law aren't always the same," Spicer said.

I was damn glad to finally hear a judge—or anyone—say that, because that's how I'd always felt.

"To settle these issues, Mr. Lomax, you'll need a lawyer."

I was gonna get me a lawyer, all right, once I got out of jail, and I was gonna get him good. His name was Henry Guinn. I shrugged. "There's not much I can say, then, I guess."

"So you plead guilty to disorderly conduct?"

"Sure. Why not? It ain't right, but it's the law."

Spicer smiled. "Now you're beginning to understand. I'm fining you twenty-five dollars for disorderly conduct. Now, as to carrying a weapon illegally, how do you defend yourself?"

Even though I figured it wouldn't do any good to explain, I went ahead anyway. "I'd just arrived in town and hadn't had time to check my gun. I tried to give it to Joe Campbell, but he ducked behind the bar. I figured he was going for a shotgun, so I fired the gun six times so he would know it was empty."

The crowd laughed.

Spicer eyed the spectators coldly. "Considering the morbid interest of the male citizens of this town in your personal welfare, or lack thereof, and considering your prolonged absence from town and the uncertainty with which the citizenry might welcome you back, I will dismiss the charge of carrying a weapon and admonish you to be more circumspect in checking your weapon in the future. Now, how do you respond to the charge of the attempted murder of Joe Campbell?"

"Well, Judge, all I can say is, I was just trying to catch up with him and check my gun so I wouldn't be accused of carrying a weapon. When he stumbled and fell, I just went over and offered it to him."

The crowd laughed. Spicer rolled his eyes.

"I offered it to him and squeezed the trigger so he would know it was empty and no longer a threat to him."

"Is it true," Spicer asked, "that you held it in his face and pulled the trigger?"

"Yes, Judge, it is. He just wouldn't believe it was empty or that I was turning it over to him. I figure his conscience was bothering him for his part in swindling me."

Spicer shook his head. "As relates to the attempted murder, the court will give Mr. Lomax the benefit of the doubt and dismiss that count. As for the accusation of swindling, Mr. Lomax, I again suggest that you get a lawyer."

"I damn well intend to get me a lawyer," I replied.

"Now, as to the second major issue before the court today," Spicer said, "we will discuss the matter of the shooting of H. H. Lomax, a shooting that has generated considerable interest in the community. The court believes it is in the best interest of Mr. Lomax and the community that this issue be resolved quickly and fairly before he or some other party is harmed." He looked at me. "You may be seated, Mr. Lomax."

Bewildered, I slid back down in my chair.

Spicer continued. "Since numerous bets were placed on where H. H. Lomax might be intentionally shot, we are here today to resolve all the questions resulting from his shooting so that this town can get back to normal. If we are ever to be considered civilized, I pray to God that never again in the history of Tombstone will so outrageous a bet be made by any man or woman.

"Now, some have claimed that no bets should be paid, since the shooting was accidental and certainly not perpetrated by the same man who originally shot bartender Joe Campbell, apparently thinking it was H. H. Lomax. Sheriff Behan, would you please stand."

Behan rose beside me. "Yes, Your Honor."

"Are you the man who shot H. H. Lomax day before yesterday?"

"I am, Your Honor."

"Was it an accidental shooting?"

"No, sir, I intentionally shot him to keep him from harming Joe Campbell or anybody else."

"Thank you, Sheriff. Had you placed any bets on where H. H. Lomax might be shot?"

"Like everyone else, I did. I figured he'd be gutshot, that or back-shot. But I bet gutshot."

"So you would in no way have profited from shooting him where you did?"

"No, Your Honor. Fact was, I was trying to protect the good citizens of Tombstone."

"Thank you, Sheriff. You may be seated." Spicer studied the crowd a moment. "It has been stated by the sheriff of Cochise County that the gunshot was intentional and that the sheriff had nothing to gain from wounding H. H. Lomax where he did, save to protect the public."

When Behan sat down, I leaned over. "What's this all about?"

"The judge is trying to settle all bets to keep you from getting killed, Lomax."

Spicer called Doc Goodfellow to the front of the court and asked him to share his professional expertise on the issue. Goodfellow stood up in the second row and fought his way to the aisle and up to the front. If there was any man in Tombstone I'd want to wash my guts, it had to be Goodfellow.

"Now, Doctor," said Spicer, "you treated Mr. Lomax after he was shot by Sheriff Behan, did you not?"

"I did."

"And where was he shot?"

"Upper left extremity, Your Honor."

"Was he shot in the arm or the shoulder?"

"Neither . . ."

The crowd gasped.

". . . or both."

"How can it be neither or both?" the judge wanted to know.

"It depends on how you define the shoulder or arm. Some shoulder muscles extend down the arm, while some arm muscles go into the shoulder."

Spicer turned to me and asked me to stand and take off my shirt.

I held my manacles in the air. "Can't take it off, Judge, not with these on."

"Very well, Mr. Lomax, unbutton it and slip it over your shoulder so everyone can see your wound."

I fumbled with the buttons until Behan gave me a hand. I didn't like the idea of a man fooling with any of my buttons, but the spectators sure thought it was funny. When Behan pulled the shirt down from my shoulder, Goodfellow stepped to me and touched the bandage.

"You can see, Your Honor, the slight bloodstain in the bandage. That is the path of the bullet, which was merely a flesh wound. If we were to draw a line straight up his shoulder from his rib cage, we would—"

Spicer interrupted. "Would you do that, please, on the bandage?"

"Sir?"

The judge dipped a pen in an inkwell atop his bench and offered it to Goodfellow. The doctor marched to the bench, took the pen, and returned to me. He drew a line from my armpit straight up to my shoulder. I understood what a piece of slate must feel like in a schoolroom.

"Now," he said, touching the pen to the point where he had started the line, "if I draw a horizontal line here, across his arm"—which he did—"I have a shape something like a slice of pie. You will note that the trail of blood on the bandage splits that piece of pie."

Goodfellow returned to the bench and gave the judge his pen. "Now, Your Honor, that pie slice of his upper left extremity can be considered either arm or shoulder. It's a little of both but not all of either. Does that make sense?"

Spicer nodded. "It does to me, but I'm not certain

it will to those of weak mind before me. Thank you, Doctor."

Goodfellow turned me around so the spectators could see the pie slice on my bandages. One fellow whistled at me. Doc Goodfellow helped pull my shirt back over my shoulder and button it up, then slipped back to his seat.

Spicer wrote a few notes before he addressed the spectators. "Faced with the evidence presented by Doc Goodfellow, the court has two options before it. First, the court can inform all parties, which in this case would seem to be every man in Tombstone, that their bets are void and no money is to change hands. Or the court can declare all parties who bet either upon the arm or shoulder to share in the winnings. This is the option the court shall take in the interest of Mr. Lomax's safety. Were the court to do otherwise, someone else might shoot Mr. Lomax and possibly end his life just to settle a bet."

The men in the courtroom groaned as if they were disappointed that I had been given a reprieve of sorts. Reluctantly they got to their feet and streamed out of the courtroom until only a handful were left.

Spicer eyed me with distaste. "You certainly don't have many friends in Cochise County, Mr. Lomax."

"They liked me when Allen Street burned down."

Spicer snorted. "Now, then, as to the fine. Do you have twenty-five dollars on you?"

Behan shook his head. "Your Honor, he had barely twenty dollars when he was arrested."

"Very well," Spicer said. "You are sentenced to twenty days in jail to pay off the remaining five dollars of your fine."

I could only sigh and say, "Yes, Judge." I had ridden into Tombstone thinking I would have enough money awaiting me to buy a bigger house and a bigger bed and invite any willing woman to share it with me, and she'd accept whether she liked me or not because she couldn't help but like my wallet.

As it turned out, thanks to a swindling lawyer and a dumb, ugly bartender who fancied himself a philosopher,

I had to spend twenty days behind bars to earn five dollars.

Behan took me back to jail, where I lingered a few days, each day requesting that Henry Guinn be sent for. I figured he was as big a coward as his wife was fat, so I was surprised one day after I'd finished my noon meal of stew and hard bread to see Henry Guinn himself enter the sheriff's office. He took off his bowler hat and stared through his thick glasses at me.

"It's about time you showed up, Guinn. What happened—did you finally get a break from feeding your wife?"

Guinn tapped his shiny shoe against the floor. "Sheriff, I did not come here so that my wife and I could be insulted."

"You're a lawyer, dammit. What did you expect?"

"I expected to be paid, Lomax, and that's the cause of all your trouble. You didn't pay me the money you owed me. Fortunately I had seen your weakness of character and had written into our contract a proviso just to handle that condition."

"You swindled me is what you did."

"The wind blows from all directions, Lomax. It seems you swindled Joe Campbell out of the saloon originally."

"I did not."

"You beat him with crooked cards."

"They were his own cards, dammit."

"No matter. A thief's a thief."

"I couldn't agree more." I'd seen rattlesnakes with more sense of right and wrong. "And how come Joe got the saloon? I thought he was too religious to run a saloon."

Guinn laughed. "It's my saloon, not his. He just tends bar."

"Kind of funny, ain't it?" said Behan. "Everybody here believes Henry's so religious, and yet he owns the Stallion Mare." He scratched his head. "Damnedest name I ever heard, but that's Joe Campbell. He doesn't make a lot of sense, now, does he?"

Guinn nodded. "He's dumb enough to do what I

want and believe what I say. After all, we go to church together, but you wouldn't know much about church, would you, Lomax?"

"I know I never hid behind the church to hide my wrong."

The lawyer held his nose in the air and lifted a satchel. "There's no wrong here. I brought the papers to show you. They've got your signature, and they're all legal. I've got a copy, the courts have a copy, and you had a copy. Whether you still do or not, I wouldn't know."

With a wave of my arm I motioned him to leave, but he would have none of it.

"No, sir, I'm not leaving until you look over these papers. I want you to understand everything was legal and you've no grounds to contest my actions. Why? Because you authorized them yourself."

Guinn came over to my cell but stopped just short of my reach. One by one he reviewed our legal dealings. I knew it didn't matter that what he had done was wrong—it was legal—and I couldn't fight him without hiring a lawyer, which is what got me in trouble to begin with.

When he was done, he shoved all the papers back in his satchel. "That's the sum of it, Lomax. You can fight, but you won't win."

I shrugged. "What can I say?"

Guinn smiled. "You can say good-bye to Tombstone once you get out of here. You'd be doing yourself and all of us a big favor."

Behan laughed. "Hell, we got rid of the Earps and Holliday. If we can just get rid of you, Tombstone might be respectable again."

I shook my head. "Too many lawyers and politicians for it to ever be respectable."

Behan laughed again. "It's the politicians and lawyers that run the world."

"Run it into the ground," I corrected as I fell on my bunk.

Lawyer Guinn and Sheriff Behan cackled, enjoying their joke on me and all of Tombstone.

After Guinn stepped out of the office that day, I

never had another conversation with him, though I guess you could say I was ultimately responsible for changing his life. I wanted to get even with that son of a bitch. I spent my jail time figuring out ways I could do it without having to spend the rest of my life behind bars for doing such a valuable deed.

I could shoot him, knife him, hang him, blow him up, push him down a mine shaft, trample him with a horse when he crossed the street, or poison him. Of course I'd have to make sure Amelia Guinn wasn't around or I'd have a real problem, because there wasn't a gun powerful enough to shoot through her, a knife long enough to reach any vital parts, a rope strong enough to hang her, dynamite enough to rattle her, a mine shaft wide enough to accommodate her, a horse brave enough to tackle her, or poison strong enough to kill her.

When the day finally came for my release, Behan unlocked the cell door and let me out. "You can have all your belongings, save your gun, which you can't carry on the streets."

I grumbled.

"I'd suggest, Lomax, that you just get on your donkey or your mule or whatever you're riding and get the hell out of Tombstone forever. You're as popular around here as the smallpox. But whatever you do, stay away from Joe Campbell and Henry Guinn."

I took my things, including my blankets and gunnysack of supplies I'd bought in San Simon. As I walked out of the jail, I vowed never to return no matter what I did to Henry Guinn.

I went straight to the O.K. Corral and searched out John Montgomery. He grinned. "Glad to see you got out in time."

"Time for what?"

"Time to pay for another month of stabling Flash. He's been getting fat and lazy. And I stabled your donkey after you were jailed."

"Keep the donkey. I'll be leaving Tombstone soon," I said.

"How soon?"

"Soon as I tie up a few loose ends."

"You thinking about getting an attorney over the saloon?"

I nodded. "I plan to get an attorney."

Montgomery laughed. "I won't ask which one." He went off to get Flash.

I must've waited about five minutes, but it was worth it when Flash came out. He was fat and sleek, and the sight of me seemed to put a lift in his step. I ran over and grabbed the reins and patted him on the neck, and he nuzzled my cheek with his nose. I felt damn proud. Even if no one else was glad to see me in Tombstone, at least my mule was.

I tied my gunnysack to the saddle and cinched down the three blankets I'd used for bedding. As I mounted up, I thanked Montgomery for taking such good care of him. I never returned to the O.K. Corral.

Having been in jail for so long, my legs were stiff, and it took me a few minutes to get comfortable astride Flash. I rode him over to my burned-out house, dismounted, and tied him to the hitching post. Wading through the burnt planks, I wondered if my tin box had survived the fire and the looting that had likely followed.

Kicking at the debris, I made my way over to the bedsprings, which had collapsed onto what was left of the wooden floor. With some effort I was able to unsnare the springs and lift a few floor planks, including some that were merely scorched rather than burned all the way through.

If my luck had been nothing but bad since returning to Tombstone, it picked up a bit when the toe of my boot hit a metal box. I scrambled to knock away more debris, then bent over.

Just as I did, Flash brayed, and I heard a terrible screech. Claws sank into my buttocks and scratched and ripped at my britches and my flesh. Thrashing and hollering, I fell forward into the blackened bedsprings.

Satan had returned.

I swatted at the cat, trying to knock him off, but, pinned as I was by the bedsprings, he was hard to reach. I finally got an arm loose, reached around, and grabbed him by the neck. With some effort I managed to jerk him free and fling him far enough that I could get up and prepare for another charge. I was ready for him, but he had had enough. He slouched away behind the outhouse and stood peeking around the corner, waiting for me to turn my back again.

I made certain I faced the tomcat as I brushed the soot and char off me. I squatted once like I was about to pick up the tin box, then shot up, just to see if he was stalking toward me, but Satan was too smart to fall for that. He stayed where he was, watching me out of those evil eyes.

I bent down again, then shot up.

Satan was still watching me.

Then I squatted and stayed a little longer, figuring he might take the bait, but he didn't. I tried to trick him a couple more times but couldn't, so I focused on working the tin box from beneath the debris.

When I stood up, Satan was gone. But that made me nervous, and I was tempted to go back to Sheriff Behan and ask for my gun so I could kill that damn cat.

I tucked the tin box under my arm and rode a couple miles out of town to stay the night. My behind being pretty much ripped, the trip was a bit uncomfortable.

"You son of a bitch," I said. "I'll get you yet." I felt like a fool threatening a cat that wasn't even around.

After making my camp I finally opened the box. I found my stock certificates, all of them in companies that had gone broke, plus $115 that I'd apparently overlooked when I left Tombstone back in January.

And there were the bundled letters from Hattie Ketcham. I started to use them to build a fire but decided to reread them just for the heck of it. The envelopes were stiff from the heat, but they held together when I opened them. I read the letters in order. They brought back some good and some bad memories, especially the first ones when it looked like Tombstone might be the place where I might finally make a go of it.

Dearest Henry:
    I enjoyed our time together last night. You were

*the handsomest man in the hall, both in and out of
your suit. Isn't that naughty?*

*I can't remember having more fun. You are so
brave to sneak out with me since you know what you
would face if we were caught. That's what makes it
so much fun.*

I can't wait until we can get together again.

Lovingly, Hattie

Although the incident mentioned in the second letter wasn't funny at the time, I couldn't help but laugh as
I read it aloud.

Dearest Henry:

*I can't believe you-know-who didn't catch us in
bed together yesterday. I'd never been in bed before
when the whole house moved.*

*I'm sorry about the scratches on your behind. I
had fun. Can't wait to see you again.*

Hattie

By the following letters the trouble had begun between me and Hattie. Ultimately that meant trouble
between me and Holliday and the Earps and all of Tombstone.

Dearest Henry:

*I'm sorry I got angry. The thought of you being
with that woman bothers me still. I hope one day
soon we can get together again when no one's
around.*

Hattie

When I got to the final letter, it was apparent everything had gone to hell between me and Hattie.

Henry:

*Don't lie to me this time, you son of a bitch. I
heard you slept with Big Nose Kate, and you're not
gonna deny it like the last time I found out you were
sleeping with a whore. I'm tired of keeping our little*

secret. I'm gonna tell you-know-who. If I do, your
life won't be worth a bucket of warm spit. If you
don't want anyone to find out, then I want a hundred
dollars to keep quiet. If I don't get it, I'll start
spreading the word with you-know-who first. It hurts
me that you would sleep with that sow. I thought you
were brave enough to stand up for me, but you're
just another coward.

Hattie

I thought about those letters long and hard and how
for all the time Hattie and I had been together, clothed
and unclothed, I'd never gotten any liver for my pup.
Odd how things work out sometimes.

Come dark I built a campfire and burned the worthless stock certificates and considered burning the letters
from Hattie as I tried to figure out how to get even with
that worthless lawyer Henry Guinn. About the time the
fire was dying on me and I was toying again with the
idea of burning the letters, it struck me that the lawyer
Guinn and I had the same first name. I guess I'd never
wanted to admit that a man with the morals of a snake in
a profession that was even lower could share my name.

Granted, I was from Arkansas and maybe wasn't as
well educated as Henry Guinn, but I was smarter, by
God. Just look at his wife. I was never dumb enough to
get hitched to a woman that broad or ugly. And I was
smart enough not to become a lawyer, which said a lot.

Then it hit me as hard as Til Walteree had when he
broke my wisdom tooth: I could sure put those letters to
good use.

I started laughing and couldn't stop for a while.
Even when I finally settled down, I couldn't go to sleep
I was so anxious for the next day. I was going to buy
some new clothes, then leave Tombstone forever.

But not without getting even with Henry Guinn, his
wife, and Satan first.

Chapter Twenty-three

Come morning I felt frisky as a colt. I was going to get my revenge if it killed me, and I decided to start with Satan.

I emptied my gunnysack of supplies into my saddlebags. I was going to need the gunnysack for Satan and the letters for Amelia. After saddling up Flash, I pulled myself aboard and headed back to Tombstone and what was left of my place.

I tied Flash by the outhouse and picked my way through the debris, carrying the gunnysack with me. I started digging through the rubble like I was looking for a few more belongings. By the ruined stove I found a flatiron, grabbed it by the handle, and kept rummaging around, waiting for that damned cat.

I must've spent a half hour or more digging through the ashes and was about to give up when Flash stirred by the outhouse. Out of the corner of my eye I spotted Satan stalking me.

He seemed wary, like he knew something was amiss. I tried not to look directly at him but kept him in view as he slipped to the edge of the foundation and peeked over the stones. I toed at the rubble and bent over, flatiron in one hand, gunnysack in the other, wriggling my butt at Satan to give him an inviting target.

The tomcat eased up onto the foundation and slipped through the debris, coming closer and closer.

Watching his approach between my legs, I kept

wriggling my butt. My hand quivered with anticipation. Then Satan crouched, muscles tightened, and leaped.

I stood up and spun around, my arm drawn back.

Satan flew through the air at me.

I pulled the trigger on my arm and swung the flatiron for him.

The flatiron met Satan right in front of my belt.

I didn't kill the son of a bitch, but I stunned him long enough to drop the gunnysack over him. He'd been in one before and knew what it was like, so it wasn't but an instant before he was clawing and biting and scratching and screeching. I managed to jerk the sack up and close the neck. Satan was convulsing so much I feared he might get free, but I held on for dear life, knowing if he did escape I'd likely be scratched to shreds.

I eased over to the bedsprings, pulled a piece of wire free, and wrapped it around the neck of the gunnysack. Only then did I feel safe, but the way Satan was fighting I figured he'd cut through the burlap in a few minutes. Holding the neck of the sack with both hands, I made my way through the debris, careful not to step on any nails. Once clear of the house, I fell to my knees and thumped the sack against the ground.

Satan screamed the first time and the second time, but then he must've understood that I just wanted him to settle down. He quit fighting and took to whimpering and moaning. Just to be on the safe side I took the sack to the nearest water trough and dunked it. Satan struggled for a moment, then seemed to concede defeat, so I jerked the sack out of the water and poked it with my finger until I heard him, wheezing and gasping.

He'd live for certain, but he'd likely have better manners as a result.

I went over to Flash, who didn't much care for the idea of having a sackful of mean cat hanging over his rump, but he didn't put up much of a protest. He'd seen what I'd done to Satan and probably figured I'd do something worse to him.

I mounted Flash and headed down the street, then turned on Fifth and rode past the Stallion Mare. The name still didn't make any sense to me but must've made perfect sense to Joe Campbell, him being a philosopher and all.

I aimed Flash toward the Miner's and Merchant's Store on the corner of Fourth and Allen Streets. It had about the best selection of clothing in town. I'd decided to leave Tombstone in style, and that hundred or so dollars I'd found needed spending, anyway.

After dismounting and tying Flash, I stepped inside. I must've looked awfully dirty, with soot and such on my hands and face, but after I announced my intentions, a couple clerks came to my assistance and took me into the back where I could wash up. Then they showed me clothes all the way from San Francisco and Denver. Before I knew it, I'd bought a fine ready-made suit, new shirt, new drawers, new shoes, new socks, and a bowler hat. I also had them throw in a box of .45-caliber ammunition.

They bundled it up for me after I paid nearly thirty-five dollars. Then I stepped outside and marched to the nearest barbershop. For two dollars I got a shave and a haircut and told the man to start heating water for a bath. After tending to my hair and whiskers, the barber led me into a back room and poured my bath.

"I don't want to be bothered," I said, "because it'll take a lot of soaking to get all this dirt off."

The barber nodded. "I don't get many bath customers this early in the morning."

I was going about my business, washing my hair, bathing like I was the president, when I heard a familiar voice up front ask for a haircut and a shave. It was Henry Guinn, the lawyer who shared my name. I grinned. I had a few things planned for him, if everything worked out.

"You're in earlier than normal today, Henry," said the barber.

"Got a trial in court that'll take a day or two. Just trying to get a jump on that."

I wondered who he'd be swindling before the trial ended.

"More overlapping land claims?" the barber asked.

"Yes, sir. It never ceases to amaze me that people

can spend their hard-earned money on land with unclear title."

It sure bothered me that a lawyer could steal my land and business just because I owed him a few bucks. If he'd been decent, he'd've gone to Til Walteree and told him I owed the money, and Til would've paid him. But Guinn didn't want the money. He wanted the property and the business, the son of a bitch.

I listened to the two of them talk for a minute. Then Henry Guinn paid the barber and stepped outside, closing the door behind him.

No sooner had he gone than I heard the barber grumble, "Bastard. Never does leave a tip, now, does he."

After I finished my bath, I stepped out of the tub, dried myself off, and put my new clothes on, taking the money and the letters from Hattie Ketcham from my dirty pants and putting them in the pocket of my new coat. I felt as good as a poor man can feel. I was tempted to leave my old clothes to be thrown out but decided I might need them down the line, so I bundled them up, carried them back to Flash, and rode him over to Hop Town. I found my laundryman and told him to have my clothes done by the next morning, as I'd be leaving town.

"Okay, Romax. You not many friends in Hop Town no more."

"How's that?"

"Much money rost. Nobody think you get shot in shoulder or arm. Most bet back or gut."

"Sorry to disappoint you all."

"We solly, too. Lose bunch of money."

I started back through town, figuring it was time to visit Amelia Guinn. We hadn't gotten along that well, so I knew I had to take her some kind of peace offering like the soldiers always did with the Apaches. I stopped at a mercantile on Allen Street. Inside I looked around at all the groceries and decided nothing would be more appropriate than a twenty-pound sack of sugar. If anything could sweeten a sour relationship with a woman who weighed as much as a locomotive, a sack of sugar had to be the thing.

After paying for it, I stepped across the street to a

saloon and bought a bottle of liquor, which I figured I'd
need if things didn't go well with Amelia. I started to un-
cork the bottle and take a deep swig but decided it
would be unwise to approach her with liquor on my
breath. Even if her husband did own my saloon now, I
doubted she realized that. So in my sober state I led
Flash down the street toward the Guinn residence. It
was near ten o'clock in the morning when I stepped up
on the porch and knocked on her door.

Standing there with the sack of sugar cradled like a
baby in one arm and my hat in the other, I smiled as best
I could when she opened the door. She was uglier that
morning than I ever remembered. It took her a moment
to recognize me.

"My husband's not here, and I don't have anything
to say to you."

I nodded as humbly as I could. "I know we haven't
gotten along well for a while, but I'm leaving town tomorrow, and there are just some things I wanted you to
know so people will quit talking behind your back."

She seemed skeptical. "The mud stains are still on
my drapes."

I extended my arm and offered her the sugar. "Here's
a gift of apology."

Amelia licked her lips, then cocked her head and
eyed me. "You sure it ain't poison?"

"Get a spoon and give me a bite."

She jerked the sack from me faster than a politician
takes a bribe. "That won't be necessary. Now, what is it?"

I looked both ways down the street. "I'd feel better
telling you inside."

After studying me hard, she nodded. Stepping out of
the doorway, she pointed to the closest chair, then settled
into a sofa across the room. "Speak."

"I always thought you were a fine woman. It was
your husband I didn't care for."

"He's a decent man."

I grimaced. "That's what I mean to talk to you
about." I dug into my pocket and pulled out my letters
from Hattie Ketcham. "These may persuade you otherwise."

She shook her head and crossed her arms over her ample chest. Her head stopped shaking before all her fat did.

"I understand you might not believe it, and I'll be glad to burn these letters if you prefer, but I just couldn't stand the thought of leaving Tombstone and having the citizens of this town laughing at you because your husband was seeing saloon girls."

"It's not so."

Waving the letters before her, I shook my head. "There's things about your husband you don't know. He kept increasing my bill to pay off a saloon girl who was threatening to tell you she was treating your husband. Your husband owns the Stallion Mare Saloon now."

"No, Joe Campbell owns it. He sent all the girls packing. They don't work there anymore."

"Joe's too dumb to own the saloon. He named it, but your husband's taking all the profits. You just ask him."

"Maybe I will."

I waved the letters at her again. "If you're not interested in these letters, I'll put them in your stove and burn them right now."

She licked her lips. I could tell she was curious. "Maybe just one," she answered.

I leaned forward in my chair and offered her the first one. As she reached for it, I was afraid she'd start an avalanche, with so much of her fat leaning my way. But I didn't make any loud noises, and the danger passed.

The first letter was the one about me being the handsomest man in the hall, in and out of my suit. As Amelia mouthed the words, her puffy face turned red. She looked up at me and let out her hot breath. "Anybody could've written this."

"Anybody could own the Stallion Mare Saloon, but it's your husband. You ask him straight up, see what reaction you get." I tucked the remaining letters back in my pocket. "Maybe it's best we stop here. I don't care to ruin a marriage, even if he is billy-goating around on you. If you don't mind people laughing behind your back, it's none of my concern."

Amelia held out her hand for the second letter. It

was the one about not believing "you-know-who" hadn't caught us and the whole house moving. Again Amelia mouthed the words until she reached a line that made her shout. " 'Sorry about the scratches on your behind.' Who is this Hattie?" she demanded.

"She's a saloon girl that worked down at the Stubborn Mule. She used to slip away from the saloon in the day and come down here when you were doing your grocery buying."

I didn't think Amelia's face could get any redder, but it did. She was so mad I feared her face would turn plaid.

"Maybe I best stop. The rest will be too painful."

"No, dammit," she said. "Give me those damn letters."

She grabbed the two from my hands, almost tearing the third one in her haste to read it. This time she read the entire letter aloud: " 'The thought of you being with that woman bothers me still.' " She stared at me. "Who's 'that woman' that she's talking about?"

I sighed. "I'm not certain. It's either you or possibly Big Nose Kate."

"That foreign harlot that pulled a gun on me in my own home?"

I grimaced. "Afraid so."

Amelia looked like she was going to explode at me or her husband—I wasn't certain which. If she exploded at me, I figured it would take me a week to get all the tallow off.

She ripped open the next envelope and read the final letter, mouthing the words silently. She looked up at me. "It was Big Nose Kate." As she read the rest of the letter, I could've sworn steam was coming out her ears. "The little whore called me a sow and threatened to tell me if Henry didn't pay her a hundred dollars."

I nodded. "That's when your husband started upping my bills."

Amelia flung the letters to the floor and pushed her way up from the sofa. "I'm gonna go kill that Hattie."

"Hattie's gone. Left about the same time Big Nose Kate did, so neither of them's around. I heard your husband may be seeing other women, but I don't know. Don't care to. Just want folks to stop laughing at you."

Amelia began to cry as she waddled over and threw her arms around me. I feared she would smother me if I didn't get out of her grasp.

"I'm sorry, ma'am," I said as I broke free, "but I wouldn't want anyone walking by to see this and think the things about you they already-think about your husband."

She seemed touched. "Thank you. I guess I shouldn't've been so mean to you before."

"You didn't know. I hope you can work things out with your husband."

Trying to keep from laughing, I backed toward the door and out onto the porch, then turned toward Flash. I saw the gunnysack with Satan inside and had a final idea. Quickly I carried it to the door.

"Ma'am," I said, "you told me once you wanted a cat. Well, I've no need for this one, since I'll be leaving. He could use a good home. He's a bit wild, so be careful."

After handing her the sack and saying good-bye, I watched her through the window. Amelia kept sobbing and wiping tears from her eyes as she undid the wire around the neck of the sack. No sooner had she removed the wire than Satan burst out, clawing at her face and chest. As big a target as Satan had, he could've scratched and clawed all afternoon on the woman and never hit the same spot twice. But Amelia slapped him across the room.

Satan had met his match.

Quickly I mounted Flash and went back down the street. I ate a large meal at an eatery since I knew I'd be leaving the next day. Mostly I hung around waiting to hear what Amelia did to her husband.

About sundown I went to see Johnny Behan and asked for my pistol and gun belt back. He gave it to me when I promised I'd be leaving Tombstone after I picked up my laundry the next day.

"You've probably caused more trouble in Tombstone

than we'll ever know about," he said. "I'm glad to be shed of you."

Since I still had some money on me, I could've bought a night in a hotel room, but I decided to sleep on the ground next to the shell of my house. I got a pretty good night's sleep, though sometime well after midnight I heard the godawfulest scream I ever heard in my life. It must've awakened half the town. To this day the recollection still sends chills up my spine.

I finally went back to sleep and was awakened after sunrise by something purring by my face. Then I felt fur rub across my cheek. I about died when I opened my eyes and saw Satan in front of me. I figured he wanted to wake me up before he clawed out my eyes, but something was different about him. He seemed tolerably well behaved. Then he rolled over on his back and moaned, and I understood why he had changed.

Amelia Guinn had made a gelding out of him.

"We had our differences," I said as I reached out to stroke his fur, "but I'd never've done that to you."

I got up, saddled Flash, rolled up my bedding, and rode out to Hop Town to pick up my laundry, Satan trailing me the whole way. I felt sorry for him. I wasn't certain whether the Chinamen might eat him, so I stopped Flash and picked him up, letting him ride between me and the saddle horn.

My laundryman asked me if I'd heard about the lawyer Guinn getting knifed during the night.

"No," I said, grinning, "but it doesn't surprise me."

With that I turned Flash toward Tucson, and the three of us left Tombstone, never looking back.

The other side of Contention I drank the bottle of whiskey to help forget the money I'd lost in Tombstone, but at least I was leaving Cochise County alive. That was more than could be said for Tom and Frank McLaury, Billy Clanton, Frank Stilwell, Curly Bill Brocius, Morgan Earp, and Johnny Ringo.

A few years later I ran into Til Walteree in Denver. He told me that Ike Clanton had been killed in a robbery. Johnny Behan ultimately went to the Yuma Territorial Prison, but as a warden rather than the prisoner he deserved to be. The most surprising thing Til told me, though, was that Amelia Guinn had married Joe Campbell after she knifed her husband and ended their marriage.

The way Til Walteree told the story, it wasn't any ordinary knifing, either. It seems Satan wasn't the only one Amelia had made a gelding that night.

I don't know whether the story is true or not, but I sure like to believe it is.

ABOUT THE AUTHOR

A native West Texan, PRESTON LEWIS is the author of eighteen western novels as well as numerous nonfiction articles on western history. In 1993 Lewis won a Spur Award from the Western Writers of America for his story, *Bluster's Last Stand*. The author currently resides with his family in Lubbock, Texas.

Of all the fellows I met during my years wandering about, not one was more likable than Billy the Kid. Something about the kid won you over. That's why I'm glad I didn't kill him when I had the chance.

THE MEMOIRS OF H. H. LOMAX

BY SPUR AWARD WINNER

PRESTON LEWIS

THE DEMISE OF BILLY THE KID

He rode with Billy the Kid and knew the illustrious and infamous men of his time: Geronimo, Jesse James, Wyatt Earp, Wild Bill Hickok. Hardheaded and resourceful, H. H. Lomax was an unknown player in the drama of the American West . . . Or the most accomplished liar of his era. ____56541-9 $5.50/$6.99 Canada

---

I never much cared for Jesse James. He was about as likable as a rabid mongrel, but sorry though he may have been, he was downright lovable compared to his momma. Some said Jesse James finally ran me out of the Ozarks, but that wasn't the case. My conscience and his momma were what sent me packing.

THE MEMOIRS OF H. H. LOMAX

BY SPUR AWARD WINNER

PRESTON LEWIS

THE REDEMPTION OF JESSE JAMES

He rode with Billy the Kid and knew the illustrious and infamous men of his time: Geronimo, Jesse James, Wyatt Earp, Wild Bill Hickok. Hardheaded and resourceful, H. H. Lomax was an unknown player in the drama of the American West . . . or the most accomplished liar of his era. ___56542-7 $5.50/$6.99 Canada